They made love, but would
they be married?

Royal AFFAIRS

MISTRESSES
& MARRIAGES

Fantastic novels from bestsellers:
Day Leclaire, Jennie Lucas
& Laura Wright

THE
Royal AFFAIRS
COLLECTION

Royal AFFAIRS
DESERT PRINCES & DEFIANT VIRGINS

SARAH MORGAN · SUSAN MALLERY · KIM LAWRENCE

Royal AFFAIRS
PRINCESSES & PROTECTORS

LUCY MONROE · RAYE MORGAN · DAY LECLAIRE

Royal AFFAIRS
MISTRESSES & MARRIAGES

DAY LECLAIRE · JENNIE LUCAS · LAURA WRIGHT

Royal AFFAIRS
REVENGE SECRETS & SEDUCTION

JENNIE LUCAS · ROBYN DONALD · DAY DECLAIRE

Royal AFFAIRS:

MISTRESSES
& MARRIAGES

DAY LECLAIRE

JENNIE LUCAS

LAURA WRIGHT

MILLS
BOON
&

All the characters in this book have no existence outside the imagination
of the author, and have no relation whatsoever to anyone bearing the
same name or names. They are not even distantly inspired by any
individual known or unknown to the author, and all the incidents are
pure invention.

Mills & Boon, an imprint of Harlequin (UK) Limited, Eton House,
18-24 Paradise Road, Richmond, Surrey TW9 1SR

ROYAL AFFAIRS: MISTRESSES & MARRIAGES
© Harlequin Enterprises II B.V./S.à.r.l. 2011

The Prince's Mistress © Day Totton Smith 2007
Caretti's Forced Bride © Jennie Lucas 2008
Her Royal Bed © Laura Wright 2005

ISBN: 978 0 263 88964 2

024-0811

Printed and bound in Spain
by Blackprint CPI, Barcelona

The Prince's Mistress

DAY LECLAIRE

USA TODAY bestselling author **Day Leclaire** is a three-time winner of both a Colorado Award of Excellence and a Golden Quill Award. She's won *RT Book Reviews* Career Achievement and Love and Laughter Awards, a Holt Medallion and a Booksellers' Best Award. She has also received an impressive ten nominations for the prestigious Romance Writers of America's RITA® Award.

Day's romances touch the heart and make you care about her characters as much as she does. In Day's own words, "I adore writing romances and can't think of a better way to spend each day." For more information, visit Day on her website, www.dayleclaire.com.

To Jada Andre, who can't be thanked often enough. You've been an unbelievable help.

One

Mt. Roche, Principality of Verdon, Verdonia

Prince Lander Montgomery gripped the phone and spoke in a low, forceful voice. "You owe me, Arnaud. You've been in my debt for years. It's time for you to pay up, and I have the perfect way you can do it."

"I don't owe you a damn thing," Joc snapped. Even from half a world away his voice was as clear as though he stood in the same room. "You and your cronies made my life hell at Harvard. You're lucky I haven't tried to even the score. But now that you've taken the time and trouble to remind me of those good ol' days, I may reconsider."

Lander glared in disbelief. "Payback? After all this time?"

"Why not? When you have as much money as I do,

payback can be a real bitch. A fact you'll soon discover firsthand, Your Highness."

"You have a convenient memory. I'd almost think you'd forgotten about graduation night." Lander paused. "Not to mention the promise you made."

Joc snarled a curse. "I was out of my mind when I made that promise."

"No doubt. But still, you made it. Or doesn't the infamous Joc Arnaud honor his promises? Given your background, I thought honor was everything."

There was a moment of dead silence and Lander wondered if he'd pushed too hard. Then, "What do you want, Montgomery?"

Lander fought to disguise his relief. Years of practice maintaining an impassive facade came to his rescue and was reflected in the calmness of his voice. "I want to discuss a business proposition. I'm throwing a charity ball this Saturday. I understand you'll be in the vicinity."

"If you consider Paris in the vicinity."

"It's a hell of a lot closer than Dallas. Where should I send the invitation?"

"Corporate headquarters. And make it two. There's someone I'd like to invite to your little shindig."

"I'll courier them to you today."

"You never did say…" A hint of curiosity climbed into Joc's voice. "What do you want from me?"

Lander smiled in satisfaction. When it came to Arnaud, curiosity was a good thing. A very good thing. "Not much. I just want you to save Verdonia."

She was late. Unforgivably late.

Juliana Rose mentally willed the cab to hurry, to cut through the heavy traffic overflowing the streets of

Verdonia's capital city of Mt. Roche and reach her destination while she could still enjoy what remained of the evening's festivities. Even if she made it to the palace within the next five minutes—highly unlikely—she didn't doubt for a single moment that she'd be the last guest to arrive.

Peering through the window, she struggled to see how much farther they had to go. In the distance the palace of Mt. Roche topped a nearby hill. It gleamed silvery gold beneath an early June moon, its graceful turrets and glittering stonework reinforcing its fairytale appearance. A hunger built deep inside, a hunger to believe in fairy tales and happily-ever-after endings, even though she'd learned long ago that such things were impossible—at least for her.

This was her very first ball, a reward for all her charitable work for Arnaud's Angels. The fact that the fates were busily conspiring to prevent her from enjoying the fruits of her labor simply underscored her suspicion that some things were never meant to be. Besides, wasn't it considered a major no-no to arrive after the royal family? Would they even let her in? Or would she be turned from the door before she had the chance to peek inside? Well, she'd find out whether they'd let her in soon enough. And if they didn't... She shrugged philosophically. She had a briefcase full of work back at her apartment and a dozen potential candidates who would benefit from Angels' benevolence.

As the cab turned onto the winding approach to the palace, Juliana struggled not to fuss with her hair or tug at the scrap of beaded silk that bared more of her breasts than she found comfortable. Instead she folded her hands in her lap and cleared her mind by silently working her way through a complex mathematical equation. She'd stumbled across the trick as a child, starting with simple multiplication tables to calm herself whenever she'd been upset. Since then, she'd refined the technique, increasing the level of difficulty until it took all her focus and concentration to work her way through the problems. To her relief, the exercise worked, easing her tension and allowing her to regain her poise.

At long last the cab pulled through the palace gates and cruised slowly around the sweeping circle to an entryway as elegant as it was imposing. "Lion's Den," the driver announced in near perfect English. But then, most Verdonians were fluent, since it was their second language. Even the children she worked with spoke English as well as she spoke Verdonian.

"Why do you call it the Lion's Den?" Curiosity compelled her to ask.

He shrugged. "Prince Lander is the Lion of Mt. Roche."

"So you call the palace the Lion's Den?"

He acknowledged her amusement with an answering grin. "Well…perhaps not to His Highness's face."

"No, I imagine not."

With a quick word of thanks, she added a generous tip to the fare and exited the cab. She could practically hear the clock ticking a frantic warning that time was passing, but she refused to rush, choosing instead to soak in the beauty of her surroundings. Normally she wouldn't have dared attend an affair like this. But she was in Verdonia, a small European country that rarely gained media attention, and far—she hoped—from the intrusive focus of the paparazzi. No one knew her real name here, that she was an Arnaud. Instead, she'd been using her first and middle name. She was just Juliana

Rose, charity worker, invited to the ball as a generous afterthought.

Tonight she had an opportunity she'd never experienced before. Tonight, she'd be able to cut loose from her conservative image and allow a tiny piece of her natural personality to take over. To shine as hot and brightly as she dared without worrying about who was watching or taking note of every word she spoke, or dress she wore, or man who danced with her.

Tonight she could be herself and damn the consequences.

Footmen lined the great hall, unobtrusively directing her along the corridor. As she suspected, she was the only guest not yet in the ballroom. The spiked heels of her sandals fired off a rapid tattoo against the endless expanse of marble flooring. With every step she felt more and more like Cinderella, though if she were fortunate her Elie Saab gown wouldn't dissolve into rags on the stroke of midnight any more than the cab she arrived in would revert to a pumpkin with a mouse for a driver.

Passing between huge Doric columns she found herself on a large curved landing overlooking the gathering. A majordomo guarded the wide staircase that led downward into the mass of glittering partygoers. She paused to absorb it all, to savor every single aspect of this moment out of time. Flowers of endless variety and hue overflowed urns and vases, filling the room with a lush, heady scent. Elegant French doors were thrown wide, allowing a soft warm breeze laden with the advent of summer to filter through the throng, and causing the candles that lit the room to flicker and dance. Eventually her attention drifted to the staircase leading downward. And that's when she saw him, positioned at the foot of the steps as though he'd been waiting for her.

He was tall. Even standing a full story above him she could tell his height was impressive. He wore his black tux with casual ease, his chest and shoulders a virtual wall of immovable masculinity. Thick, wavy hair swept back from his face, streaks of sun-bleached blond competing for supremacy over the rich nut brown.

She could see his chiseled features were striking, with high arcing cheekbones and a strong, square jaw that warned of a stubborn nature. But it was his mouth that fascinated her the most. It sat at odds with the hard, forbidding lines of his face and jaw. That mouth betrayed him, the lips full and sensuous and perfectly designed to give a woman pleasure. There was a volcano of passion brewing beneath that mountain of calm control, passion requiring only a single spark to ignite an explosion. The knowledge stirred a secret smile, one that faded the instant she realized he was watching her.

While she'd been studying him, curious and unguarded and exposed, he'd been busy returning the favor. Their gazes locked and held for an endless moment. Heat pooled low in her belly, lapping outward in ever-increasing demand. Never in all her twenty-five years had she experienced anything quite like it. She'd heard of women who'd been struck by that sort of sexual lightning bolt, had even scoffed at the possibility, but she'd never believed it possible.

Until now.

Now, she was faced with an urgent demand she could no more restrain than deny. She knew this man. Oh, they'd never met. But somehow she recognized him. Connected with him on some primal, instinctive level.

For instance, she knew with every fiber of her being that he was a strong man. Powerful. A leader. And she knew that he'd taken one look at her and decided he would have her. He wanted her, wanted to sweep her into his arms and carry her off to his own private lair. To lock her away and possess her body, heart and soul until he'd had his fill of her.

The knowledge almost had her stumbling backward. Pride kept her locked in place. He wasn't the first of his kind she'd had to sort out. She'd spent her entire life dealing with strong, powerful men. They were nothing but trouble. They demanded full control and considered everyone and everything within their world a challenge to either conquer, absorb or destroy.

She also knew that if she were smart she'd turn around and flee the palace. The safest recourse open to her was to hail a cab and return to her apartment where she could hide herself in precious anonymity. There was only one problem.

She wanted him, too.

Flight or confrontation? Rationality or insanity? She hesitated for a telling second before lifting her chin. To hell with it. She'd never before thrown discretion to the winds. Tonight would be her one chance and she intended to seize it with both hands. Gathering up her silk chiffon skirting, Juliana started down the steps and toward whatever fate the gods decreed.

Prince Lander Montgomery stood at the bottom of the staircase leading to the ballroom and stared at the vision standing, still as a statue, in the shadows on the landing above. She was absolutely magnificent—statuesque, with the sort of figure capable of making grown men weep. Her skin rivaled the color and beauty of the white lilies that dotted the floral displays, and set off hair that at first appeared brunette. But then she stepped into the light, and flames erupted from the darkness, smoldering like hot ruby coals. It reminded him of the fire that hid in the richest of Verdonia's world-renowned amethysts, the spark of hidden red that would heat the blue and purple to a blistering inferno and had made the unusual gems some of the most coveted in Europe.

She wore an elegant silver gown, the low-cut corsetted bodice and capped sleeves forming a triangle that framed her neck, shoulders and breasts. Her gaze drifted across the ballroom and a smile broke free, chasing the aloof expression from her face and completely altering her appearance. In the space of a heartbeat she went from cool and regal to warm and vibrant. And then she glanced in his direction.

Heaven help him, it was one of the most intimate looks he'd ever received—open and direct, and as arousing as a lover's caress. A matching hunger consumed him, a ravenous need. One look and he knew he had to have her. It didn't matter why. It didn't matter how. He'd never felt such urgency before, had never felt on the bitter edge of control. Not over a woman. He'd always been the one in charge, the one to set the terms. It was his right and one he'd taken full advantage of.

Until now.

She handed her invitation to the majordomo and then swept down the staircase toward him, crystal beads glittering with every movement. Lander found himself blessing whichever designer god had created her gown, mesmerized by the way the silver material clung to her shapely hips before flaring outward. Layer after layer of tissue-thin skirting lifted and fluttered to show off a spectacular pair of legs.

It was like a scene straight out of *Cinderella*. Except this prince had no intention of falling madly in love. In lust, perhaps. Hell, definitely. But love belonged right where Cinderella found it—in a fairy tale.

Reaching the final step, she hesitated. She continued to stare straight at him, her eyes the color of gold-flecked honey. He read barely suppressed excitement there combined with an inner fire that burned so fiercely he could feel the scorching heat from where he stood. It drew him, stirring an uncontrollable desire. It also roused the predator in him. He wanted to have her focus that iridescent gaze on him and only him, to discover the cause of her suppressed excitement. Free it. Just as he wanted to free her inner fire and bask in its searing intensity.

A ripple lapped outward among the nearby guests, warning of gathering interest. Verdonia was a small country, the people attending tonight's charity gala familiar with one another. This was the first ball since his father's death, a traditional affair Lander had known his father would have wanted them to hold, despite being in mourning. And into the darkness this exotic stranger had appeared, cutting through their grief with fiery brilliance. It wouldn't be long before one of the un-attached males—or even a few of the attached ones—approached her.

Before that could happen, Lander closed the distance between them. She was tall. In her four-inch heels she easily hit six feet. "Welcome," he said simply. "I've been waiting for you."

Wariness clouded her eyes and she retreated a pace. "Do you know me?"

Odd question. Did she think they could have met in the past and not remember each other? Not a chance. "No, I don't know you. But I hope to change that."

Her relief was palpable, a fact he found intriguing. "My mistake," she murmured. Her husky accent held the unmistakable sultriness of the American south and tugged at something visceral deep inside him. "I thought perhaps we'd met and I'd somehow forgotten."

"No. It was my rusty attempt at a pickup line." Lander's mouth twisted. "It would appear I'm seriously out of practice."

For some reason his admission succeeded where the line hadn't. "In that case, you can practice on me. I promise I'll go easy on you." She leaned forward and lowered her voice. "I wasn't certain they'd let me in if the royals had already arrived. I don't suppose you know the proper protocol? Is there someone I should speak to? Apologize to?"

As a pickup line it worked far better than his had. "Prince Lander, for instance?" he suggested with a teasing smile.

To his surprise, alarm flared. "Definitely not him. I'm just here for the party, not to hobnob with any luminaries. In fact, the first one I see will be the last, because I'll be out the door in two seconds flat."

He fought to keep his face expressionless. How interesting. Unless she were the best liar he'd ever met, she didn't recognize him. That had to be a first. Nor did she want to know him, which meant keeping her far from anyone who might give his identity away.

"As it happens, I do know the proper protocol," he

responded in a grave voice. "You've missed the receiving line. Fortunate, since it's damn boring. But it's a serious lapse in etiquette to arrive so late. You'd be smart to get onto the dance floor as quickly as possible before someone notices and has you removed."

Alarm flitted across her face before she caught the wicked gleam in his eyes. Her smile flashed, filling her expression with a sweetness as unexpected as it was appealing. "I don't suppose there's anyone here who knows how to dance?"

He made a show of looking around before shaking his head. "I've seen these men in action. It's not worth the risk. Considering how late you are, it's either me or the dungeon."

Her eyes widened and she managed to appear suitably shocked. "The dungeon, huh?"

"I'm afraid so." He shrugged. "Blame it on Prince Lander. He takes this whole I-am-lion-hear-me-roar stuff pretty seriously."

"So it's either dance with you or be dragged off to the dungeon. Tough choice." She pretended to consider. "I suppose I'd be safer in the dungeon."

"True." He held out his hand. "But safe isn't always as much fun."

"And rarely does it give us our heart's desire." She came to a swift decision. "I'll dance with you."

With that, she accepted the hand he offered. The instant they touched it was as if time slowed to a crawl. Outside of their tiny world, sound grew muffled. Light dimmed. Movement paused. Her fingers were long and supple within his, revealing both strength and softness. He found he didn't want to release her, didn't want to sever the connection between them. Rather he wanted to draw her closer, to taste her, inhale her, touch far more than just her hand.

Her breath quickened as he continued to stare, the pulse leaping at the base of her throat. Her lips parted in anticipation and in that twilight of stillness he could feel the heady rush of scented air as she swayed toward him. It was all the agreement he needed, the most subtle of feminine signals giving him permission to take what he wanted. He tugged her into his arms, and just like that, time clicked back into its normal rhythm. He had enough self-possession—barely enough—to turn his actions into the first steps of the waltz the orchestra was performing.

Sweeping her onto the dance floor, he circled the room. She fit beautifully within his hold, her height making her a perfect match. He kept the dance simple and basic. She followed him without hesitation and he increased the intricacy of his movements, delighted when she matched him step for step.

Her scent tantalized him, and he drew it deep into his lungs. "What's the perfume you're wearing? I don't recognize it."

"You wouldn't. It was a gift from—" She broke off self-consciously. "It's a special blend, number 1794A."

He couldn't help but wonder who had given it to her. A former husband? A current lover? Aw, hell. The fact that he cared was a bad sign. A very bad sign. He gritted his teeth, searching for something to say that would distract him from the futile path his thoughts were taking. "What have you named it?"

She tilted her head to stare at him blankly. "Named it?"

"You're kidding, right?" Okay, now he was distracted. "You have a perfume blended just for you and you haven't named it?"

She shrugged, disconcerted. "Was I supposed to? I didn't realize."

"Most women would have." Hell, most women would have named the perfume after themselves.

"I'm not most women."

"So I'm discovering." And he found that fact fascinating. "I just realized we never introduced ourselves. Tell me your name."

"Juliana Rose." The mischievous expression in her eyes accentuated the burnished gold flecks. "And shall I call you Prince Charming?"

He shot her a swift, suspicious look, but couldn't detect so much as a hint of guile. "There are those who'd disagree," he replied, sidestepping the question.

"That's because you threaten your partner with the dungeon if she refuses to dance with you. I don't suppose there's any chance of a tour of the palace?"

"I could show you the gardens. But the rest will have to wait for another night."

Her smile flashed. "In other words, we're allowed in the gardens but the main part of the palace is off-limits."

"Something like that."

"And here I thought you were an influential man with unlimited power."

He stiffened. "What makes you say that?"

"Instinct."

"Do you know me?" he demanded, throwing her earlier words back at her.

In response, she eased away from him, distancing herself. A wash of cold air cut between them, while wariness stole the open warmth from her expression. "Should I?"

"Verdonia is a small country."

"I'm not Verdonian."

"No. American, if I'm not mistaken. And you still haven't answered my question."

"Okay, fine. Yes, I'm American." It wasn't what he'd asked, and she damn well knew it. The contest of wills was brief. It took a strong person to stand up to him. And though he believed Juliana possessed unusual strength, it was no match for his. With an exclamation of annoyance, she conceded, "No, I don't know you. As far as I'm concerned we're two strangers who have the opportunity to enjoy a single evening together before going our separate ways."

"Instead of happily-ever-after we indulge in happy-for-one-night? Is that why you came here?" he demanded. "So you could meet a stranger and spend an evening with him? Is that the current American euphemism for a one-night stand?"

Instead of reacting in anger she grew more remote, more regal. "I came because I received an invitation to the ball," she said with devastating simplicity. "And I have to settle for a single evening because that's all I've been given. After tonight I return to real life. You see, I discovered long ago there's no such thing as a happily-ever-after ending. One night at a royal ball won't change that."

"Then I suggest we make the most of the one night we have together. Have you ever been to a ball before?"

"No." Her voice dropped, the wistful quality underscoring her words hitting him low and hard. "At least, not to anything like this."

"I'm surprised."

"Really? Why?"

"Because you look like you belong. You act like it."

"I don't," she replied shortly.

"I'm not so certain. You're wearing a couture gown. Your shoes are handmade and would have cost the average citizen a month's pay." He could sense her dismay and wondered at it. "Shall I continue?"

"If you must."

"You walked into the palace as though you were a Verdonian princess. Proud. Confident. At ease with your surroundings. It tells me that even if you've never been to a royal ball, you're accustomed to elegant affairs."

"I may have been to one or two," she conceded.

She'd aroused his curiosity. "Why is it so difficult for you to acknowledge that fact?"

"Because it's in my past. This gown?" She swept her hand over the silk chiffon skirt. "The shoes? Even my invitation are all gifts. If they hadn't been I wouldn't be here. It's not a lifestyle I enjoy. Not any longer."

Lander didn't have a single doubt there was a man involved in that decision. Had she been some wealthy man's mistress? A plaything for the rich and powerful? Any man would have been delighted to have such a woman gracing his arm, not to mention his bed. The thought infuriated him, rousing a primitive possessiveness he'd never before experienced and one he fought to restrain. What did it matter who or how many men she'd been with? Right now she was in his arms. And if he were extremely fortunate, later tonight would find her in his bed.

"So you've chosen to leave this sort of lifestyle behind," he managed with impressive lightness. "Or you have until now."

"Well…" He caught a hint of self-mockery. "It *is* a royal ball. What woman could resist indulging in that sort of fantasy for one night?"

The dance ended and she stepped free of his embrace before he could prevent it. "Then allow me to make your night as special as possible."

His offer gave him the excuse to touch her again, to take her hand and gather her close. To put an unspoken stamp on her that read *mine*. He'd learned over the years how to throw up a protective wall on the rare instance he needed privacy, a subtle signal for others to keep their distance. Most recognized and obeyed, and this occasion proved no different.

Of course it helped that his staff ran interference whenever he gave them that certain look. Footmen shifted their positions. Matrons were intercepted and their hopeful daughters distracted by accommodating friends. It all occurred with the beauty and timing of an intricate dance with no one, he hoped, the wiser—especially not the woman on his arm.

A clear path opened to the buffet set up in an anteroom adjacent to the ballroom, and Lander headed in that direction. Helping himself to one of the fragile china plates embossed with the Montgomery family crest, he filled it with a selection of tidbits. He dipped a strawberry in the molten chocolate fountain and offered it to her. To his amusement, she bit into the strawberry, her eyes half closing as she savored the rich dark chocolate.

"Come on. I know someplace private we can go to eat this."

Bypassing the scattering of linen-covered tables, Lander led Juliana through the open French doors to the gardens beyond. Subtle lighting glowed along the gravel walkways and in the trees and shrubbery. He hooked a sharp right onto a path that most overlooked.

"You know your way around," she observed.

"I've been here once or twice before."

The path dead-ended at a small lattice-covered gazebo. Vines twined up the posts and across the top, dripping fat white rose blossoms. Their fragrant scent hung heavily in the air, ripe and eager to lend assistance to a scene set for seduction.

Lander plucked one of the plumpest roses, and after thumbing off the thorns, threaded it behind her ear. He allowed the back of his hand to trail along her cheek and down the endless length of her neck. He was amazed at the softness of her skin, the color and texture putting the rose to shame. Even the scent of her rivaled the most potent flower.

"How did you come to be here?" he demanded.

"Does it matter?"

"No. Right now it doesn't matter in the least. Only one thing does."

He tossed aside the plate he carried. Neither of them were hungry, at least not for food. Sliding his hands up along the bare length of her arms, he dipped his fingers into the heavy mass of auburn curls and tugged her close. She came willingly, lifting her face to his.

Night shadows turned her eyes black, the moonlight picking out the occasional glitter of gold that slipped past the darkness. Her heart thudded against his, tripping light and eager. A soft smile tilted her mouth and he wondered if her lips were as soft as her skin.

His younger brother, Merrick, had been labeled the impulsive one in the family practically from the moment of his birth, with his stepsister, Miri, close but not quite as bad. Lander had always chosen a more disciplined route. Steady. In charge. He allowed little to sway or influence him.

But he had only to look at Juliana to want with a ferocity beyond his control. He didn't care that the Verdonian election to choose whether or not he'd be the next king was only months away. He didn't care that the press had him beneath a microscope. He didn't even care that in all likelihood the woman he held within his arms wouldn't make an appropriate wife, let alone an appropriate queen. All that mattered was finding a way to carry her off to his bed and lose himself in the fiery heat of her.

Taking his time, he lowered his head and captured her mouth. Lightly. Just a gentle sample. Just enough to test flavor and texture. But that was all it took. One taste and he was lost. His mouth returned to hers and her hands curled into his shirt, anchoring him in place. Not that he planned on going anywhere.

The kiss seemed to change with each and every breath. First fast and impatient, two people discovering a new, irresistible sweet—and desperate to sate their craving of it. Then curious, each eager to explore every detail about the other. Next came slow and languid as they savored what they'd discovered, relishing the ability to please, before the want grew too strong, the urgency too powerful to deny. The kiss turned stormy again. Demanding. Pulsing. Hard and reckless. Robbing them of all thought. He heard her moan and inhaled the sound, reveling in the helpless sign of desire.

With each passing minute, with every hungry, biting kiss, his need for her coalesced into one inescapable certainty. Once she found out who he really was, there would be hell to pay. But he didn't care. It would be worth it. Because no matter what obstacles he had to overcome, no matter who stood in his way, this woman was his and he intended to have her.

Two

She was lost. Totally lost.

Juliana opened her mouth to his and drank greedily, aware that if there had been a bed here in the middle of their private glade, she'd have been on her back, opening herself to this man, giving herself to someone she'd known less than an hour. The knowledge had her shuddering in a combination of disbelief and desire.

His hands drifted from her hair to her shoulders before skating down the naked length of her spine. He cupped her hips, tugging her against him until she was locked tight against his pelvis. She struggled to think, to speak, to plead. But even that was beyond her. All she could do was moan her encouragement. His hands were large and hard and she wanted them on her, wanted them to touch her in the most intimate ways possible, just as she wanted to touch him.

Impatient, she snagged his bow tie and ripped it from its mooring. The pearl studs holding his shirt closed scattered beneath her urgent fingers. And then finally, *finally,* she hit hot, masculine flesh. She ran her hands across his chest and downward over hard, rippled abs.

He returned the favor, finding the crystal button at the nape of her neck and slipping it through its hole. The cap sleeves of her gown slid down her arms and he eased back, tracing the swell of her breasts above the corsetted bodice. Gently he slid the silk downward, baring her. They both stood motionless for a long moment. The only sound was the desperate harshness of their breathing. Moonlight silvered them, giving ripe flesh an unearthly glow. The scent of roses mingled with that of desire.

"God, you're beautiful," he murmured.

"I want you. As crazy as that sounds, I do." She laughed unevenly. "Maybe it's something in the air."

"Or maybe we were meant to be here, like this."

"Fate?"

He shrugged. "It's as good a reason as any."

As though unable to resist, he reached for her, tracing his fingertip down the swell of her breast to her nipple. His face remained taut and hungry, filled with a determination she found impossible to resist.

It took two attempts before she could speak. "I don't even know your name." That simple fact both bewildered and excited.

"We know this." His hand cupped her breast and he leaned down to feather a kiss across the tip, eliciting another helpless moan. "This is all that matters."

She hovered between common sense and lust. She craved this man, craved his touch, his kisses, his body.

It didn't matter that she'd only met him a scant hour ago. It had only taken one look, one single touch, for her to be willing to compromise the values and mores she held most dear.

She'd never done anything like this before nor wanted a man quite so desperately. Even with Stewart, with the man who'd ultimately betrayed her, she'd never come close to experiencing such a total rending of control. If she'd learned nothing else from her past, it had been to live with the utmost caution. To keep rampant emotions in tight check. As a result, she'd turned logic and rationale into her own personal religion. And yet, here she stood, ready to dive headfirst into a fast-moving river leading straight over a waterfall. Not that she cared. This one man, along with this one moment in time, governed every thought and deed.

"We can't do anything here," she felt compelled to protest. "Someone might find us."

"In that case we have two options. We can stop. Or we can take this somewhere else." He made the suggestion without inflection. And though he continued to hold her, he didn't use those clever hands to try and influence her decision. "It's up to you."

He was offering her a clear-cut choice, an opportunity to back out while there was still time. But she'd already made that choice. There was only one option available to her. She lifted her arms and wrapped them around his neck. Finding his mouth with hers, she sank into the kiss, offering herself without saying a word. It was glorious. Delicious. A fantasy beyond compare. If this were a dream, she hoped never to awake. His arms offered a world she'd never known, but one that she wanted more than anything. A world of passion and seduction, and oddly enough, protection. If she were very lucky, this night would never end.

She snatched a final kiss before pulling back. "I'd like to go somewhere else," she said answering his question. The ease and simplicity of her response amazed her. How right it felt and how deliriously free she felt saying it. "I'd like to go with you very much."

With an exclamation of triumph, he swept her into his arms. She grinned up at him about to demand that he carry her off to his fairy-tale castle and have his wicked way with her, when the sound of someone clearing his throat came from the edge of the copse. Instantly her "prince" spun them around into shadow, putting his back to whomever had joined them. He lowered her to the ground, refastening her gown to conceal her nudity.

"Bad timing, Lander?" a laughing voice asked.

"Damn it, Joc. Two minutes more and we'd have been gone."

Juliana stiffened. No. Oh, please no. It couldn't be. A single, swift glance confirmed her worst fears. She gave herself a few precious seconds to catch her breath while mustering what little poise she still retained. Circling the man Joc had referred to as Lander—and why did that name send a warning bell screaming though her fogged brain?—she stepped into a patch of moonlight.

"Hello, Joc," she greeted her brother.

"Juliana?" He uttered her name in sharp disbelief.

Lander's gaze switched from one to the other, his eyes narrowing. "You two know each other?"

"I work for Arnaud's Angels," she responded calmly, shooting her brother a look, warning that she didn't want him to reveal their relationship. To her relief, he gave a subtle nod of understanding. "I didn't realize Mr. Arnaud would be here tonight."

"No," Joc murmured dryly. "Obviously, you didn't."

"If you'll excuse me…Lander, is it?" She knew that name. How did she know that name? If only she could think straight. "I'll leave you two gentlemen to your business."

Joc lifted an eyebrow. "Don't be rude, my dear. As a representative of Arnaud's Angels you owe His Highness more respect than that. After all, he is your host."

Lander started to speak, but after making a sound of disgust, fell silent.

Juliana stilled. "What are you talking about?" But deep down, she knew. His name had sounded familiar, and perhaps if she hadn't been so drunk on kisses she'd have recognized it sooner.

Joc released a bark of disbelieving laughter. "Didn't you realize? The man you've been kissing is Prince Lander. Or to be more precise, Prince Lander Montgomery, Duke of Verdon. The Lion of Mt. Roche."

Oh, no. It couldn't be. What wicked-humored fate had put her in the path of the one man she wanted most to avoid? And why hadn't she figured it out sooner? How was it possible that the very first time she'd chosen to cut loose, she'd selected to do it with him? When it came to ignorant fools, she took top prize in both categories. Lifting her chin, she faced Prince Lander with what little remained of her tattered dignity.

"How very amusing," she said, her tone making it clear she was anything but amused. She swept him a deep, formal curtsey. "I'm delighted I could provide Your Highness with tonight's entertainment."

"It wasn't like that and you damn well know it."

She could hear the frustration underscoring his words, but didn't care. He'd kept his identity from her for reasons of his own, even after she'd made it clear that she had no interest in meeting Prince Lander. Maybe he'd remained silent because she'd warned him that she'd run if she came across anyone of consequence. Otherwise, he'd have revealed his name if only in the hope that it would have her tumbling into his bed all that more quickly.

More quickly? She almost groaned aloud. How much faster could she have tumbled? It had only taken him a brief hour to sweep her off her feet, and that was without pulling rank, as it were. Murmuring an excuse, she skirted her brother and returned to the palace. She hesitated in the shadows just beyond the spill of lights from the ballroom, struggling to regain her self-control.

How could she have been so idiotic? How could she have let a man—even a prince—rob her of every ounce of intelligent thought? But from the moment she'd first seen him, she'd been utterly lost, willing to go anywhere he demanded, give anything he requested, do whatever he required. The knowledge ate at her. With one painful exception, she'd never allowed a man so much control over her. And yet in the space of a single hour, Prince Lander had not only demanded that control, but had been given it without a single word of protest. Had she learned nothing from her past? Clearly not.

Taking a deep breath, she stepped into the light and headed across the ballroom, walking casually, if determinedly, toward the nearest exit. Before she'd taken more than a half-dozen steps, a hand landed on her shoulder, spinning her around.

"I'm sure you don't intend to leave without dancing with me," Joc stated. Not giving her a chance to protest,

he swung her onto the dance floor. "So, tell me...
What's a nice girl like you doing in a palace like this?"

"Oh, ha-ha. The more interesting question is, what are
you doing here?" Juliana retorted in a furious undertone.

"Visiting you, of course."

Blithe and casual. Typical of him. But she wasn't
buying it for a minute. She knew that beneath that
good-ol'-boy routine hid the soul of a brilliant, hard-
as-nails businessman. Whatever reason Joc had for
being here, it was neither blithe nor casual. "You
came all the way to Verdonia just to visit me? Try
again, big brother."

"Maybe I should ask what you're doing with
Prince Lander."

As usual, he'd turned the tables on her with annoying
ease. She focused on the dance for a full minute before
replying. "I didn't know he was a prince."

"Or you'd never have been with him?"

She hated the gentle concern in Joc's voice almost
as much as she hated the question. "Not a chance."

His breath escaped in a sigh. "Just as well. I wouldn't
want any sister of mine mixed up with a Montgomery."

Her head jerked up at that. "Why not?"

"We have a...history."

"What sort of history?" she pressed.

"That's not important."

Impatience lined Joc's face, warning her to drop
the subject. It was a striking face, lean and golden, with
the blood of their Comanche ancestors contributing to
the impressive bone structure. Black eyes, black hair
and what some would call a black heart completed the
package, though she knew better. Joc was the kindest,
most generous man alive. Unless crossed.

"Explain something to me, Ana—"

"Juliana," she corrected. "I don't use my nickname, anymore."

"And why is that?" he demanded. "Why don't you want him to know who you are? What does it matter if I tell him you're Juliana Rose Arnaud, my sister, rather than Juliana Rose, charity worker? You won't be seeing him again." He waited a beat before pushing. "Will you?"

"No." But how she wanted to.

Deep grooves formed on either side of his mouth. "It's because you're my sister, isn't it? That's why you only use your first and middle names these days. Because you're afraid of the attention you'll receive if anyone finds out you're Ana Arnaud, sister to the infamous Joc Arnaud."

Tears filled her eyes and she blinked them back before lifting her gaze to his, praying that he wouldn't be able to tell how close to the edge he'd pushed her. She lifted a hand to his cheek. "It's not that. You know I love you. I'm proud to be your sister."

"Then what stopped you from telling Montgomery the truth?"

She shivered at the coldness of the question…and the underlying hurt. "I haven't told anyone. I want the focus to be on the charity, not on me. Now that I know Lander is a prince, it's even more imperative that I remain silent. He's in the public eye. If the media gets a whiff of our involvement, they'll be all over us. I can't handle that. Not again." Not ever again. "Don't you see? It's not just what will happen to me. It's not fair to throw Prince Lander to the wolves without any warning."

"Is that the only reason? Because if it is, I can take care of the media."

The hard look in Joc's eyes worried her. There was

another reason she couldn't be with Prince Lander, but she didn't dare mention it. It would only anger her brother. "I came to Verdonia to escape scandal, not stir up more. Besides, it isn't like I'm seriously interested in Prince Lander."

"Liar." He hesitated, no doubt torn between whatever history stood between the two men and his love for her. "I may not care much for your choice, but if you're serious about him, I can fix things," he offered grudgingly. "Though to be honest, I'd rather you kept your distance. I don't trust the man. Not with you."

"What you saw in the garden, it was just a bit of harmless fun. Nothing consequential. And it's not like I'll be in Verdonia for very much longer. A few more weeks at most." Could Joc hear the desperation in her voice? Probably. Her brother was as skilled at reading people as he was at making money. In fact, she doubted he'd have amassed his current fortune if he hadn't possessed both abilities. "Tomorrow I'll be back at work and tonight will have been nothing more than a sweet dream. Just a meaningless interlude."

"And Montgomery?"

She took a deep breath. "Since you don't want me to see him again, I won't be seeing him." For some reason the realization caused a stab of pain.

"Montgomery's a powerful man. If he wants you, he'll find you."

She shook her head. "He won't waste time trying. After all, it was only one dance."

"And one kiss," Joc added. "No big deal."

She flinched. "Exactly." She deliberately changed the subject. "I guess I have you to thank for the ticket to the ball, as well as the dress."

"Considering how hard you've been working, you deserve it," he answered, accepting the new topic with good grace. "It only seemed appropriate to send a suitable dress and shoes. I'm willing to bet you didn't bring anything with you."

"Good guess. Maybe that's because I'm here to work, not play."

"Speaking of which, the reports I've received have been glowing."

"Thank you." His acknowledgment of her accomplishments delighted her. Although Joc wasn't stingy with his praise, he also didn't offer it gratuitously. "And thank you for tonight. It's been—" Amazing. Incredible. A dream come true. "Very nice."

He leaned forward and kissed her brow. "You're welcome. I don't suppose you're ready to come home now?"

"Home?" It took her a minute to catch his drift. "Oh, you mean to the States?"

"Of course I mean to the States." Amusement competed with impatience. "Honey, as wonderful a job as you're doing here, I need you back in Dallas. You're my best executive accountant."

"Was," she stressed. "I *was* your best executive accountant. Now I head up your European branch of Arnaud's Angels."

He waved that aside. "A total waste of your talent."

Her mouth tightened. "I don't happen to agree. The children need me."

"You mean…you need the children."

Sometimes it didn't pay to be subtle with her brother. "I'm not returning to Dallas."

"It doesn't have to be Dallas, if you'd rather not."

His instant willingness to compromise warned of his seriousness. "You can work out of whichever city suits you."

"What suits me is the job I'm currently doing. Considering how much work there is for me in Europe, I may never return home." Her hand tightened on his shoulder. "I need you to back off, Joc, and let me live my life my way. Either I continue with Angels or I offer my services to some other charitable organization. I guarantee they'll snatch me up in a heartbeat."

To her surprise, he let it go. "Fine, fine. If that's what you want, stay in Verdonia. Hell, stay wherever in Europe you want." A frown touched his brow. "So long as it's away from Montgomery, I can live with it."

Lander stood on the sidelines, watching Joc and Juliana dance with an ease that spoke of long intimacy. Damn it all! It might have been a replay of their years at Harvard. For some reason, they'd constantly found themselves in competition. On the playing field. In the classroom. And in their most contentious battles, over women. After the first few years where they'd taken loutish delight in poaching, their attitudes had changed. Lander hadn't wanted any of the women Arnaud had been with, anymore than Joc had wanted Lander's.

But that changed the moment Lander had met Juliana. Now only one question remained…was Juliana fair game? And what did he do if she wasn't?

The dance ended. But Joc didn't release his hold on his partner. Rather, they spoke quietly for a moment before he bent forward and gave her a second kiss, this one on the cheek. It took every ounce of self-control for

Lander to keep his shoulder glued to the wall instead of striding across the room and planting his fist in Arnaud's nose. If that kiss had landed any closer to Juliana's mouth he might have, regardless of the consequences.

The couple reluctantly parted—at least, it appeared reluctant to Lander—and the crowd chose that inopportune moment to surge forward, blocking his view. When next he could see, only Joc remained, who offered a nod of acknowledgment and headed toward Lander, joining him on the sidelines.

"I think it's time we spoke, don't you?" Joc asked.

Screw that. "Where is she?"

"Gone."

"Is she yours?" Lander demanded with single-minded intensity.

Anger flared in Joc's gaze. "That's a hell of a thing to ask. Juliana doesn't belong to any man. Not me. And for damn sure not you. Not now. Not ever."

Not ever? He'd see about that. "If she's not yours, I want to know where I can reach her."

"Did you hear what I said?"

"I heard. Are you telling me she's off-limits?"

A silent battle of wills ensued with Joc blinking first. "Is she that important to you?"

"Yes."

Joc shrugged his concession, but Lander could see the wheels turning. Ever the businessman, he was no doubt trying to figure out how to turn the situation to his financial advantage. "Fine. But don't you have more important issues to deal with than some woman you only met tonight? Isn't that why you called me?"

It shouldn't have taken Lander a full minute to switch his focus from Juliana to affairs of state. But it did. Aw, hell. He scrubbed a hand across his face. He had it bad. Without another word, Lander led the way to his private office. It was a large room with floor-to-ceiling windows that offered an unparalleled view of each day's sunrise. The room also overlooked the front of the palace, and Lander made a point of crossing to the window just in time to see a distinctive flash of silver silk disappear into the back of a cab.

Deliberately forcing himself to redirect his focus to the current problems plaguing his country, he turned to face Joc Arnaud. His nemesis stood in front of a map of Verdonia, his hands clasped behind his back.

"So when will you be crowned king?"

"Either in two months—" Lander shrugged "—or never."

"Never?" Joc swiveled, his brows climbing. "I don't understand. Wasn't your father king? I assumed when he died that the crown would fall to you. Isn't that how those things work?"

Lander inclined his head. "In a true monarchy that would be correct. But in Verdonia it's a little different. We have a popular vote among the eligible royals."

Joc frowned. "You and your brother have to compete for the throne?"

"As a second son Merrick's not in the running. No, the eldest royals from each principality are the only ones eligible."

"Well, hell. Who are you up against?" Joc leaned in and tapped the southernmost principality. "I gather you represent Verdon."

Lander joined Arnaud in front of the map and indicated the principality farthest north. "Prince Brandt von Folke is the eligible royal from Avernos."

Joc traced the principality snuggled between north and south. "And this one in the middle? Celestia, is it?"

"There aren't any eligible royals. You have to be twenty-five to rule Verdonia and Princess Alyssa won't turn twenty-five until after the election. She's my brother, Merrick's, wife. They married just a few days ago."

"A political affair?"

Lander nodded. "It started out that way. She was going to marry Brandt until Merrick intervened."

"Why would Merrick inter—" Joc broke off, his brow furrowed. "Oh, I get it. If Alyssa and this Brandt fellow had married, it would have united the royal families of Avernos and Celestia. Wouldn't that have ensured Prince Brandt the popular vote?"

"Astute as always," Lander commented. Joc's talent at grasping the salient points and analyzing how they affected the big picture had always—reluctantly—impressed the hell out of him. "Yes, Brandt would have won the election if Merrick hadn't interfered. He abducted Alyssa and married her himself."

Joc barked out an incredulous laugh. "Gutsy."

"Would have been if he hadn't fallen in love with her."

"I don't know." Joc's expression turned dubious. "You certain he wasn't ensuring you the win by uniting the Montgomerys with her people? Sounds damn convenient if you ask me."

Lander fought back a stab of anger. "I think he'd have claimed it was quite inconvenient. But if you saw them together—" he shrugged "—they appear disgustingly happy."

Joc glanced across the room and brightened. Crossing to Lander's desk, he helped himself to a Havana Corona from the humidor. "Okay, so now that you've caught me up on the political situation, why don't you explain what I'm doing here." Making himself at home, he clipped the cigar and passed it to Lander before repeating the process for himself. "I gather there's a serious reason or you wouldn't have imposed on our…friendship."

Lander didn't bother couching his words. "I need your help." He took his time lighting his cigar, before lifting his gaze to stare at Arnaud through the haze of pungent smoke. "Verdonia's in trouble."

"I assume you mean financial difficulties. I suppose you expect me to bail you out just because I owe you over a half-forgotten college debt?"

"If it were half-forgotten, you wouldn't be here." He allowed his comment to hang, before adding, "And I'll only accept your help if you can do it aboveboard."

Joc bit down on his cigar, fury burning in his gaze. "You have a hell of a nerve." A hint of rawness ripped through his voice. "My father may have walked the wrong side of the line. At least, that's what the feds claimed. And he may have fathered a pair of bastard children on my mother and then refused to give them his name. But I'm not, and never have been, my father. I only deal aboveboard and if you've had me investigated, as I'm sure you have, you damn well know that."

Lander inclined his head. "That's the only reason we're talking. Tell me something, Arnaud. How many failing businesses have you turned around?"

"Too many to count."

"Right now Verdonia is a failing business. I need your skill—and maybe a few Arnaud business interests relocating here—to get my country turned around."

Joc worked on his cigar before slowly nodding. "If

there's money to be made helping, I'll help. But I'll want an airtight contract before I let go of one thin dime."

"Perfect. First we'll talk money." Lander opened a decanter and splashed a couple fingers of single malt into a crystal tumbler. He held it out. "And then we'll talk women."

Three

Juliana cuddled Harver in her arms as she spoke quietly to the baby's mother. Born with a cleft palate, the little boy would be another of Arnaud's Angels. At least, he would if Juliana had her way. She had doctors standing by once she received approval from Harver's parents for the operation.

The mother was understandably fearful, while the father appeared suspicious of the offer of such an expensive procedure for free, despite her having explained everything with meticulous care. It helped that the surgeon was Verdonian, his calm voice of reason allaying most concerns. At long last the parents signed the consent forms and Harver was carried off for the necessary testing in preparation for his surgery.

After wishing the parents well, and receiving a fierce hug from Harver's mother, Juliana gathered up her paperwork and filed the various forms and folders in her briefcase. As always, an irrepressible excitement bubbled through her now that her task was completed, now that she knew another baby would receive the life-altering procedure. How could Joc think an accounting job, no matter how lofty the position, could compare to this?

She exited the hospital, her high spirits giving a swing to her step as she headed toward a nearby cab stand. A light breeze tugged at her hair, loosening a few of the curls that she'd secured at the nape of her neck with a clip. She hadn't gone more than a dozen paces when a black stretch limo pulled up beside her. She sensed who it was even before the door swung open to reveal Prince Lander.

Dismay filled her. So he'd found her. She shouldn't be surprised. It was bound to happen. Her grip tightened on her briefcase as she inclined her head. "Your Highness."

"Please, get in, Ms. Rose," he said. "We need to talk."

Just because he was a prince didn't mean she had to go with him. She'd made enough of a fool of herself the previous evening without making it worse in the harsh light of day. "No, thank you. I think we said everything we needed to last night."

"Perhaps." He paused a telling moment. "But we didn't do everything we planned, did we?"

She fought to control the flush that heated her cheeks. "Fortunately. Now if you'll excuse me—"

"I'm not going anywhere. And neither are you." Determination settled into the hard lines of his face. She recognized that expression. She should. Joc wore it often enough and it always signaled an unwillingness to budge from his position. "Now are you going to get in, or do I continue to draw attention to us by following you?"

He couldn't have found a more effective way of convincing her to join him. Caving to the inevitable, she slid in beside him, placing her briefcase between them. Let him read whatever he wished into that small, pointless gesture.

"Okay, speak." She closed her eyes, drawing on every ounce of self-control. "Please excuse me, Your Highness. I apologize if that sounded rude. How can Arnaud's Angels be of assistance to you?"

"I'm not interested in your charitable work," he bit out. "I'm interested in you, as you damn well know."

"Yes, sir. I believe you explained that last night. Perhaps we didn't have an opportunity to finish that conversation, after all. So allow me to finish it now."

She forced herself to turn and offer her coldest stare. It was a major mistake. She'd mapped out precisely what she'd intended to say, worked it almost like a mathematical equation—the words, the intonation, the expression she'd use. But in the space of the two heartbeats it took for her to fall into his intense gaze, every last thought vanished from her head. She could only stare at him in complete and utter bewilderment.

"Fine," he prompted. "Finish it."

"Finish it." She moistened her lips. "Right. I'll do that right now."

Held by those brilliant hazel eyes, she racked her brain, struggling to remember what she was supposed to finish. Something. Something about…finishing. Her confusion must have shown because his mouth twitched. And then a chuckle rumbled deep in his chest. "Hell, woman. We do have a bizarre effect on each other, don't we?"

She couldn't help it; his laughter proved too contagious. Shaking her head, she gave in to her amusement. "What am I going to do about you, Your Highness?"

"Whatever you want. And make it Lander."

"Thank you." She regarded him with sudden suspicion. "How did you find me? Joc?"

"No. He refused to help."

She could be grateful for that much, at least. For some reason their shared amusement had her relaxing enough for her brain to function again. "I remember what I was going to say."

"Something about finishing?" he offered with a slight smile.

She nodded gravely. "Finishing things between us."

"Excellent. I'll instruct my driver to drop us off at the palace so we can finish what we started last night."

She fought to keep from laughing again. She didn't want to be charmed by him. Yet she was. Utterly charmed. Enthralled. Entertained. Filled with an impossible yearning. It had to stop, and stop now. "I meant finishing, as in ending things between us," she clarified.

"Why?"

The simple question caught her off guard. "Last night… It wasn't meant to happen."

"But it did. You wanted me. You can't deny that."

Honesty came hard, but she refused to shy from it. "I don't deny it. I wish I could blame it on the moonlight. Or on too much to drink."

"It wasn't even close to a full moon. And you didn't have anything alcoholic."

"No, I didn't." If only she had, it would be some balm to her pride. "I take full responsibility for what happened."

"Noble, but unnecessary." Irony laced his words. "I seem to recall you weren't alone in that garden."

"But I let you—" She'd let him kiss her. Incredible, amazing kisses. And he'd touched her. Just remembering had her aching to have his hands on her again.

He studied her, pinning her with a look that had her brain misfiring again. "Are you feeling guilty because of Joc?"

She blinked in bewilderment. "Joc? What does he have to do with this?"

"He asked for two invitations when I invited him to the ball. I assume he sent the second to you. And I'm also guessing he might have had something to do with your designer gown, as well. Didn't you tell me it was a gift?"

He didn't know. Relief swept through her. He'd assumed she and Joc were lovers. Her brother had promised he wouldn't tell Lander of their connection, but she'd been concerned that the prince might have guessed the truth. She nodded. "Joc arranged for both the clothes and the invitation."

"Is that why you want to end things between us? Are the two of you involved?"

"Not the way you mean."

His eyes narrowed in thought. "In that case, there can only be one other reason. It's because of who I am, isn't it?"

She couldn't hold his gaze. "Yes."

"Hell." She could hear the ripe frustration vented in that single expletive. "You're probably the first woman I've ever met who didn't want to have anything to do with me once she knew who I was."

"Takes all kinds," she joked.

"Explain it to me."

She forced herself to look at him, to be as honest as possible. He deserved no less. "I don't like living in the spotlight. Being with you, even for a short time, would mean precisely that."

"Been there, done that?"

"Yes."

"With Joc."

He didn't phrase it as a question or ask for a confirmation, so she didn't offer one. Instead, she reached for the door. "May I go now, Your Highness?"

He gave an impatient shake of his head. "I'll take you home." Before she could protest, he signaled his driver. "Samson Apartments," he instructed.

"How do you know where I live?" When he simply smiled, she released her breath in a sigh. "Why do I bother asking? You're Prince Lander, Duke of Verdon. I suppose all you have to do is wave your royal scepter and your every command is granted."

"If that were true, we wouldn't be having this conversation. We'd both be in my suite at the palace and you'd be gracing my bed."

There was nothing she could say to that, so she closed her mouth and turned her head to stare out the window. The drive through the city was accomplished at a record pace, and in short order they pulled up outside her apartment complex.

"I guess this is goodbye," she said, reaching for the door handle.

"It is." He paused a beat. "If that's what you really want."

"We settled this already."

"You can leave." He shifted closer and covered her hand with his, preventing her escape. His breath stirred the curls at her temple while his voice murmured seductively in her ear. "You can get out and we'll never see each other again. Or you can stay. Think about it. We can have one evening together before we go our separate ways. No one has to know. I can arrange that. No media attention. No spotlight. Just a man and a woman doing what men and women have done throughout the ages. One night, Juliana."

One night. The insidious words were all too tempting. She could see it, as clearly as though it had already happened. A night she'd never forget, held within the arms of a man who filled her with a desire beyond anything she'd ever before experienced. Limbs intertwined. Heated flesh sliding against heated flesh. An intimate exploration as soft and gentle as it was hard and fierce. She'd never allowed herself to give in to such basic, primitive demands. For the first time, she wanted to.

"Don't," she whispered.

"Because you're not interested in what I'm offering?"

She shook her head. "Because I am."

He tucked a lock of hair behind her ear, his mouth following the same path as his fingers. "Then why resist?"

She fought back a moan. It was an excellent question. Why did she resist? She was far from home. No one knew her true identity. Nor did anyone know about the various scandals in her past. Hadn't she been cautious her entire life, watching every step she took? And even that hadn't prevented her from tripping. Now she had an opportunity that would never come her way again. A chance to seize what she wanted. Have the sort of fling she'd never dared indulge in before—never been tempted to indulge in.

"If I come with you," she began hesitantly, "what would you expect from me? Where would we go?"

"I expect nothing more than what you're willing to give. And we can go anyplace you'd like."

He interlaced her fingers with his and lifted them from the door handle. She allowed it, realizing as she did so that she'd just committed herself to insanity. She didn't know whether to laugh at her daring or call herself every sort of fool. Perhaps both.

"Can we go somewhere other than the palace?" she asked.

He inclined his head in agreement. "Someplace private."

"You're actually allowed privacy?"

"Allowed? No. But every once in a while I take what I need." His smile came slow and deliberate. "And right now what I need is you. Give me a moment to arrange everything."

The entire time he was gone she sat in utter disbelief. What had she done? How could she have agreed to see him again when she knew the potential consequences? Last night she could blame on moonlight and roses, on wanting so desperately to believe in fairy tales that she'd behaved in ways she never would have believed herself capable. Now, with a clear, bright June sun shining down on her, she couldn't delude herself any longer. The facts were as black-and-white as a column of numbers. It didn't matter how many times she totaled the figures, the bottom line didn't change. And the bottom line right now was she'd just agreed to spend the night with Lander.

Her mouth firmed. So what if she had? Why shouldn't she indulge in a single night of bliss before returning to real life? It wasn't that she deserved it, or had earned it. She simply wanted it. Wanted the fantasy. Wanted the intense pleasure she'd shared with Lander to continue a short time longer. She slid her hand over the plush leather seat. For once she'd be greedy. She'd put aside all her fears and worries and grab with both hands what fate had so generously provided. As for tomorrow?

She lifted her chin in defiance. Tomorrow could take care of itself.

A few minutes later Lander returned to the limo. "Everything all right?" he asked.

"Perfect."

"I was hesitant to leave you alone in case you had second thoughts."

"Oh, I had second thoughts. And third and fourth and fifth."

"You're still here."

She offered a blinding smile. "Yes, I am."

He cupped her chin in response. Lifting her face, he took her mouth in a slow, deliberate kiss. She was curious to see what would happen, whether she'd react to him the same way as before. To her dismay she found it far different.

Last night she'd been lost. Totally and utterly lost. It had been like discovering a glorious private world, filled with beauty of sound and taste, scent and sensation. She'd been intrigued by what she'd discovered, but able to explore only the smallest part. Last night she'd barely stepped into that world.

Today it exploded around her, everything twice as intense, twice as spectacular, twice as overwhelming. And it left her utterly bewildered. A kiss was supposed to be just a kiss. A sweet joining of lips. A mild physical pleasure. Not this blistering desire that melted all intelligent thought. That had never happened to her before.

Lander reluctantly released her. "We're in serious trouble. You realize that, don't you?"

"We can handle it," she insisted. Did he catch the hint of desperation in her voice? "One night. That's all we can have. After that, we go our separate ways."

"Hell, woman. We can barely handle a simple kiss. You think after I make love to you, we'll be able to walk away from each other?"

"You promised!"

A hint of anger glinted in his eyes. "I've never broken my word, and I don't intend to start now, no matter how much I'd like to."

She'd have to be satisfied with that. "Where are we going?" she asked, intent on changing the subject.

"I have access to an apartment on the outskirts of the city. It's a secure location. With luck, no one will discover we're there."

To her relief, he was right. The limo pulled into a deserted underground garage and dropped them off by a private elevator before departing again. In less than two minutes the elevator whisked them upward, opening onto a penthouse suite. Lander locked the elevator in place to ensure they didn't receive any surprise visitors, before joining her in the middle of the foyer.

"It's lovely," Juliana murmured, struggling to conceal the distressing awkwardness sweeping through her.

"Feel free to look around."

Taking him at his word, she wandered from the foyer into a great room walled on two sides with windows overlooking the city of Mt. Roche. Adjacent to that she found a formal dining room with a compact kitchen beyond. Lander didn't follow her. Instead, he took up a stance between the foyer and great room, his gaze on her entire time. Returning to her starting point she glanced toward the one section of the apartment she hadn't yet explored.

"Don't," Lander said.

She looked at him, startled. "Don't what?"

"It's the bedroom. You're welcome to check it out." He tilted his head to one side. "But somehow I don't think you're ready for that."

She wrapped her arms about her waist. "Is it so obvious?"

"What's obvious is that you're not ready for any of this." He straightened from his stance and approached. "If I were less selfish, I'd take you home. But I can't. I want you too much. And I think you want me, too."

As nervous as she was, she couldn't deny the truth. "You know I do."

"If you were willing to give me more than one night, we could avoid tonight's dilemma. We'd have the time to take our relationship slow and easy. What do you say? Wouldn't a gradual progression suit you far more than fast and reckless?" Wordless, she shook her head and he accepted her refusal with a shrug. "In that case, will you stay, or should we end this now?"

She hesitated. How could she have thought herself capable of a one-night stand with him? To go into it so cold-bloodedly when she'd never indulged in one before. She glanced uneasily across the foyer. If Lander hadn't locked the elevator, she'd be over there right now, stabbing at the button, determined to escape. She needed an out, even just the promise of one, so she wouldn't feel quite so much like a mouse caught beneath a cat's paw.

She cleared her voice. "If this doesn't work—"

"I'll take you home." Amusement rippled through his

words and she realized he'd been able to read her thoughts as though she'd shouted them aloud. "In the meantime, no pressure. I'll open a bottle of wine and we can talk."

"Sounds perfect."

And it was. They decided to watch the sunset from the balcony off the great room. Lander chose a French Beaujolais that went down as smooth and light as the conversation. He asked about her work with Arnaud's Angels, a subject dear to her heart. As they talked and drank, Juliana could feel her tension ease. They finished their wine just as the sun vanished behind the Mt. Roche skyline. The city lights sparkled in the growing darkness, winking up at the stars dotting the velvet canopy overhead.

Lander rose, offering his hand. "Are you hungry? I arranged for dinner to be delivered. It won't take long to heat."

She gazed up at him, wishing with all her heart that Lander were an ordinary man, or that she didn't have a past that curtailed any possibility of a relationship. That she were the sort of woman he could be seen with in public. Or he was in a position not to care about propriety or scandal.

Taking his hand, she stood. "Thank you, I'm starved. I worked through lunch today."

He maintained his stance, his face cast into shadow, while hers was bared by the light seeping onto the balcony from the great room. "What were you thinking about a minute ago?" he asked unexpectedly.

She regarded him warily. "Nothing important."

"Did you know that your eyes darken when you're not being honest?" He cupped her face, sweeping his thumbs along her cheekbones. "The brown swallows up the gold. Tell me the truth. What were you thinking?"

"That I was sorry we don't have longer than tonight," she confessed.

"That's your choice, not mine."

"Trust me when I say I have a valid reason."

"Tell me what it is."

"Maybe after dinner." He shook his head, rejecting the possibility, and she sighed. "My eyes, again?"

"Dead giveaway."

"Joc could always tell when I was lying, too. Now I know why."

She'd made a mistake mentioning her brother, she realized. Lander's hazel eyes didn't darken as hers had. Instead they flamed with odd green sparks. He shifted closer, joining her inside the circle of light. It sliced across his face, revealing the fierceness of his expression.

"I think it might be wise to leave your boss out of our conversation tonight." His voice scored the balmy dark with a wintry coldness. "Unless you want this night to end far differently than planned."

She considered backing down. But it had never been her style. She might be unwilling to reveal her true relationship with Joc or confess to the various scandals in her background. That didn't mean she'd allow him to believe she was one of her brother's women. "Are you jealous? Is that why you don't want me to mention Joc?"

"Yes."

He'd surprised her with his honesty. "Then allow me to reassure you. He and I aren't lovers. Not now. Not ever."

"Your relationship is strictly professional?" Lander asked dubiously.

"No," she admitted. "It's more than that, and always will be. We've known each other most our lives."

"Let me guess. He's like a brother to you."

She couldn't help but smile. "Exactly."

"I find it impossible to believe there's a man alive who could be around you for any length of time and not want you in his bed. Especially a man like Joc."

"Look at my eyes and tell me what you see. Truth… or lie?"

He took his time, his hands continuing to skim across her face as if he could absorb the information through his fingertips. After an endless minute his mouth curved to one side. "Truth."

"Is there anything else you want to ask me about Joc? Now's your chance."

"Not a thing."

"Good." She grinned. "In that case, let's eat. I really am starving."

She helped him heat their dinner and carry the meals to the table. "My stepmother was quite disgusted that we weren't expected to learn any domestic chores," he told her as he thanked her for her help. "But my father explained that it would have shocked the staff if we showed up in the kitchens expecting to cook our own meals or the laundry room to clean our clothes. My brother, Merrick, and I got off easy. Our stepsister, Miri, wasn't so lucky. When she joined our family, she learned the consequences of being stepdaughter to a king. Poor thing."

Juliana cupped her chin in her hand and gazed at him across the candlelit table. "Why poor thing?"

He shrugged. "She found it difficult to deal with the restrictions and all the protocol." His brows drew together. "Wasn't there a movie a while back along those lines? Something about an American girl who discovers she's a princess and has to learn how to act the part?"

"I remember it. Cute movie."

"Well, Miri lived it. Merrick and I had been trained for our roles since birth. Miri was seven when she came to live with us. It took a while before she fit in. And Merrick and I didn't make it easy for her, either. At least, not at first."

Something in his tone roused her curiosity. "What happened to change that?"

Lander's mouth compressed. "Merrick and I overheard someone telling her that she wasn't a 'real' princess. It was true, of course. She wasn't a princess. But I don't think she understood that until then. I'll never forget the expression on her face. It devastated her. From that moment on, Merrick and I closed ranks. She was our sister, if not by birth then by choice, and we weren't about to let anyone hurt her like that again. When my father discovered what happened, he adopted her and had her crowned Princess Miri."

"What a wonderful thing to do," Juliana marveled.

"My father was an amazing man." Lander's declaration held equal parts love and sorrow. "Not a day goes by that I don't miss him. I can only hope that if I'm elected I'll make half the king he did."

"I'm sure you will."

"Thanks for the vote of confidence, but everything considered, it won't be easy. Verdonia is facing some challenging times."

It didn't take much to read between the lines. "I've heard rumors about the amethysts. There's growing concern that the mines are played out. What will happen if it's true? Aren't the gems Verdonia's economic mainstay?"

"We'll find alternatives to help bolster the economy.

I'm considering a number of possibilities." Determination filled his expression. "It might take a while, but we're a strong people. We'll adapt."

Juliana lowered her gaze, a puzzle piece clicking into place. She'd wondered why Joc had come to Verdonia. He'd claimed it was to see her, to pressure her back into her old job. But she'd had trouble buying that. Now she suspected she had the answer. If Verdonia faced financial difficulties, who better to call in than financial wizard Joc Arnaud?

She didn't have long to dwell on the matter. Lander leaned forward and took her hand in his. "So, tell me, Juliana. Have you made a decision?"

His question caught her by surprise. "About what?"

"About tonight. Do you want an out?"

Didn't he know? Hadn't he sensed her decision? "I don't need an out." She fixed him with an unwavering look. "I'm staying."

"In that case, let's try a little experiment." Releasing her hand, he rose and crossed to her side. When she would have stood to join him, he pressed her back into her chair. "No, no. You don't need to move. Just sit for a minute."

"What are you going to do?" she asked, torn between apprehension and amusement.

"Just this." He released the clip anchoring her hair at the nape of her neck and filled his hands with the curls that tumbled free. "Soft. And much prettier loose."

"It's too curly." Her voice had grown thick and heavy. "It gets in the way."

"It won't get in my way."

His hands drifted downward to her neck, circling her throat. Sliding his palms along the lapels of her suit coat, he reached the first button and flicked it through the hole. One by one, he released them until the jacket parted. Still standing behind her, he turned his attention to her blouse. Again he took his time, unfastening button after button.

Her breath quickened with each one he loosened, and she fisted her hands around the arms of her chair. It seemed to take forever before he finished. Was he waiting for her to protest? To change her mind? It wouldn't happen. It was as though her inhibitions were released with each practiced flick, freeing her to express every sensation crashing through her. At long last he finished, sliding both jacket and blouse from her body.

"Nice," he commented, tracing the scalloped lace edging her bra. "Very nice. Who'd have guessed you were hiding something this sexy under such a prim business suit? Which is the truth, do you suppose? The suit or the lingerie?"

"What makes you think they're not both the truth?"

His index finger dipped beneath the lace and stroked. "Are they? Or is one truer than the other? Siren or businesswoman? Which is the better fit?"

"This morning, trying to change a baby's life, it was the businesswoman. Although I'm not sure that's even an accurate description. Perhaps *advocate* suits best. As for tonight…"

She stood, praying her legs would hold her. The instant she turned to face him, he kicked the chair out of the way. "What about tonight?" he asked.

"I'm not a siren. But I am a woman, a woman who wants you." She stepped closer. "You're wasting time. Are you going to take me or just talk about it?"

Four

Lander didn't need any further prompting. He swept Juliana into his arms and carried her to the bedroom. He didn't bother turning on the lights. A half-moon shone through the windows offering the perfect amount of illumination. He released her legs and allowed her to slide down his body, inch by luscious inch. The moon turned her into a palette of charcoal and silver—skin kissed with silver moonbeams, eyes as inky as the coal-black sky. Even her hair picked up the shades of the night, dousing the flames, if not the heat the color imitated.

He lowered his head, burying a kiss in the silken juncture of shoulder and throat. "One night," he whispered against her heated skin. "I swear I'll make it unforgettable."

He could feel her hands on his head, her fingers trembling as she threaded them into his hair. "I want unforgettable," she told him, holding him close. "Even more, I want to give it to you, as well."

"You already have."

He feathered kisses across her face, determined to taste every part of her. He was so intent on his exploration that he barely felt her unbutton his shirt or loosen his belt buckle. He fought against the urge to take, quickly and thoroughly. Juliana deserved more. If they only had one night, he would make certain they took their time and enjoyed every single second.

He found the zip at the side of her skirt and lowered it. To his amusement she rested her hands on his shoulders, and gave a rolling shimmy that sent the skirt drifting to the floor before nudging it aside. It left her standing in a pool of moonlight, clad in stockings and heels and a bra and thong. She paused then, and he caught a hint of vulnerability in her upturned face.

He traced her cheekbones with his thumbs. "What's wrong?"

"Nothing. I mean—" She made a small, fluttering gesture. "Nothing's wrong, exactly. It's just that I've known you barely a day."

"And yet you're standing in my bedroom, practically nude, about to make love to me."

He could feel a flush gather along her cheeks. "Yes."

"And it feels wrong."

"No." She shivered from the sudden chill that seemed to have invaded the room. Instead of wrapping her arms around herself or reaching for her clothes, as he half expected her to do, she shifted deeper into his arms, drawing warmth from him. "It feels right. It scares me how right it feels. How could that be in just a few short hours?"

She'd stunned him with her confession. Even more

unnerving was how her observation mirrored his own subconscious thoughts. Holding her, loving her, having her in his bed, his apartment, his life, did feel right. It wasn't a possibility he was willing to deal with, not when they only had this one night available to them.

This rightness, it had to result from the novelty of the situation. No more than that. Just lust. Once sated it would diminish, easing from this clawing necessity to something more manageable. Something that didn't tear him apart inside. Years from now when this time with Juliana came to mind, he'd smile reminiscently, savoring the faded memory the same way he savored a fine port or a Cuban cigar.

He glanced down at the woman he held, certain their reaction to each other was simple sexual attraction. How could it be anything more? Resolution filled him. He'd make the most of what they shared in the next few hours. Give her a memory she'd never forget, something she could savor, as well. And then it would end.

"It feels right because it is right," he reassured. For now. Knowing he had to be fair, he added, "We can stop. If it's only sex, it'll pass. We'll come to our senses, eventually." Maybe.

She laughed at that. "I don't think this will pass, not until we've done something about it."

Nor did he. "Then let's see how right we can make it."

There wasn't any talking after that. Focus narrowed, tightened. He could sense the slow build within her, the gradual drift from sweet want to desperate need. He curbed his impatience, the instinct to take her fast and thoroughly. To mark her as his. Instead, he continued on a slow, languid path, savoring each progressive step.

He unhooked her bra while she made short work of

his unbuttoned shirt. His slacks came next, along with her heels. He knelt to roll her stockings down the endless length of her legs, pausing periodically to kiss the path the drift of silk bared.

She clung to him for balance, shuddering beneath his caresses. "Hurry," she urged.

"Not a chance." He gave his undivided attention to the inner curve of her thigh, catching her as she sagged in his arms. "This is too important to rush."

Clothes ringed them in a tangled circle. Snatching a final kiss, he lifted her into his arms. He stepped from the circle of clothes and moonlight toward the shadowed bed, following her down onto the plush comforter. Her dark curls flowed out around her, captivating him. She was one of the most beautiful women he'd ever seen. Satin soft. Warm and generous. Filled with a hunger that matched his own. She returned his look, seducing him with a laugh as she melted against him.

"What would make you happy, love?" He filled his palms with her breasts and gently nipped at the rigid tips before laving them with his tongue. "This? Or how about…"

He trailed kisses downward, over the valley of her belly to the edge of her thong. Hooking his thumbs in the elastic riding her hips, he tugged, baring her. The perfume of her sex threatened to drive him insane. He found her with his mouth. Loved her. He heard her choked cry, her pleading words escaping in swift, desperate pants. Her muscles bunched, buttocks and thighs rippling beneath the strain, while she gathered up fistfuls of the comforter. Within minutes a high keening sob broke from her and she shattered in his arms.

"No, no." Her head moved restlessly back and forth. "It can't be over."

He soothed her with a gentle touch. "It's not over, love. It's just beginning."

He covered her body with his, stroking initially to calm, then to arouse. He'd promised himself when they'd met that he'd explore every inch of her body, and tonight he intended to do just that. They exchanged kisses, tentative at first, then with growing ardor. He'd anticipated a slow burn, building bit by bit, log heaped on burning log. But it was nothing like that. Wildfire exploded, sweeping fierce and reckless in one direction then another, overrunning sense and sensibility until they were both caught up in a maelstrom beyond their control.

His hands played over her until he heard the hitch in her breath that warned of her approaching climax. He sought out the heart of her, cupping the source of the fire. He'd done this to her. His touch had brought her to the brink once again. The knowledge roused something indescribable in him, awakening an emotion he couldn't put name to or fully understand. It was primal and viscerally male. A word echoed in the deepest recesses of his mind. A single word, chanted over and over again, like a mantra, offering both promise and intent.

Mine.

Juliana's voice joined the chorus. "Please. Please, Lander. Take me now. Make me yours."

He levered above her and dipped himself in her liquid heat. She wrapped her legs around him, locking him tightly against her. He surged, deep and hard, stroking into her. He'd never in his life felt anything like it. So snug and sleek. Almost virginal. She gasped out his name and when he moved even that one word was lost to her.

Still, he heard her singing, a soft musical cry of urgency and delight. Of wonder. Of rapture. And somehow he knew—knew without doubt or question—that it was a song she'd never sung before. That the woman in his arms wasn't almost virginal. Until just seconds ago, she'd been a virgin. She'd given herself to him without condition or hesitation, despite there being no future in it for either of them.

He mated their bodies, filling her again and again, whispering words, endless words, he couldn't afterward recall. They poured from the very heart of him as he poured his heart and soul into her. She arched beneath him, and the building came, faster and more powerful than before. It pounded unrelentingly until they reached the dizzying crest, teetering there for an endless second. The climax came, so hard and merciless, that all they could do was surrender to its taking, clinging to each other in its aftermath.

Breathless, they collapsed in a tangle of slick arms and legs, utterly spent. He had no idea how long they lay there while their bodies cooled, then chilled. Flinging out a hand, Lander snagged a section of comforter and pulled it over them, cocooning them in a silken nest.

Forever passed before passion eased and his brain began to function again. "Why, Juliana?" He rolled onto his side, levering himself upward onto an elbow. "Why didn't you tell me?"

To his frustration the bed remained in shadow, concealing her expression. Even so, he could hear the wariness in her voice. "Tell you what?"

"Don't pretend. You've never done anything like this before. Why now? Why me?"

She shrugged. "Because it felt right."

"That's not good enough."

She sat up, and this time the moon did find her, cutting across her face and lapping over her bared shoulders. "Do you think I wanted it to be you? That I wasn't hoping for more than you have to offer? More than I can give you? But when you touch me…" She turned her face away. "Is it just me? Or do you feel it, too? Isn't that why I'm here?"

"Hell. I'm sorry." He snagged a rope of curls and tugged until she looked at him again. "It just caught me by surprise. I find it hard to believe that there hasn't been a man in your life before this."

"There was a man."

A possessive stab caught Lander by surprise. "Obviously things didn't work out, because there's no question in my mind that he never had you in his bed."

"No." The intense pain in that single word had him wanting to gather her up and protect her from everyone and everything that might hurt her again. "He wanted to seduce me for reasons of his own. I found out before I made the ultimate mistake."

Possessiveness turned to cold anger. "A Verdonian?"

"No, Your Highness." A hint of gold flickered in her eyes, highlighting her amusement. "Not a Verdonian. The dungeons and torture rooms won't be needed."

"I'd have done it," he growled.

"Let's forget about Stewart." She rolled on top of him and captured his mouth with hers. "Isn't there something else you'd rather be doing?"

It was an offer he couldn't resist. The remaining hours of the night flowed from one unforgettable moment into another until exhaustion overtook them and they finally slept. When next Lander awoke, sunlight enveloped the room, filling it with a sparkling brilliance. But the warmth had fled.

Juliana was gone.

Juliana lifted her face to the first rays of the morning sun. Rather than hail a cab, she decided to walk for a while, needing the exercise to help center herself. Initially, her steps were light and joyous, the blood singing through her veins. Last night was the most incredible of her life. She'd never imagined lovemaking could be so earth-shattering. The fact that one man could make her feel so loved and cherished, amazed her every bit as much as it confused her. But Lander had done that and more.

A secret smile swept across her mouth and a passing pedestrian returned the smile with a wink and a grin. She shook her head, marveling. Imagine a lifetime filled with nights like the one she'd just experienced. Greeting each day locked in Lander's arms, having the right to stay there as long as she wanted. And imagine waking each morning filled with a jubilance and contentment that surpassed anything she'd dared believe possible. She hugged the emotions close, reveling in them.

Until she remembered.

Lander could never be a part of her life. She'd never know what it felt like to awaken in his arms, because it would never happen. She'd agreed to give him a single night, no more. And he'd accepted the offer and promised not to ask for another. Even if he wanted to see her again, to continue their relationship, it was impossible.

Maybe he'd have succeeded in tempting her if he could have guaranteed that their affair would remain secret. But she'd had enough experience with the paparazzi to know better. Eventually they'd discover Lander was seeing her. And once they did, they'd ferret out her identity. Her real identity. When that happened, it would cost Lander big-time. He might very well lose the election because of her and she couldn't bear it if that happened. Besides it wasn't like she'd be staying in Verdonia much longer. Soon she'd move on to another European country.

Her energy drained away, her earlier euphoria fizzling like a spent firecracker. Hailing a cab, she sat in the back, fighting tears. She tried to run through a series of mathematical equations to calm herself, but even that was beyond her. Ten minutes later she arrived outside of her apartment building. Paying the driver, she entered the complex and took the elevator to the tenth floor, grateful that she had no work pending and could take the day off to lick her wounds. To her dismay, even that was denied her. Stepping into her apartment, she found Joc waiting. She took one look at her brother and burst into tears.

"Aw, hell," he muttered, gathering her into his arms. "What did that bastard do to you?"

"Nothing. Everything." She fought to regain control with only limited success. "I'm sorry, Joc. I don't know what's the matter with me."

"I told you to stay away from him. Naturally you didn't listen and now he's made you cry." Beneath the brotherly concern she heard a ferocity that alarmed her. "No one's made you cry since Stewart."

His comment stopped her cold. She remembered all too well what he'd done to Stewart for that single affront. The only jobs still available to him involved mops and buckets of soapy water.

"No!" She pulled back, fisting her hands in her brother's shirt. "Now you listen up, big brother. You stay out of this. Lander didn't make me cry. I'm serious. He didn't."

He greeted her reassurance with skepticism. "Then why are you so upset?"

"Because he wanted to continue the relationship and I refused to even consider it."

It wasn't precisely accurate, but she didn't doubt for a minute that if she'd made the offer, Lander would have accepted without hesitation. He'd wanted her to stay with him. The desire had been buried in every whispered word, in each hungry kiss, in his first tender caress, straight through to his last. He'd overwhelmed her with want, seduced her with a need she'd never realized she possessed. If she'd been able to find the least little excuse for remaining with him, she'd have seized it without hesitation. But there hadn't been any reasonable excuses. The risk was too great, protecting Lander's reputation paramount. That far outweighed her petty wishes.

Joc shook his head. "You're not making a bit of sense. That alone is peculiar, considering you're one of the most rational, analytical women I know. If Lander still wants you, then what's the problem?"

"You know what the problem is."

A muscle jerked in his jaw. "You're afraid people will find out who you are and dig up old history about you. And you don't want to be in that sort of media frenzy again."

"Yes." She let go of his shirt, trying to smooth the wrinkles as assiduously as she tried to smooth the pain from her face. "You were right to warn me away from him. He's a prince. I'm no one. I'm worse than no one.

If his people find out who I am or about my background, he'll lose the election."

"You don't know that, not for sure," he protested.

"Yes, I do." She took a step back and offered her most implacable expression, the one she used when dealing with recalcitrant clients. "It's over, Joc. I had my one night with him. That's all I asked for or wanted, and it's exactly what I received." It would be foolish to hope for more.

"Are you certain? I can fix this, if you want."

"I'm positive. And no, I don't want you to fix a thing." She managed a quick, bright smile. "Seriously. Stay out of it."

Joc met her smile with one of his own, his a hard flash of white against his sun-darkened skin. "Okay, Ana." He tucked a tumble of curls behind her ear. "After all, haven't I always given you everything you wanted?"

"Yes, you have." But he couldn't help her this time, she realized. What she wanted wasn't his to give.

The instant the door closed behind her brother, the dam broke and with it came the realization that by allowing herself to become emotionally involved with the one man she couldn't have, she'd totally and completely ruined her life.

Lander stared at Arnaud in stunned disbelief. "What did you say?"

"You heard me." Determination was carved into every line of Joc's face. "I want you to marry my sister. In fact, our negotiations hinge on that very point."

Lander sliced his hand through the air, cutting him off. "Forget it. Maybe if you'd approached me a week ago. *Maybe* I'd have considered it. I'm that desperate. But not now."

"Because of Juliana."

He hadn't felt this possessive toward a woman ever. "Yes, because of Juliana."

"I thought it was a one-night stand."

"You bastard! Did she tell you that?"

"I have no intention of betraying her confidence." A hint of mockery crept into Joc's voice. "As far as I'm concerned you have two choices. I can either beat you to a bloody pulp for messing with Juliana, or I can make you pay for what you did to her by forcing you to give up your precious freedom. Personally, whaling on you for a bit holds far more appeal."

In two strides Lander was across the room and had Joc by the throat and up against the nearest wall. "What's your relationship with her?" he demanded. "She swore you weren't lovers, something I can verify as fact. So, why are you throwing up roadblocks between us? Why put your sister in the middle of all this? You want Juliana for yourself, don't you?"

To Lander's surprise Joc didn't try and break his hold. "I want Juliana to be happy."

"And marrying your sister will make her happy?" That didn't make sense.

"I believe so." Joc actually had the nerve to laugh. "Why don't I show you a picture of my sister."

"What the hell good will that do?" He released Joc with an exclamation of disgust. "You think I'm going to take one look at her and fall madly in love?"

Joc shrugged. "It could happen." He removed a snapshot from his wallet and spun it in Lander's direction. "Why don't we try it and see."

Lander caught the photo midair. Flipping it over, he stared at the picture in sheer disbelief.

"My sister. Juliana Rose Arnaud. I always called her Ana." Joc shrugged. "I guess the nickname carries bad memories, so she doesn't use it anymore."

It took Lander two tries before he could speak. "This has been a setup from the beginning, hasn't it?" He shot Joc a furious glare. "I call you for help and who shows up at the ball while I'm waiting for you, but your sister—a sister who's conveniently forgotten her last name's Arnaud. She falls into my arms like a ripe peach and after we spend one unforgettable night together all of a sudden I find out the two of you are related. And coincidence of all coincidences, the very next day you're holding our contract for ransom."

Joc shook his head. "Clever plan. I wish I could actually take credit for it. But I can't, because it didn't go down that way."

"I don't care how it went down. I suggest you get the hell out of Verdonia while you still have your head attached to your shoulders."

Joc held up a hand in an appeasing gesture. "Look, I swear there was no setup. I tried to warn her about you, Montgomery. I can't tell you how many times I advised her to give you a wide berth. But Juliana has a soft spot for jackals like you and once your relationship took a turn for the worse, this seemed an obvious solution."

"Not to me."

A hint of anger glittered in Joc's black gaze. "Maybe you should have thought of that before your North Pole got overruled by the southern half of your equator. Now let's talk turkey because this is how it's going down. I'm making a one-time offer. You refuse, I walk. And your precious country can go bankrupt for all I care."

Son of a— "What do you want?"

"Your end of our business arrangement is simple. Get my sister to fall in love with you. Should be easy since she's halfway there already. Marry her. Treat her like the queen she deserves to be. Live happily ever after. Hell, have babies if you're so inclined." He paused, shooting Lander a keen look. "Think you can do that?"

Babies? An image of redheaded toddlers racing through the palace came all too easily to mind. He took a step back, mentally and literally. "I think you're interfering where you don't belong."

The two locked gazes for an endless minute. "But you'll do it, won't you?" Joc demanded. "You'd do anything to save your country, including marry my sister."

Lander ground his teeth in silent fury. "Yes," he finally bit out.

"Even if it means being related to me?" Joc pressed harder. "And even if our connection causes you to lose the election?"

It very well might. Lander turned away and allowed the possibility to settle into his heart and mind. Not that it took much thought. He'd seen Arnaud's plan for Verdonia. It was a good one, one that had an excellent shot at ensuring full financial recovery. Setup or not, if the price he had to pay for that was marriage, he'd do it. If it meant saving Verdonia from economic disaster, he'd have married a two-headed goat, and Juliana was far from that.

Still, he didn't like Joc's tactics anymore than he liked suspecting someone as open and candid as Juliana of deceit. Granted, she'd concealed her full name from him, but he had a feeling that was a one-time aberration. What he liked least of all was being forced to marry on command. He'd always been the one in charge of his own destiny. He'd always been the one to command. It rankled more than a little to play puppet to Joc's puppeteer.

Turning, he asked, "I gather she's not to know about the addendum to our contract?"

"That would be a definite deal breaker."

It confirmed Lander's suspicion that if this was a setup, Juliana had played the part of unwitting pawn. "Just one question." He approached. "Why? You can't honestly believe this is in your sister's best interest?"

He didn't think Arnaud would answer. Emotions swept across the Texan's face. Anger. Stubborn determination. And—hell, could it be?—an odd vulnerability. "You're wrong, Montgomery," he said at last. "This is in her best interest. I couldn't protect her growing up. I'm not even much good at protecting her now." His expression hardened. "But you can do what I can't. You can give her everything she needs, everything I've never been able to."

Lander wanted to argue the point. This was a huge mistake, one he didn't doubt he'd live long to regret. But he didn't see any other choice. He wanted to explain what a disservice it was to Juliana to be married for financial gain rather than love. That she wouldn't appreciate this sort of manipulation any more than he did. But he knew from long experience that once Arnaud set his mind to something, he was impossible to budge. There might be room for negotiation later on, a better opportunity to apply calm reason to reckless obsession. Until then, Lander had no choice.

"Do we have a deal?" Joc asked impatiently.

"Yes, it's a deal."

He took Arnaud's hand in a tight grip, grinding bone against bone as he fixed the man with a fierce stare.

"Someday you'll find yourself boxed into a corner like this. Remember me when that happens, Arnaud. Remember, and know that you brought it on yourself when you forced this agreement on the woman you should have protected, and the one man who will do whatever it takes to see that you pay for your arrogance."

Five

Juliana finished the last of her paperwork, signing her name with a swift practiced stroke, before shoving the folder to one side of her desk. Swiveling to face the window, she leaned back in her chair and closed her eyes. Exhaustion threatened to overwhelm her. The past three days had been hideous, perhaps because she'd chosen to work nonstop rather than pacing herself. But at least it had kept her from obsessing over Lander and that one unforgettable night.

A knock sounded at her door, and she stifled a groan. The clock on the wall warned it was well past seven. The office staff should have long since cleared out, with the possible exception of her assistant. She heard him push open the door but didn't bother to open her eyes. "Colin, I thought I told you to go home an hour ago," she complained. Her assistant didn't answer, but she could hear him approach, no doubt to get the last of the papers she'd signed. "Didn't you have a date tonight?"

To her shock, he put his hands on her, his fingers digging into the knots of tension ridging her shoulders. Her eyes blinked open and she shot straight up in her chair. "Good Lord. Colin?"

"Gone."

"Lander!" She swiveled around, staring up at him in disbelief. "What are you doing here?"

"I came to see you, of course."

He plucked her out of the chair and into his arms. For an instant she allowed herself to relax against him before common sense prevailed and she fought her way free of his hold. "Please don't take this the wrong way, but…why?"

"Because of this."

Lowering his head, he teased her mouth with his. She had every intention of stopping him, of pulling back from those coaxing lips. Of telling him firmly and un-equivocally that she had no interest in seeing him ever again. Her good intentions lasted all of two seconds.

With a groan she gave up and fell into the embrace. She twined her arms around his neck and practically inhaled him. He walked her backward the two paces to her desk and lifted her onto the wooden surface. Her skirt hitched upward and he planted his hands on her knees and parted them. Stepping between, he tugged her tight against him.

"What are we doing?" she demanded, torn between laughter and tears.

"What we were meant to do."

"We agreed to a single night."

"Your choice, not mine. And like a fool, I didn't push

hard enough." He broke off to kiss her again, deep, drugging kisses. "But I've decided I want to renegotiate the terms of that agreement."

She started shaking her head before he'd finished speaking. "No. No, I can't. You have to trust that I have an excellent reason. Several of them, actually."

"Give me one."

She struggled to balance truth with caution. "You have an election coming up. You need to focus on that."

"My personal life has never interfered with my duty to my country. You should know, that takes primary importance over everything. Always," he emphasized. Sweeping the clip from her hair, he forked his fingers through the mass of curls. "But that doesn't mean I don't have time for you, as well. What's your next excuse for ending our relationship?"

"A point of clarity, if you don't mind. We don't have a relationship."

He merely smiled. His hands dropped to her legs, sliding upward, gathering her skirt as he went. "Tell me what you call it."

She shuddered beneath his touch, struggling to maintain an ounce of reason in the midst of this insanity. "A one-night stand."

His grip tightened on her thighs. "Don't." The single word sounded harsh, almost guttural. "Don't denigrate what happened between us."

"I'm just being honest." She struggled to tidy a messy situation, regardless of the pain it caused. To fit it neatly into its appropriately labeled box, a sealed box etched with "one-night stand" on the lid in indelible marker. "And though I can't explain all the problems it will cause if we continue to see each other, it's important you believe me. That you believe that it's best for Verdonia."

He dismissed her assertion with a shrug. "Why don't you let me decide that. There's only one question you need to answer. Was our one night together enough?"

She closed her eyes, dropping her head to his shoulder. "Please don't ask me that."

"Too late." She could feel his smile against the side of her neck. "Be honest, Juliana. You want more, just as I do."

The temptation to admit the truth was overwhelming. "Yes," she whispered. "I want more. But I'm begging you to walk away. There's so much you don't know about me."

His mouth traced a path along her neck to a sweet spot just beneath her ear. "In time, when you learn to trust me, you can tell me all your secrets."

Didn't he understand? With an effort, she lifted her head to look at him. "You're better off not knowing."

"At some point you'll tell me." He repeated the assertion with casual certainty. "You won't have any choice."

"You're probably right." She released her breath in a sigh. "If I agree, there are conditions."

"Name them."

"No one can know about us. And I mean no one."

"Agreed. Next."

"No falling in love."

To her surprise, that gave him pause. "You think you can order love? Where have I heard that before?"

"I don't know." Where had he? "But we can try."

"Sex and nothing but sex?"

It sounded so crude. So harsh. Not that she had any other option. She couldn't afford to fall in love with Lander. "Would that be so wrong?"

"Yes." He lifted her chin, forcing her to meet his

green-flecked eyes. She caught a hint of amusement, softened by tenderness. "Yes, it's wrong. But you'll need to discover that for yourself. What other conditions do you have?"

She hadn't a clue what else. Maybe if she'd anticipated this conversation, she'd have had a list prepared. Neatly numbered and bulleted, of course. But she'd ended things between them. She distinctly remembered doing it, even though it had ripped her apart. She'd cried over him and everything. And yet here he was, standing between her thighs with her skirt hiked to her hips and eighty-six combined inches of leg locked around his waist.

She shook her head. "I don't know. I'll give you the rest when I can think straight."

"In that case, I'm not sure I want you thinking straight." To her surprise, his grip firmed on her hips, pulling her so tightly against him that his belt buckle bit into her abdomen. "If that's everything, I suggest we get on with it."

"Excuse me?" She wriggled in discomfort. "You can't mean—"

"I do mean," he confirmed. "Right here and right now."

Had he gone crazy? She eyed him uncertainly. "Some women might want to make love on top of a desk, but I'm not one of them."

"Really?" A slight smile curved his lips and his gaze ran over her, lingering. "What happened to sex and nothing but sex?"

She became vividly aware of how she must look, her hair rioting around her shoulders, her skirt flipped back to expose everything from her waist down, her legs clasped about him. Heat scored her cheekbones and she had trouble meeting his gaze. "Not here," she whispered. "Not like this."

"I don't understand. I thought you said it's just sex, no emotion involved." He ran the tip of his finger over the swell of her breast. He'd touched her in a similar manner on a number of occasions, but this time it felt different. Careless. Distant. Carnal. "It's not like we need a bed. We can do it right here." He glanced around. "Or up against the wall over there. Or on the floor. Rug burns, but what the hell. I'm hungry, I eat. Isn't that how it works?"

She unwound her legs from his waist and shoved at his shoulders. Not that it did any good. He remained as unyielding as granite. "Please, move. I want to get off the desk."

"I'm serious, Juliana. Explain it to me. What does it matter where?" His hands dropped to her thighs. "Or how?"

She covered his hands with hers, attempting to stop those clever fingers from exploring any further. To her horror, tears pricked her eyes and her throat closed over, making it a struggle to respond. "It just does, okay?"

His hold eased. Gentled. Cupping her face, he leaned forward and kissed her. "And that, my beautiful Juliana, proves my point. Sex alone will never be enough for either of us because it's innately wrong." Stepping back, he helped her off the desk. With a few swift tugs, he straightened her clothing. "I'm sorry if I upset you."

She wobbled on her heels, struggling to regain her composure. "If that's how you feel—that it can't just be about sex, then why did you agree when I suggested it?"

He shot her a wicked look. "Oh, I'd have been willing to give it a try, if you insisted."

"Magnanimous of you," she muttered.

"I thought so." His smile faded. "But in the end, we'd have failed."

"And one of us would have gotten hurt." She rested her head against his shoulder. "So why are we doing this?"

His arms slid around her. "Because we don't have any other choice."

He made it sound as though fate had set something in motion, something they could neither change nor escape, assuming they wanted to. She felt a sudden urge to run. To return with Joc to Dallas. She was good at running. She'd done it often enough. Her breath trembled in a sigh. She'd done it often enough to know it never worked. If people wanted to find you, they could. If they wanted to expose you, they did.

Chances were, running and hiding wouldn't work this time, either. But until the truth came out—and it always came out—she'd enjoy however much time she had with Lander and hope it was enough. It would have to be.

"So what now?" she asked.

"Now we play."

She glanced up at him, intrigued. "Play?"

"You look confused. Haven't you ever played before?"

She thought about it before slowly shaking her head. "Not really."

"Then it's past time you started."

The nights following flew by as though part of a dream. During the daylight, Juliana worked harder than she thought possible so she could enjoy those few precious nighttime hours with Lander. It became like a game. Late each afternoon she'd receive a phone call giving her a different location to meet, each in a section of the city free from curious eyes. And every evening she'd escape work and race to wherever she'd been directed.

She always found a different vehicle waiting for her, the only thing they had in common a unifying anonymity in appearance that guaranteed they'd fade in with every other car on the busy streets of Mt. Roche.

The first night she was driven to an underground garage, and had expected to find herself back at the apartment complex where she'd made love to Lander. But that hadn't happened. Instead, she ended up in one of the downtown malls. Even though all the shops were lit, to her astonishment not a soul stirred. She and Lander spent the entire night wandering through the mall, laughing at the insanity of having the entire place to themselves. Every once in a while she'd catch a glimpse of the security guards who shadowed their every move. She hadn't noticed them the night she'd spent at his apartment, but she had an uneasy feeling they'd been there, regardless.

Most of the time she could ignore their presence and dart from store to store, trying on clothes or jewelry or shoes, or wandering through the bookstores or among the craft stalls. Just as exhaustion set in, dinner miraculously appeared at a small table inside a trendy café. They dined by candlelight, soft music playing in the background. When they'd finished, Lander escorted her back to the car she'd arrived in, which, to her astonishment, delivered her home again.

The next night Lander arranged for a private showing at a movie theater. Another evening found them wandering through a wild animal park on the outskirts of the city. He took her ice skating. Swimming. He even arranged for a night at a spa. But not once did he take her back to the apartment and make love to her as she longed for him to do.

He must have been aware of her confusion, just as he must have been aware of how much she wanted to be in his arms again. She didn't understand it. As impossible as it seemed, it was almost as though he were… wooing her. But that didn't make a bit of sense.

On the tenth night, her car pulled into another underground garage. Once again she thought perhaps it was the apartment complex, and hope flared. But when she stepped from the vehicle, one of Lander's private bodyguards whisked her along a set of unfamiliar corridors dotted with security. He paused before a heavy steel door, guarded by his hulking counterpart.

Opening the door, he gestured for her to enter. "Please go on through, Ms. Rose," he said. "Tell His Highness that I'm here if he needs anything."

Before she could ask the guard where she was, the door clanged shut behind her. Subdued lighting suffused the room, and it took a minute for her eyes to adjust. Once they had, she was astonished to discover she stood in a museum.

"It's one of my favorite places to come." Lander spoke from the shadows across the room. He flicked on a light switch, flooding the room with a brighter glow. "Do you like museums?"

"Yes," she confessed. "Very much."

"This one has it all. Art. History. Science."

The hours flowed one into the next as he led her through each wing. As they explored the section detailing Verdonia's rich history, Lander brought it to life with stories that gave added depth and color to each exhibit. Later, they ate picnic-style on the floor in front of a

Monet and a Renoir with a Rodin sculpture guarding them from the corner. And they talked, endlessly.

The evening concluded in a small secure room housing the crown jewels of Verdonia. "The ones not in use," Lander teased.

To her astonishment, he opened the cases and lifted out various pieces for her to try on. "I'm afraid to touch them," she told him. "I half expect your guards to burst in here and arrest me."

"I have to admit, you're the first woman outside the royals who's ever had the opportunity to do this." He fastened a necklace dripping with diamonds and amethysts around her neck. "What do you think?"

Mirrors lined the back of each display case and she stood in front of one to look, watching the gems dance and glitter with her every breath. "It's stunning."

"It was a wedding gift from my father to my mother, along with these." He lifted out a tiara and settled it in her curls. Then he slipped a ring on her finger, the central stone a huge amethyst, the purplish-blue depths flashing with red fire. "This ring's called Soul Mate, which is actually what the Verdonia Royal symbolizes."

"Verdonia Royal? Is that what the amethyst is called?"

"That particular color. There's not another shade quite like it anywhere else in the world. We also have pink stones which are far more common, but popular, nonetheless."

"A Rose de France? I've heard of them."

He glared at her in mock anger. "Please. Celestia Blush."

She swept him a deep, graceful courtesy. "I beg your pardon, Your Highness. I misspoke. I swear it won't happen again."

"See that it doesn't."

Rising, she studied the circle of Blushes that surrounded the Royal. "Does the Blush have a special meaning, too?"

Lander nodded. "It signifies the sealing of a contract. When it's set in a circle like this it denotes a binding agreement, in this case a marriage."

"It's beautiful." She glanced at him hesitantly. "You must miss your mother very much."

"She died when I was very young, Merrick little more than a baby. My memories are more…impressions. Feelings of warmth and comfort."

His expression remained open, so she risked another question. "You said it took a while to adjust to your stepsister's advent in your life. What about your stepmother's?"

"She's an impressive lady." An odd smile curved his mouth. "Did you know she designed her own engagement ring?"

"Really? What does it look like?"

"There's a replica of it over here."

She joined him in front of a display case and stared at the ring. It was quite different from the one belonging to Lander's mother. Three gem stones—a diamond, an emerald and a ruby—made up the central portion of the ring, the trio surrounded by a circle of alternating Verdonia Royals and sapphires.

"It means something, doesn't it?"

"Yes." A poignant quality had crept into his voice. "And once Merrick and I figured it out, we became a family."

"Birthstones?"

"Clever, Juliana. Yes, they're birthstones. The three in the center represent Merrick, Miri and me. All of them are of exact equal weight, cut and clarity."

"And the circle of amethysts and sapphires? Your father and stepmother?"

"The amethyst, ironically enough, is my step-mother's birthstone. The sapphire, my father's. And if you look carefully at the gold filigree that makes up the rest of the ring, it spells out two words in Verdonian."

It took Juliana a moment to find the words hidden in the pattern. "Love and…unity?"

"A circle of love and unity around the three most precious people in their lives. She's a special woman, my stepmother." He paused a beat. "You'd enjoy meet-ing her, as she would you."

His comment brought her down to earth with painful swiftness. Her reflection bounced back from a dozen different mirrors, mocking her. She stood in fantasy, arrayed in jewels she had no right to wear. A tiara worn by a queen. A necklace given as a royal wedding gift. A ring that connected two soul mates.

It hurt. It hurt to know that she would never be the re-cipient of such gifts. Oh, not the gems. She didn't care about those. It was the love and commitment and promise they stood for. Perhaps the women in her family were never meant to know those things. Certainly, her mother had never received as much from her father, though she'd kept hoping against hope, right up until her death.

Without a word Juliana turned her back on Lander, at the same time turning her back on a reflection that was just that—a reflection of reality. "I don't think I can work the clasp," she said, relieved that she sounded so calm. With luck she'd concealed her inner turmoil. "Would you mind?"

"Are you certain? I thought we could—"

She rounded on him, not so calm anymore, the

turmoil slipping from her control and spilling loose. "Could what? Indulge in a little make-believe? Were you going to put on a crown and play Prince Charming to my Cinderella again?"

He twined a length of her hair around his fingers. The curls clung to him like the roses had clung to a midnight arbor in a dream they'd shared on a night not long ago. "I've hurt you. I'm sorry. That wasn't my intention."

Pain threatened to overwhelm her, and it took a full minute to recover her equilibrium. "Thank you for a lovely evening, but it's time for me to return home now."

Home. Not that she actually had one. Her Verdonian apartment wasn't a true home. An image of a Texas hacienda flashed through her mind, filling her with a vague yearning. Nor was Dallas. Not any longer. She'd lost all that at the tender age of eight. Her mouth twisted. Or rather, she'd lost the illusion then. The pretense of hearth and home.

Without a word he reached behind her and unclasped the necklace. The tiara proved more problematic, tangling in curls that seemed reluctant to part with it. When she would have yanked it free, Lander stopped her, gently coaxing it loose.

"There," he said at last, dropping a kiss on top of her head. "Not a single hair lost."

His comment knocked her off-kilter. He hadn't been careful out of concern for the tiara, but so he wouldn't hurt her. Her breath escaped in a gusty sigh. "What are we doing? What are *you* doing?"

"Don't you know?"

She shook her head. "To be perfectly honest, I haven't a clue."

"You're a smart woman. You'll figure it out eventually."

"I don't want to figure it out eventually." She studied him, attempting to analyze the situation. She should be able to logic it out. To add it up or puzzle it through, or apply reason to the problem and come up with a simple solution. One plus one always equaled two. But no matter how hard she tried, nothing made sense. "You're playing some sort of game. I wish I knew what it was."

He paused in the process of returning the pieces of jewelry to the display cases. "This is no game."

"Are you trying to seduce me?" She shook her head as soon as she'd posed the question. "That doesn't make sense. I vaguely recall you did that already."

He lifted an eyebrow. "If it's such a vague memory, I must have done something wrong." He locked the case. "Perhaps there's another explanation. A very simple, very obvious one."

"Wait. You forgot the ring." She slipped it from her finger and held it out to him. "The only explanation that makes any sense is that you're still trying to prove that what we feel isn't lust. Like you did in my office."

He took the ring from her. But instead of returning it to the display case, he pocketed it. "Close, but not quite there."

"I give up. Tell me what's going on."

"What about love?"

He shocked her so that she couldn't think of a single thing to say. Taking her arm, he escorted her through the door protected by his bodyguards and to the car that had delivered her to the museum. The engine started with a soft purr and they exited from the garage onto a rain-slicked street. Lightning speared the sky while thunder cleared its throat. Heavy droplets pounded the front windshield, their descent as fast and dizzying as her thoughts.

In no time they pulled into a garage, and this time she recognized it as the one to his apartment. He parked the car and glanced at her. There wasn't an ounce of question in that silent look, just heated demand. She gave him her response by exiting the car and slamming the door. Then she stalked to the elevator, thunder rumbling approval with every step she took.

"It's not possible," she announced the minute they stepped from the elevator into the apartment.

A crash of thunder shook the building and Lander waited until it had died before asking, "What isn't possible?"

"True love. Fairy-tale romances. Happily ever after."

He glanced her way, the soft glow from a nearby lamp providing enough illumination to reveal his curiosity. "You don't believe in love? Or you don't believe in love at first sight?"

"I'm not sure I believe in either one," she confessed.

"Interesting, considering what happened when we met."

Her throat tightened. "What did happen, exactly?"

"Why don't I show you instead."

He lowered his head and sampled her mouth. Her lips parted beneath the onslaught. It was such a sweet joining, thorough and tender. When he would have pulled back, she thrust her fingers deep into his hair to prevent him and deepened the kiss. She couldn't deal with tender right now, couldn't handle all that it suggested about their relationship. But she'd accept thorough— accept it, as well as give it. She drank with greedy abandonment, consumed with a driving need to seize what he'd been promising for the past ten days.

The storm broke overhead, and the air quickened,

filled with an energy and electricity that fueled their taking, one of the other. It was fast. Edged with violence. A battle for supremacy between male and female. He drove her toward the bedroom just as lightning flared, turning the room a stark blue white and revealing a man pushed past reason. Exhilarated, she pushed harder.

"Show me more," she demanded, ripping at his clothing.

"Until there's no more to show." He stripped her with swift economy before dealing with the few remaining pieces of his own clothing. And then there was no more talking. The first moment of intense rapture caught them both by surprise, a swift, needy explosion of sheer ecstasy that mirrored the storm raging overhead.

"Tell me now that you don't believe in love," he demanded as he drove into her, sending her soaring again. "Deny it if you can."

Her breath caught on a sob. "I can't. You know I can't."

And as the heavens opened, flooding the earth, Juliana opened herself, heart and soul, no longer able to hide from the truth. She loved this man. Loved him more than she believed possible. It was as though her revelation gentled the storm. The thunder lost its voice, fading to a distant grumble, while the lightning flashed a soft farewell.

In that perfect moment they came together again. Slowly. Easily. With piercing sensitivity. Moving together in exquisite harmony.

Juliana closed her eyes, forced to accept the truth. They moved together in the ultimate expression of love.

Six

Lander woke, delighted to discover he still held Juliana in his arms. Rain-washed sunlight spilled across the bed and into her eyes, causing her to stir. With a gasp she sat up, one elbow just missing his jaw, the other nailing his gut with pinpoint accuracy. Whereas the night before she'd been all grace and poetry in motion, the morning turned her awkward and uncertain. He found it unbelievably endearing.

"Good morning," he said, once he could draw breath.

She gazed up at him, blinking the remnants of sweet dreams from her eyes. "I overslept, didn't I?"

"A bit." Unable to resist, he buried his hands in her hair, realizing as he did so how much he enjoyed the soft, springy texture, as well as the way the curls clung to his fingers. He gave her a slow, lingering kiss. "But if that means waking with you in my arms, rather than finding you've slipped out the door, so much the better."

"It's definitely better," she confessed with an abashed smile. "If not conducive to good work habits."

In that moment she looked as far removed from the self-confident businesswoman as he'd ever seen—not to mention the seductive siren who'd first captured his interest. He wasn't certain which aspect of her personality appealed the most. Right now he found the rumpled urchin a fascination he'd love to spend the rest of the morning exploring.

Before he could suggest it, a tiny frown crinkled her forehead. "What time is it, do you know?"

"Ten."

She nearly hyperventilated. "Work. Office. Late. Very, very late."

He shrugged, unconcerned. "Tell them you're with me."

That gave her pause, if only for an instant. At least it gave her enough time to calm down. "Wait a minute. Are you telling me that sleeping with the Prince of Verdon gives me a free pass at work?"

A smile slashed across his face. "Duke of Verdon," he corrected. "Prince of Verdonia. And I've been thinking of making it a royal decree. Any woman who sleeps with me is excused from work the next day. How does that sound?"

She inched toward the edge of the mattress. "You'll have them lining up at the palace doors."

He scooped her close before she could escape. "There's only one woman I want at my door, and that's you."

He saw the delight blossom in her face and felt the eager give of her body. She laughed up at him and that momentary indulgence completely altered her appearance. A mischievous pixie peeked through the regal facade of the Fairy Queen, and Lander found he couldn't take his eyes off her.

She was so beautiful, her eyes tilted at the corners, just enough to give them an exotic slant, while specks of gold glistened hungrily in the honey brown. The sunlight danced across the spill of auburn curls turning them to flame against the elegant angles of her face. And her body. Lord help him. Plump and rounded where it needed to be and long and lean everywhere else, with skin so milky it looked as though it had been painted on by a master artist.

His arms tightened. "Stay," he whispered. "Just this once."

"Just once? I tried just once. It didn't work, as I'm sure you recall." With a regretful sigh, she rolled away from him, and as much as it pained him, he let her go. "I'm sorry, Lander. I have to get to work."

"The children are depending on you, aren't they?"

"Yes." She gathered up her clothing and hugged the pieces to her so that all he could see was acres of leg vanishing into crumpled green silk.

He swept back the covers. "Give me a minute to dress and I'll drive you."

"No, don't bother. I'll just catch a cab back to my apartment."

"Why bother with a cab if I'm willing to do it?" It didn't surprise him when she avoided his gaze, not that he needed to see her eyes to guess what she was thinking. "It's because you're afraid someone will catch us together, isn't it?"

"Too many people already know. It's going to leak sooner or later." She did look at him then, and the pain he read there struck like a physical blow. "We don't have much longer."

He erupted from the bed and dragged on a pair of jeans, not bothering to fasten them. "We have as long as we want," he insisted, stalking toward her.

"My work in Verdonia is almost finished. I've already been up north in Avernos for six weeks. And I spent more than two months in Celestia. I may need to go back there for an additional week or so after I'm finished here, but…" She trailed off with a sigh of regret. "There are other countries. Other children. Europe's a big place."

He couldn't resist touching her. Needed to, for some reason. "How much longer here, in Mt. Roche?"

"A few days," she whispered. "Maybe a week."

"It's not enough."

"It'll have to be."

She ended the discussion by vanishing into the bathroom, emerging a short time later wearing her clothes from the night before. She'd somehow managed to tame her hair, ruthlessly knotting it at the nape of her neck. In her business suit, all neatly tucked and buttoned, she looked every inch the self-possessed professional. Lander took one look at her and all he could think about was freeing that glorious mane and rumpling her tidy suit until he'd released the heart of passion that beat within the woman of calm reason standing before him.

"I'll send a car for you tonight," he said.

She caught her lower lip between her teeth. "Maybe we should take a night off. I'm getting behind on my work and—"

"Your work isn't going anywhere."

"No, it isn't," she conceded. "But the children are hurt by any delay."

Hell. She'd gotten him with that one. "I wouldn't want that. Are you certain I can't give you a ride?"

"Thank you, no."

He could hear the unspoken "Your Highness" in her tone, the polite curtsy buried within her words. His hands folded into fists. "I'll call you. If we can't see each other, you can at least take five minutes to talk."

She attempted a smile, but he caught the faint wobble and realized she wasn't anywhere near as in control as she'd like to pretend. He took a step in her direction intent on breaking through the vestiges of that control, but she flung up a hand, stopping him at the last second.

"Don't." Her voice broke on the word. She shot a swift, hunted glance toward the door. "Please let me go."

It wasn't what either of them wanted. He could change her mind with a single touch, but he didn't have the heart to stop her, to hurt her any more than she was already hurting. "I'll call you later," he repeated, more forcefully this time, and stepped aside.

She broke for the door, snatching up her purse as she went. He didn't waste any time. Dressing as swiftly as she, he made a beeline for the elevator. Juliana was already gone, but had sent the elevator back up for him. He shook his head as he stepped inside and stabbed the button for the garage.

He found her fascinating. Passionate. Kind. Wary. Like a wild creature in need of help, but fearful of becoming trapped. He could sympathize. Soon she'd discover they were both trapped in a situation not of their making, one with only a single solution. He fingered the ring he'd taken from the museum. It weighed heavily in his pocket. It was time to end this nonsense once and for all, he decided. Time to spring the trap.

He commandeered the car from the previous night and started it with a roar. Pulling out of the garage, he turned onto the street fronting the apartment complex. To his surprise, a crowd had gathered there. He glanced over as he passed, and what he saw had him slamming on his brakes and screeching to a halt.

Damn it to hell! Someone had sprung the trap ahead of him.

The elevator ride to the lobby seemed endless, stopping at every other floor. She'd been a fool to get involved with Lander. She'd known it from the start. At least with Stewart she could claim a certain level of naiveté. She'd been woefully inexperienced. Unfortunately, with Lander she could make no such claim. She'd committed the ultimate folly. She'd allowed herself to fall in love. To believe—if only for a moment—in fairy tales and happily-ever-after endings. It had been a mistake, one she'd never make again. She had no right to involve herself with a man who would be king. None.

The doors opened on to the lobby, and after returning the car to the penthouse, she walked briskly toward the exit, the rapid-fire chatter of her heels marking the speed of her passage. She never even looked up as she pushed through the doors leading outside, never saw them until she'd burst right into their midst.

"What's your name, miss?" The question was asked in Verdonian.

Flashbulbs exploded in her face and she flung up a hand to protect herself. "What…?"

Dozens of men and women hemmed her in on all sides, pressing, pressing, pressing. Microphones were shoved toward her, along with tape recorders and camera lenses. Everything took on a surreal quality. Noises grew too loud—the shrill, demanding voices, the desperate thrum of her heartbeat, the labored sound of her breathing. Odd, unwanted sensations heightened—the harsh feel of the sunlight scouring her face, leaving it naked and vulnerable to prying eyes. The stab of heat her panic induced, countered by the dank chill of fear. The stench of too many perfumed bodies, pulling, pulling, pulling.

"How long have you been seeing Prince Lander?" Verdonian again.

"What's he like in bed?" American. Female. City-slick and cynically amused. Followed by, "Who are you? You look familiar. You're not from Verdonia, are you, sweetie?"

Oh, God. Had she been recognized? "Please—"

"American," another crowed. "Definitely American."

She tried to push her way clear, but they weren't about to allow that. They reminded her of a pack of hyenas cornering a foolish gazelle who'd strayed too far from the herd. She was struck with a hideous sense of déjà vu. Another time, another place, but with the same rabid mob mentality, pushing, pushing, pushing.

"Did you know your father was already married?" the voices had shouted at the helpless eight-year-old she'd been back then. "How does it feel to be a bastard?"

The flashback to that hideous, long-ago moment only lasted an instant, but it was enough to cause her chest to tighten. "Please, move." She could feel the panic gnawing at the edges of her self-control and she fell back a pace only to be shoved stumbling into the center ring once again. "I don't know what you're talking about. I need to get to work."

"Where do you work?"

"Do you work for Prince Lander?"

"I wouldn't mind that sort of work." Laughter erupted at the American reporter's comment. "Hell, I'd be willing to pay for the pleasure, if it meant spending the better part of my day in bed with Prince Lander."

The laughter had cut off in the middle of the woman's comment, so the final words rang crude and unpleasant in the morning air. An uncomfortable silence descended, though Juliana remained too shocked and confused to judge the cause.

And then she heard him. He uttered just a single word, one that sang of salvation, even if it sounded more like a growl than a song. "Move."

As one, the reporters and paparazzi parted and Lander stood there looking as much like the Lion of Mt. Roche as she'd ever seen him. His hair swept back from his face like a mane, the sunlight picking out the streaks of blond among the tawny brown. Fierce green lights burned in his gaze, and every line of his face held an implicit promise of violence. He sliced through them with a jungle cat saunter, and took what belonged to him—her.

He caught her by the hand and she felt something slide onto her finger before he turned with her, facing the press. He eyed them one by one, his gaze lingering for a fraction of an instant on the American reporter.

"Remove her." Security closed in, security Juliana hadn't even noticed encircling the mob until then. "Escort her to the airport and see her on the first plane out of Verdonia." He cut off the woman's furious protests with a single glare. "No one treats my fiancée with such disrespect and continues working in this country." He lifted Juliana's hand to his mouth with old-fashioned gallantry and kissed it. "No one."

Every last person drew a collective breath, including Juliana. Before anyone could fire a single question, Lander draped an arm about her shoulders and whisked her through the crowd to his car. It sat in the middle of the street, the engine idling, the driver side door hanging ajar. He bundled her into the passenger seat before climbing behind the wheel. In the next instant they shot down the road, security cars clearing a path in front and behind.

"Are you okay?" Lander spared her a swift glance. "Damn it. You look like you're going to faint. Even your lips are white." He took his hand off the wheel long enough to stroke her cheek. "And your skin is like ice."

"It was… It was—" She drew in a deep, shuddering breath, striving to speak through chattering teeth. "I don't handle crowds like that very well."

"No one does. I'm sorry. I swore I'd protect you from that sort of media circus and I failed." A muscle jerked along his jawline. "I promise it won't happen again."

"Of course it will." It always did. Numb acceptance vied with a visceral fear. She twisted her hands together in silent agitation and suddenly realized she was wearing a ring. Glancing down, she gaped. It was Soul Mate, though she didn't have a clue how it had come to be on her finger. She thrust her hand beneath his nose, her fingers trembling so badly that red sparks exploded outward from the center of the amethyst. "What? How…?"

"I slipped it on your finger right before I announced our engagement."

For some reason, she couldn't get her brain to wrap around his explanation. "But we're not engaged."

He shot her a swift, humorous glance. "We are now."

Disjointed bits and pieces from her rescue coalesced into a less-than-cohesive whole. The *snap, snap, snap* of the reporters' jaws as they bit off pieces of her for public consumption. Her helplessness and fear. And then Lander had arrived, her knight in shining armor. And he'd said…he'd said, *No one treats my fiancée with such disrespect….*

She closed her eyes. That's right, she remembered that part. He'd called her his fiancée. He'd made that one reporter leave for being disrespectful. Then he'd lifted her hand and— She sucked air into her lungs and her eyes flashed open in shock. Her *left* hand. He'd lifted her left hand and kissed it, so that everyone would notice the ring he'd surreptitiously slipped onto her finger. She'd seen the astonished delight on the faces of the reporters. Had cringed from the speculation in their eyes as they'd scribbled their notes and recorded the moment for posterity with their cameras and video. She'd just been too far gone to comprehend the significance of what had happened.

"No!" She looked around with a rising sense of desperation. "Pull over. Pull the car over, right now. You don't realize what you've done. We have to go back and fix this before you're ruined. You have to tell the press we're not engaged. Please, Lander!"

He shot her another look, one of deepening concern. "Two more minutes and we'll be there. Hang on until then."

He was as good as his word. He spun into the winding drive that led to the palace and zipped up the road and through the gates at a rate of speed that spoke of long practice, and yet had her closing her eyes out of sheer panic. When they slowed, she peeked through her lashes in time to see him turn onto a small access road that circled toward the back of the palace.

"This way," he said as soon as they'd exited the car.

He led her through a warren of walkways and it was everything she could do to keep from battering him with a barrage of questions and demands—questions as to why he'd claimed they were engaged, and demands that they return to the apartment complex and tell the press the truth. A few minutes later they found themselves once again in a small, familiar glade at the path's end. In the center of the clearing stood the trellis gazebo she remembered so well, the structure barely visible beneath its canopy of white roses. Their heady perfume scented the air, stirring bittersweet memories of the last time she'd been here.

"Back to where it all began," she felt compelled to say.

"It didn't start here." He closed the distance between them. "It started in the ballroom when I looked up and saw you standing above me. I'd never seen anyone more beautiful than you."

"Love at first sight?" If only that were possible. "I already told you I don't believe in that. It's the stuff of fairy tales and fantasies and—" Her voice broke before she managed to harden it. "And make-believe."

"Don't." He gathered her close. "It'll all work out. I promise."

"How can it?" She pushed away from him. "You just don't get it. You think I'm Cinderella. But I'm not. I'm the ugly stepsister. You have to go back to the apartment. You have to tell all those reporters that you made a mistake. That you were just joking about our engagement."

"But I wasn't joking. And it's not a mistake." Even though she'd pulled free of his embrace, he didn't let her move beyond his reach. If she'd been the imaginative sort, she'd have suspected he was stalking her. "Besides, mistake or not, it's too late to take it back."

She stilled. "What do you mean?"

"By now the information is everywhere," he explained matter-of-factly. "Newspapers. Television. The Internet. All of the media outlets will be trumpeting the news. And every last one will be in the midst of a pitched battle to be the first to identify you."

She fought to draw air in her lungs. "Oh, God. You have no idea what you've done."

"What's wrong?" The sensation of being stalked intensified as he caged her against the gazebo. "Why are you in such a panic?"

Soft white roses kissed her face and shoulders while the vines snared her hair, delicately coaxing the curls loose from their confinement at the nape of her neck. "I warned you there were things you didn't know about me."

"Like what?"

Tears blinded her. *Say it! Just say the words.* "I'm illegitimate, Lander." There. It was in the open now. She'd claimed the awful truth. Even after all these years it still had the power to wound, stirring some of the most traumatic memories of her life. "I was eight when I found out, in a manner not that different from what happened outside the apartment complex. It was…it was a big scandal at the time. My mother, my brother. We were crucified by the press."

"Easy, sweetheart. It's all right."

"No, it's not all right!"

She covered her face with her hands, struggling to contain the flood of emotions, with only limited success. It was time to get this over with, to tell him the truth and be done with it. Past time, if she were honest. She'd known this moment was coming but had been too much of a coward to face it any sooner because her desire for Lander had outweighed basic common sense. Now she had no other choice but to deal with the situation and put an end to their involvement, once and for all. Slowly she dropped her arms to her sides and stood before him like a prisoner facing a firing squad.

"No one in Verdonia knows my name yet. But that American reporter recognized me. Once she's had time to think about it, she'll remember where she's seen me." Pain underscored each word, despite her best attempts to keep her voice emotionless. "And she'll be angry because you made her leave the country. She'll want to get even. She'll put things in the paper. Or online. Or go on some hideous talk show and air all the sordid details."

"What sordid details?"

She forced herself to speak unemotionally, though it was one of the toughest things she'd ever done. "My name is Juliana Rose…Arnaud. I'm Joc's sister. Most people in the States know me as Ana Arnaud, rather than Juliana. When it gets out that I'm the illegitimate daughter of a crook, the sister of a man who amassed his fortune through—what the press regards as—questionable means, you'll be crucified."

Lander's hands tightened on her shoulders. "It doesn't matter who your father is, or your brother. I'll protect you."

"It's not me who needs protecting!" She drew a ragged breath, staring at him in disbelief. "You say none of this matters, but you're wrong. It does matter. Don't you understand what I've done? I've ruined your reputation. At the very least, I've cost you the election. No one in Verdonia will want their king married to a bast—"

He stopped her with his mouth, cutting off the word before it could be fully uttered. It was as though he refused to have the air they breathed sullied with such an ugly declaration. Every last thought in her head evaporated beneath the heat of his embrace. He took her to new heights with that kiss, reassuring her without words. Adored her. Gentled her. Loved her.

"I don't care," he said between kisses. "The circumstances of your birth aren't what matter to me."

"My illegitimacy should matter. Don't you understand—"

"Trust me, Juliana. I understand more than you know." He snatched another kiss while she puzzled over that. Reaching behind her, he removed the clip at the nape of her neck, and with a swift flick of his wrist, sent it spinning over the nearest hedge. "God, I've wanted to do that since the first time you wore your hair in that annoying knot."

Before she could utter a single protest, he sank his fingers deep into the loosened strands and tumbled it into a fiery halo around her face. In between swift, teasing kisses he stripped off her suit jacket and released the top three buttons of her blouse. The entire time he edged her closer to the gazebo until they scaled the half dozen stairs and stepped inside.

Shadows draped the interior, and the scent of roses hung more heavily in the confined space. Intent on putting some distance between them, Juliana retreated to the padded wrought-iron bench in the middle of the gazebo and attempted to do up her blouse. Before she could get more than a single button through its hole, Lander sat next to her and swung her legs across his lap. Removing her heels, he tossed them through the archway onto the verdant grass beyond.

"What are you doing?" she demanded.

"Making love to my fiancée."

She stared at him, wide-eyed. "Stop calling me that. It's not a real engagement and I'm not making love in the palace gardens where anyone could stumble across us."

He shrugged. "Okay, then we'll talk some more. Have you told me everything you need to?" He smiled at her with such tenderness that it nearly broke her heart. "Any more confessions, my scandalous wife-to-be?"

"Aren't you listening? I'm not your wife-to-be. You haven't asked and I haven't accepted. This is nothing to make light of, Your Highness. It's serious."

He sobered, the laughter dying from his eyes. "I promise I'm not making light of it. The circumstances of your birth don't make any difference to me, or to how I feel about you. Nor does your relationship to Joc. But it infuriates me that you've been made to feel ashamed of something beyond your control."

Dear God, she'd have to tell him all of it. It was the only way to get him to understand. "It isn't just the circumstance of my birth," she insisted. "There's something else. Something worse."

If she were going to get through this next part she needed every ounce of control she possessed. She fixed her gaze on where Lander had tossed her shoes, one sitting as neatly as if she'd placed it on the grass, the other facedown, its stiletto heel stabbing skyward like a finger of doom. She retreated into a math equation to help clear her mind, working it through step by step. She'd nearly finished when Lander spoke.

"Would you mind telling me what the *hell* you're doing?"

She blinked. "I'm sorry. What did you say?"

"I asked what you were doing. It's like…you went away. One minute you were here and—" he snapped his fingers just shy of her nose "—the next you were gone. This isn't the first time it's happened, either."

"Oh. That."

"Yes. That."

"I was solving a second-order-linear-difference equation."

"Second order linear—"

"Difference equation. With constant coefficients." A reluctant smile broke through. "It's a mathematical equation. It helps reduce stress."

"And you do that in your head?"

Her brow crinkled in a frown. "I'm not sure I always get the answer right, but that's not the purpose."

"Of course not," he muttered. "Damn, woman, you never cease to amaze me." He gestured for her to continue, bringing them back on point. "Okay, let's hear it. What's the other scandal in your background? I don't suppose it has anything to do with a certain man named Stewart?"

"I'm afraid so."

She started to lace her fingers together, but finding she still wore Soul Mate threw her off stride and she hesitated, not quite certain what to do with her hands. Lander settled the matter for her. He pulled her closer and twined her arms around his neck. It seemed easiest to submit rather than to protest. He'd release her soon enough—once he heard all she had to say.

Juliana rested her head on his shoulder. "I used to be an accountant," she began.

"Too bad you didn't tell me when we first met. I might have offered you a job working for me. Our chief executive accountant, Lauren DeVida, left when my father died." His voice rumbled deep and soothing against her ear. "I assume you worked for your brother as an accountant?"

"Before heading Arnaud's Angels, I was his CEA."

"See? I was right. You'd have been perfect as Lauren's replacement. I'd bet you'd find keeping track of our amethyst exchange far more interesting than Joc's wheeling and dealing." He twined a rope of curls around his finger and gave it a playful tug. "And I'm sure you'd be as devoted to me as Lauren was to my father."

"No, I wouldn't," she retorted. "Because I no longer mix business and pleasure."

"Ah. Cue Stewart's entrance into your life," Lander guessed.

Juliana nodded, her cheek rubbing against downy-soft Egyptian cotton. "And then came Stewart. It's not a pretty story."

"Let me guess. Stewart worked in Arnaud's corporate headquarters, and the instant he discovered you were Joc's little sister, he moved in." When she stared at him in astonishment, he shrugged. "It's an old story, sweetheart."

She grimaced. "Then I guess this next part won't surprise you, either. He decided to steal from Joc and use me to do it. I was so madly in love with him—" She offered Lander an apologetic look. "Or thought I was, that I didn't catch on to what he was doing until too late."

"I assume when it all came out, you were vilified right along beside him, despite being the innocent in the story?"

It took her a long moment before she could bring herself to speak. "Thank you for believing in me. Not many people did, because of who my father was."

"And your brother."

There was a harsh undercurrent to his voice that disturbed her. "Joc may have gotten his start skating a slippery line. But as soon as he found his footing, he made sure all his dealings were dead honest. It's become a point of honor with him. Unfortunately, the press has a long memory and a suspicious nature. They've never forgotten those early days."

"You're a loyal sister."

"I have reason to be. He's always done everything in his power to protect me." She returned to the issue at hand with painful deliberation. "As for my part in Stewart's scam... Though I didn't help him, at least not directly, I wasn't innocent, either. I made it easy for him to pull it off. I was careless with passwords which allowed him access to computer documents he shouldn't have seen. I also let slip information that I should have kept confidential."

"Did he embezzle money?"

"No, he was too slick to remove it directly from any of Joc's accounts. Instead, he used insider knowledge to line his own pockets. You see, Joc has hundreds of businesses under dozens of corporate umbrellas. Stewart was able to gain access to records on outstanding bids, and on proposed buyouts and sell-offs. He acquired client lists, employee records, profit-and-loss statements." She splayed her hands across Lander's shoulders. "Basically, he used his position for insider trading. In addition, he influenced clients, revealed bids to competitors. You name it. If he could profit from it, he did it."

"I assume you discovered what he was up to."

"Eventually. But not until it was too late to fix. The scandal broke within weeks of my figuring out what was going on. By then it couldn't be covered up."

"Your own brother fired you?"

"No, I quit. I couldn't let Joc take the fall for my error in judgment." She removed Lander's ring and held it out to him. "You do understand why you have to call off the engagement? Why you have to tell the media it was all a huge misunderstanding? Even though Joc corroborated my side of things, there's always been a suspicion that I was more involved than anyone could prove. Especially since my last name is Arnaud, a fact that only added to the taint of suspicion."

"What I see is a young and naive woman taken advantage of by an experienced scam artist. You aren't the first person to have that happen, and you sure as hell won't be the last." He took the ring as she'd expected he would, then stunned her by saying, "The engagement stands. And just so you know, in my world a marriage always follows an engagement. Always."

Her eyes widened. He couldn't be serious. A fake engagement was one thing. But marriage? "You can't—"

"Think about it, sweetheart. How would it look if five minutes after I announce our engagement, I claim it was all a mistake? They have photos of you wearing my mother's ring." He took her left hand in his and slid Soul Mate back into place. "I wouldn't have given this ring to someone without due consideration, and the people of Verdonia know that."

Her fingers trembled in his grasp. "If you don't put a stop to this, you'll lose the election."

"Then I'll lose the election," he retorted implacably. "Better that than my honor."

His tone warned that their discussion was at an end, something she recognized from a lifetime's experience dealing with Joc. She inclined her head in apparent agreement, but she couldn't bring herself to give voice to the lie. When he pulled her back into his embrace, she went willingly enough. But inside she wept for the loss to come.

She told Lander about her relationship to Joc, expecting him to release her from their impromptu engagement. To distance himself from her. It was one thing to maintain an arm's-length business dealing with someone, even a man suspected of amassing his fortune through dubious means; it was another to marry into the family. Once the people of Verdonia discovered she was Ana Arnaud, the stain on Lander's reputation would be irreparable. Which left her with only one choice.

If Lander's honor prevented him from breaking their engagement, she'd have to see to it personally.

Seven

"You can't do this, Ana."

"Yes, Joc, I can and I will." Juliana put the finishing touches on her makeup, then slipped a pair of plain pearl studs through the holes in her ears. "If Lander refuses to stop this insanity, I'll do it for him. The press conference stands."

"Maybe Montgomery doesn't want to end your relationship. Maybe he's in love with you. Maybe he used the situation to force you into an engagement you'd never have considered otherwise. Have you thought of that?" Joc paced from one end of the bedroom to the other, before pausing behind her. "Well? Have you?"

It took her an instant to control the wild surge of longing, the reckless hope that flared to life before she could tamp it down. "Doubtful. It's a question of honor, not love."

Joc seized her by the shoulders and spun her around. "Why do you say that? Do you consider yourself unlovable?"

"Stop it, Joc." She wriggled free of his hold. "This isn't about love, and you know it. Lander feels responsible. He pursued me after I tried to end things between us, pushed us into an affair—not that I required much pushing. It's only natural that when the press found out about us, he felt honor bound to act. He practically told me as much."

"Bull."

She drew herself up. "Excuse me?"

"You heard me. Do you think I'd be so easily trapped into a marriage I didn't want? Hell, no. Nor would Lander. He could have found some other solution if he'd wanted. A less extreme one than announcing your engagement." Joc planted his fists on his hips and lowered his head in thought. "Didn't you tell me Lander had his mother's ring on him."

"Right. It was in his pocket. So?"

"So…" Joc lifted his head and pinned her with a keen gaze. "So, what was it doing in his pocket?"

She stared blankly. "I…I don't know." How *had* it ended up there? She struggled to recall. "I handed it to him when we were at the museum. And I think he stuck it into his pocket instead of returning it to the display case."

"Wait a minute. Take me through this step-by-step. His mother's engagement ring was at a museum, the national one here in Mt. Roche?"

"Yes. He was showing me the crown jewels after hours last night."

Joc cocked an inquiring eyebrow. "Just showing? If

it was all just showing, how did the ring end up outside the case? There had to be a bit of touching going on for that to happen."

"Okay, fine," she responded defensively. "Maybe I was also trying on some of the pieces."

He grinned. "Montgomery let you wear the crown jewels of Verdonia?"

"He might have." Her cheeks warmed. "No big deal."

"Yes, it is a big deal. Have you any idea how much expense and effort that would take to secure the premises so you two could play?" Joc glanced at her finger, then frowned. "Speaking of your engagement ring. Where is it?"

"I sent it back."

"Damn it, Juliana!"

"That's enough, Joc. The subject isn't open for debate. In case you've forgotten, there's a pack of reporters gathering outside my apartment. It would look odd if I wore Lander's engagement ring to a press conference announcing the end of our engagement."

She turned her back on her brother and started to pull her hair into a sleek knot at the nape of her neck until a memory of Lander tossing her clip into the shrubbery intruded. She hesitated, combing her fingers through the strands and watching the curls riot around her face and shoulders. Maybe she'd leave her hair loose. Just this once.

Joc came to stand behind her. "Okay, I won't debate the matter with you or try and explain why you're the biggest idiot I ever met. But I'd think, at the very least, you'd be curious to know why Lander stuck that ring in his pocket instead of returning it to the display case. Admit it. Aren't you curious?"

"No, I'm not." She glared at her reflection. She was being ridiculous. The only reason she wanted to leave her hair loose was because Lander liked it that way. With ruthless intent, she scraped back every last curl, anchoring the weighty mass with a spare clip. "He could have been stealing the ring, I suppose."

"Very funny." Joc leaned in, whispering close to her ear, "Maybe he took it because he'd been planning to propose all along."

Hope flamed anew. Was it possible? It did explain his keeping the ring. The next instant pain subdued every last spark of hope. No, no, no. She didn't dare allow herself to think along those lines. She'd drive herself crazy wondering about the what-might-have-beens. What might have been if she didn't bear the Arnaud name. If she hadn't been illegitimate. If she hadn't fallen for a scam artist and ruined her reputation beyond repair. She shook her head, forcing herself to focus on her one and only goal—protecting Lander.

"I have to go." She turned to confront her brother. Stubborn determination had settled into the crevices of his face, warning he wouldn't easily give up the argument. She didn't understand it. Why was he pushing this? She released her breath in a sigh. "What do you want, Joc? I mean, really."

"I want you to stay away from the press for a few days. Allow the situation time to settle down."

"You mean, do nothing?" She couldn't believe he was suggesting such a thing. "You always taught me that whenever a problem arose, you had to deal with it right away, before it had a chance to escalate. That's what I'm doing. Besides, if I don't act now, Lander will be the one paying the consequences. There's not much more the press can do to me."

"You don't give your fiancé enough credit."

"My fiancé," she repeated. Her eyes narrowed. "What are you up to? I would have thought you'd do everything possible to help me straighten out this mess, instead of throwing up roadblocks to maintain the status quo."

"I just want you happy. And I think Lander will make you happy."

Her expression softened. "That's sweet, especially considering your earlier opinion." She raised on tiptoe and planted a kiss on his cheek. "Thank you for caring."

"You aren't going to listen to me though, are you?"

"I can't. There's too much at stake. An entire country at risk."

She checked the mirror a final time. She'd chosen to wear her most conservative dress, the unrelenting black of the raw silk relieved by a simple strand of pearls and matching earrings. She'd also kept her makeup to a minimum, just a hint of blush, a swipe of mascara and a touch of lip gloss. Satisfied, she collected her purse and turned to leave.

"Are you coming?" she asked her brother. "Or am I on my own?"

"I wouldn't miss this for the world. If you need me, I'll be right behind you."

Her mouth twisted wryly. "Lurking in the shadows?"

He lifted a shoulder. "I do my best work from there."

Juliana took the elevator to the lobby, struggling with nerves. It didn't help that each blinking number mocked her descent, as though marking her fall from grace. She dreaded the next fifteen minutes with a passion that left her shaking. She couldn't think of anything worse than facing a horde of frenzied reporters. But she'd do it. She didn't have any other choice.

The doors parted, opening like the gates to hell. "Here goes nothing," she murmured bleakly.

She walked steadily across the lobby. The media circus milled just beyond the double glass doors with two uniformed apartment security guards all that kept them from storming the building. Sparing her brother a hunted look, she forced herself to push open the doors. Just as she stepped outside, she felt something tug at the back of her head, and the next instant her hair sprang free. Damn it! Somehow she'd lost her clip, not that she could do anything about it now.

A stray breeze kicked up as she stepped onto the landing outside the doorway, and fiery curls rioted about her face and shoulders. She shoved at the windswept barrage, then gave it up as a lost cause. Forcing herself to move forward, she paused at the head of the steps that led down into the sea of journalists. More than just journalists, she realized with a start. People from all walks of life swelled the press corps ranks. How had they known she'd be here, giving a press conference? Someone must have tipped them off.

A late-afternoon sun spotlighted her, shining into her eyes, which proved a blessing in disguise since it made it impossible to pick out individual faces. Questions pelted her from the moment she appeared, so many she couldn't single out one from another. She lifted a hand, and the clamor died to an unnerving silence, giving her an opportunity to speak.

"Thank you all for coming." She hesitated at the top of the steps, relieved to have at least that much space between her and the seething mob. Since her voice carried well from her position, she elected to remain where she was. "I'd like to make a statement, after which I will not be taking any questions."

Steady. She could do this. She had to; there was no other choice. "I'm here to announce that I'm formally breaking my engagement to Prince Lander. I'd like to assure all of you that I am both honored and flattered by His Highness's proposal and I wish—" To her horror her voice broke and it took her a heartbeat to gather up her control once again. She felt Joc edge closer and signaled him that she was okay and to stay back. "And I wish circumstances could have been different. Unfortunately, I wasn't forthcoming about my background with Prince Lander. He had no idea of my true identity when he proposed, since I was using my first and middle name in an attempt to protect my anonymity."

She bowed her head. "I was a fool. I should have told him the truth the moment we met, explained why any sort of serious relationship between us was out of the question." Looking up she offered a wistful smile, one that trembled around the edges. "Maybe some of you can understand how I felt. I wanted—just for a few hours—to believe in the fairy tale. To believe that I could find true love and live happily ever after. It was selfish and rash of me, not to mention unfair to Prince Lander. And for that I apologize to him, to you and to the people of Verdonia. I should have refused Prince Lander's proposal right from the start. Because I didn't, because I was self-indulgent, he's in this mess and it's all my fault."

"You still haven't told us your name," someone called from the middle of the pack of reporters.

No she hadn't. She drew a deep, calming breath and

stared over the heads of the crowd, into the setting sun. "It's Juliana Rose…Arnaud." She twisted her hands together and the absence of Soul Mate made her feel as though part of her had been cut away. "Most of you know me as Ana Arnaud."

All hell broke loose. The questions came fast and furious, one over top of another. She held up her hands. "Please. There's nothing left to be said. Be assured that Prince Lander had no idea who I was when he announced our engagement. This was all my fault, one I've now corrected. Thank you for coming."

She turned from the deafening shouts and escaped inside her apartment building, followed close behind by Joc. She'd done the right thing, even though it hurt more than she could have believed possible. The people of Verdonia needed Lander, a need far more urgent and vital than her own.

It was her fault they'd become engaged. Her fault that he felt honor bound to offer such an extreme solution to their predicament. And her fault that he stood to lose the election by insisting they marry. The only way he'd be the next king of Verdonia was if she released him from their engagement and ended their relationship. It struck her as the ultimate irony that his honor insisted he marry her, while hers insisted they part.

"It's better this way," she told her brother as they waited for the elevator.

"If this is better, then why are you crying?"

She lifted a hand to her cheek, surprised when her hand came away damp. How odd. She hadn't realized she'd been crying. "They're tears of joy for being out of this mess," she lied.

"It's interesting that your tears of joy look exactly the same as tears of misery. Why is that do you suppose?"

Her chin quivered. "When I figure it out, then we'll both know."

Lander faced the members of the press with calm determination. They all stood respectfully, waiting to hear what he had to say. No one shouted out comments or questions as they had with Juliana. The fact that they gave him the respect they refused to give her, annoyed the hell out of him. Not that he allowed his feelings to show.

"Thank you all for coming." He hesitated before admitting, "It would seem I'm in need of your help."

His opening statement was greeted with murmurs of surprise and a few encouraging smiles. So far, so good. "My fiancée, Juliana Arnaud, is under the mistaken impression that the people of Verdonia won't accept her as my wife. I'd like to see what we can do to change that."

"We?" one of the reporters asked.

"We Verdonians. You see, I believe she thinks her illegitimacy is an unacceptable stigma." Lander gave a what-can-you-do sort of shrug. "I've assured her on numerous occasions that this isn't true. That Verdonians judge people on their merits, not on their lineage. But she's having trouble accepting that fact. She feels that should we marry, it'll cost me the election."

Another of the reporters raised his hand and Lander pointed to him. "Your Highness, you referred to Ms. Arnaud as your fiancée. Are you saying the engagement *isn't* off?"

So, it was Ms. now, was it? That wasn't what they'd called her when they'd been shouting questions the night before. "As far as I'm concerned, it's not off. Ms.

Arnaud has a different opinion." Lander offered a smile that encouraged them to join him on his side of the dilemma—and once joined, to help. "I'd like to try and change her mind."

"I don't understand, Your Highness," a man in front spoke up. "What do you expect the Verdonian citizens to do?"

"First, I'd like to introduce all of you to the Juliana Arnaud *I* know. A woman who's kind and intelligent and compassionate, who puts honor before self-interest. If her press conference yesterday proved nothing else, it should have proved that she only wants the best for me and the people of this country." He leaned forward, speaking earnestly. "Juliana is a woman who, at the tender age of eight, discovered her father was a crook masquerading as a respected businessman. Imagine discovering not only that, but that your father had two families, one legitimate, the other not. And then imagine spending the next thirteen years branded with that illegitimacy and judged by it—hounded by some—despite the fact that you're the innocent byproduct of your parents' affair."

A woman in the middle of the pack raised her hand. "I don't see that the circumstances of your fiancée's birth have any importance. But other aspects of her background certainly do. According to my sources, she was suspected of helping her lover steal from her brother. That concerns me, as I'm sure it does most Verdonians. Any comment?"

He used silence to his advantage, waiting until it had stretched to the breaking point before responding. "First, Ms. Arnaud and the individual in question were never lovers." He paused to add impact to his statement.

"Secondly, she never helped this person, nor knew what he was up to until too late. She was thoroughly investigated and cleared by the authorities, but condemned by the jury of public opinion simply for being an Arnaud. The worst you can accuse her of was an unfortunate excess of naiveté. As soon as she discovered this man's duplicity, she reported him and resigned her position as a point of honor."

"Why is she in Verdonia?" questioned another reporter.

"I'm glad you asked." He'd hoped someone would. "She works for Arnaud's Angels, a charitable organization providing medical treatment to children in need. If you check, you'll discover that Verdonia has benefited greatly from the generosity of Angels, and that's largely thanks to Juliana."

"What do you hope to gain by this press conference, Your Highness?" came the final question.

He answered with absolute sincerity. "This is the woman I want to marry. I'm hoping the people of Verdonia can do what I've failed to do. Let Juliana know how you feel. Let her know that you'd welcome her as your princess." He held up Soul Mate, allowing the lights from the cameras to flicker off the brilliant amethyst. "I'd like all of you to help me put this ring back on her finger."

Juliana yanked the door open. The minute she saw who stood there, she started hyperventilating. "You… I…" She flapped her hand toward her living room where the television was replaying Lander's press conference for the umpteenth time that day. "What were you thinking?"

He strolled past her. "Oh, good. You're watching it."

She finally managed to wrap her tongue around the words clogging her brain. "Have you lost your mind?"

she demanded. "Have you any idea what you've done with that little performance you staged?"

He lifted an eyebrow in a regal fashion. "If you're going to speak to me like that, perhaps you should address me as Your Highness."

"You think I'm being rude? Too bad! I had it all fixed. I protected your honor. I fell on my damned sword for you." She pointed a shaking finger at the screen. "Why would you do…do *that* after all I went through to put an end to a bogus engagement?"

"Because I never considered it a bogus engagement, merely a premature one." He approached, and she realized she'd caged herself with a lion, a lion in deadly pursuit. He backed her against the edge of her couch and pinned her there. "I didn't want you to fall on your sword for me, Juliana. There was no need. I had everything under control."

He was too close, muddling her thoughts and rousing emotions she had no business feeling. Not anymore. "You consider that—" she gestured toward the television again "—under control?"

He tilted his head to one side. "What do you think is going to happen as a result of what I did?"

"I suspect everyone will erroneously believe we're engaged again."

A swift smile came and went. "Besides that."

"You'll lose the election," she stated flatly.

The fierceness of his frown had her catching her breath. She didn't know why, perhaps watching the respect and deference he'd garnered during his talk with the press had affected her in some strange way. But more than anytime since they'd first met, Lander struck her as every inch the royal. "I'm going to tell you this one final time, and then

I'll consider the topic closed. My relationship with you will not affect the outcome of this election. Are we clear?"

She nodded, wide-eyed.

"Topic finished?"

"Not quite," she dared to say. "I have one final question."

"One and only one." He folded his arms across his chest. "Ask."

"Why won't it affect the outcome?"

"Because within the next couple of weeks all of Verdonia will fall in love with you. I guarantee it. What you watched today is just the beginning."

She wanted to believe him. More than anything she hoped it was true. But she didn't dare. She'd spent too many years hardening herself against the callous stares and objectionable assumptions people made about her. That sort of thing didn't change overnight, not even by royal command. "How can you be so certain your people will accept me?" she asked.

His gaze held so much tenderness it brought tears to her eyes. "Because everything I said was true. You are kind and intelligent and compassionate. Most of all, you're honorable. As soon as the country sees that for themselves, they'll realize that not only do you belong here, but we need you."

She didn't know what to say to that, which was just as well since her throat had closed over. Taking her hand in his, he slipped Soul Mate back onto her finger. She started to stammer out a protest, one he stopped with a simple shake of his head.

"Don't refuse it. Not yet. Listen to me first."

"This is insane, Lander. We don't know each other all that well. It's happening too fast." The excuses flooded from her in a nervous rush, the one that concerned her the most, coming last. "You can't want to marry me."

"You're wrong. I do want to marry you. And I think you want to marry me, too." He gathered her up, fitting her into his embrace. They locked together as though they were missing puzzle pieces, finally made whole. His hand swept across her cheek in a light caress before his fingers forked into her curls and he tilted her face up to his. "There's no hurry, Juliana. We don't need to get married tomorrow or next week, or even next month. Wear the ring. If you decide our relationship is a mistake, you can always return it. In the meantime, we'll take it slow and easy."

She moistened her lips, afraid to believe. Afraid to trust or hope. Those qualities had been lost to her so long ago, she barely remembered possessing them. "Why don't we take it slow and easy, and then decide whether or not that ring belongs on my finger?"

He shook his head. "Everyone will be looking to see if you're wearing it. So, it's all or nothing, sweetheart. Right here and right now we either make a commitment or call it quits and go our separate ways. Your choice."

"But—"

"That's my offer. I refuse to go back and forth with the media playing 'is she or isn't she.'" He held her with a demanding gaze, his eyes an intense greenish gold. "Take a chance, Juliana. Trust me."

Oh, God. Trust. He would use that particular word. She leaned into him, closing her eyes against the urge to throw caution to the winds and give in to sweet temptation. "What happens if it doesn't work out?"

"You walk away, and I let you." She opened her eyes to discover the hard lines bracketing his mouth had softened. "I'm hoping you won't walk, because I'm not sure I can keep my side of that particular deal if you do."

His admission filled her with joy, a joy she forced herself to curb. She had another concern that might end everything before it ever began. "There's something else I need to know. Not about the election," she hastened to add.

"Why do I have the feeling I'm not going to like your next question?"

"Maybe because it has to do with Joc."

"Ah." His voice soured. "That might be it."

She caught her lip between her teeth. "You two don't like each other, do you?"

Lander shrugged. "We've had our differences."

"Then…what's he doing here in Verdonia? If you're not friends, why is he here?"

Lander's face lost all expression, filling her with apprehension. "I assume he came here to see you."

Not a chance. Joc adored her, she'd never doubted that. But he adored business more. If he'd come all this way, there was more drawing him to Verdonia than trying to talk her into resuming her old job at corporate headquarters. Her brother was a strong believer in the adage, "killing two birds with one stone." "Tell me, Lander. Do the two of you have some sort of business deal in the works?"

He shook his head. "You should ask your brother about that."

Her heart sank. "I'll take that as a yes. When he danced with me at the ball, he…he warned me about you. He warned me to stay away from you." She grimaced. "Now that I think about it, he pretty much warned me to stay away from you every time I saw him."

A smile of satisfaction eased the grimness from Lander's expression. "You didn't take his advice."

"No, I didn't." She gripped his arm, the amethyst on her ring glittering with red-blue fire. "I need you to tell me the truth. If we continue our relationship, will it hurt your business deal with him?"

He stared at her for an endless moment, his jaw tightening with growing tension. His eyes had darkened with some emotion she couldn't quite decipher, but it worried her. "Throwing yourself on your sword again?" When she stared at him in open dismay, he relented. "It hasn't and it won't."

Juliana couldn't disguise her relief. "You promise?"

"I promise."

His reply was so short and abrupt she wondered if she'd offended him again. But then he lowered his head and kissed her, putting an end to any further discussion, and she realized that he was far from offended. She tumbled back onto the couch with him and lost herself in his embrace. Somehow it would all work out. Somehow the people of Verdonia would accept her, maybe even love her. They had to.

Because she'd just realized that she was madly in love with their future king. And, though he hadn't said he loved her, too—the only dark cloud on the horizon—for the first time in years, she'd begun to trust again.

Lander flipped open his cell phone and placed a call. "It's done," he announced as soon as Joc answered.

"She's wearing your ring again?"

"That's what 'done' means, Arnaud," Lander snapped. He fought for control, fought even harder to keep his voice pitched low, though his intensity still came ripping through. "If your plan backfires, if she's hurt because of this, I will find a way to make you pay."

"You make sure she doesn't find out about our contract and she won't get hurt."

"This is wrong, Arnaud."

There was a momentary silence that Lander took for agreement. "I want her happy," Joc said gruffly. "For some reason, you make her happy. Since you're what she wants, you're what she gets. As for the contracts, they should be ready to sign by the end of the month. We don't sign until you two are married, so I suggest you keep things moving at your end."

Hell. "I promised her time."

"Take all the time you want…so long as it doesn't go past the end of the month. Juliana's not stupid. You take too long sealing the deal and she'll figure out what we're up to. Get her to the altar and fast."

Lander snapped the cell phone shut, wanting nothing more than to hurl it at the nearest wall. So much for honor. He didn't know who he was more disgusted with, Joc or himself. The only part in all this that brought him any pleasure was Juliana. He didn't know what to call what they had. Not love. He wasn't the type to allow his heart to rule his head. But he wanted her. He cared about her. And he looked forward to having her for his wife. Whatever that was, it would have to do.

He could only hope it would prove enough for Juliana.

Eight

"Your Highness, please." The dressmaker fluttered behind Lander as he entered the bedroom. "You can't be here. It's bad luck to see the bride in her wedding dress before the ceremony."

"Of course I can see her, Peri. My palace, my rules."

Across the room sheer pandemonium broke out. He grinned as Peri's assistants fell over each other to hold up lengths of fabric in an effort to hide Juliana from his view. From behind the makeshift barrier, he heard a crash, followed by a muffled oath, the sound of ripping silk and another louder curse. Then, "Damn it, Lander! What the hell are you doing here?"

He laughed, in part at the exasperation in his darling bride-to-be's voice and in part at the shocked expressions of the dressmaker and her assistants. "Why, I came to visit you, of course."

"I was with you not thirty minutes ago. You couldn't wait another thirty until I'm through here?"

"No, I can't." He settled cautiously onto a dainty davenport. When it proved sturdier than it appeared, he flung one leg over the armrest and settled back against the cushions. "The latest newspapers just arrived and I wanted to share them with you."

"I try and avoid newspapers whenever possible. I usually find them depressing, if not downright unpleasant."

He winced at the hint of vulnerability threaded through her comment. "These are neither depressing nor unpleasant. In fact, in the few days since our press conferences, they've all been rave reviews. For instance…" He selected a newspaper at random and turned to the appropriate page. "May I be the first to inform you, you are officially the cat's meow."

The assistants dropped the fabric they held, revealing a hand-painted dressing screen. Lander could see Juliana's silhouette on the far side as she was assisted in removing a billowing gown that one of the dressmakers whisked away for further alteration. Lord, she was gorgeous. All long, sweeping lines and soft, feminine curves. She poked her head around the side of the screen. In her haste to hide from him, her carefully knotted hair had become delightfully unknotted. For some reason, he found those bountiful curls fascinating.

"The cat's meow?" Her eyebrow winged upward. "Should I assume you're the cat?"

"You may so assume."

"Really?" She pretended to be disappointed. "I thought you were a lion."

"Cat. Lion." He shrugged. "If you don't like that nickname, how does Angel Ana grab you? It's the most popular of the dozen or so choices, although Angel seems a little much to me. And not terribly accurate, based on the words I just heard come out of that angelic mouth of yours."

Her eyes narrowed and he could see the warning flash of gold from clear across the room. "Would you please tell me what you're talking about?"

He held up a stack of newspapers. "I told you. I'm talking about these news articles."

She gripped the edge of the screen in alarm. "All those? They're all articles about me?" she asked in disbelief.

"Well, and me, too." His brows drew together. "At least, I think I'm in here somewhere. Probably listed in one of the footnotes as Angel Ana's bridegroom."

She started to come around the screen, only to be shoved back in place by one of Peri's assistants, who then bustled around the room, pretending not to listen as she straightened bolts of satin and tulle. "Are you trying to tell me that the press is saying nice things about me?" Disbelief underscored the question. "The press never has anything nice to say. You must have read it wrong."

"Did not." He riffled through the papers. "Here's one that's fairly illustrative. And I quote, 'Verdonia's princess-to-be, Angel Ana Arnaud, has the entire country at her feet. Standing before a crowd of reporters and local citizens, vibrant red hair tousled by the wind—'"

"Darn clip."

"'Angel Ana confirmed her engagement to Lucky Lander is back on—' Oh, there I'm mentioned. See? I'm also known as—damn, I hope Merrick and Miri don't read this, I'll never hear the end of it—Lander the Love-struck, and Lovelorn Lander."

"They actually had the nerve to call you that?" Juliana asked faintly. "And the reporters are still breathing?"

"Breathing, just not functional. And you're interrupting. Let me read you the best part of the article. Where was I? Oh, yes. And I quote once again. 'All of Verdonia rallied in their efforts to encourage Ms. Arnaud to accept Prince Lander's offer of marriage. Now that she's once again wearing his ring, the entire country is celebrating the good news.' There, you see? Rave reviews."

"I don't understand." She sounded sincerely puzzled. "Usually all they want to print about me is scandal."

He tossed the papers aside and stood. "People are coming forward from all over Verdonia, sweetheart. All in support of you and full of reports of your many good deeds and kindnesses."

"You've helped so many of our children," one of the assistants offered.

"They even support you in Avernos," the dressmaker concurred. "As well they should."

Lander chuckled. "I'll bet that has von Folke's tail in a twist. What I wouldn't give to see that."

"Now, Your Highness," the dressmaker scolded, making shooing motions toward the door. "You need to go now so I can finish my job."

"Yes, yes. I'm leaving." Before anyone could stop him he crossed the room in a half-dozen swift strides. Yanking Juliana from behind the screen, he gave her a long, thorough kiss. "To hell with bad luck," he muttered against her mouth.

The instant he released her, Peri and her assistants ringed him, urging him toward the door. They almost succeeded in ousting him when he noticed piles of silk folded on top of her bed. "What are these?" he asked, detouring in that direction.

"Nightgowns. Please, Your Highness—"

He dug in his heels and gave the garments his full attention. "I'm not going anywhere until I see what you have here." He shook out each piece and studied it with an experienced eye. "I like this one. A definite yes for the green. This one's perfect. Great color. Please, God, yes. And—fair warning—" he swiveled toward Juliana and held up one of the selections "—if I ever see you in this, I rip it off and it goes directly into the fire."

"In that case, I'll be sure to wear it on our wedding night," she returned.

"Huh." He tilted his head to one side, considering. "Not a bad plan. Okay, fine. In another two weeks you can wear this one."

"Two weeks!" Juliana shot out from behind the screen again. "What are you talking about…two weeks?"

"Didn't I mention?" he asked with the utmost casualness. "We have an official wedding date."

"There must be some mistake," she began.

Returning the nightgowns to the bed, Lander cut her off. "Ladies? If you'll excuse us?" Without a word, the dressmaker and her assistants vanished from the room, leaving him alone with his bride-to-be. "Problem?"

Regarding him warily, Juliana snatched up her silk robe and belted it. "What happened to taking our time? To having a slow and easy engagement period?"

He approached and caught the ends of her belt. One hard tug sent her tumbling against him as the robe came undone. "We can wait, if that's what you'd prefer." He slid his arms inside her robe and around her waist. "I just felt the timing was good."

"Why? Why so soon?"

He shrugged. "It gives the country something to focus on other than my father's death. Instead of grieving, they have the opportunity to celebrate. It also pulls the focus off the amethyst crisis, giving me time to get to the bottom of the problem without worrying about media scrutiny."

"And the election?" She gave him a searching look. "Our marriage will help with that, too, won't it?"

"Now you're going to win the election for me?" He smiled in genuine amusement. "I seem to recall that just a few short days ago you were certain you would be responsible for my losing."

She shot him a teasing look, relaxing. "Hey, that was before I became the cat's meow. You marry me and the election's in the bag."

His amusement faded. "Tell me something, Juliana. Do you think I'd marry you…or not marry you, if it meant winning the election?"

She didn't hesitate. "No, of course not." She nibbled on her lower lip. "Do you really want to go through with this so quickly? You don't have any doubts at all?"

He found he could answer with absolute sincerity. "None."

She took a deep breath and then nodded, undisguised happiness giving her face a breathtaking radiance. "Then it looks like we have fourteen days in which to finish organizing a wedding. Maybe you'd better call Peri back in. We have a lot to do if we're going to be ready on time."

"Later." He took her mouth in a lingering kiss, one she returned with utter abandonment. "Much later."

When Lander finally left Juliana's room, he found

himself thinking that while his bride thought two weeks far too soon for the ceremony, he found it an endless wait. He groaned in frustration. He'd never make it. Someone would slip up before then. Somehow she'd find out about that ungodly bargain he'd made with Joc. If the truth came out before the wedding could take place, she would walk. Hell, she'd run. And Verdonia would be ruined.

He shook his head in frustration. He should be worried about putting his people first, about his country's economic future. Instead, all he could think about was Juliana. If she found out the truth, it would be worse than anything she'd experienced before. Being told in such a harsh manner that she was illegitimate had been bad. Having Stewart betray her trust and the public scandal that had resulted from that betrayal, had been worse. But this…this would destroy her. And it would be all his fault.

A rolling drum of thunder woke Juliana on her wedding day, while a white staccato blaze of lightning greeted her the instant she opened her eyes. Rain peppered the windows blown there by a gleeful wind that rattled the sashes and shutters in a vain attempt to invade her bedroom. Before she had an opportunity to do more than groan in dismay, the lights flickered on overhead and an entire platoon of determined women bustled in, Lander's stepmother, Rachel, leading the parade.

"Perfect weather for a wedding," she announced. "An excellent omen."

Juliana sat up in bed and drew her knees toward her chest, eyeing the intruders with sleepy annoyance. They were all Montgomery family members, the connections so convoluted she needed a detailed genealogy to keep them straight. But it was tradition for them to help Juliana prepare for the wedding and keep her company, so she accepted their presence with good grace.

"A downpour on my wedding day is considered lucky?" A yawn interrupted the question.

"Without question." To a woman, the others gathered in the room nodded in agreement. "Rain on your wedding day means you'll be blessed with fertility and good fortune."

Juliana glanced dubiously toward the window. "And what does thunder and lightning mean?"

"It signifies a very passionate love affair." Again the nods of agreement. Rachel came and sat on the edge of her bed. "Normally your mother would be performing the task I am today," she said, taking Juliana's hand in hers. "Lander told me she died when you were only ten. I hope you don't mind that I'm substituting for her."

Juliana shook her head. "Not at all. In fact, I appreciate it very much. It makes this part so much nicer."

Rachel brightened. "That's a relief." She tugged at Juliana's hand. "Up you go. You can't believe how much there is to do if we're to get you to the chapel on time."

The first item on Rachel's checklist was for Juliana to have breakfast with her and Lander's stepsister, Miri, so they could discuss the day's schedule. The two women were unmistakably mother and daughter, both with midnight-black hair as straight as Juliana's was curly. Both had the same unusual bottle-green eyes and flawless complexions, just as both were delightfully unreserved.

To Juliana's surprise, she sensed a certain strain between them and couldn't help but wonder if they'd just had an argument, or if the thread of discord she sensed indicated that they disapproved of the wedding. Juliana could understand if that were the cause. She'd only conversed with Rachel on a handful of occasions. And she'd never met Miri before. No doubt they questioned the speed with which the wedding was taking place.

She waited until they'd been served before tackling the issue with customary directness. "Do you disapprove of Lander and me marrying so quickly?"

Both woman glanced at her, startled. "No," they said in unison. It broke the tension and they all laughed.

Rachel leaned across the breakfast table and patted Juliana's arm. "You can't govern love. Or the speed with which it happens. Lander's father and I only knew each other a week before he proposed. Merrick met his bride no more than two before they wed. And yet, I've never seen a couple more in love." Juliana couldn't mistake the sincerity in the older woman's voice. "I'm delighted for you and Lander, and wish you only the best."

"Thank you." Relieved, she turned to Miri. "Lander speaks of you all the time. I'm sorry we haven't had an opportunity to meet before this. Have you been away?"

It was as though she'd hit them with a live wire. Both women jolted in shock and after exchanging one startled look, were careful to avoid the other's gaze. Juliana frowned. Oh, dear. If she didn't miss her guess, she'd just discovered the source of the strain she'd noticed earlier.

"My daughter has been enjoying a brief vacation," Rachel explained smoothly.

Miri's chin jerked upward in clear defiance and she tossed her waist-length hair back over her shoulder. "Actually, I was hiding out on the Caribbean island of Mazoné after helping Merrick abduct his wife."

"Miri!"

"Give it up, Mom. I'll bet Lander's already told her."
She shot Juliana a challenging look. "Hasn't he?"

Juliana dabbed her mouth with the linen napkin. So
much for asking what she'd assumed was an innocuous
question. She'd opened up a veritable can of worms
with that one casual inquiry. "He told me just the other
day that Merrick had abducted Alyssa and that they
ended up falling in love. But he didn't mention your part
in the affair."

"I took Alyssa's place at the altar in order to give
Merrick time to get away."

It was everything Juliana could do to keep her jaw
from dropping open. She snatched up her teacup and
buried her nose in her Earl Grey until she could control
her expression. "Let me get this straight." She couldn't
come up with a delicate way to phrase her question.
"You're married to Prince Brandt, the man Lander will
face in the upcoming election?"

"It's not legal." To Juliana's amusement, both women
spoke in unison again.

"At least, we don't think it is," Miri added.

"What's he like?" Juliana asked, curious to know
more about Lander's rival for the throne.

"He's tall, dark and handsome, of course."

"How can you call him handsome?" Rachel demanded. "He's too austere to be considered handsome."

"I don't agree. You just think that because his features are more severe than the Montgomerys', which
sometimes makes him look hard." An odd quality crept
into Miri's voice. "To answer your question, Juliana,
he's self-contained yet passionate. And he has this old-
world charm about him. He puts honor and duty and responsibility before everything else. Everything. And

once he makes up his mind about something, he's impossible to sway."

"Interesting."

Juliana had learned to make swift assessments of people. Like her brother Joc, her judgment was rarely wrong—with the one disastrous exception of Stewart. Instinct told her Miri's feelings toward Brandt ran deep. Secrets burned in those spring-green eyes, as well as pain. Not wanting to add to her pain, Juliana deliberately changed the subject, addressing Rachel.

"So, what's next on my checklist?"

"After we've finished breakfast, you'll meet with Father Lonighan. He'll give you his formal blessing for the union and offer marital advice."

"Have fun with that."

"Miri! Then you have an hour to soak in your bath before the fun part begins." Rachel ticked off on her fingers. "A massage, facial, manicure and pedicure."

"Good Lord," Juliana murmured faintly.

"Then Miri and I will return to help with your hair and makeup."

Miri grinned. "What she means is, we'll watch while the experts take care of it. Then, in accordance to Verdonian tradition, Peri will sew you into your gown."

"Yes, she told me about that part," Juliana said. "But if I'm sewn in, how do I get out again, later?"

Rachel and Miri exchanged quick, mysterious smiles which worried Juliana no end. "You'll see," was all they'd say.

The rest of the day proceeded as outlined and the hours flew by. In no time she was having her hair fashioned into a gorgeous Gibson Girl hairstyle with ringlets framing her face and teasing the nape of her neck. Then the tiara she'd tried on at the museum was added to the arrangement. She hoped Lander would appreciate that she'd chosen something his mother had worn as a bride on a day very much like this one. She had the odd notion that it connected the two of them spiritually, one generation to another. As though aware of her feelings, Rachel gave her hand an understanding squeeze.

"Lander asked me to give this to you," she whispered, and offered Juliana a square jeweler's box.

Opening it, Juliana found the most striking pair of earrings she'd ever seen nestled inside on a velvet bed. They were a teardrop confection of diamonds and amethysts, both Royals and Blushes. Her hands trembled so badly she could barely put them on.

And finally came the gown itself, with Peri sewing her into it. As soon as she'd finished, she stepped back and nodded in a combination of approval and pride. The fitted bodice glittered with tiny amethysts of every shade. Layer after layer of tulle swept out from the narrow waistline in an endless train behind Juliana that folded and hooked to form an elegant bustle to make for easier maneuvering both before and after the actual ceremony.

And then they brought out her veil. A glorious confection of lace and tulle, it, too, glittered with amethysts. The lace and gemstones had all been set in an intricate pattern of swirls that managed to obscure her features while still allowing her to see. Now she understood how Miri had managed to fool Brandt when taking Alyssa's place at the altar.

As soon as Rachel twitched the veil into place, Juliana was escorted from her bedroom suite to the front of the palace where a flower-bedecked horse-drawn carriage awaited. Joc stood beside it wearing a dove-gray tux and looking more handsome than she'd ever seen him.

At some point the storm had passed, leaving the air scrubbed clean of humidity and filled with the delicious scent of early summer. A soft mist rose around the carriage, giving everything a fairy-tale quality. They rode through streets lined with Verdonians who cheered her passage. In no time they arrived at the chapel and Joc literally lifted her from the carriage and swung her to the flagstone entranceway.

"You know I only want the best for you," he said gruffly.

"Of course I know that."

"I'd hug you, but you're all—" He gestured to indicate her veil and dress. "I don't think I can wade through all that and back out again without getting it messed up."

She smiled, though she doubted he could see it through the veil. "I appreciate your restraint."

He offered his arm. "You ready?"

She took the question seriously. Was she ready? There were certain aspects of her future life with Lander that worried her, mainly living as a public figure. She'd spent a lifetime fighting the negative labels affixed to her name. How long would it take before she went from acclaimed to infamous again? It could happen. Public favor was a fickle thing.

And then she thought of Lander and how she felt about him. How much richer her life had become now that he was a part of it, and nothing else mattered. Nothing. "I'm ready," she said, and slipped her hand into the crook of Joc's arm.

Music drifted from the dim interior, Handel's "Minuet." They paused in the foyer where attendants straightened Juliana's gown and unhooked the train, spreading it behind her. "His Highness said he cut these himself," one of the women whispered, handing her a bouquet of fragrant white roses. "He said you'd know where they came from."

The gazebo. Tears sprang to Juliana's eyes and she started to lift the heavy blossoms to her nose, but the veil prevented her. As though realizing she was on the verge of ripping through the layers of lace and tulle, Joc urged her toward the sanctuary. The rippling majesty of horns broke into Stanley's "Trumpet Voluntary" the minute she appeared.

And that's when she saw Lander. He stood at attention waiting for her, dressed in full military whites, including a chest rippling with medals and an ornate saber belted at his hip—the Lion of Mt. Roche at his most majestic. Late-afternoon sunlight struck the stained glass windows on the west side of the chapel. The colors shattered, forming a rainbow of hues leading from where she stood to where she most wanted to be.

And then she was walking toward him. No, not walking. Floating, as though in a dream. The wedding service began, vanishing into the mists of memory almost as soon as it occurred. She vaguely recalled Joc joining her hand with Lander's. Father Lonighan spoke at length, his deep voice rumbling over her. Through it all, her full attention remained on the man professing to love, honor and cherish her, to protect her from all harm.

One of the clearest moments of the ceremony, a shard so piercing in intensity that it would forever remain a part of her, was when he slipped a pair of rings on her finger. The first was a heavy band of gold studded with Verdonia Royal amethysts. The second had her catching her breath. Instead of Soul Mate, he slid a far different ring on her finger, a delicate confection of diamonds and amethysts in a trio of unusual shades that complemented the earrings he'd given her earlier.

"I had it designed just for you," he murmured so only she could hear.

"Does it mean something?"

"Of course." His hazel eyes glowed with tenderness. "We'll see how long it takes you to figure out."

There wasn't further opportunity to speak. Father Lonighan gave them a final blessing, and the ceremony concluded with their being declared husband and wife. As tradition dictated, Lander had waited until the very end to lift her veil.

"I've never seen you look more beautiful," he told her.

Cupping her face, he took her mouth in the sweetest kiss they'd ever shared. Her eyes drifted closed as she lost herself in his embrace. The only thing that would have made the moment more perfect would have been if he'd told her he loved her. Just as the kiss ended, trumpets flared to life in a triumphant recessional. Lander took her arm and escorted her down the aisle and then outside where a roar of cheers greeted their appearance. The sun dipped low on the horizon spreading a rosy glow across the city. With a laugh, Lander swept his bride into his arms. Her train caught the breeze and billowed around them as he carried her to their waiting carriage. And in that moment Juliana didn't think she'd ever been happier.

Nine

After the wedding, Lander hosted a dinner reception for close friends and relatives. Laughter flowed as easily as the sparkling wine, both bright and effervescent and full of good cheer. During those brief hours, Juliana knew what Cinderella must have experienced after she'd married her prince. A rightness. A completion. For the first time in her life, Juliana felt loved and cherished. She felt like a real princess.

Toasts followed the dinner, some funny, some poignant, others heartwarming. Just as the last glass was raised, the majordomo appeared, inviting the guests to adjourn to the balcony to watch the fireworks display celebrating the royal marriage. When Juliana would have followed, Lander caught her hand and urged her in the opposite direction.

"We'll watch them from a more private location," he told her.

She didn't need any further encouragement. Gathering up the voluminous skirts of her wedding dress, she raced with him through the deserted corridors. At least, they appeared deserted. If security was stationed between the dining hall and Lander's private wing of the palace, they remained well hidden.

The two of them arrived at his bedroom suite breathless with laughter. She couldn't say what they'd found so amusing. Perhaps it was just their happiness bubbling over like uncorked champagne. Or maybe it was being alone together at last, the joyful anticipation of the hours to come. Pushing open the door, Lander swept Juliana into his arms and carried her across the threshold.

When he set her on her feet, she glanced around, her breath catching in her throat. Candles lit the room, dozens upon dozens of them on every surface, encircling them in a soft, warm glow. White rose petals were strewn across the carpet, providing a romantic pathway from door to bed. More of the petals were scattered on the satin sheets, their fragrance filling the room. Soft music issued from hidden speakers, and she paused to listen for a moment. It sounded so familiar. And then she realized why. The songs were selections from their wedding service.

"You did this, didn't you?" she asked in a broken voice.

"I'm forced to admit, I didn't light the candles. But, the rest…" He nodded. "I wanted it to be special for you."

"Thank you."

In the distance she heard a faint boom signaling the start of the fireworks, and she crossed to a set of French doors that opened onto the balcony. Lander joined her there, coming up behind and wrapping his arms around her waist, enfolding her in the warmth of his presence.

They watched the initial fireworks in silence, a blaze of color and explosion of sound that celebrated their union.

Gently he turned her. "Come. Let's get you out of that gown."

"I'm sewn into it, you know. I'm told it's traditional." Did he hear the sudden nervousness in her chatter? But then, how could he miss it? "No one's explained the origins to me."

"I believe it's to ensure the safe passage of the bride from her family's loving arms to that of her husband. Proof that no one has touched her during the interim."

"I've got news for you. There's plenty of touching that can go on without the bride removing her dress."

"Not if it's done right."

Juliana's mouth twitched. "Good point." She lifted an eyebrow. "So how do you propose to release me?"

"Like all good Verdonian husbands, I come prepared." He picked up a jeweled dagger resting on the bedside table. "This is called a *koffru.*"

"I'm almost afraid to ask."

"You should be. It's a bride cutter."

"Lovely," she said dryly. "You're going to cut me with that thing?"

He responded to her jibe with a grin. Pulling her close, he spun her around so her back was to him. "It's not you I plan to cut. It's your gown."

"Don't ruin it!"

"Trust me, wife."

After sweeping her veil to one side, he sliced through the seam holding the back of her gown together with delicate precision. Inch by inch the knife skimmed down her spine until he reached her waist. And then it dove lower still, to a point just past her hips. Finished, he slid the dress from her body as well as the layered petticoat beneath. Offering her his hand, he helped her step free of the yards of satin and tulle. She stood before him, oddly self-conscious considering that they'd already been lovers, her only covering a few flimsy scraps of lace, her stockings, heels and garter, and her amethyst-studded veil and tiara.

"So beautiful," he murmured as he unhooked the veil and set it aside. When she would have removed the tiara, he stopped her. "My job." He slid the tiara from her hair, freeing the few curls that insisted on clinging to the jeweled hairpiece. "I wondered if you'd choose to wear this." His voice deepened. "It's in honor of my mother, isn't it?"

"Yes." Tension gripped his jaw, while sorrow cut brackets on either side of his mouth. Seeing him like that nearly broke her heart. "I wanted her to be a part of the ceremony in some small way."

"Thank you for that. She would have appreciated the gesture." He placed the tiara out of harm's way before turning back to her. "And now my favorite part."

One by one Lander removed the pins restraining her hair, catching the loosened pool of curls in his palms. Behind her fireworks lit up the night sky, flinging brilliant flashes of color across the hard, masculine planes of his face. Rich, vibrant sparks of green glowed in eyes filled with unmistakable hunger.

She reached for him with trembling hands, fervent and unabashed, fumbling with buttons and zips as she helped him remove his clothing. If she lingered over the corded muscles she found beneath his dress whites, he didn't complain, though she could feel the tension gathering across his shoulders. Nor did he complain when she followed the plunging vee of crisp, masculine hair that darted from chest to abdomen and farther still. She followed that line until she found the heart of his passion. She cupped him, stroked him, playing along the full length and breadth of him. It made her keenly aware of her own femininity and of his unrelenting maleness.

He took her mouth with a groan, plying her with fierce, desperate kisses. Her few remaining garments were a barrier swiftly eliminated and then it was her turn to be filled with an unnerving urgency, one painful in its intensity. He stroked her, the sensations growing hotter, headier, more concentrated. Just when her legs were on the point of giving out, he lifted her in his arms and carried her to the bed.

She drank in the aroma of the roses surrounding her, felt their silken caresses against her bare skin. But they were overlaid by another aroma and another caress, a more elemental, pervasively masculine one. He braced himself above her, touching, barely touching. Sliding with excruciating slowness. Rousing sensations that had her fevered one moment and chilled the next.

"Please, Lander. Now," she urged. "Make love to me now."

He didn't need a second invitation. He lowered himself to her, crushing the rose petals against her skin in an explosion of scent. Palming her thighs, he parted her legs, releasing his breath in a rough sigh as she welcomed him home. He surged into the liquid warmth, sealing their wedding vows as he sheathed himself fully within her.

"My bride," he whispered. "My princess. My wife."

He moved then, taking her with the utmost tenderness and care. Stroke built upon stroke, gathering the heat, driving it toward a burning need, escalating toward a frenzied desperation that left her utterly exposed, utterly abandoned to this most intimate of embraces. Her muscles tensed in anticipation of the ultimate surrender. When it came it stormed through them, demolishing every defense in an explosive release, one echoed by a final barrage of fireworks.

And in that moment of shattered completion, they became husband and wife in body, as well as name.

"Damn it, Joc. Could we get this over with?" Lander growled. "Juliana will wake any minute now. Considering it's our first day of marriage, I'd like her to do it in my arms, rather than waking to a cold bed."

"The final contracts are right here. All we have to do is get these lawyers to agree on the remaining two points and we're done. A few months from now, new business will flow into Verdonia, and hot damn—" he rubbed his hands together "—you've got a source of revenue to fill in the gaps left from the declining amethyst trade."

Lander grimaced. "It can't be soon enough. The Royals are becoming scarcer by the day. If something's not put in place to augment that lost income—and soon—it's going to have a disastrous effect on our economic stability. Nine months, a year from now, we're going to be hurting."

"We'd have an easier time finalizing our plans if you had an executive accountant working with us. What happened to yours?"

"She left after my father's funeral."

"Any chance she'd be willing to come in and lend a hand?"

"None. Lauren made that clear before she left. She

took my father's death pretty hard. I guess she'd been with him since—" Lander shook his head "—must have been before the death of my own mother. I believe she's somewhere in Spain enjoying an early retirement."

"I'm tempted to call Ana in and have her go through everything."

"Not a chance in hell."

Joc waved him silent. "I know. I know. It was just a thought."

"A bad one. We'll cope using our current accountants, not to mention the team of lawyers we both seem to have in excess." He shot a fulminating glare in the direction of the conference table. "Will they never finish?"

A light knock sounded at the door. Before Lander even saw the tumble of auburn curls and the gold-spiced eyes, he knew who it would be. Sure enough, Juliana poked her head around the door. She was dressed in a simple off-white silk shell and billowing skirt that had him remembering how beautiful she'd looked in her wedding gown. Even though her face was bare of makeup, she'd taken the time to put on the earrings he'd given her as a wedding present. It took every ounce of his self-possession to keep him from sweeping her into his arms and carrying her back to their bedroom.

"Oh, there you are." Relief brightened her face. "I thought I'd lost you."

"Not a chance." Lander pulled her into his arms, not giving a damn who was watching, and kissed her. "Good morning, wife. I'm sorry I wasn't there when you woke up," he said, and meant it.

"What's going on?" She glanced at her brother. "Hey, Joc. What are you doing here?"

"Business," he replied easily. "Just moving some of

my interests over here. You know me. Spread the wealth around."

"Right." She smiled at her brother. "Lander wouldn't discuss it, but I had a feeling you two were in negotiations over some deal or another."

"Oh, we're long past the negotiation stage. We should be done within the hour."

"Why did you have to wait until this morning to finalize everything?" To Lander's amusement, she shifted into scold mode. "In case you didn't realize, your timing stinks, Joc. That's not like you. You usually have impeccable timing."

"Sorry, Ana." Joc worked to appear suitably chastised. "I guess your wedding threw it off. If it makes you feel any better, we're at the sign, seal and delivery stage. As soon as that's done, you two lovebirds can take off on your honeymoon."

Juliana laughed, slanting a mischievous glance up at Lander. "I've worked with Joc on countless contracts. I know all about the delivery stage. One of the first things my brother taught me was to always wait until every last precontractual condition has been met before signing any agreement. He drummed the importance of it into me during every negotiation." She lowered her voice in a mocking imitation of Joc's Texan drawl. "Don't sign based on promises, Ana. Wait until they've done what they said they'd do before putting your name on the dotted line. It's all about leverage. It's all about getting what you paid for." Her gaze flashed from husband to brother. "So, what's left to do? Anything I can help with?"

"No!" Joc and Lander replied in unison, far too emphatically.

Juliana froze, and the tiniest of clouds drifted across

her expression. The silence thinned. Sharpened. Became painfully acute.

"Your Highness?" One of Lander's team of lawyers rose. "Excuse me, sir, but we can't move to the next stage until Mr. Arnaud has signed the papers indicating that you've fulfilled all the preconditions to the contract."

Juliana stiffened and the clouds from earlier deepened, piling darkly across her face and dimming the brilliance of her eyes. She untangled herself from Lander's embrace and took a quick step in her brother's direction. "What conditions are they talking about? What did Lander have to do in order to get your business?"

"It's not important," Joc dismissed the question. "Details. Nothing for you to worry about."

One look warned Lander she wasn't buying her brother's glib reply. He signaled the lawyers, jerking his head toward the door. "Out."

They didn't wait for a second invitation. Within thirty seconds they'd cleared the room. The minute the door closed behind them, Juliana spoke again, her analytical brain focused to a pinprick. "Joc, did you ever refuse to do business with Lander because he and I were having an affair?"

Lander relaxed ever so slightly, as did Joc.

"No, Ana. I didn't."

She spared Lander a swift, wary glance that had him freezing up again. "Maybe…maybe all this time I had it backward," she murmured. "Let's try it from this direction. Did you ever refuse to do business with Lander unless he and I became involved? No, you wouldn't have done that. You wouldn't have settled for anything less than—" She broke off, wide-eyed.

"Ana—"

She stumbled backward toward the door. "Oh, no. Tell me you didn't do that. Tell me *that* isn't one of the conditions of your contract."

Lander took a step in her direction. "Honey—"

She held up a hand. "I'm so stupid. How could I still be so naive after Stewart?" She shook her head, curls frothing around her face. Her complexion had turned as pale as her ensemble, stretched fragile and translucent across her elegant bone structure. Her heart fluttered at the base of her throat like the wings of a wild bird fighting the bars of her cage. "One plus one always equals two. Always. You'd think I'd remember that."

Joc frowned in confusion, but Lander instantly understood. He wished he could deny the conclusions she'd reached, but how could he when she was all too right? He'd never before seen such a look of devastation on a woman's face. The fact that that woman was his wife nearly destroyed him.

"Am I actually written into the contract, Joc?" she asked with amazing composure. "Section C, Subparagraph Four, Line Sixteen. In exchange for my basing X, Y and Z business in Verdonia you will marry my sister. If I read those contracts on the table over there, will I find my name in them?" When neither man twitched so much as a muscle, she swept relentlessly onward. "No? Not there? Then you must have decided my future over brandy and cigars. I'm a gentleman's handshake, aren't I? Marry my sister and I'll do this contract with you."

"Sweetheart, don't—"

Her composure shattered, her breath escaping in a sob. "Oh, God. You don't have to say another word. I get it. I do. My marriage is nothing more than a business deal." Her laugh was a painful splinter of sound. "Do I have all the details right? Have I missed anything?"

"Listen to me, Juliana," Lander began.

But she had no intention of listening. Before he'd even gotten the words out, she'd turned and made a beeline for the door. Flinging it open, she darted into the corridor. She heard Lander giving chase behind her. He caught up with her just as she burst into their bedroom suite.

Slamming the door closed behind them, he snagged her arm and spun her around. "Listen to me, damn it!"

"Listen to what?" She could hear the fury in her own voice and fought to modulate it, fought for a measure of restraint. Once upon a time, she might have succeeded. But this hurt went too deep to keep inside, the pain too raw to bottle up. "Whatever you have to say to me will either be a lie or an excuse. Which one were you planning on using?"

"Neither. I was planning on giving you the truth… and an explanation."

She cut him off with a swipe of her hand. "You don't need to explain. You did that weeks ago. I just wasn't paying close enough attention."

"I have no idea what you're talking about." He forked his fingers through his hair, the lion rumpling his mane. "What did I explain to you? Where? When?"

Her breath came far too quickly, her thoughts racing too fast for coherency. "We were in my office. Don't you remember? You were trying to convince me to continue our relationship after our one-night stand. And when I told you it wouldn't be in Verdonia's best interest, you said—" Her eyes fluttered closed as she strove to calm down enough to recollect his exact words. "You said your personal life has never interfered with your duty to your country, that duty takes primary importance over everything. Always."

Oh, God, why hadn't she listened? Why hadn't she understood? She'd been so caught up in the dream, in the fairy tale, that she'd forgotten what reality was all about. Well, she remembered now. It had come crashing down on her with a vengeance, destroying her from the inside out. "But I get it now, Lander. Marrying me meant that Verdonia would be protected from economic ruin. You didn't marry me because you loved me. You married me to protect Verdonia."

"You're right. You're absolutely right." Desperation had him pacing, and he ate up the length of the room with long, swift strides. "Joc came to me with his proposition. Said he had a sister he wanted me to marry."

"Me."

He swiveled to face her. "No, not you. Ana Arnaud." He closed in on her and she drew inward, flinching away from him. "I told him to go to hell. I told him I might have considered such an outrageous suggestion the week before, but not then. I'd met someone, I told him. Juliana Rose. But the joke was on me, wasn't it? Because when he showed me a picture of his sister, damned if Juliana Rose and Ana Arnaud weren't one and the same person. An interesting coincidence, don't you think?"

Her eyes narrowed. "Coincidence? You say that like you think—" Her breath escaped in a hiss and her control snapped. "You believe I was in on it?" she demanded, livid. "You think I plotted with Joc to force you to the altar?"

"The possibility occurred to me. You show up at the first ball we'd thrown since my father's death. You're using your first and middle name, conveniently omitting your last. Your brother arrives the same evening. We spend one unforgettable night together, and all of the sudden Joc is talking contracts and marriage."

She shook her head in disbelief, too full of anguish to speak, afraid she might break if she tried. If that happened, all her most private emotions would come spilling out in a hysterical flood. Once loosened from her control, she could no more call those emotions back than she could gather up a single raindrop out of a downpour.

Lander started toward her again. "So, yes. I admit it. I considered the possibility that you and Joc were setting me up. And you know what I decided?" He pursued her until he'd backed her against the bed. "I decided, who cares if that's how it went down? I wanted you. You wanted me. And then there was Verdonia to consider. With the amethyst mines played out, the country's on the verge of economic collapse. So, hell yes, Princess. I agreed to marry you. What would you have done?"

"I'd have told you the truth," she argued bitterly. "Given you a choice."

"Really?" He cocked an eyebrow, his expression skeptical. "Would you have agreed to marry me if I'd been upfront with you?"

She hesitated. Would she have? "I don't know," she conceded.

"At least you're honest about it." He lifted a shoulder in a weary shrug. "I suspected that might be your answer, and I couldn't afford to take the chance you might refuse my proposal. When the press found out about us—Joc's doing, I assume—I took advantage of the situation and had my ring on your finger before you had an opportunity to react."

"You put your country first, just as you warned you would."

He wanted to deny it, she could tell. "Yes. And let me be clear about something else, as long as we're being so damned honest. I'd do it all over again. The situation is too critical for me to leave anything to chance."

Resolution took hold, hard and implacable. "I can't live like that. I wish I could, but I can't." She looked around the room, seeking an avenue of escape. "I have to leave."

He reached for her. Fingers and curls seemed to find each other of their own accord, snaring and tangling. Clinging. Joining. "You're my wife."

"Bought and paid for." Her voice broke on the final words. Helpless tears gathered in her eyes. "That makes me property, not a wife. At least not a real one."

He snatched a kiss, then another. She remained helpless beneath the onslaught, her body softening, responding, betraying her need. "Stay," he demanded between kisses. "We'll find a way to work this out."

The tears fell then. Hopelessness drove them, a despair so deep and pervasive that nothing he said or did could make it right again. After Stewart, she'd thrown up a protective wall and hidden behind it, afraid to allow anyone access in case they hurt her again. Lander had pulled down that wall, brick by brick. He'd set those emotions free and she'd allowed it to happen, because she'd wanted—more than anything—to find love.

A coldness slipped through her veins, stealing the warmth his arms provided. She'd believed this man fulfilled her in every way possible, aligned her, balanced her. She'd thought she'd found her soul mate. And instead it had been an illusion. What he'd offered hadn't been real. What she'd hoped to find with him hadn't existed. Now all that remained was an empty shell.

She untangled herself from his embrace. He didn't want to release her any more than she wanted to go. Fingers and curls fought her, resisting, before being forced to part. No matter what it took, no matter how difficult, she had to walk away. She had to run. She wouldn't survive the pain if she didn't.

"I'm sorry, Lander. I can't stay." Her voice wobbled, not that there was any way to prevent it. "I'm going to ask Joc to take me back to the States while I consider my options. You two can decide how best to settle any outstanding contractual issues."

She started to remove her wedding rings and earrings, and he stopped her before the rings left her finger. "Keep them," he ordered.

Her gaze lifted to lock with his, a desperate, searching look. If only he'd say the words, just three simple words that would make all the difference in the world. But either he didn't know them, or he didn't feel for her what she felt for him. Time to concede defeat. It was over, the fairy tale ended before it had even begun. Without another word, she turned and left her husband.

Juliana was already on Joc's plane when her brother arrived. After shooting her a single look of concern, he gave his full attention to the pilot and attendants, issuing instructions in a low voice. He must have asked for privacy because they were immediately left alone in the spacious cabin.

"Ana, I'm so sorry." He came to sit on the armrest of the seat across the aisle from her. "I screwed up. I know that. But I swear I was acting in your best interests."

There had never been any question in her mind about that. Her brother had spent most of his life caring for her. Protecting her. Trying to provide everything she could ever want or need. But this…! "Why did you do it, Joc?" The blistering anger from earlier had gone, leaving behind a cold, bottomless fury. "How could forcing Lander to marry me possibly be in my best interests?"

"Because you deserved to be a princess." Determination filled his voice. "To be a queen, if that's what the people of Verdonia decide."

"How dare you!" she snapped. "What made you think I wanted to be a princess, let alone a queen?"

He stilled, taken aback. It had been a long time since anyone had ever questioned the rightness of his decisions, and having his little sister do it clearly left him unsettled. "Do you think I don't know how hideous the past seventeen years have been?" he tried to explain. "How you've suffered at the hands of the media? For a while I thought you'd come to terms with it. Put it behind you. You seemed to love your job." His expression darkened. "Until Stewart."

"And because of that you forced Lander to propose to me? To marry me? Was a contractual marriage supposed to protect me somehow? To ensure I live happily ever after?" Her mouth worked. "How could you do that to either Lander or me?"

"Don't you see? It's because I love you so much that I want what's best for you."

"You can't order the world and everyone in it to your convenience."

His jaw took on a stubborn set. "Why not?"

"Joc!"

He waved that aside. "Listen to me, Ana. There's something I haven't told you about my relationship with Montgomery. *I* owe *him.* That's why I came to Verdonia. That's why I agreed to help him."

Her brows pulled together. "What are you talking about?"

"We had a rather contentious relationship at Harvard." His mouth twisted. "I guess that would be a generous description considering how much I hated the man."

"You hated Lander? But, why?"

Joc's eyes were black with emotion. "You know why. Because he represented everything we weren't. He had the name, the heritage, the perfect life. He was the golden child. So I went after him to prove who was better. Grades, women, sports. You name it, I had to beat him. And in the end, I did. I graduated just ahead of him." He grimaced. "The bastard even had the nerve to shake my hand when he congratulated me."

Juliana shook her head. "I don't understand. How does that translate into your owing him?"

"His cronies decided that the only way I could have come out ahead of Montgomery was if I cheated. They beat the snot out of me, determined to get me to confess."

Understanding struck. "Lander rescued you, didn't he?"

"Yeah. I've never seen anything like it. He mowed through every last one of them and then carted me off to the hospital. I swore to him that day that if he ever needed anything, if it was in my power, I'd give it to him." His gaze fixed on her. "So, you see, he didn't have to marry you. If he'd refused, he knew damn well I would still have lived up to my part of our agreement.

There's only one reason he went along with my condition. He loves you. You have to believe that."

"But I'll never be one hundred percent certain," she shot back. "If someday he decides he does love me, I'll never know if it's what's actually in his heart or if it's part of his contract with you. I'll suspect every word he says. Every gesture he makes. Every gift he gives me. I'll never know. Not for sure."

Her brother stared at her in stunned horror. "No. That's…that's not right."

She bowed her head. "None of this is right." She pushed herself to her feet. She'd never felt so tired before, nor so defeated. "I'm going into the back to lie down. Please ask the attendants not to disturb me."

He caught her hand and squeezed it. "I'll watch out for you."

"You always do." She couldn't bring herself to look at him. "The problem is, I'm all grown up now. It's time I watched out for myself, even if it means falling down on occasion and skinning my knee. It's time to let go, Joc. You have your own life to live. Now let me live mine."

She didn't wait for his response. It didn't matter what Joc said or did anymore. Her declaration had been as much for her own benefit as it had been for her brother's. There had been the ring of truth to her words, a message from herself to herself. It was past time she took charge of her life. Long past time.

Ten

Juliana never did recall those first bleak days back in Dallas. They passed in a blur of pain and confusion, as well as a desperate, bone-deep despair. The minute she landed in Texas, she yearned to turn around and fly right back to her husband. But she couldn't. Not the way things stood between them. By the end of the first week, she knew she had to follow the advice she'd given herself on that last hideous morning in Verdonia. It was time to take charge of her life. There were decisions to make and a resignation to tender to her brother, something she intended to do that very day.

It didn't take long to drive into the city. Joc owned a full city block worth of office building in the heart of Dallas, a soaring glass and chrome structure that stabbed skyward in a gradually narrowing column. It was simply labeled Arnaud's. Security waved her through to Joc's private elevator, and upon exiting she found his personal assistant, Maggie, sitting in her usual spot outside his office.

The older woman looked up from her typing and smiled at Juliana over the top of her reading glasses. "Hey, there, girl. Or should I say, Your Highness?"

"You should not." Juliana cast a determined glance at the door leading to Joc's inner sanctum. "Is he around?"

"Can't you tell from the growls and snarls coming from in there?"

"That bad?"

"The worst I've seen him in a long time. Maybe you can snap him out of it."

"I'll see what I can do."

"His employees would be most grateful."

Taking a deep breath, Juliana entered Joc's office. She found him standing with his back to the door, staring out of the floor-to-ceiling windows at the Dallas skyline. "Damn it, I want some answers," he snapped as she slipped into the room. Realizing he was on speaker phone, she remained silent.

"You heard me." Juliana jumped in shock at the sound of her husband's voice. "I don't want her back in the country. I don't care what you have to do, just keep her with you in Dallas. Is that clear?"

"You don't give me orders, Montgomery."

"I do about this. I won't be changing my mind. If she tries to return, I swear I'll ban her from the damn country."

She must have made some small sound because Joc spun around. The words he uttered were some of the coarsest she'd ever heard him use. "Would you care to repeat that for your wife's benefit, Your Highness? She just walked into my office. Judging by her expression, I'd say she overheard every word you said."

An endless pause followed. Then the man she loved more than life itself replied, "If she heard, there's no point in my repeating it. I'll assume my message has been delivered and we can be done with this nonsense." He made the statement in a flat, emotionless voice, one so unlike his own, if she hadn't known it was her husband, she'd have thought she was listening to a stranger.

It took her three tries to answer him. "I'll have my wedding rings messengered to you first thing tomorrow."

"Don't bother. I don't want them back." And with that, the connection went dead.

Juliana stared blindly at her brother while she fought to breathe. "I…" She tried again. "I just came by to tender my resignation. If you'll excuse me—"

"Ana, wait." He started toward her. "There's something you don't know."

But she didn't wait. Turning, she walked steady as a rock from the office. Later, much later she'd break. But not here. And not now.

As Lander hung up the phone, he knew that he'd completely and utterly lost his wife—the one woman he'd ever truly loved.

Who'd have thought him capable of that particular emotion? How had that happened? When had it happened? Before their wedding, he knew that much. Certainly before he'd implemented the design for her wedding rings. Maybe it had happened the first time he'd seen her, when he'd mistaken love for lust. Leaning back in his chair, he closed his eyes, images of Juliana flashing through his mind.

His bride floating up the aisle toward him in that spectacular wedding gown and veil, her eyes gazing at him through layers of tulle, glowing a brilliant brown seasoned with gold. His wife, her skin more silken than the sheets she lay on, opening herself to him, crying his name as he brought her to completion. His princess, breaking their engagement in order to protect him, while facing down a pack of snarling reporters. She'd done all that for him. How could he do any less for her?

Even so, it hurt. A deep, immeasurable hurt. He'd thought his love for Verdonia outweighed everything. That he was incapable of the sort of love touted by poets and romantic fools. But that wasn't true. He was more than capable. It had hidden within, asleep until Juliana had come into his life. And what had he done with it when it had been gifted to him? He'd done everything in his power to destroy it.

"Excuse me, Your Highness." His majordomo stood in the open doorway to his office. "The Temporary Governing Council has requested your presence."

"Thank you, Timothy. Will you inform them that I'm on my way?"

"Yes, sire. Immediately." He hesitated. "Is there anything I can do to help?"

"There's nothing." Lander offered an encouraging smile. "Everything will be fine. I haven't done anything wrong, any more than my father did. The truth will come out."

"Yes, sir. Of course it will. No one doubts that for a minute."

Lander only wished that were true. Unfortunately, someone somewhere had pointed the finger in his direction, blaming the Montgomerys for the amethyst crisis. And he wasn't certain he could prove them wrong. The TGC, put in place to govern Verdonia until after the election, had no choice but to act on the allegations.

Added to that, news of Juliana's return to the States on the morning following their wedding had leaked almost as soon as she'd stepped onto Joc's plane. He'd anticipated the resulting public outcry and had been prepared to deal with it. But when news of the investigation had broken later that same afternoon, her disappearance had only added fuel to the fire of suspicion. Why would she have left the day after her wedding if she hadn't believed her husband guilty of wrongdoing? The fact that she'd flown out with her brother had only made the entire affair more suspect. Even the infamous Joc Arnaud had refused to stand by Prince Lander, the gossips had whispered.

The scandal threatened to rip his country apart. Until he could get it straightened out—*if* he could get it straightened out, he wanted Juliana well away from the media bloodbath.

The minute Juliana hit the street, she hailed a cab. "Drive," she instructed the cabbie as soon as he pulled curbside.

"Where do you want me to go?"

"Anywhere. In circles for all I care."

Sliding into the back, she began to shake, her hands trembling so badly the diamonds and amethysts on her rings flashed with urgent fire. She stared blindly at them as she fought for control, and when her cell phone rang, it was all she could do to answer it. She expected to hear her brother's voice. Instead her mother-in-law responded to her abrupt greeting.

"Have you heard?" Rachel asked without preamble. "About Lander?"

"I…I spoke to him ten minutes ago." If those few terse sentences could be considered speaking. "Has something happened to him?"

Rachel groaned. "He hasn't told you about the charges, has he?"

"Joc tried to tell me something when I left his office, but—" As her mother-in-law's comment sank in, she straightened in her seat. "What's wrong, Rachel? What charges are you talking about?"

"He and his father are accused of…misappropriation, I guess is the most tactful word."

Misappropriation? Did she mean…*theft?* "Did I hear you right? Lander's been accused of embezzling money?"

"Amethysts. He's been charged with skimming a portion of the outflow and selling the gems on the black market. Apparently, there's conclusive documentation to back up the accusation."

"That's a crock, and you know it," Juliana declared irately. She thrust a hand through her hair, sending curls flying. "Lander would never do anything so dishonorable. Nor would he be party to anything that would harm Verdonia."

There was an instant of silence, then Rachel whispered, "Thank you, Juliana. I was so afraid you left because you believed he was guilty."

"I left because I found out he didn't love me," she responded without thought.

"No! Whatever gave you that idea?" There was a momentary pause and then Rachel continued. "Never mind. That's none of my business." She hastened to change the subject. "Your brother told me you were the best there is when it comes to accounting and finance. Would you be willing to examine the records and see if there's something our people have missed?"

Juliana didn't hesitate. "I'll be there as soon as I can." Of course, returning to Verdonia meant facing Lander again, something she wasn't prepared to do. Not after their phone conversation. "There's one condition."

"Name it."

"I don't want Lander to know I'm in Verdonia."

"Oh. I…I guess I can do that. At least, I can promise I won't tell him. I can't promise that he won't find out from some other source. Will that be acceptable?" When Juliana reluctantly agreed, Rachel added, "Tell me, my dear. Did you ever figure out what your wedding rings meant?" Without waiting for an answer, she hung up.

Juliana flipped her cell phone shut, and after a momentary hesitation, held out her hand. She stared at the rings curiously. They were such a beautiful set. Her mouth curved upward in a wistful smile as she remembered the moment when Lander had slid the band and engagement ring onto her finger. She recalled that he'd said the design meant something, as well. Something she was supposed to figure out. With everything that had happened in the interim, she'd forgotten until Rachel's reminder. Now she looked, really looked at the pair.

The wedding band itself was set with an unbroken circle of Verdonia Royal amethysts. Royals, for soul mates. Hah. As if. But the engagement ring, was another matter. On the outer portion of either side were a scattering of tiny Blushes set in gold filigree. Farther inward the amethysts grew progressively larger and changed in color to a shade she'd never seen before, becoming mixed with diamonds until the very middle where a huge diamond and a matching Verdonia Royal were connected in a swirl of gold.

What had Lander said about the Blushes? That they symbolized a contract. Wasn't that how their engagement had begun, as a contract? She might have been unaware of it, but that didn't make it any less true. She frowned in concentration. The Blushes were only on the outer rim. As they grew in size, they also changed to an unusual reddish-purple color that was neither Blush nor Royal. She wasn't sure what this new shade symbolized. None of the jewels Lander had shown her had contained anything similar. But at the center of the ring the stones were the deepest, richest purple-blue she'd ever seen. A diamond and a Royal mated together. She shook her head. No. It couldn't possibly mean what she thought.

The tears came then, tears of regret mixed with a surge of hope so expansive and strong that it drowned out every other emotion. It took two circuits around the block before she'd recovered sufficiently to decide on her next step. Fumbling for her cell phone, she punched in a number. Her brother answered on the first ring.

"I need three things from you and I need them an hour ago," she announced.

"Name them and they're yours."

"I need your jet. My old team of accountants. And the meanest, nastiest, sharkiest bunch of lawyers you have on staff. I want to be airborne before nightfall."

"Going somewhere?"

"Verdonia."

Joc let out a sigh of relief. "About damn time."

"Lander! Lander, where are you going?" Rachel called breathlessly.

He paused, his hand on the knob of the conference room door, and glanced over his shoulder at his stepmother. To his surprise, she approached at a near run, alarm clear in her eyes. "I'm checking in with my lawyers and accountants, of course. I've called down at least six times today for an update and haven't heard a word."

"Maybe if you left them alone so they could get some work done—"

"This will only take a minute."

He pushed open the door and stepped into the room. Everyone froze, and the animated conversation came to an abrupt stop at his entry. And that's when he heard it, a soft gasp. He knew that tiny hiccup of sound, had heard it every time he'd kissed his wife, every time he'd made love to her, every time he'd brought her to completion. Slowly he turned his head and there she was, standing off to one side of the room, staring at him.

Of course her eyes gave her away, brilliant flecks of gold burning within the honey brown. He flinched at what he read there. Apprehension, longing, wariness. Even a heartrending hint of sorrow. But worst of all was the unadulterated pain.

He didn't hesitate. He was beside her in an instant. Cupping the back of her neck, he tumbled her into his arms. His mouth took hers with an intense kiss that told her more clearly than words how much he missed her. His tongue breached her lips and she responded to him the way she always did, with a generous passion that threatened to unman him. She wore her hair up in a style similar to the one on their wedding day, and he thrust his hands into those perfectly arranged curls and set them free.

At long last he pulled back and gazed down at her. "You're here."

"Yes, I'm here," she agreed breathlessly.

"Don't take this the wrong way, but…why?"

"I thought I could help."

Help. She meant help with the embezzling charges. Damn it! If the media got wind of her presence they'd be all over her. If she thought her previous experiences had been bad, it would be nothing compared to this. And there wouldn't be anything he could do to protect her. "I left specific instructions with Joc—"

"Yes," she cut in. "I heard those instructions, remember?"

Hell. Lander thrust a hand through his hair. "We need to take this someplace private where we can talk." He started to urge her from the room, only to discover that they were already alone. He paused, tempted to carry her off to their rooms while no one was watching and allow his hands and mouth to do his speaking for him. Duty battled desire for supremacy. Duty won. "You shouldn't be in Verdonia. You need to leave before word leaks of your return."

"I'm not going anywhere. At least, not yet." She stepped away from him and folded her arms across her chest. "Why didn't you tell me about these charges you're facing?"

"You left, remember?"

Hot color scorched her cheeks. "Vividly. I also remember the reason I left."

"And still you came back?" he couldn't help but ask. He didn't understand it. After everything he'd done to drive her away, here she stood.

She waved that aside as though it weren't important. "Why did you tell Joc to keep me out of Verdonia?" she countered. "Was it to protect me?"

He shrugged. "You've had enough trouble with the media to last a lifetime. You don't need any more."

"Falling on your sword, Lander?"

He managed a brief smile. "We seem to make a habit of it, don't we?" His smile faded. "Not that it matters. You're returning to Texas right now, even if I have to put you on the plane in handcuffs."

"Just one last question before I go." She hesitated before rushing into speech. "I couldn't help noticing that all the Verdonian wedding rings you showed me at the museum had names. Does mine?"

The change of topic caught him off guard and he answered automatically. "Of course."

"What is it?"

He should have seen the question coming and diverted her before she could ask. "We can discuss this later." He attempted to dismiss the subject. "The plane—"

"Can wait." One look warned she wouldn't be budged from her stance. "If you want my cooperation, we'll discuss it now."

He made the best of a losing hand. "If I tell you the name, do you agree to leave? To get on whatever plane brought you here and return to Texas within the hour?" At her nod, he bit out, "Metamorphous. Your ring is called Metamorphous."

"Ah." A strange smile tugged at her mouth. "I'd hoped it was something like that."

He started for the door. "If we're careful, I think I can get you to the airport with no one the wiser."

"In a minute." She laced his hand in hers and tugged him toward the conference table where papers were piled high. "I want to show you something first."

"We had an agreement, Juliana." Determination filled

him. This time he wouldn't fail. If she didn't come soon, he'd take more drastic action. Whatever necessary, so long as he protected her. "You promised you'd leave."

"I'll be quick." She shoved her loosened curls back from her face. "Normally I wouldn't allow a client in here while I'm working."

She was chattering from nerves, and his eyes narrowed as he watched her. "I'm not your client."

"It wouldn't matter if you were, not anymore." She edged around the table away from him and gathered up a sheaf of papers. Tidying them, she reached for another. "I'm through with my investigation."

He took the comment with calm stoicism. "Don't let it worry you. I know you did your best. Now if you don't mind—"

"I always do my best." And she smiled at him.

He saw it then. The quiet satisfaction. The breathtaking radiance that eased the lines of strain from his wife's face. "You figured out what happened to the amethysts," he marveled.

"Yes. Lauren DeVida happened to them."

"Our chief executive accountant?" He couldn't disguise his shock. "Not a chance in hell. She was devoted to my father. Devoted to Verdonia."

"No, she was pretty much devoted to stealing amethysts. I have to admit, she was good at it," Juliana reluctantly conceded. "She was really good."

"But not as good as you." There wasn't a doubt in his mind.

She struggled to appear modest. "No one's that good."

He sat down across from her. "Are you sure it was Lauren?"

"Sure enough that the accountants are reporting to

the Temporary Governing Council as we speak." She reached out and squeezed his hand. "She was like family, wasn't she?"

"Yes. My father adored her. We all did."

"Huh." Juliana's brows pulled together in thought. "I hadn't considered that possibility."

"What possibility?"

She riffled through some of the documents. "When were your father and Rachel married?" She flicked a piece of paper across the table toward him. "Was it around about this date?"

"Not around. Exactly."

"That's when the scam began. It ended the day your father died."

Damn it to hell. What had Juliana once said? One plus one always equals two. "You think Lauren was in love with my father, don't you?"

She nodded. "And when he married Rachel, that adoration turned vindictive. From what I've been able to uncover, she set up the entire operation to make it appear that your father, you and Merrick had run it. There are even documents that implicate Rachel and Miri. I'm guessing she sent copies of some of this to certain interested parties."

"Von Folke."

"It's possible. I haven't found any proof of that."

Lander glanced around the room, taking in the controlled chaos. "What's left for you to do here?"

"Nothing. As soon as we let everyone back in, copies will be made. Reports written." She shrugged. "Details finalized."

"You're certain? There's no question that it's finished?"

"I'm positive."

"That leaves one last task for me to deal with." Without warning, he circled the conference table and swept her up into his arms.

She released a muffled cry. "What do you think you're doing?"

"I'm taking a page out of Merrick's book."

"I…I don't understand." A heartbreaking ache underscored her words. "Are you still sending me home? I know I promised to go, but—"

"I'm abducting you, not sending you home," he explained gravely. "It worked so well for Merrick that I thought I'd give it a try."

"You're going to—"

He silenced her with a kiss. When he came up for air again, he said, "Abduct you. Yes. Would you prefer to be tied up?"

"That won't be necessary." Looping her hands around his neck she released a disgruntled sigh. "It would seem I don't have a choice." She peeked up at him, her eyes shining like burnished gold. "Do I?"

"You can fight. But I recommend cooperation. That way you don't invalidate Section C, Subparagraph Four, Line Sixteen of my contract with Joc."

She stiffened within his hold. "Dare I ask?"

"I believe it has to do with love, honor and cherish until death do us part."

Something shifted in her expression, a slow undoing, a helpless breaking signaling the final release of a lifetime's worth of barriers. Without a word, she closed her eyes and lowered her head to his shoulder. He carried her from the room. In no time he had a limo arranged to transport them to the apartment building where he'd first made love to his wife.

"I should have sent Joc packing the minute he proposed that outrageous contract," he told her, once they were inside.

"Why didn't you?"

"Verdonia," he said simply. "And then later, there was no reason to terminate our agreement. Why would I? It gave me everything I wanted." He reached for her. Now that she'd returned, he couldn't seem to keep his hands off her. "It gave me you."

"Oh, Lander." She clung to him. "You should have told me you were in trouble sooner," she informed him fiercely. "I would have been on the next plane back to you. We could have had this resolved a week ago."

It was all he needed to hear. She lifted her face to his kiss at the same instant as he lowered his. Their mouths collided, setting the mating dance into motion. Clothes were shed with overwhelming haste. Limbs entwined. And then they were on the bed, with nothing between them but a desperate urgency.

They surged together, the crest building, the subtle upheaval like waves fomenting before a distant storm. Juliana undulated beneath him, arching into the ebb and flow of their mating, the depth and intensity increasing before the steady advance of the tempest. And then it was on top of them, breaking loose from all restraint. Crashing and clawing at emotions drawn bow-string taut. Howling for release. They were swept high into the storm's embrace, and in that instant, she came undone, shattering in his arms.

Lander watched her, reveling in the knowledge that he'd brought her to crisis. Humbled by the fact that his hands, his mouth, his body, his touch—and his alone— could cause such an intense climax. The storm lashed out with a final violent kick. Roaring through him. Furious. Wrenching. And he followed her into the very heart of it, clinging to the one person in the universe who completed him. Who sheltered and fulfilled him.

His bride. His princess. His wife.

Much later, Lander rolled onto his back and scooped Juliana tight against him. By then dusk had settled in, leaving the room in semidarkness. He slid his fingers into her hair, filling his hands with her curls. He experienced a loosening deep inside, the knowledge that his world would only be right when it was like this—with his wife in his arms and his hands on her.

"Why did you return?" he felt compelled to ask.

Her calm gaze remained fixed on his, filled with an absolute certainty. "I returned because I realized you loved me as much as I loved you."

His brows drew together. "Of course I love you."

"You never said the words," she replied simply.

Hell. How could he have overlooked something so obvious? "Then how did you know?"

"The wedding rings. I'd forgotten what you'd told me on our wedding day, about their having a special meaning. But then Rachel reminded me." Her voice softened, grew richer. "That's when I put it all together."

"What did you put together?"

"That you loved me." She held up her hand, her rings giving off a subdued flash of fire. "The Blushes on the outside represent how our relationship began, as part of a contract. But then the stones change and grow, just as our feelings for each other changed and grew. At the very heart, it's a metamorphous from contract to soul mate."

"I couldn't have put it better myself." He smoothed

her hair away from her face. "I love you, Juliana. I have for a long time. But I knew you wouldn't believe words alone. They're too easy."

"Even so, you put the words in the ring. I found those, too. In the gold filigree. It says 'true love' in Verdonian. There's only one thing I don't understand."

"And what's that?"

She ran her fingertip over the stones set between the Blushes and Royals. "The meaning of these other amethysts. The ones between the pink and purple. They're such a unique color. Not quite red, not quite blue, nor purple. Yet, all of them mixed together. I've never seen an amethyst quite like it."

"My father came across the stones years ago. Apparently just these few were coughed out of the mines. Nothing like them has been found since."

"They're so distinctive."

"So is their name."

"Really?" She looked up at him, innocent curiosity reflected in her face. "What are they called?"

He stroked her ring, touching each stone in turn. "The Celestia Blush. The sealing of a contract. The Verdonia Royal. To represent soul mates." His finger lingered on the final group of stones. "And these were named by royal proclamation on our wedding day. This color is now known as the Juliana Rose, and will forever after symbolize true love."

She wept then, helpless tears of disbelief and joy. He held her patiently until they'd eased. Wiping the dampness from her cheeks, she wound her arms around his neck. Her eyes shone brighter than the sun as she kissed him three times, each deeper and more passionate than the last. The first kiss sealed their marriage contract. The second was reserved for soul mates. And finally, she gave him the kiss of true love.

"You should know that you've done something for me no one else has ever been able to do," she whispered against his mouth.

"What's that, Princess?"

She laughed away the last of her tears. "You've made all my dreams come true."

He smiled contentedly. "Now that sounds like the perfect job for a prince."

* * * * *

Caretti's Forced Bride

JENNIE LUCAS

Jennie Lucas grew up dreaming about faraway lands. At fifteen, hungry for experience beyond the borders of her small Idaho city, she went to a Connecticut boarding school on a scholarship. She took her first solo trip to Europe at sixteen, then put off college and travelled around the USA, supporting herself with jobs as diverse as petrol station cashier and newspaper advertising assistant.

At twenty-two, she met the man who would be her husband. After their marriage, she graduated from Kent State with a degree in English. Seven years after she started writing, she got the magical call from London that turned her into a published author.

Since then life has been hectic, with a new writing career, a sexy husband and two babies under two, but she's having a wonderful (albeit sleepless) time. She loves immersing herself in dramatic, glamorous, passionate stories. Maybe she can't physically travel to Morocco or Spain right now, but for a few hours a day, while her children are sleeping, she can be there in her books.

Jennie loves to hear from her readers. You can visit her website at www.jennielucas.com, or drop her a note at jennie@jennielucas.com

To Tatia Totorica
A great writer, a great critique partner,
a great friend

CHAPTER ONE

CLIMBING out of his Rolls-Royce, Paolo Caretti pulled his black coat close to his body and stepped out onto the sidewalk. Sunrise was just a slash of scarlet above New York's gray skyline as his chauffeur held an umbrella to block the freezing rain.

"Paolo. Wait."

For a moment he thought he'd imagined the soft sound, that his insomnia had finally caused him to dream in daytime. Then a small figure stepped out from behind the tall metal sculpture that decorated the front of his twenty-story office building. Rain plastered the woman's hair and clothes to her body. Her face was pale with cold. She must have been standing outside of his building for hours, waiting for him.

"Don't turn me away," she said. "Please."

Her voice was soft, throaty, low. Just like he remembered. After all these years he still remembered everything about her, no matter how much money he made or how many mistresses he'd taken to wipe her from his memory.

His jaw tightened. "You shouldn't have come."

"I…I need your help." Princess Isabelle de Luceran took a deep breath, her light brown eyes shimmering beneath the streetlights. "Please. I have nowhere else to go."

Their gazes locked. For a moment he was taken back to spring days picnicking in Central Park, to summer nights making love in his Little Italy apartment. When, for four sweet months, she'd made his world bright and new and he'd asked her to be his wife…

Now, he looked at her coldly. "Make an appointment."

He started to step around her, but she blocked him. "I've tried. I've left ten messages with your secretary. Didn't she give them to you?"

Valentina had, but he'd ignored them. Isabelle de Luceran meant nothing to him. He'd stopped wanting her long ago.

Or so he'd told himself. But now her beauty was seeping through him like a poison. Her expressive hazel eyes, her full mouth, those lush curves hidden beneath the ladylike coat—he remembered everything. The taste of her skin. The feel of her lips kissing down his belly. Her soft hands stroking between his legs…

"You're alone?" He clenched his jaw, struggling to get himself under control. "Where are your bodyguards?"

"I left them at the hotel," she whispered. "Help me. Please. For the sake of…who we once were."

To his horror, he saw tears blending with rain to fall in rivulets down her cheek. Isabelle? Crying? Her hands trembled. Whatever she wanted, she must want it badly, he thought.

Good. Having her on her knees begging for a favor was a very pleasant image. It wouldn't make up for what she'd done, but it might be a start.

Abruptly, he moved closer, tracing a finger down her wet cheek. "You want a favor?" Her skin felt cold, as if she were indeed the ice princess the world believed her to be. "You know I'll make you pay for it."

"Yes." Her voice was so quiet he could barely hear her over the sound of rain. "I know."

"Follow me." Taking the umbrella from his chauffeur, he turned on his heel and strode up the wide concrete steps. As he entered through his building's revolving door, he nodded a greeting to the security guards in the foyer. He could hear the click-click-click of Isabelle's high-heeled boots across the marble floor behind him.

"Good morning, Salvatore," Paolo said to the first security guard.

"Good morning." The elderly man cleared his throat. "It's a cold one today, isn't it, Signor Caretti? Makes me wish I was in the old country, where it's warmer." His eyes trailed to Isabelle. "Or San Piedro, maybe."

So even Salvatore had recognized her. Paolo uneasily wondered what his executive secretary would do. Valentina Novak, though highly competent, had one weakness: celebrity tabloids. And Isabelle, the princess of a tiny Mediterranean kingdom, was one of the most famous women in the world.

As Paolo left the guard station, he heard Salvatore whistle through his teeth. He couldn't blame the man. Isabelle had been a lovely, fresh-faced girl at eighteen; she was more beautiful now. As if even time itself were in love with her.

Angrily shaking the thought away, Paolo strode to his private elevator and pressed the button for the penthouse level. As soon as the elevator's doors closed, he turned to her.

"All right. Let's have it."

Isabelle's voice was low. Desperate. "Alexander's been kidnapped."

"Your nephew?" He gave her an incredulous stare. "Kidnapped?"

"You're the only one who can save him!"

His eyebrows rose, still disbelieving. "The heir to the throne of San Piedro? Needs *my* help?"

"He's not just the heir now. He's the King." She shook her head, wiping her eyes. "My brother and sister-in-law died two weeks ago. You must have heard."

"Yes." He'd unwillingly heard the details from Valentina, who'd told him the couple had died in a boating accident in Majorca, leaving their nine-year-old son behind. And that wasn't the only gossip she'd shared…

Grinding his teeth, he pushed the troubling thought away. "I'm sorry."

"My mother is officially regent until he comes of age, but she's getting older, and I'm trying to help." She took a deep breath. "I was at the London economic summit yesterday when I got a frantic call from Alexander's nanny. Alexander was missing. Then I received a letter demanding I meet the kidnapper at midnight tonight. Alone."

"Don't tell me you're actually considering following his instructions?"

"If you don't help me, I don't know what else to do."

"Your nephew has a national army, bodyguards, police. Get them involved at once."

She shook her head. "The letter said if I contact anyone in an official capacity I'll never see Alexander again!"

He gave a harsh laugh. "Of course the kidnapper would say that. Don't be a fool. You don't need my help. Go to your police. Let them handle it." As the *ding* sounded and the doors opened on the penthouse level, he turned away from her. "Go home, Isabelle."

"Wait." She put her hand on his wrist. "There's more. Something I haven't told you."

He stared down at her hand. He could feel the electricity through his cashmere coat, his tailored jacket, his finely cut shirt. He had the sudden desire to close the door behind him, to push her up against the wall of the elevator, to pull up her skirt and taste her. He yearned to lick the rain off her skin, to pull off her sodden clothes and warm her with the length of his body...

What the hell was wrong with him? He felt nothing for Isabelle de Luceran but scorn—both for her shallow nature and for the naïve boy he'd been when he'd loved her.

So how was it possible that five minutes with her

made his body combust into flame? Even through his clothes, her touch burned his skin.

He jerked his arm away.

"I'll give you one minute," he ground out. "Don't waste it."

He strode out onto his private floor, crowded with employees who managed his global holdings. Valentina stood up from her desk. As always, she was the picture of well-groomed efficiency: her stylish red suit accentuated her curvy figure, and her bright auburn hair was pulled back in a neat chignon. Her only jewelry was the gold Tiffany watch he'd given her last Christmas.

"Good morning, Mr. Caretti." She spoke rapidly, chewing on her full lower lip with white, even teeth. "Here are the numbers you wanted from the Rome office. Palladium is up two percent on the Nymex, and I've taken several calls this morning from reporters about the rumor of a buyout offer. Then, of course, all those calls from a woman claiming to be…"

Blue eyes widening, she sucked in her breath, staring at Isabelle.

"You told them Caretti Motors is not for sale," Paolo said. "Correct?"

The thirty-year-old redhead looked as if she might swoon. "Yes. No. That is—"

"Hold my calls," he bit out. Grabbing Isabelle's wrist, he dragged her into his office and closed the door behind them. Tossing his coat on the plush black leather sofa, he turned on a small lamp to illuminate the dark, spacious room.

"Thank you," Isabelle said softly, rubbing her wrist. "I appreciate that you—"

"Say what you have to say, and get out," he interrupted.

Her caramel-colored eyes narrowed. She took a deep breath. "I need your help."

"So you said," he replied coldly. "But you didn't explain why you need *my* help instead of going to the police or the bodyguards who protect San Piedro's king. Or, better yet," he added scornfully, "your fiancé."

She looked at him in surprise. "You know about Magnus?"

Paolo folded his arms, trying to calm the tension he felt in every muscle. "You're famous, Isabelle. I hear about your life whether I want to or not."

But it was more than that.

Isabelle.

And Magnus.

Together.

He was still reeling. Ever since Valentina had started sighing over their "glamorous" affair, he'd wanted to hit something—preferably Magnus's meek, handsome face.

"I'm sorry," she said in a small voice. "I don't try to end up in the tabloids. They chase me. It's how they sell papers."

His lip curled.

"It must be hard," he agreed sardonically. He could hardly believe she was trying to pretend she didn't love every minute of her fame. Her whole shallow existence had been built on the temple of her vanity and insatiable appetite for adoration. Even he himself had once been stupid enough to—

Stopping the thought cold, he clenched his jaw. "So why don't you ask your fiancé for help?"

"He's not my fiancé. Not yet."

"But he soon will be."

For the first time she looked away. "He proposed to me a few days ago. I haven't given him my answer yet, but I will. Once Alexander is safe, we will announce our engagement."

It was exactly what he'd expected, and yet involuntarily, he stepped toward her. Isabelle—Magnus's bride? The thought ricocheted through his body like a bullet.

"And as for why I can't ask him for help," she said, "he would insist on calling in the police and working through proper channels." She shook her head fiercely. "I can't be that patient. Not when some criminal has Alexander."

The irony of it rose like bile in his throat, nearly choking him. "So that's why you've come to me?"

"I've read about you as well." Her eyes met his. "You're ruthless. Well-connected. Magnus has told me about—"

"About what?" he interrupted harshly.

"About how you focus only on yourself," she said. "You ignore the pain of others. You'll drive right past accidents. You're almost inhuman in your determination to win."

He clenched his jaw. Of course Magnus hadn't told her about their past—he was even more ashamed of it than Paolo was. "That's why I always win every race and Magnus takes second place."

"People whisper that…you're truly your father's son," she said quietly.

He'd heard it so many times that he didn't even flinch. "So you're seeking one monster without morals to fight another?"

"Yes."

"Thank you."

"Alexander's bodyguards could be involved. I need an outsider, and you're the only one ruthless enough to bring him home safe. No one must ever know he was kidnapped. It would make my country appear weak and corrupt—as if we couldn't even protect our king."

"So you want me to keep the whole thing secret, even from your future husband?" He raised an eyebrow. "Hardly a sound foundation for marriage, Princess."

"Insult me however you want. Just bring Alexander home!"

He watched her. "And you're sure Magnus didn't send you to ask me?"

"Of course not." She lifted her chin. "He would be horrified if he knew. He wouldn't want me to get involved."

"Such a perfect gentleman," he said sardonically.

She bristled. "He *is* perfect! He's handsome and charming. Wealthy and influential beyond belief. The tenth richest man in the world!"

"I always knew you'd sell yourself to the highest bidder, Isabelle."

"Just as I always knew you'd replace me with the cheapest-looking tart you could find," she snapped. "I'm just surprised it took you a whole hour."

He exhaled with a flare of nostril. The night Isabelle had so abruptly ended their affair he'd gotten drunk and slept with his next-door neighbor—a girl trying to break into Broadway whose name he could no longer remember. For a moment he wondered how Isabelle knew about it. Then he decided he didn't care.

"What did you expect me to do?" he replied acidly. "Spend my whole life celibate? Mourning your loss?"

A pink flush stained her cheeks. "No," she muttered. "That would be pathetic." She bit her bottom lip, and in spite of his dislike he couldn't help but be aroused. Her lips looked tender. Full. And he remembered their sweetness. It had been so many years, and yet he could still remember how those lips had felt, kissing down the length of his body…

"Of course a man like you couldn't be faithful for longer than a day." She straightened her shoulders, haughtily raising her chin. "It's why I'm glad I found a man I can trust."

As she'd obviously never trusted *him*. Paolo's hands clenched. He had to change the subject before he lost control and did something utterly insane…like grab Isabelle by the shoulders and kiss her until she forgot Magnus and every other man she'd taken to her bed in the last ten years. Before he made love to her right here on his desk, punishing her, pleasuring her, branding her forever as his own.

"Go ask Prince Charming for help, then," he said harshly.

"He can't help me. I told you. You're the only one who can." She took a deep breath. "Please, Paolo. I know that I hurt you…"

"You didn't hurt me." He glanced out the wide windows. From the view on the twentieth floor, misty clouds hung low over the city, covering it like a shroud. "Just tell me one thing—who benefits from your nephew's kidnapping?"

Her eyelashes fluttered against her cheek. "Politically? No one. We're a small country."

"Ransom?"

"That has to be it. But if the kidnapper asks for a large sum, it will be hard for us to pay it. We cannot raise taxes when half our factories have moved offshore. Our economy is struggling. If it weren't for tourism…"

"Struggling?" He looked at her pearls, her designer coat, her expensive high-heeled boots.

She flushed. "My clothes are given to me free by designers. Everyone wants publicity." She glanced uneasily at the door. "Speaking of which—would any of your employees call the press about my visit?"

"I trust them implicitly." And, unfortunately, he also trusted that as soon as Valentina had recovered her senses she'd started phoning all her friends in the Tri-

State area. She was normally the epitome of discretion, but with her passion for celebrities there was just no way she'd be able to keep silent. "Let's make this quick. What about Magnus?"

"Magnus?"

"Would he have any reason to kidnap your nephew?"

Her eyes widened in shock. "No! Why would he?"

"Perhaps he wants his own children to inherit the throne."

She looked at him like he was mad. "His children?"

"His future children. With you."

Their eyes met.

"Oh," she whispered. "Those children."

An echo of primal, almost animal fury went through him at the thought of Isabelle pregnant with another man's child. Once he would have killed any man who'd tried to touch her...

She exhaled. "I love San Piedro. You know I do. We're rich in culture and tradition. But we're just three square miles. Magnus owns more land in Austria alone. The von Trondhem bloodline dates back to Charlemagne."

"Are you trying to convince me to marry him, or yourself?" he said acidly.

She looked at him. "He's a good man."

"Right." Forced to concede her point, he scowled. He'd raced against Magnus von Trondhem for five years now on the circuit of the Motorcycle Grand Prix. And as far as he could tell he really was a Boy Scout—the kind who was afraid to tilt his motorcycle an extra degree in a turn beyond what the manual advised. The son of an Austrian prince, rich and respected, he was also bland and boring enough to let Isabelle lead him by the nose.

The perfect husband for Isabelle, he thought. The husband she deserved. And yet…

"So will you help me?" she whispered.

Help her? Paolo didn't want to go near her. Just looking at her from a few paces away made his whole body rise. Her skin looked soft, so soft. Her beige wool coat, belted at the waist, accentuated her petite, curvaceous figure. He could see the rapid pulse of her slender throat beneath her old-fashioned pearls. And she still used the same lotion, the same shampoo: he caught the delicate scent of Provençal roses and Mediterranean oranges. The scent, which he remembered so well, made him instantly hard.

And he realized two things.

First: he hadn't forgotten her. Not by a long shot. He yearned for her like a starving man longed for bread.

Second: there was no way in hell he was going to let another man have her.

He wanted to take her to bed until he'd had his fill. Until his desire for her was completely satiated.

Until he could toss her aside as carelessly as she'd once discarded him.

"Please," she whispered. Her tawny skin was pale with cold and her long chestnut hair was wet with rain, but when she looked up her eyes were the color of honey in paradise. She placed her small hand over his larger one. "Will you?"

For a moment he looked down at her hand. Then, with a shudder of desire, he looked out the windows, towards the Hudson River and all of Manhattan beneath him. The sun had risen at last, trickling pale and wan through the gloom. Far below, he could see taxis crawling down the street, and pedestrians scurrying ant-like down sidewalks. Dreary and dark, the city was endless shades of gray.

Except for her. Even desperate, wet and cold, she glowed with color and light. Even in the belted coat, she drew him with her heat. Made him yearn and feel.

Made him realize that every woman he'd been with for the last ten years had been a pale imitation.

He tried to remember the last time he'd felt this way. But all he could recall was making love to her long ago in his dingy one-room apartment in Little Italy, far from her dorm at Barnard College. He remembered the way she'd felt when he touched her. The way she'd tasted. Her sweetness, the beads of sweat on her skin. His mattress on the floor—the sound of the springs moving beneath her body. The slow, quiet whir of the fan. And the heat. Most of all the heat.

Paolo's eyes suddenly narrowed.

Ten years was long enough.

He still desired her.

So he would have her.

"Paolo?"

"Very well." He turned back to her carelessly. "I'll help you. I'll save your nephew. I'll keep it quiet. And I will destroy any man who tries to stop me."

Her eyes flashed relief. "Thank you, Paolo. I knew you would—"

"And in return—" he looked down at her with dark eyes "—you will be my mistress."

His mistress?

Isabelle stared at him in horror. "You can't be serious."

He gave her a brief, humorless smile. "You have some objection to becoming my lover? Strange. You had no objections before. In fact, you did it for pleasure, with no return favor required."

It was heartless of him to remind her of that. Lover? The word was meaningless on his sensual, lying lips. Paolo Caretti didn't know anything about love. And she certainly couldn't trust him. He'd proved that long ago. So why was she surprised to discover he still had no heart?

"One thing hasn't changed," she choked out. "You're still as selfish as ever."

"More so." He came closer to her, his eyes as dark and fathomless as the midnight sea. "You would enjoy being in my bed. I promise you."

She shivered as he reached out to stroke a long tendril of her hair. He might know nothing of love, but pleasure was another matter. Darkly handsome, he had the same strong physique, the same broad shoulders she remem-

bered. The same Roman profile and chiseled jawline.
The same dark, intense eyes.

It was true he now wore a black Savile Row suit
instead of a blue mechanic's jumpsuit, and his fingernails were clean instead of dirty with engine grease, but
he was more dangerous to her than ever.

Because Paolo wasn't just her first. He was her only.
And if she spent time with him she would risk far more
than her heart…

"No," she whispered. "I can't. I'll give you anything
else you want, but not that."

He turned back toward his desk, dismissing her.
"Good luck finding your nephew."

She swallowed. She was at his mercy and she knew
it. She would pay any price to cuddle Alexander close
again. To have him squirm in her embrace like always,
his sweet, exasperated voice complaining, "Aunt
Isabelle, I'm not a little boy anymore!"

But, king or not, he *was* a little boy. He always would
be to her—though he'd grown up far too quickly over
the last two weeks. Every morning he'd met Isabelle and
his grandmother at the breakfast table red-eyed with
grief, but she hadn't seen him cry. He'd gone through
the motions of his new royal duties with quiet dignity,
showing the type of man he would someday become.
The king San Piedro needed.

So it was pointless to pretend there was anything she
wouldn't do to save him. Even sell herself to Paolo Caretti,
the one man she'd sworn to avoid for the rest of her life.

But…she couldn't become Paolo's mistress. In addition to her own private reasons for wanting to stay away from Paolo, nothing must prevent her marriage to Prince Magnus von Trondhem. Since the textiles industry had moved offshore, San Piedro had been in economic freefall. They desperately needed the influx of business and money that Magnus would provide. Without it, more factories would close. More shops would go bankrupt. More families would be desperate.

Isabelle rubbed her eyes. She couldn't let that happen. She had to save Alexander. Save her country. Compared to that, her own feelings—her own *life*—meant nothing.

"I can't be your mistress," she said quietly. "I am engaged to be married."

"No, you're not. Not yet. You said so yourself."

She shook her head. "That's just a technicality."

"Suit yourself," he said, turning away from her. "If you'll excuse me…"

"Wait."

He looked at her, raising a dark eyebrow.

She swallowed. He had her, and they both knew it. "One night," she said, nearly choking on the words. "I'll give you one night."

"One night?" He lifted her chin. "And you would give yourself to me completely?"

"Yes," she whispered, unable to meet his eyes.

She waited for waves of guilt to crush her at the thought of cheating on her future fiancé. Even though she was being blackmailed, even though it was to save a child, shouldn't she feel horrible at the thought of deceiving the perfect man she was to marry? After all, she above all people had seen the damage that infidelity could do.

But her heart felt nothing.

Because I don't love Magnus, she thought. *And I know he doesn't love me.* The one small blessing in all of this.

To save Alexander, Isabelle would give herself to Paolo for one night. That was nothing. To save her country, she would soon give herself to Magnus for the rest of her life.

And she would forever keep secrets from them both...

"One night?" Paolo mused. "You hold yourself very high."

A very unladylike curse went through Isabelle's mind. "A child is in danger. If you were any sort of gentleman you wouldn't ask me to be your mistress as the price for your help!"

"He's not my child," he said coolly. "He's King of San Piedro, with a hundred bodyguards at his beck and call. You could have half of Europe searching for him already, but you chose to come to me instead." He came closer. "And, as you have already pointed out to me so succinctly, I'm not a gentleman."

His gaze devoured her whole. He leaned forward, his lips inches from hers. She could feel the muscles of his thighs pressing against her legs. Her knees felt weak. She hadn't eaten or slept for two days. She'd barely made it to New York without the paparazzi catching her, and ditching her bodyguards at the hotel hadn't been easy. All she'd been able to think about was Alexander. Where was he? Was he being well treated? Was he scared and alone?

Paolo was right. She didn't need a gentleman. She didn't need someone who was kind and civilized and knew how to properly tie a cravat.

She needed a hard-edged warrior who was strong and ruthless. She needed a man who was invincible.

She needed Paolo.

But at what cost? How much was she willing to risk?

"Why do you want me in your bed?" she whispered. "To soothe your pride? To punish me? You could have any woman you wanted!"

"I know." He ran his hand down the side of her neck to the bare skin of her collarbone above her wool coat. "I want you."

Hearing him speak those words made her weak, and his fingertips caused heat to sweep across her body like a brush fire. How many nights had she dreamed of him—reliving every moment he'd ever taken her in his arms? How many days, while sitting through long speeches that would make any sane person want to stab herself with a pencil, had she fantasized about the way he'd once touched her?

For ten years she'd longed for him. Even knowing he was forbidden to her forever. Even knowing that if she gave herself to him again it would risk far more than her marriage. Far more than her heart.

"Why?" she managed. "Why me?"

He shrugged. "Perhaps I want to possess something other men only dream of."

"Possess?" At that, she raised her chin. "Even if I become your mistress, you will never truly possess me, Paolo. Never."

He looked down at her, his eyes dark. "Ah. Now there's the Princess I remember. I knew you couldn't stay a meek little mouse for long." He stroked her cheek. "But we both know you're lying. You *will* give yourself to me. And not just for your nephew's sake, but because you want to. Because you cannot resist."

She couldn't deny it. Not when just his slightest touch sent her senses reeling, made her body combust beneath the chill of her wet clothes.

"Would you keep our night a secret?" she asked in a low voice. "Could you?"

His lip curled. "You mean, would I call reporters to brag about my good fortune?"

"That's not what—" She took a deep breath. "No one must know that Alexander was ever kidnapped. And my marriage…"

"I get it." Clenching his jaw, he held out his hand. "Let me see the letter."

She gave him the scribbled note out of her coat pocket. Isabelle already knew it by heart, the strangely formed letters demanding that she go alone to the palace garden in San Piedro at midnight tonight and tell no one.

"How did you get this?"

"It was left outside the door of my suite at the Savoy."

"You haven't left yourself much time," he said, handing the letter back to her. "What was your plan if I refused?"

"I don't know."

"No other plans? No one else to ask for help?" he said softly. "Perhaps I should demand more of you. A month of nights. A year of them."

Horrified, she stared up at him.

He gave her a smile. "Fortunately for you, I tire of women easily. One night with you should be more than enough." He stroked her cheek, the edge of her jawline, the sensitive crook of her neck. "And so you agree to the terms?"

She pressed her hands against her belly. She wanted to say yes. And, if she were truly honest with herself, it wasn't just to save Alexander.

But it was too dangerous. Giving herself to Paolo, even for one night, risked everything she held dear—her marriage to Magnus, her heart and, worst of all, her secret. Dear God, her secret…

"Please, Paolo." She licked her dry lips. "Isn't there any other way you'd consider—"

He cut her off with a kiss. His lips crushed hers as his tongue penetrated her mouth, mastering her, enslaving her.

"Say yes," he growled. He kissed her again. "Say yes, damn you."

"Yes," she whispered, sagging in his arms.

He abruptly let her go. She nearly lost her balance as

he opened his cell phone and dialed. "Bertolli. Get every man on the list. Yes, I said every man. I will pay ten times the going rate. It must be flawless. Tonight."

Knees shaking, she sank into a chair, feeling as if she'd sold her very soul. She watched as he efficiently and effortlessly organized the invasion of her country. He turned away, barking orders into the phone, all business. As if he'd already forgotten she was there.

But she knew he hadn't forgotten her. He could feel her, as she could feel him.

She touched her lips. She'd spent ten years trying to forget Paolo Caretti. She'd given up what she loved most in order to stay out of his ruthless, vicious world. But now she was being drawn back in. She could only pray she wouldn't be irrevocably caught in his web.

His mistress for one night. That was the price. She would be used at his will and at his pleasure. And, worse still, he would make sure she enjoyed it. Just thinking of what was ahead, she clutched the arms of her chair as the world seemed to hover and spin around her.

All she could do now was pray that Paolo never discovered the secret she'd been hiding. The greatest secret of her life.

CHAPTER TWO

THE moon was hazy and full over the palace garden as Isabelle sat on a bench inside the hedge maze.

She shivered. She was still wearing the same blouse and skirt, covered by the belted wool coat, that she'd worn since she'd abruptly left London for New York. She was exhausted, grimy, and most of all she was afraid.

Afraid that at any moment Alexander's kidnapper would come out of the dark shadows like a wraith.

Afraid he wouldn't, and she'd lose him forever.

Paolo will find him, she told herself fiercely. Paolo Caretti was vicious and ruthless. If half the rumors were true, he was nothing like the young mechanic who'd once spoken of his father's criminal ties with revulsion, who'd seemed determined to build an honest life for himself.

Her mother had been right. *Blood will tell.*

But then, Isabelle had known Paolo couldn't be trusted from the moment when, mere hours after he'd proposed to her, he'd jumped into bed with another woman…

A twig snapped behind a far hedge. She leapt to her feet, her high-heeled boots sinking into the soft grass.

Don't be afraid, she repeated to herself, trying to steady the beat of her heart, the clammy shake of her hands. Don't be afraid.

"Who's there?" she whispered, despising the tremble in her voice.

No answer. Paolo had gone into Provence chasing a lead, but twenty of his men, along with her two most trusted bodyguards, were hidden invisibly throughout the garden. They awaited the kidnapper like death on gossamer wings.

In spite of that, she stared at the shadowy hedge with all her might, hardly able to breathe. All she could see was moonlight on dark green leaves. She could smell eucalyptus and pine, and hear the roar of the sea pounding the nearby cliffs.

Suddenly she heard voices in the darkness, a crash, rapidly running footsteps.

It's Paolo, she thought, her heart in her throat. He's come to tell me that Alexander's dead.

She closed her eyes, remembering the feel of the little boy's arms around her. Remembering his sweet face when she'd rocked him to sleep as a baby. The sound of his laugh as he'd toddled down the marble hallways of the *palais* on unsteady feet. If Alexander was dead, she didn't want to live. She squeezed her eyes shut, swaying on her feet. *Please let him be all right. Please. I'll do anything. Just let him be all right...*

"Aunt Isabelle!"

Her eyes flew open as she felt the little boy's arms around her.

"Alexander," she whispered. Pulling back, she looked at him in the moonlight, felt his cold, thin arms, saw the big grin on the face that was usually serious and pale. "Alexander," she breathed, and at that moment she realized she was weeping. "You're here. You're safe."

The boy gestured to Paolo, who was standing behind him like a dark guardian angel. "He found me. I'm fine, Aunt Isabelle! *Zut alors.*" He grimaced, squirming in her arms. "You're squashing me! I'm not a little baby, you know!"

"No, you're not," she agreed, smiling until her cheeks hurt. Tears were streaming down her face.

Behind him, Paolo folded his arms. "We tracked him to an abandoned *mas* thirty miles from here. He was tied to a chair in the farmhouse's unheated cellar. But he never cried—not once." He glanced down at Alexander. "You're a brave kid."

Man and boy faced each other. They had similar coloring. The same dark eyes and dark hair. The same penetrating frown as they each took the other's measure.

Alexander shook his head. "There's no point in being afraid." His voice wobbled a little as he added, "When you're King, you do what you have to do."

He was repeating a phrase that Isabelle had heard her brother say many times. Though a faithless husband, he'd been a wonderful father. Maxim had loved

Alexander so much. But then, he and Karin had spent so many years trying to have a child.

"Thank you for saving me, *monsieur*," the boy said, sounding far too old for his age—like a medieval king speaking to one of his knights.

"It was nothing," Paolo replied gruffly, taking off his black cashmere coat and slinging it over the boy's shivering shoulders. He turned to the man beside him. "Bertolli, take the King back to the palace as quietly as possible. Go through a side door and ask for…?" He looked at Isabelle.

"Milly Lavoisier," she said. "His nanny."

Alexander's face lit up. "Yes. Milly. She'll be missing me." He gave them a mischievous grin, and for the first time looked like a nine-year-old child. "She'll give me ice cream for this. For sure."

"Alexander, Milly knows the truth," Isabelle said, "but you must keep this a secret from everyone else. People must think you went on a skiing trip with me."

"I know, Aunt Isabelle." The boy drew himself up with dignity. "I can keep a secret."

"Of course you can." The boy was a de Luceran, after all. Secrets were the family trademark.

But there was a catch in her throat as she kissed his forehead. She held him tight in a hug, but was forced to let him go when he pulled away impatiently. The boy disappeared through the hedge maze with Bertolli, musing aloud over the flavors of ice cream he would choose, and whether Milly would give him two scoops or if he should try for three.

"You were right," Paolo said after he was out of earshot. "A former bodyguard betrayed him."

"Which bodyguard?" she demanded.

"René Durand."

"Durand," she whispered. In spite of his impeccable résumé, Isabelle had never liked the man. She'd tried to convince herself that his hard, cynical eyes were normal for a bodyguard, and that she had no reason to feel uneasy. She'd allowed him to be hired as one of Alexander's *carabiniers*. Her mistake.

"I should have turned him in to the police," she said fiercely.

"He's done this before?"

"Two months ago I caught him stealing a Monet from the palace—brazenly carting it out the back door as if he owned it. He gave me all kinds of excuses and pleaded with me to give him the benefit of the doubt. So I let him go."

"Well, there can be no doubt now," Paolo said. "I found him writing a ransom note. He's deeply in debt and has a grudge against you. If you want my advice, Durand should be put in solitary confinement. Or better yet—" he watched her from beneath heavily lidded eyes "—just have him disappear altogether."

"What?" she gasped.

"As the old saying goes, dead men tell no tales."

"No!"

"You said you wanted secrecy…"

A moment before she'd been ready to kill René

Durand with her own bare hands, but the idea of Paolo making him "disappear" sent a chill over her body.

"Not that way," she said sharply.

For a moment he looked at her in the moonlight. His face was hidden by shadow as he said quietly, "You're taking a risk, Isabelle. Being civilized can be a weakness. He hates you. If he ever gets the chance, he might try and hurt you or the child."

She drew back. "We will be fine. Just give him to the captain of the *carabiniers*."

He clenched his jaw. "You're making a mistake."

"Fortunately, after tomorrow I'll no longer be your responsibility. Magnus—"

"Magnus will protect you?" The hard angles of Paolo's face were edged with a translucent silver light as he gave a derisive snort. "If you believe he could protect anyone from anything, love must have truly made you blind."

"I—"

"He has money to hire bodyguards, of course. And, as you pointed out, he's the tenth richest man in the world," he said coldly. "So of course you love him. Let me be the first to wish you joy."

She opened her mouth to say she didn't love Magnus. Then closed it again. Admitting she didn't love him would just make her a bigger target for Paolo's scorn. She already had enough of a bull's-eye on her back for his pointed barbs.

"Thank you," she said over the lump in her throat. "I can't wait to be his wife."

"I'm sure you'll be very happy together, Princess."

The ice in his voice made her shiver. This was the man she had to spend the night with—share her body with? This ruthless, unfeeling man?

What had happened to the boy she'd once loved?

He was just an illusion.

Paolo would never believe that she didn't care about Magnus's money beyond how it would help her country. But the Prince came from a good family, he was kind, and—let's face it—she had to marry someone. She was nearly twenty-nine, and as her mother and counselors had so often reminded her, her duty required that she take a husband.

And Isabelle did long to have children of her own.

The fact that she didn't love the Prince, far from being a problem, was a huge bonus. It meant he could never hurt her. The one time she'd fallen in love it had caused her only grief. She'd been foolish to disregard her mother's example. Selfish to follow her heart. And she'd nearly disgraced her whole country because of it.

It was best to avoid having feelings altogether.

But there was no point in trying to explain that to Paolo. He seemed determined to hate her. He would never understand anyway. How could he, when he'd never loved anyone but himself?

She wished she'd never made such a devil's bargain. She wished she could stay at the palace and spend the warm spring day with Alexander, planning his upcoming coronation, helping him teach his little dog

Jacquetta to do tricks. Making sure that he still remembered how to play. Making sure he always remembered he was loved.

Instead, she had to leave and give herself to Paolo Caretti—the only man who'd ever taken her body, the only man who'd ever taken her heart.

Isabelle shivered. His dark power was almost frightening. The people of San Piedro still slept, unaware that a coup had been prevented. What could possibly stop a ruthless billionaire with his own private army? He had no morals at all. It was why she'd known that she couldn't marry him. Known he couldn't be the father to her children…

"You can spend the rest of tonight at the palace," Paolo told her now, coldly turning away. "Tomorrow I will return to collect on our bargain."

"Tomorrow?" Her nerves couldn't wait that long! "Why not now?"

Clenching his jaw, he turned back to face her.

"Whatever the rumors say, I'm not a heartless monster. I'll allow you to spend some time with your nephew."

She wanted to be with Alexander more than anything, but her promise to Paolo was hanging over her head like an execution. Knowing she had to give herself to him, she was filled with dread…and anticipation. She wanted to get it over with so she could return to her calm, passionless life. A life that made sense. A life without passion—without pain.

She took a deep breath.

"I owe you a debt. I want to pay it." Before anyone—Magnus, the paparazzi, her mother—discovered their liaison, she wanted Paolo Caretti permanently out of her life. It was her only hope. Because he was too smart not to see what was right in front of his eyes. Sooner or later he'd figure it out. She couldn't let that happen. Not now. Not after everything she'd sacrificed.

"I'll go with you now," she said quickly. "Take me to…to…" She tried to think of someplace close to the palace, but not too close. "To your villa."

His eyebrows rose. "You know about San Cerini?"

"Of course I do." Since he'd purchased the property three years ago, she'd often watched the villa's lights across the bay. Wondering if he was there. Wondering if he was alone.

And knowing he wasn't. Paolo Caretti's list of conquests—mostly models and actresses, with a few heiresses tossed in for good measure—was legendary around the world. Something like pain went through her every time she thought about it. She told herself it was just because she pitied the woman he would someday take as his wife. If his wife loved him, she would never know a moment without heartbreak.

"Fine," he growled. "My villa. Tomorrow."

"No." She raised her chin stubbornly. "Tonight."

Moonlight cascaded over his handsome face, shadowing the chiseled lines of his cheekbones and Roman profile. "Do you really want to fight me, Isabelle? You know you'll lose."

How dared he order her around as if she were his slave? His arrogance infuriated her.

"I'm not one of your little tarts," she said haughtily. "I have responsibilities. One night, that was our bargain. So let's just go get it over with, shall we?" She made a show of glancing at her watch. "We'll have to hurry, if you please. I need to get back to the palace by 6:00 a.m. I have appointments—"

"Get it over with?" He pushed her against the rough branches of the hedge. "Get it over with? We could consummate our bargain right here. Would that be convenient enough for you?"

The hedge was sharp, full of branches stabbing into her back. She could feel his anger like a riptide, threatening to pull her under, threatening to drown her.

She'd been furious with him, and before that she'd felt hurt, but now, for the first time, she felt afraid. All the rumors she'd heard came crashing through her mind: that for all his sophistication and good-looks, Paolo Caretti was nothing more than a thug in an expensive suit. That he crushed people without remorse, taking everything he wanted—both in business and in bed.

Pushing aside her fear, she lifted her chin. "Let me go."

He grasped her hip, pressing his leg between her own. "I could just wrap your legs around me and take you here. Is that what you want, Isabelle?"

"You're hurting me!"

Abruptly, he released her.

"There is no question of getting our affair *over with*,"

he said scornfully. "You are mine when I want you. That was the bargain. To take whenever and however I please."

"Just—just for one night," she stammered, hating how weak she was against his strength.

"Yes. One night." His eyes were dark and mesmerizing. Even without him touching her, she could feel it up and down her body. "Not for a half-night, sandwiched between a rescue and your morning appointments."

"But I—"

"Tomorrow morning you will be waiting for me at the back entrance of the palace. At ten o'clock." He gave her a coldly measuring appraisal that caused her cheeks to burn. "And you won't wear a rumpled suit that has gone back and forth across the Atlantic. You will wear a sexy dress and your hair down. You will do everything you possibly can to please me."

"You really are an insufferable bastard," she whispered, yearning to slap his handsome, arrogant face.

"I know what I am." Leaning forward, he stroked her cheek with a tenderness belied by the hard look in his eyes. He gave her a sensual, predatory smile. "Now, go get some rest. You're going to need it."

CHAPTER THREE

PAOLO was ten minutes late the next morning, when he pulled up behind the stables in a cherry-red Ferrari.

Furious, Isabelle bent to look at him through the open passenger window of the ultra-flashy car. "This is your idea of being discreet?"

He shrugged. Leaning across the gearshift, he lazily pushed open her door. "Get in."

For a split second Isabelle hesitated, longing to slam the door back in his face. But she couldn't do that. It wouldn't suit her plan.

Careful with the short hemline of her dress—she didn't want to reveal too much, not yet—she climbed down into the leather seat, placing her overnight bag in her lap. "You're late."

"And you're beautiful. I'm surprised."

"What do you mean by that?"

He gave her a sharp, glinty grin. "Let's just say I didn't expect you to follow my orders so well."

He'd demanded that she try to please him, so naturally her first desire had been to take a mudbath in the nearest pigsty, but, grinding her teeth, she'd put her simmering anger aside and done her best to obey. She wore a red silk dress with a low-cut bodice and spaghetti straps, while her high-heeled espadrilles showed off her brand-new pedicure. Her long brown hair cascaded in big curls down her bare shoulders, and her lipstick and mascara were expertly applied, courtesy of her stylist. She usually hired him only for royal functions, but today she felt no guilt at the expense.

Her one-night stand with Paolo was as important as anything she'd ever done for her country. Perhaps *the* most important thing.

Paolo, on the other hand, was wearing faded jeans and an old white T-shirt so tight it showed every ridge of his hard-muscled torso.

"You look nice, too," she said ironically.

"I don't have to dress up for you." His hands turned the steering wheel with casual confidence as he pressed on the gas, speeding the Ferrari through the palace's back gate with a loud roar. He gunned down the cobblestoned hilly streets of the town, attracting startled stares from tourists returning from the flower market in the old square.

She flinched, hunching in her seat and covering her face with her hand.

"You're doing this to annoy me," she said through clenched teeth.

He lifted a dark eyebrow. "I am bowing to your

wishes, *Princess*, and getting us out of San Piedro as quickly as possible."

"Stop calling me Princess."

"Isn't that your title?"

"You say it with a sneer. I don't like it. Please stop."

"As you wish, Your Serene Highness."

She flinched. Arguing with him only made things worse. She turned away as they drove along the coastal road. Looking out the window, she felt her heart start to rise in spite of everything. She was done with London's stifling economic summit, done with New York's gray sleet. Alexander was safe, she was home, and it was spring. Through her open window she could smell the seasalt and fresh air. Far beneath the cliffs she could see the blue waves of the Mediterranean sparkling in the morning light.

Paolo's villa, San Cerini, was directly across from the palace, on the other side of San Piedro Bay; traveling by speedboat it would have taken no time at all, but traveling the circuitous route by land took longer. Isabelle had taken the road many times. Magnus's family, like all the best families of Europe, also had a villa on this exclusive stretch of coastline…

Paolo's lips turned downward as they went past the von Trondhem gate. He pressed down on the gas, speeding the Ferrari faster along the curves of the cliff.

Isabelle gripped the leather edges of her seat, feeling as if any moment they might skid off the edge and plummet into the water pounding the rocks below.

He glanced at her out the corner of his eye. "Am I going too fast?"

"No," she said tensely. She'd be damned if she'd ask him to slow down. He'd frightened her in the garden last night, but she'd sworn to herself that it would be the last time she would ever let Paolo affect her. She leaned back against her black leather seat, taking a deep breath as the wind whipped through her hair. "The sooner I'm in your bed, the better."

He pushed down on the gas pedal. "I couldn't agree more."

Seconds later Paolo was driving his Ferrari down the *allée* of palm trees to his villa. With a careless wave at the guard, he went through the gate. The circular driveway went around an enormous fountain of carved stone. She looked up at the statue in amazement.

"Do you like it?" Paolo said. "The carving is from an old Russian fairy tale. This villa was built over a hundred years ago by a St. Petersburg émigré richer than half the world."

It was monstrous. A fierce firebird three times taller than a man rose triumphant from a stone sea, clutching a dying sea dragon in its vicious claws. The firebird's fierce power reminded her of the fountain's owner. Would Paolo crush her, too? She stared at it, licking her lips.

Then she saw he'd been watching her. Purposefully, she settled back against the car seat, doing her best to exude nonchalance and boredom. "A monster is your villa's mascot? Appropriate."

He abruptly stopped the car and got out. Servants immediately appeared, but to Isabelle's surprise he glowered them back.

He wrenched open her door himself. "This way, Princess."

In spite of all her proud defiance she was afraid. She was now entering his demesne—under his complete control. Feeling like a doomed French aristocrat on her way to the guillotine, Isabelle closed her eyes, relishing the sun's warmth on her skin for one last time. She had the sudden impulse to flee, to fling herself into the driver's seat and use the keys hanging in the ignition to drive the Ferrari far, far away—to a place where she'd never see Paolo again. To a place where she could forget he even existed, forget the hot kisses that had seared her with fire.

But she knew, to the depths of her soul, that no such place existed.

"Perhaps you'd like me to carry you?"

The threat of him flinging her over his shoulder like a sack of potatoes was enough to make her immediately hand him her overnight bag. He slung it over his shoulder, but still waited for her with his other hand outstretched.

With a deep breath, she placed her hand in his own.

Instantly she regretted it. A current of electricity went through her at his touch. His fingers tightened, intertwining with hers, and his eyes glittered at her with dark, sensual promise. She knew they would be in bed together long before the sun set.

Good, she told herself. Her plan was working.

But the nervous butterflies in her belly had nothing to do with any plan. She was attracted to him so much that it terrified her. She feared he was too strong for her. It would be too easy to succumb to his power. Almost impossible to resist…

With servants trailing in their wake, Paolo led her through the front door. It was strange for her to finally see the inside of the famous San Cerini. First built by the Russian nobleman in the nineteenth century, Paolo had had it expanded and rebuilt to the security of a fortress—and the luxury of a palace far more lavish than anything Isabelle knew at home.

She'd spent many hours, lonely in her bedroom, watching the lights of San Cerini across the water. Wondering which actress or heiress or artist's model he was entertaining that night. And tonight she would be the one in his bed. She would be the one to glory in his touch, to be ignited by his caress.

She could only pray that as she surrendered her body in his bed she would somehow have the strength to keep both her secret and her heart guarded…

After giving orders to a matronly housekeeper, Paolo turned back to her. "Come with me."

Isabelle allowed him to draw her through the spacious high-ceilinged rooms and up the sweeping marble stairs. She allowed him? There was a laugh! As if she had any choice in the matter! Who could stop Paolo Caretti from doing anything he wished?

Especially since her own traitorous body yearned to obey his every command…

She stopped in the doorway of his bedroom.

Thrilled.

Terrified.

My plan, she reminded herself as her body shook with conflicting emotions. *Stick to the plan.* She had to convince him to seduce her as quickly as possible. She would keep her heart frozen, layered in impenetrable frost. Then she would leave and make sure their paths never crossed again. As simple as that.

Or perhaps not so simple. Paolo picked her up from the doorway, sweeping her in his arms as if she weighed nothing.

"What—what are you doing?" she gasped.

His dark eyes looked down at her. "Carrying you over my threshold."

"But I'm not your bride!"

"You agreed to marry me once," he said softly. "Do you remember?"

A shiver raked through her. His enormous suite, overlooking San Piedro Bay in one direction and the Mediterranean Sea in the other, was the perfect setting for any honeymoon. The bedroom had high, plastered ceilings, exquisite tapestries, Louis XV furniture. Through the wide windows she could see a stone balcony overlooking the sea, and palm trees swaying in the fresh spring breeze.

It was perfect in every way—except Paolo Caretti

wasn't the man she was supposed to marry. Within months she would be Prince Magnus's bride, and for the rest of her life it would be easy to keep her heart hidden and cold.

She blinked hard, willing away incomprehensible tears.

Paolo kissed her shoulder, trailing his fingers along her collarbone. Then he drew back, looking into her eyes. "Are you crying, *bella*? Is this truly so distasteful to you?"

"No," she whispered. And that was the problem. She sucked in her breath as she felt him stroke the bare skin of her back. "You can have any woman you want in the whole world," she said. "Why me? Who am I to you?"

He pushed her back against his bed, and for one intense instant the mockery disappeared from his eyes.

"You're the one who got away," he said softly.

She couldn't hide the shiver that went through her as he kissed her neck, running his hands up and down her body through the red silk. She gasped as his weight pushed her into the soft mattress. Caressing her everywhere, suckling the tender flesh of her ear, he spread her legs beneath him. Only their clothes separated them.

He had to be almost twice her weight, but every hard pound of him felt like pure pleasure against her. His body was so muscular, so heavy, so fine. She wanted to pull off his shirt and caress his naked skin. To plunder his mouth in a hot, hard kiss.

But she didn't move. She couldn't. Except for that hot summer in New York, she'd spent her whole life following the rules and being good. No matter how she wanted to live dangerously…

He kissed her. His tongue teased hers as he reached for the bodice of her halter dress, caressing her breasts through the fabric. At the hard demand of his lips on her own, desire pounded through her blood. His kiss ignited her body. He made her feel things she did not want to feel, drugging her senses. He made her whole body tremble.

It was as if she'd been sleeping for ten years and now, suddenly, she was awake.

Somehow, her arms reached for him of their own accord. She pulled him against her, relishing the warmth of his hard, muscular chest through his cotton T-shirt. She felt everything and everywhere he touched. She felt far too much.

His hands reached beneath the silk to cup her breasts, squeezing her tight nipples between his rough fingertips. Grasping her backside, he thrust her hips upwards, moving his hips between her legs. She tried to remain still, then realized she was already swaying against him, desperate to be closer, desperate to feel him naked inside her.

As if he'd read her mind, he pulled up her dress. She could feel the silk moving up her thighs with agonizing slowness, the slippery fabric caressing her skin like water.

"Bella," he said in a low voice. *"Sì.* You are so beautiful…"

Reaching beneath her lace panties, he softly stroked her. She gasped aloud, arching her back against his fingers.

Lowering himself on the bed, he moved his head between her legs. She had the sudden realization of what he meant to do. She tried to pull back—she couldn't possibly allow—

Pushing the panties aside, he tasted her. When she tried to buck her hips away, he held her firmly in place, tempting her to accept the pleasure. Her head fell backward as he teased her with his mouth. He licked with light brushing strokes, then pressed harder, deeper, spreading her wide with the full roughness of his tongue. He tantalized her, pushing his tongue deep inside her as his finger swirled softly over her slippery, sensitive nub. His tongue and his hand switched places and he pushed a thick finger inside her, sucking and licking until she was dripping wet. He pushed in another finger, stretching her. He added a third, and she gasped. The pleasure was so great she thought she might die.

She gave a soft, soundless cry as her whole body tightened and exploded. He paused. But he didn't stop. And before she understood what was happening she felt the pleasure start to gather tension through her body again, like dark clouds in a storm…

She whimpered. She couldn't take much more. But she didn't want his fingers. She wanted…

Breathlessly, she grabbed a belt loop of his jeans. She couldn't say what she wanted—she couldn't even think of the words—but her meaning was plain.

He stopped, looking down at her with a strange expression in his eyes. "You are mine, Isabelle. For always."

His growl cut through her sensual haze. No matter how lost she was in pleasure, the risk of what they were doing was still too terrifying to think about. "For one night," she panted. "Your mistress for one night."

"No," he said in a low voice. "For always."

He abruptly let her go.

Still spread wide across his sheets, she stared in bewildered shock as he got off the bed, leaving her bereft and vulnerable.

"What is it? Why did you stop?"

He looked down at her. "That's enough. For now."

She actually considered begging him to return to bed. So much for being made of ice! She sat up, her cheeks hot with shame. He obviously meant to prolong his torture until she would do or say anything he wished. And that was what frightened her most. She had to get this over with *now*—before she felt anything more. Before she became so intoxicated by forbidden emotions and pleasures that she'd give away everything she held dear...

She took a deep breath and forced herself to do the unthinkable.

Plan B.

"No," she said.

His eyebrows lifted. "No?"

"We're not going to wait." She stood up from the bed. Her hands shook as she untied the halter behind her back. "You're going to take me here. On this bed. Right now."

Unzipping her red dress, she let it drop to her feet. Wearing only her translucent lace bra and panties, it took all of her courage to meet his eyes.

The arrogant billionaire who had power over half the world looked as if he were suddenly having trouble breathing.

Encouraged, she stepped out of the dress, leaving it crumpled on the floor. The bra was made of deep blue silk lace, edged with ribbon and utterly see-through; the thong panties were tied with ribbon bows on each side and could be pulled off her hips with one tug. She bent to unlace her espadrilles, giving him a good view of her breasts, already clearly on view through the flimsy triangles of silk lace. Slowly, lingeringly, she pulled the sandals off her feet, tossing them aside like a stripper she'd once seen in an American movie.

"Where did you learn to do that?" he muttered.

She looked at him, praying he wouldn't see how inexperienced she felt, how totally out of her league. He'd been with so many women—would he sneer at her efforts? Or—worse—laugh? She swallowed, then, meeting his eyes, raised her chin defiantly.

"It's only morning. I'm not going to stay all day and then give you my night as well. A bargain is a bargain. Take me all day." She leaned defiantly on her tilted hip. "Tonight I'm going home."

Part of her was amazed at her own brazen behavior. But she wanted him to take her hard and fast, before she completely lost her reason. Before her heart started to remember the desperate way she'd once loved him.

And, most of all, before he discovered her secret: nine years ago she'd had his baby.

Alexander was their son.

"Please," she whispered. "Just let me return home to the people I love."

He wrenched his gaze up from her breasts.

"Nice try," he said evenly. "But you're not going anywhere."

Let me return home to the people I love.

Her words hit Paolo like a fierce mistral wind, smothering the warmth of the spring sun.

He'd meant to coldly lure her into a short-term affair—just long enough to satisfy him and leave her wanting more. True, she'd left him once, but he'd been barely more than a boy then. Much had changed. *He* had changed.

He'd arrogantly assumed that Isabelle, like every other woman, would melt like butter in his experienced hands. Instead, as he'd felt her arms twine around him on the bed, pulling him into a sweetness even sharper than he remembered, he'd been the one who started to fall.

He'd felt a tremor go through his body—a shock of desire such as he'd never known. Her kiss had sent him reeling like an untried boy. One moment in her arms, against the warmth of her skin, had sent him back in time; one hot caress and he'd forgotten all the other women he'd ever had. God help him, but he'd actually had the momentary delusion of wanting Isabelle as his wife.

He was glad she'd reminded him about Magnus.

Paolo's jaw clenched as he looked at her. Half-naked. Impossibly beautiful.

And totally in love with another man. A weak-chinned, entitled-since-birth, *civilized* prince. But why should he be surprised? She wasn't the first woman who'd chosen Magnus over him…

"Kiss me," Isabelle whispered now, putting her arms around him.

She was so petite, so soft. He felt her full breasts pushing up against his chest, her hip rubbing against his thigh. His whole body was aching for her. Painfully. As if he'd been hard for a decade, wanting her…

She leaned forward, stroking his chest.

He'd thought he could control his desire for her. He was accustomed to controlling everything—well, except the ability to sleep, damn it. But looking at her now, so seductive and powerful, in nothing more than a few scraps of flimsy lace, he wanted her almost more than he could bear.

While *she* wanted to hurry through their bargain. She wanted to marry someone else, give *him* children, give *him* all her tomorrows.

No.

One night of pleasure was suddenly not enough for Paolo. Not nearly enough.

Isabelle was meant to belong to him and no other man.

"Paolo?"

He looked down at her, feeling her tremble beneath him like a fragile bird. "We made a bargain. One night.

Not a day. Not a throwaway quickie. One full night." His lip curled. "So you'll just have to wait. Both you and that precious fiancé of yours."

"You can't keep me here—"

"I can." Picking the red dress up off the floor, he tossed it at her. "Put this back on. It's bright daylight and the windows are wide open. You look like a *puttana*."

He had a brief image of her face blanching with humiliation as he turned from her. He pushed aside his stab of regret. He knew she didn't deserve that insult. Her fire was what he'd always loved the most about her: she was sweet innocence wrapped in sin.

But the innocence was a lie. He'd learned that the hard way. It was just how she lured men into loving her—before she crushed them beneath the weight of her scorn.

Clenching his jaw, he turned away.

"Where are you going?" she whispered, holding the red dress in her arms like a scarlet slash against her pale belly.

Without answering, he stalked out the door and down the hall toward his study. He disliked his bedroom anyway. The room was a cage—the place where he hadn't had a decent night's sleep since he'd bought San Cerini. His insomnia had started here. But it hadn't stayed here. It now followed him everywhere: his New York penthouse, his Irish estate. He'd exercised until he dropped. Boxed in a fight club till he was covered with blood. Even made love to anonymous women for hours on end. Nothing had helped.

So? he told himself harshly. Insomnia just gave him

more time to work. In the last three years his net worth had quadrupled. His global holdings—comprising steel factories and metal commodities trading, as well as the famous Caretti Motors—had turned him into a billionaire. He now had everything any man could want.

And if surviving on three hours of sleep a night made him abrupt and rude at times—well, people knew not to test him. His employees knew to get it right the first time.

Paolo pushed the door open to his study. His bookshelves included everything from a biography of Glenn Curtiss to a paperback history of nitrous oxide; his sleek black desk had a view overlooking the bay. When he was at San Cerini he was nearly always here, or in his ten-car garage, tinkering with engines. Engines calmed him. Engines made sense. If he took care of them, they took care of him.

Unlike people.

Damn it, he'd asked her to marry him.

He grabbed a bottle of expensive Scotch from the cabinet. The night before she'd planned to leave New York for the summer, he'd looked down at her, sleeping in his arms. "Marry me," he'd whispered, never expecting that she would.

But she'd opened those beautiful eyes and said, in a trembling voice, "Yes." Joy had washed over him such as he'd never known. They'd slept all night in a lovers' embrace on his tiny worn mattress on the floor.

The next day, while she'd been at Barnard, packing up her room, he'd sold his only possession of value—

the old engine he'd been tinkering with for a year—and traded it for an engagement ring. Determined to propose properly, he'd used his landlady's kitchen to prepare fettuccine from his grandmother's old recipe. Setting up a card table at the center of his studio apartment, he'd covered it with borrowed linen and mismatched dishware, crowning the table with a centerpiece of a candle in an old wine bottle.

But somehow, in spite of all his care, everything had fallen apart. Isabelle had been nervous and distracted over dinner, barely eating two bites of pasta. And when he'd finally knelt on one knee before her, holding out the precious ring and asking her to be his wife, she'd changed in front of his eyes.

Snatching the engagement ring from his outstretched hand, she'd stared at the tiny diamond in disbelief. "My *husband*? Are you out of your *mind*?" She had barked a laugh, then tossed the ring back scornfully into his face. "I've just been slumming with you, Paolo—having a bit of fun. I assumed you knew that. Marriage? I'm Princess of San Piedro. You're nobody."

Paolo poured himself a double Scotch, staring through the wide windows toward the palace across the bay. The same view he'd brooded over his very first night in the villa, watching the lights of the *palais* shimmer across the dark water.

Love made a man deaf, dumb and blind.

But he should thank her, really. The engagement ring had bought back his engine—the eventual prototype of the Caretti motorcycle engine—and her scorn had spurred him into becoming richer and more powerful than he'd ever imagined. And, though he'd been ruthless at times, he'd never sunk to his father's level. He'd made his fortune with no help from the old neighborhood.

The only time he'd ever used those connections was this past week—at Isabelle's request—to find her nephew.

But he saw now that, no matter what he did, she would always see him as a lowlife. No matter how many billions he had in his bank account, his net worth would always be zero to her.

He took a long drink of the single-malt Scotch, draining the crystal glass to the dregs. He could handle it. He didn't care what people thought of him—now. As a child it hadn't been so easy. His father had been constantly in and out of jail…his mother had abandoned him when he was three months old. Alone, he'd been an easy target. But by the time he'd been in fifth grade he'd learned how to start a fight, how to launch himself at opponents far bigger than he was and make them take back their words. It had been a valuable experience. It had made him stronger.

But that didn't mean he wanted his own children to endure the same.

He wanted to give his future children a bloodline so exalted that, coupled with his wealth, they would always be treated well. Give them a mother who would love them enough to stay…

Suddenly his eyes narrowed. Too good to be his mistress, was she? Too good to marry him?

I'm Princess of San Piedro. You're nobody.

"Signor Caretti, is everything all right?"

An anxious servant stood in the open doorway of his study.

"Sì." A cruel smile curved his lips. "Everything is fine."

He would show her. He'd lure her. Caress her. Woo her. Make her laugh. Make her love him. And most of all...

"Your new motorcycle has arrived, *signore,*" the young man said. "It is waiting in the garage. Signor Bertolli is already checking it over."

"Excellent." Paolo rose from his desk. As he went down the sweeping stairs towards his ten-car garage, he'd already come to a decision.

If Isabelle wouldn't willingly give him her respect, he would just take it. He would *own* the most famous princess in the world, possess her completely.

He would seduce her. Get her pregnant.

Paolo would force her to become his wife.

CHAPTER FOUR

AFTER he'd left the bedroom, Isabelle stumbled backward, sinking onto the high mattress. She curled up in a ball, clutching the noxious red dress against her belly. A warm breeze, sweet with spring honeysuckle and sharp with the salty tang of the sea, swayed the curtains as she stared out blindly through the wide windows.

The memory of the way she'd stripped in front of him, demanding that he make love to her, replayed in her mind. She—a princess of San Piedro, a scion of the proud de Luceran bloodline—had debased herself to the man she feared and despised. And all she'd gotten for her trouble was his rejection.

The only man she'd ever loved, the father of her child, had just called her a *whore*.

"Oh." She gasped aloud from shame, covering her face with her hands. But even with her eyes closed she could still see the curl of his lip, still hear his scornful words. She'd have willingly jumped off the balcony and let herself be swallowed by the sea if it had meant she'd never have to face him again.

But she was Princess of San Piedro. Her country needed her. Her son needed her. Shamed or not, she had to go on. Get up. Get it over with.

With a deep breath, she forced herself to open her eyes. Slowly she straightened her spine, unfolding her body. She rose from the bed, still wearing only her lace bra and panties. Then she stared down at the expensive bit of red silk crumpled up in her hand. Her eyes narrowed with hatred.

She stalked across the priceless Savonnerie carpet to the Louis XV marble fireplace. Tossing the dress into the fireplace, she took a match from a nearby wrought-iron log rack. Lighting the match, she lit the expensive red dress on fire and watched it burn.

It was finished.

She would die before she tried to seduce Paolo again.

When there was nothing but ash left, Isabelle turned on her heel. She briefly hesitated when she saw a plush white robe hanging from the bathroom door, then grabbed it. Wrapping her body in his robe, she rang the bell.

A few moments later his housekeeper appeared. She had rosy cheeks, and salt-and-pepper hair pulled back into a bun.

She looked at Isabelle with critical eyes before she lowered her gaze with a brief curtsy.

No doubt the woman was thinking the same thing that Paolo had said: she was nothing better than a harlot.

Her cheeks went hot, but she raised her chin, staring the housekeeper down. "I am Isabelle de Luceran."

"Ne sono, Principessa. I am Signora Bertolli."

"Somewhere in this heap of bricks is my overnight bag. Please find it for me."

"Sì, immediatemente."

A few minutes later, she reappeared with the overnight bag. "Shall I unpack for you, *Principessa*?" Not waiting for an answer, she opened the bag. "Ah, such beautiful clothes," she said wistfully.

Looking at her, Isabelle felt some envy of her own. Signora Bertolli likely had a snug little cottage, a husband to take her to the movies. Children. Family dinners. Conversations in the kitchen. Everything Isabelle had once dreamed of.

Everything she'd once thought she would have with Paolo.

The day after he'd first proposed in bed she'd gone back to her dorm, still reeling at her decision. She knew her family would never accept him as her husband, and neither would her people, but she didn't care. She was ready to defy them all.

She had found her mother's bodyguards outside her door, and Queen Clothilde sitting stiffly on her unmade bed. Praying she'd convince her mother to accept the match, Isabelle had told her about the engagement.

"To a poor mechanic?" her mother had gasped in horror.

"I love him, *Maman*."

Her mother had shaken her head.

"Love." She'd spat out the word bitterly. "Men are not faithful, *ma fille*. If you marry for love you will have a lifetime of heartbreak. This man has no family, no fortune. And do you think this…*nobody* would actually enjoy marriage to you? Sacrificing his own desires? Living entirely for others? Always being criticized and watched without the slightest bit of personal freedom? He would be mocked and scorned… Isabelle—look at me when I'm talking to you. *Isabelle!*"

She'd sunk dizzily to the bed. At the time she'd thought it was just the sensation of her heart breaking. She'd forced herself to sit quietly as her mother proved why it would be best for everyone, including Paolo, if Isabelle ended the affair. Ignoring her body's warnings, she'd finally, tearfully, agreed.

She'd gone to Paolo's apartment for dinner and crushed his hopes with the words her mother had suggested—coldly, cruelly, making sure he'd never miss her.

She'd known it was the right thing to do. He'd deserved far better than a life with her. But still it had nearly killed her.

An hour later, as they had prepared to leave for San Piedro, Isabelle's dizzy spells had abruptly intensified. The Queen's doctor had examined Isabelle on the private plane. They'd soon discovered that, at the tender age of eighteen, she was leaving New York with far more than just a broken heart…

"Will you be staying for long, *Principessa*?"

Signora Bertolli's question brought Isabelle back to the present. "No. I intend to leave tonight. Stop unpacking, please. Just leave the bag with me."

The woman gave a dignified nod and turned to go.

"Wait."

She halted, looking back at her. *"Sì, Principessa?"*

"Do you know where I might find Signor Caretti?"

"I believe he's in the garage. Shall I take you there?"

Her jaw hardened. "I'll find him."

Minutes later Isabelle was dressed in prim white underwear, a pale pink cashmere sweater set, her grandmother's pearls and a demure knee-length skirt. Her quilted leather handbag bounced against her hip as she stalked across the villa, crossing the garden in her beige peeptoe pumps.

When she saw Paolo she would be cold. Bitingly polite. She would cut him down in the most ladylike way. She would force him to realize he could not insult her and keep her prisoner.

She would not stay here.

She had a child to raise and a man to marry… One out of love, the other out of duty.

Paolo, she would say, *I made a good-faith effort, which you refused. I therefore consider myself absolved of our agreement…*

She heard Paolo's voice ahead, speaking in Italian.

And, furthermore, you can go to hell. Although of course she wouldn't say that last bit. Repressing her own feelings for the sake of diplomacy had been drummed into her since birth. But Paolo had a way of making her hot all over, causing her to lose her reserve. She hated that. A princess always had to stay in control. She certainly never swore at a man in public, no matter how richly he might deserve it...

She saw Paolo and stopped dead in her tracks.

He was standing at one of the open garage doors, kneeling in front of an old upside-down motorcycle with a large single-cut file in his hand. Next to him, a boy about Alexander's age peered into the engine.

"Look at the casing now," Paolo said.

The boy looked. "It's so much better! I thought those old bits of gasket were stuck on there for good!"

"Not with the right file," Paolo said, his voice strong with approval and affection. "See how easily twenty years can be stripped away?"

"Are you bothering Signor Caretti, Adriano?" Bertolli called from the back of the garage.

"No, I'm helping," the boy replied, then turned anxiously to Paolo. "I *am* helping, *sì*?"

"You're a great help, Adriano," Paolo told him. "I couldn't do without you, *giovannato*."

Isabelle started in shock at the warmth in his voice.

"So hire me on your pit crew," the boy pleaded. "I swear you won't regret it!"

"Adriano," his father said warningly.

"I'm sure I wouldn't regret it." Paolo ruffled the boy's hair. "You have skill and promise."

"So you agree—?"

"When you're older I will be glad to hire you, if you still wish it. But for now—school!"

"Oh, school," he replied, with good-natured grumbling.

Watching them from the shadows of the juniper trees, Isabelle felt her knees tremble beneath her.

This was the man she'd kept from his son. The man she'd told herself had no business being a father. Watching him smile down at the boy, she felt a wave of guilt crash over her. Guilt that threatened to drown her.

She tried to fight it off with all her old justifications.

She'd had no choice, she told herself desperately. Marrying Paolo would have been a disaster. Raising a baby with him outside of marriage would have been even worse. Their child had deserved to be brought up a prince, with two loving, married parents.

But now those parents were dead, a voice whispered inside her. Didn't Alexander deserve to know that he still had a mother and father on earth?

He's mourning the only parents he's ever known. The parents he loved, she argued back fiercely. It would only confuse him to know the truth.

But—

Besides, she argued more loudly, if Paolo knew the truth he might try to get custody. No matter how wonderful he might seem with children now, she couldn't risk ruining Alexander's life. His Kingship. She couldn't just blindly trust Paolo to do the right thing for his son, for all of them…

"Isabelle?"

She looked up. Paolo was standing by his motorcycle. Chrome and black steel gleamed in the noon sun as he smiled at her. "I'm glad you're here."

Looking at his smile, it was as if she'd gone back in time to the moment she'd first met him, when Paolo had arrived at her stalled limousine in a blue mechanic's jumpsuit, wrench gleaming like a lightning bolt in his hand. He'd made her laugh, flirting with her as if she were any college girl, and asked her to a movie. She'd relished the anonymity of the theater. Ordering popcorn and soda. Nearly dropping both when he put his arm around her.

Afterward, they'd climbed five flights of stairs to his tiny apartment. It had been at the door, beneath a single swaying lightbulb, that he'd first kissed her. Then he'd smiled, and for the first time in her life she'd understood the meaning of the words *warmth* and *home*…

Paolo's smile now was the same. It was exactly the same.

As he came toward the juniper trees his eyes were intent on her. She felt his look down to her toes. He took her hand, and his touch flooded her with warmth more vivid than sunlight.

"I'm sorry for what I said—about the dress." He softly kissed the back of her hand. "I didn't mean it."

Her eyes widened. All her years of social training hadn't prepared her for this. As far as she knew, Paolo Caretti had never apologized to anyone for anything.

"Can you forgive me?" he asked humbly.

She shook her head, trying to remember what she'd meant to say to him. All rational thought had evaporated from her mind like morning mist in sunlight. "I came to find you…to say…"

He waited patiently, but when she didn't continue he gently prompted, "There's something you wanted to say to me?"

"Yes. I… I…" She licked her lips as she stared up at him.

"Tell me, *bella*." Clasping his fingers firmly around hers, he pulled her closer. He looked down at her, their faces inches apart. "Tell me anything."

"I want to tell you…"

She tried to remember her planned insults, but, looking into his face all she could think was, *You have a son. We have a son.*

He raised an eyebrow at her. "Yes?"

But she couldn't risk Alexander's life just to make her own conscience feel better. What if Paolo told the whole world? What if he demanded custody?

What effect would it have on Alexander, on the whole nation, if it were known that the King of San Piedro was really the illegitimate son of a corrupt Italian-American billionaire?

And what if, demanding time with their child, he stayed near Isabelle forever? Forced to spend every day beneath the assault of his dangerous charm—his smiles, his skilled lovemaking—what chance would she possibly have of survival? Even if by some miracle she forced herself to marry Magnus, how long could she keep her heart in ice?

"Isabelle?"

"I forgive you." She could barely speak the words over the guilt choking her. Forgive Paolo? She was such a fraud! Grandly forgiving him for a verbal insult when she'd done a far greater injury to him by keeping him from his child!

"Thank you." He released her hand.

Her whole body suddenly hurt. All her life she'd tried to be silent, graceful, dignified. She'd been constantly aware of cameras rolling, people watching.

But it was still often hard to keep her emotions in check. Her family was brittle with secrets. Her mother, once so romantic, had become sharp and thin from enduring her father's endless affairs before he died. Isabelle's brother Maxim had taken a Danish princess as his wife in an arranged marriage. They'd had an amicable arrangement—until Karin had fallen in love with him and stressful years of fertility treatment had taken their toll. By the time their son was two years old, Maxim had started visiting a little house in Cannes, leaving Princess Karin as bitter and lonely as her mother-in-law.

Isabelle had promised herself that she would never endure in silence, as her mother had. She would never suffer like Karin.

She'd once thought Paolo was different from any man she'd ever known. When she'd found out she was pregnant she'd begged her mother to reconsider allowing them to marry. In addition to the scandal it would cause for Isabelle to be an unmarried mother, a child's life was now at stake. A baby needed two parents! she'd argued.

Hours after Isabelle had forced herself to fling the ring back in Paolo's face, her mother had reluctantly allowed herself to be persuaded to meet him. Isabelle still remembered how excited she'd felt, climbing those five flights of stairs. She'd felt sure her mother would accept him—how could she not love him as she did? Isabelle would marry Paolo, have his baby, and they would all be so happy…

Then she'd reached the landing.

The blond tart from next door had been silhouetted in Paolo's open doorway, wearing only a bra and shorts. In the predawn light her mussed hair and his half-naked body had made it obvious that they were kissing farewell after a night of lovemaking.

Her mother had stopped cold beside her. Before the lovers could turn around, she'd taken her daughter's hand, gently pulling her away from the scene. "Come away, *ma fille*," she'd whispered. "Come away."

Now, Paolo touched Isabelle's cheek. "I was wrong to insult you, *cara mia*," he said quietly. "You are generous to forgive my thoughtless words."

Isabelle sucked in her breath. A lifetime of secrets pressed down on her, leaving her tense enough to shatter.

"I am the one who should thank you," she managed.

"For saving Alexander. I will never forget it. I will always be grateful for what you did for him. For me."

The expression in his dark gaze changed. Brushing a brown tendril from her face, he looked down at her.

"I will always protect you, Isabelle," he said in a low voice. "I protect what's mine."

"And you still think I'm yours?" she whispered.

He gave her an enigmatic smile, brief, like a sudden April shower. Mysterious. Charismatic. Powerful. "I know you are."

She had a sudden fierce longing for it to be true. That she did belong to him—not just for today, but for always. That they could go back in time and be young and naïve again. Before she'd discovered that loving Paolo—loving any man—would lead to a lifetime of anguish and heartbreak…

But there was no point in wishing. They had one day together before she married someone else. Someone safe. Someone who would never, ever break her heart or leave her crying at night.

Turning away, she cleared her throat. "I need to make a call."

"Go ahead," he said, not moving a muscle.

Pulling her phone from her Chanel handbag, she dialed the number of the captain of the King's *carabiniers*. She spoke with the man quietly, then closed her phone.

"René Durand is in jail," she said to Paolo.

"I told you I'd take care of it."

"I needed to make sure."

"Why?" he asked evenly. "Couldn't you just trust my word?"

Trust Paolo? No. Not with her son, and not with her heart. No matter how she wished she could.

Her headache was starting to pound all the way round the back of her neck. She rubbed her forehead, blinking hard. She knew from experience that only one thing would make her feel better. Only one thing would help her forget the stress of enduring things she couldn't change.

It was an ordinary pleasure—something other people did every day—but it was a rare special treat for her. Her solace when she was desperate to forget the *princess* and the *de Luceran* in her name and be just Isabelle.

In sudden decision, she held out her hand. "Come with me."

He tilted his head. "Where?"

But even as he asked the question he put his hand in hers. And beneath the bright Mediterranean sun Isabelle gave him a smile that rose as slow and sure as the tide. "You'll see."

"Do you like it?"

Paolo could not answer her. He was afraid to move his tongue. Afraid it might make him taste more of what he had in his mouth.

"Tell me the truth," Isabelle insisted.

He looked around wildly for an escape. The outdoor terrace was warm with sunlight and surrounded by flowers beneath swaying palm trees, overlooking the jutting cliffs of San Piedro Bay.

He was tempted to jump off the balustrade and take his chances with the rocks.

"Paolo?"

He forced himself to gulp down the half-raw, half-burned egg whites mixed with undercooked asparagus. His belly lurched. He grabbed his *tazza* of scalding hot black Italian coffee, hoping that it would burn every tastebud.

But his sacrifice was all in vain. When he looked up, she was still watching him, dewy-eyed with expectation.

"I got the recipe from a book," she said with pride.

"A cookbook?" he asked faintly.

"Well, I had to modify it a little bit. I took out the hollandaise sauce and the cheese, and replaced the ham with asparagus. Do you like it?"

He looked at her. "Isabelle, I can't lie to you…"

But her face looked so vulnerable, so hungry for approval. He stopped.

His emotions had taken a turn in the last hour. He'd been coldly furious at her—until she'd surprised him with her gratitude for saving her nephew. Then she'd turned around and insulted his ability to protect her, phoning the captain to make sure that Durand was in jail. *Dio santo,* what did she think? That Paolo might have simply abandoned the kidnapper to play roulette in some Monte Carlo casino?

Then, watching her rush around the large kitchen—

his soon-to-be bride and mother of his children, so damned sexy in an apron—he'd been aroused in an almost primal way. He had thoroughly relished watching her cook.

It had never occurred to him to supervise her methods. He had made his own meals from a young age—with an absent mother and a father frequently in jail it had been a necessary skill to prevent starving to death. But Isabelle had had no such advantage. She'd had a palace of servants at her beck and call, and had never learned to cook or clean. He accepted that. He'd just never imagined what evil she might create with a pan.

"It's healthy, isn't it?" Isabelle said hopefully. "Light, but gourmet? I've been told asparagus adds a wonderful flavor and crunch."

Literally biting his lip, he managed, "I've never tasted anything like it."

Isabelle's face lit up.

"I'm so glad," she said. "It's my only real hobby. It helps me relax. I've cooked many times for the servants at the palace, but I was never sure if they really liked it or were just eating it to please me. You're the rudest person I know, so I was sure you'd tell me the truth."

Paolo suddenly felt very sorry for the whole servant class. Regular meals such as this seemed rampant cruelty. Although it was cruel to Isabelle, too, since she obviously had no idea how truly awful her cooking was. What those long-suffering servants said in private would likely have made her ears burn with horror.

"Aren't you going to finish your breakfast?"

He glanced down at his full plate with dismay.

"Shall I serve you some more?"

A shudder went through his whole body. "No."

"It's no trouble, really. I have a whole panful!"

Enough was enough. He had other ways of wooing her. Ways that were far more appetizing. Ways far more likely to get her pregnant. He didn't intend to marry her for her cooking, anyway.

Grabbing her wrist, he pulled her into the chair next to his. "Let me serve you for a change."

She shook her head shyly. "I like cooking for other people. That's the whole point. It helps me relax."

Cruel or not, it was time she learned the truth. Taking the pan, he piled several spoonfuls of the egg mixture onto an empty plate. He shoved the plate toward her, pushing a fork into her hand. "Have some."

"Really, I couldn't—"

"Eat," he ordered.

"Fine," she said with a sigh. She stabbed some eggs and asparagus with her fork. "I suppose I am pretty hungry. It couldn't hurt to—"

She tasted it, and blanched. Gulping it down painfully, she grabbed the pan and looked down at it with consternation. She looked up at him accusingly. "It's *awful*!"

"Yes."

"Why didn't anyone tell me?"

He glanced significantly at the heavy cast-iron pan. "Perhaps they were afraid you'd resort to violence?"

She dropped the pan with a loud thunk against the table.

"Oh," she moaned, leaning forward and covering her face with her hands. "All this time my servants were eating my food—and what? Tossing it into the plants when I wasn't looking? Laughing at me behind my back?"

"Both, probably."

She shook her head, but he saw tears in her eyes. "Why couldn't they just tell me the truth? Why did they have to let me make a fool of myself?"

He looked at her. "I'll always tell you the truth. Even if it hurts."

She snorted a laugh.

"I will," he said.

She wiped her eyes. "Even Magnus lied. I cooked breakfast for him twice. He said it was delicious. He asked for more."

If she'd made Magnus breakfast it had likely been after a long night of lovemaking. The thought made Paolo want to punch something—preferably the Prince's smugly handsome face. But he couldn't really blame him for lying. Hell, even Paolo might have honestly thought her food tasted terrific after a night of making love to her.

Ten years ago he'd had no money to take Isabelle to restaurants, and she'd been afraid someone might discover their affair. They'd rarely left his apartment. He'd set up pillows on the floor for seats and heated up canned ravioli and baked beans on a hotplate. They'd eaten with plastic forks from paper plates. Not very gourmet. Not very romantic.

But somehow her company had made even those cheap meals taste delicious. Isabelle had a way of making everything taste like dessert...

He looked down at his plate ruefully. Almost everything.

"Paolo?" she said softly. "Did you really mean it? You'll never lie to me?"

Tilting his head, he watched her. "I'm planning to seduce you, get you pregnant with my child, and make you my bride."

She blinked at him for several seconds, then hiccoughed a laugh. "Very funny."

"Yes," he said. "Aren't I just?"

Rising from the table, he held out his arm. "It's noon. How about we forget breakfast and have lunch instead?"

"You're going to cook for me?" she asked, looking up at him in surprise. "Just like the old days?"

He didn't blame her for sounding shocked. With all of her servants, all her glamour, why would she ever want to eat such a plain, cheap meal again? The thought set his teeth on edge. The bad old days. When he'd been young, broke, and stupidly in love. When they'd made love for hours, then slept all night long in each other's arms. Nights he'd never fully appreciated until now.

He pushed the thought away. He had other advantages now. And to force Isabelle to become his bride he would use them all.

"No, I'm not going to cook," he said. "I'm in no

mood to open up a can, and even if I were I have people to do that for me."

She looked up at him inquisitively. "So, what did you have in mind?"

He gave her a sharp smile. "I'm thinking Italian…"

CHAPTER FIVE

AFTER his private plane had landed at the Ciampino Airport in Rome, Paolo led her down the steps to the tarmac. Isabelle stopped in her tracks when she saw the motorcycle waiting for them below.

"What's that?" she demanded.

"Our ride."

Was he trying to punish her for the way she'd nearly poisoned him that morning? She made a self-conscious motion to her hair, hanging in thick waves down her shoulders, and to her knee-length pencil skirt. "I'm not sure I can…"

"You can," he said firmly. Taking the keys from the servant standing beside the gleaming beast of a cruiser, he nodded the man's dismissal. He threw his leg over the seat and held out his hand. "Get behind me."

She stood uncertainly, biting her lip like a nervous schoolgirl.

"Surely, Princess," he mocked, "you're not frightened?"

"Of course not." Terrified was more like it. "It's

just… Do you know what the traffic is like in Rome?"
She gave a nervous laugh. "It doesn't have to be a Rolls-
Royce, but I'd like a few inches of steel around me.
Can't you phone and order a car? Or, better yet, a tank?"

"Are you questioning my driving skills?"

"No, I just—"

"Then get on," he said, still holding out his hand. And
this time there was plenty of steel—in his voice.

Isabelle realized that she had two choices. She could
either admit that the idea of riding a motorcycle scared
her silly and refuse to go, or she could take his hand,
close her eyes, and hold on tight.

Her pride made the choice for her. She strapped her
Chanel purse across her chest and hiked up her slim skirt
to a scandalous position at mid-thigh. Leaning on his
arm, she climbed onto the motorcycle seat behind him.

He handed her a helmet. "Put this on."

He didn't need to ask her twice. Just the idea of
nothing but bare skin between her and the road was
enough to make her whole body tremble. He gripped the
throttle and they drove off with a roar that seemed as
loud as an aircraft engine.

She held him tight, pressing her body against his as
they drove into the city. As their bodies leaned against
every fast curve, every dangerous traffic circle, the
engine vibrated between her legs. They drove down the
crowded Via dei Fori Imperiali past the Colosseum, and
his hard backside rubbed against the bare skin of her
inner thighs. She pressed her breasts against his back as

she wrapped her arms around him, holding on tight. Through the front of his cotton T-shirt she could feel the warmth of his flat, muscular belly. Wind streamed through his short dark hair, carrying the scent of clean shampoo and heady musk, and something masculine and foreign.

He wasn't wearing a helmet. Of course not. Nothing would, or could, ever hurt him. Even a crash would leave him untouched. A man like Paolo could walk through flames unscathed.

He didn't know what it was like to be afraid. Tightening her hands around him as they drove past the Piazza Venezia, she shook her head angrily. What was wrong with her? Envying first the housekeeper, and now Paolo. She had a great deal to be thankful for in her own life. Alexander was safe. Wasn't that enough?

But years of loneliness were catching up with her. Since she'd left college she'd been afraid to have close friends. Confidantes betrayed her to tabloids. Her only real friends had been Karin and Maxim, and now they both were dead. Dead on vacation in Majorca, where they'd gone on a second honeymoon, trying to revive their marriage…

Isabelle blinked back tears, missing them.

Even when they'd been alive, her days had consisted of royal duties and required social functions. She'd rarely left the palace for fun, and she'd always slept alone. Other than Magnus's brief, constrained kisses of a few weeks ago, she'd never allowed any man to touch her. Always prim and proper in public, she'd been dubbed the "ice princess" by the paparazzi, and that was pretty much on target. For ten years she'd been as frozen as Antarctica.

But beneath the constraining safety and heat of Paolo's helmet, with the dark blur of the road just inches beneath her shoes, she had the sudden yearning to feel things again. To be brave. To be free. To let consequences be damned…

Paolo pulled the motorcycle abruptly to a stop at a trattoria near the Piazza Navona. Parking the hundred-thousand euro Caretti motorcycle crosswise in a tiny space between a Fiat and an old BMW, he reached back to help her. Encircling her waist with his hands, he gently lifted her to the sidewalk. His hands were so large his fingertips could almost touch around her.

"What are we doing here?" she asked in confusion.

He glanced back at the trattoria, and his dark eyebrows lifted sardonically. "I could be mistaken, but generally people eat at restaurants. Lunch, in this case."

He didn't seem to notice or care as strangers on the sidewalk slowed down, staring at them. Or the way people's eyes widened in sudden recognition.

"We can't eat here," she said quietly, smiling for the crowds. "Paparazzi will be on their way in seconds—if they aren't here already."

He stopped, looking down at her. "This trattoria has the very best fettuccine *alla Romana* in the world. I want you to try it."

She licked her suddenly dry lips. "But then everyone would know—"

"Know what? That you eat pasta?" His jaw hardened. "Or that you'd share a meal with a man like me?"

"I… I…" She licked her lips. It was such a small thing. And yet the prospect of taking Paolo's arm and boldly going into the trattoria, to enjoy a meal like anyone else, gave her vertigo like tottering on the edge of a cliff.

He held out his hand. "It's just fettuccine, Isabelle."

His dark eyes mesmerized her, luring her with everything she'd denied herself for the last ten years. Sensuality. Freedom. Risk.

Her cell phone started to ring. Fumbling with her handbag, she pulled out the phone and saw it was her mother's private number.

Just the thought of what her mother would say when she found out about Paolo made Isabelle's hackles rise with irritated rebellion. She tossed the phone back into the black quilted bag. Defiantly, she put her hand in his.

A slow smile spread across Paolo's face.

"Grazie, cara mia," he said softly, his voice thick with approval.

It's not that hard to be reckless, she thought in surprise as he led her into the restaurant. *Not with him to guide me…*

The interior of the trattoria was small and cozy, apparently unchanged since the 1950s. A waiter came to their table and Paolo didn't bother to open his menu. "We'll have the fettuccine *alla Romana*."

"No!" Isabelle protested, desperately scanning the menu for something healthy. Allowing herself to be blackmailed into sex was one thing, but eating fattening food was another. She must be thin, as a matter of duty, and if her mother hadn't told her that the designers who sent her free clothes certainly would.

"Maybe baked fish?" she suggested weakly. "Lettuce with lemon juice?"

The waiter looked down at her with frank Italianate horror.

Paolo's expression didn't budge. "Fettuccine. For both of us," he said firmly.

He took the menu from her hand, and as his fingers brushed hers she gave in. She'd already gone into the restaurant. By tomorrow photos would be flashed around the world, of her having lunch in Rome with the ruthless billionaire motorcycle racer Paolo Caretti. Compared to that, eating a plate of pasta seemed a small sin. Why not enjoy it?

"You're too thin, anyway," he added under his breath with a wicked smile. "I intend to fatten you up, *bella*."

"Very well." She stared up at him for several heartbeats, her lips slightly parted. "Fettuccine."

"And a bottle of wine," Paolo ordered, mentioning a specific vintage that was both expensive and exceedingly rare. With a nod of appreciation the waiter disappeared, leaving them alone.

Isabelle glanced around the tiny trattoria. Every other table was filled, but other than a few surreptitious glances none of the other patrons seemed particularly interested in taking photographs or demanding autographs.

She looked at Paolo in surprise. "I think we *can* have lunch here."

"Do I really need to explain the concept of a restaurant again?"

She smothered a laugh. "No. I get it."

"Good." He gave her a heavy-lidded sensual smile. "Because I intend to satisfy your every appetite."

Her cheeks went hot. Ever since they'd left San Cerini he'd been like this: making small talk about the weather, discussing the upcoming Cannes Film Festival, sympathizing about the state of San Piedro's economy. But beneath it all his eyes were undressing her. His expression clearly said that he was picturing her in his bed.

It was an image she herself could imagine all too well. But if that was the case why had he refused her mere hours ago, when she'd been half-naked in his bedroom?

The waiter reappeared and uncorked the wine. He poured an inch into a wine glass. Paolo took a sip, then nodded his approval. The waiter filled their two large-stemmed glasses half-full of the ruby-colored wine, then placed the bottle between them on the table.

Isabelle immediately picked up her glass, hoping the cool dark wine would calm her. But instead of numbing her senses, as she'd hoped, the tannins lingered tantalizingly on her tongue, and the alcohol's warmth spread up and down her body, tingling her scalp and toes. She licked her lips, then looked up and saw him watching her from beneath heavily lidded eyes.

He was playing with her, she thought suddenly. Like a sleek panther running down his prey. And her nerves were already so frayed that she wasn't sure she could take much more of his charm.

She put down her glass with a clang. "Why are you acting like this?"

"Like what?"

"So friendly. So flirty. I don't understand. You know that I want to end our bargain. You could have me in your bed whenever you wish. Why are you acting like we're on a date? You don't need to seduce me."

His dark eyes met hers. "Perhaps I want to."

She wanted to shake her fists in frustration. "But why?"

"Am I doing it improperly?" He tilted his head as he watched her through narrowed eyes. "I suppose your lover does it quite differently."

She frowned. "My lover?"

"Prince Magnus."

She looked at him sharply. He'd said the name with a deliberate casualness belied by the hard set of his jaw. "Magnus is not my lover."

His expression didn't change. "Who's the liar now?"

"Believe what you want, but he and I have never been in bed together. We've barely even kissed."

His eyes darkened imperceptibly. "Kissed?"

She choked out a laugh. "You've got to be joking. You're critical of me kissing a man who's proposed marriage? You, who've slept with half the actresses and models in Europe?"

Leaning back in his chair, he stretched his arms behind his head, suddenly appearing much more relaxed. "I don't sleep much. A man's got to stay busy somehow."

"From everything I've heard, you're very busy indeed," she said, irritated.

He shrugged. "Work and pleasure. What else is there in life?"

"You used to believe in other things." She swallowed. "Love, for instance."

He stared at her for a moment. "That was a long time ago."

"And now?"

"I believe in hard work. I believe in honesty." His gaze lingered over her body. "I believe in protecting what's mine."

She felt his hot glance against her skin, stroking her hair, cupping her breasts, caressing her naked thighs. She took a deep breath, struggling against her desire by stoking her anger into a flame. "But you don't believe in keeping it, do you?"

"What do you mean?"

She knew she should keep her mouth shut, but a decade of rage wouldn't let her. She raised her chin. "You only want me because you think you can't have me."

His eyebrows lowered like a dark, cold storm. "We've already agreed that you're mine."

"For today. And the minutes are passing. In a few

hours I'll be gone. That's just how you like it, isn't it? Keeping things nice and simple in your queue."

"What are you talking about?"

Her heart was in her throat. "You say you protect what's yours, but you don't. You like the pursuit, but once you possess something it loses its value. The last time we had fettuccine—"

"I don't want to talk about it," he bit out.

"You asked me to marry you." She felt tears behind her eyes, and angrily blinked them away. She would die before Paolo Caretti saw her cry again. "You swore that you loved me. You begged me to run away with you."

"And as I recall," he said acidly, "you tossed the ring back in my face. Let's not talk about the past. I find it all very boring."

"You promised me forever, but within hours you replaced me with the blond tart next door!"

"How do you know?" he demanded.

"Because I saw her!" she cried. "The next morning I saw you kissing her!"

He narrowed his eyes. "You came back to the apartment? Why? Did you have a sudden urge for more *slumming*?"

She sucked in her breath, hurting to remember the cold phrases her mother had given her, the words she'd thought she had to use to make Paolo let her go.

"Damn you," she whispered. "I loved you. But you couldn't even be faithful to me for a single night."

He took a drink of wine, then set the glass down.

"You gave me no reason to be."

She bit her lip, choking back angry words as the waiter reappeared at the table. He placed plates in front of them, offering them ground pepper and freshly shredded parmesan. He refilled their wine.

After he'd departed, Paolo took a bite of the fettuccine, appearing coldly unaffected by their discussion.

It was all Isabelle could do not to cry.

Why had she brought up the past? Stupid. *Stupid.* Sitting up straight in her chair, she twisted a large amount of pasta onto her fork and stuffed it into her mouth.

She'd meant to imitate Paolo's calm behavior, but the butter, cheese and freshly made pasta burst onto her palate like an explosion of joy. Even when she was heartsick she could feel pleasure. It surprised her. But why should it? She despised Paolo, and feared the pain he might inflict in her life, but that didn't stop her from desperately wanting him.

"Do you like it?" he asked quietly, several minutes later.

"It's delicious," she muttered. She took another bite, then realized that she'd finished the entire plate. It was the best meal she'd had in ages. If she hadn't been in a public restaurant, she might even have licked the sauce off the sprig of rosemary garnish. "I just wish I could cook like this," she sighed under her breath.

"It could be arranged," Paolo said.

"What do you mean?"

"Armando could teach you. He is a friend of mine."

"But I'm terrible," she blurted out. "Why would you want me to try again?"

"You like to cook. You said it's one of your greatest pleasures."

She shook her head, blinking up at him in confusion. "You would spend an hour with me, in the kitchen of a trattoria, watching me learn to make fettuccine? Why? What could you possibly gain from it?"

"I told you. Your every appetite." Paolo stood up, holding out his hand. "Come. It's time for a lesson."

Paolo stared out through the tiny porthole window, watching the afternoon sun drift downward as his plane flew up the Italian coast, along the shimmering blue sea.

Damn you, I loved you. But you couldn't even be faithful to me for a single night.

The tearful expression on Isabelle's face when she'd spoken those words still haunted him. He wondered if it could be true—if she'd actually loved him. Was it possible that he'd been more to her than a boost to her vanity?

No, he told himself harshly. She'd just been slumming. She'd said so herself. If she'd actually loved him she never would have flung the ring back in his face.

But still…

He glanced down at the adjacent white leather seat. Exhausted from a long, busy day, she'd fallen asleep against his shoulder soon after their plane left Rome. Her head kept falling forward in her sleep, causing her eyelashes to flutter.

He put his arm around her. Leaning more fully against his chest, she wrapped one arm around him with a contented sigh. Like a child clutching a beloved toy.

Why had she come back to his apartment that day?

He watched her chest rise and fall with each breath. She looked so peaceful. So beautiful. Almost as beautiful as she'd looked in Armando's kitchen. Her eyes had glowed as the chef taught her to make fresh pasta and properly melt butter in a pan. Every so often she'd glanced back at Paolo with a crease in her forehead, as if expecting him to criticize or complain. But he'd enjoyed watching her. The joy on her face as she'd patiently worked to learn a brand-new skill had made him catch his breath.

For all these years he'd known exactly who Princess Isabelle de Luceran was—a spoiled, vain little gold digger.

Now he wasn't sure what to believe.

While making the pasta, she'd gotten a large smear of flour across her cheek. He'd brought it to her attention, expecting her to panic and head for the nearest mirror. But she'd just laughed. No—she'd *giggled*. She'd tried to wipe it off with the back of her hand, only succeeding in making things worse.

Finally, he'd gently swept the flour away with his hand. She'd looked up at him, and her laughter had died away.

Holding her close, while she looked so damn sexy in that apron, Paolo had nearly forgotten that they were in the crowded kitchen of a trattoria. He'd nearly lowered his head to kiss her. Had wanted to pick her up and wrap her legs around his waist, to spread her across the clean, gleaming table…

He'd barely restrained himself. Now, he looked at her sleeping beneath his arm.

If what she'd said was true—

If she'd loved him, and she'd returned to the apartment to give a different answer to his proposal—

Strange to think how different things might have been if he hadn't gone to his neighbor's apartment to borrow some whiskey. At the time, his choice had seemed either whiskey or a long jump into the Hudson.

His blond neighbor had answered her door wearing only a bra and shorts. "Sure," she'd replied with a grin. "I have a ton of whiskey. Here."

He'd gone back to his apartment alone, but a few glasses later she'd knocked at his door. "Can I borrow your bed? Mine's broken," she'd said brazenly.

He hadn't wanted her. Not really. But he hadn't resisted either. He just hadn't cared. What difference did it make? Sleeping with…what was her name?…Terry? Tara?…had been the same as drinking her cheap whiskey. The same buzz, the same forgetting, the same wretched hangover the next morning.

But to think if he hadn't touched her all his young dreams of marrying Isabelle might have come true…

It's better this way, he told himself harshly. Many women had tried to get him to commit over the years, but he'd always resisted. Easily. He had no intention of loving anyone. Love made a man vulnerable. The only woman he'd ever loved had left him. Even his own mother had left him as a baby. He'd be stupid to set himself up for that ever again.

Besides, he didn't need love. He had the satisfaction of a hefty bank account. The power of having others to serve him. The triumph of being the fastest motorcycle racer on earth.

Only one thing was missing. And with Isabelle that piece would finally be complete.

He would have a home.

She would bring respectability to his family in the eyes of the world. Though at night, in his bed, she would be far from respectable...

He gently stroked her cheek. He'd seen the hurt in her eyes because she thought he'd so easily replaced her.

The truth was that Isabelle wasn't replaceable. To the contrary. She was different from any other woman he'd known. She had pride—in her family, in herself. She had dignity and self-control. It was what made her special. It was what made her valuable.

And, whatever she might think, he did value her.

She would be the perfect wife. The perfect mother of his children. She would service his needs and supervise his homes. The devotion she'd shown to her nephew proved that she was born to be a mother. And her cooking was rapidly improving...

He grinned to himself, then his smile faded.

One thing hadn't changed. On no account would he love her.

She murmured in her sleep, turning toward him with a soft, satisfied sigh. Her arm clutched him tightly, pressing her breasts against his chest.

He would possess her, body and soul.

He looked again at her full, pink lips.

He'd start with her body.

Why had he done it?

In the backseat of the limo, traveling the coast road from San Piedro airport with Paolo's arm around her, it was all Isabelle could do not to ask.

Why had Paolo allowed her to have a cooking lesson? He'd blackmailed her into becoming his mistress for one night, then given up precious hours purely to indulge her desire. He'd arranged the lesson. He'd encouraged her every step of the way.

What could he possibly gain from it? It wasn't like she would be living with him in the future, cooking his meals.

She glanced at him from beneath her lashes.

She'd felt so close to him at the trattoria in Rome. Laughing. Touching. Mashing ingredients for the pasta, melting butter and cheese in the pan beneath Paolo's hot, approving gaze. It had all been a joy. *This must be what it's like,* she'd thought. *To be normal, to be loved, to cook for my family in a snug little kitchen…*

She thought Paolo was a cold, cruel, faithless bastard. So why had he been so kind?

"We're almost home, *bella*," he murmured, pressing a kiss against her forehead.

It's a trick, she told herself fiercely. He wants something.

She just didn't know what it was yet.

But all afternoon he'd been like a knight out of a fairy tale, handsome and true. And she already felt like the wicked witch who'd stolen his child. If they really were in a fairy tale, some ogre would certainly have come round to eat her by now.

If only she could trust Paolo enough to tell him about his son…

"Alexander," she whispered, picturing the little boy's face. She stopped, her heart pounding with fear. If she did tell Paolo, would she hurt the child she'd always tried so desperately to protect?

Would Alexander, instead of being King of San Piedro, become just another illegitimate love-child whose parents had lied?

"Alexander?" Paolo repeated, looking down at her with amusement. "Are you worried about your nephew? It's only been a day, and Durand is safely behind bars. But if you want to go back to the palace for a quick visit…"

"No." Her teeth chattered. That was the last thing she wanted right now. She had to get through her night with Paolo.

Stretching out their time together was too dangerous. He tempted her to betray every promise she'd made to herself. He lured her to her own destruction.

It would be too easy to love him again…

But the sun was setting. All she had to do was get

through a few more hours. Just one night. Then she could go back to Magnus and, if he still wanted her, announce their engagement.

The thought of it made her sick to her stomach. She didn't want Magnus. She never had. And now, spending time with Paolo…

His large hand curled protectively over the bare skin of her arm. She looked at him in the twilight. The shape of his wide shoulders and finely sculpted chest was visible beneath the white T-shirt, and the scattering of a few dark hairs showed above his collar. His rugged jaw was dark with five o'clock shadow. He was so handsome he made her head spin.

His thigh, muscular and wide beneath the denim, pressed against hers as the Rolls-Royce twisted along the curves of the coast road. She relished the feel of him, the heaviness of his weight pressing on her; she closed her eyes, savoring his warmth and the pressure of his body. They were barely touching, but she could feel him from her scalp to her toes.

The car stopped.

"We're here," Paolo said. She opened her eyes. The villa was silhouetted in shadows against the vivid red and orange Mediterranean twilight.

Paolo got out and held out his hand. Her knees shook as she placed her small hand in his larger one, allowing him to help her from the car. But instead of leading her up the sweeping steps to the villa he pulled her toward the dark, lush gardens that overlooked the cliffs.

"Where are you taking me?" she asked.

He looked down at her, his heavy-lidded eyes full of intent. "Does it matter?"

No. Looking into his face, she felt mesmerized. Without a mind or will of her own...

He drew her through an old wooden door that led past the seven-foot stone walls guarding the secret garden. He led her past the intricately designed ponds, flower-beds and palm trees to the nineteenth-century gazebo overlooking the cliff.

The sun was falling, plummeting like a fireball into the sea. The fading scarlet cast his sharp cheekbones and jawline with a roseate glow. She looked at his mouth. His gorgeously cruel mouth that had given her such pleasure. That had once said, *I will always love you, bella, you and only you.*

He caught her staring and she jumped in embarrassment. She'd nearly leaned forward to kiss him—another thing she'd sworn she'd never do...

What was this spell he cast on her?

She had to get a hold of herself.

"Don't worry." She straightened her shoulders, attempting a derisive laugh. "I won't be stupid enough to try to seduce you again—"

He pushed her back against the bougainvillea-covered trellis, sweeping her hair off her cheek with his large hand.

"You don't have to try, Isabelle," he said in a low voice. "You're always seducing me. Everything you say, everything you do makes me want you."

His hands cupped her jawline and the cool breeze, infused with the fragrance of roses and sea salt, blew through her hair, spinning around her and making her dizzy.

"I want you more than I've ever wanted any woman," he said, and he lowered his mouth to hers in a deep, searing kiss.

She closed her eyes, transported by the feel of his lips on hers. The unexpected tenderness of his caress made her breathless with longing, desperate with need...

"Now, at last," he whispered darkly against her cheek, "you're mine."

CHAPTER SIX

SHE'D never been kissed like this. Never. Been kissed like this.

Her body melted against him in the shadows of the garden. She could feel his heat like a raging fire. He kissed her not with the angry, bruising passion of yesterday, nor even with the naïveté of their long-ago youth, but with something in between. With the tenderness of the boy but all the fierce power of the man.

And this time his kiss had purpose. His hands grasped beneath her soft pink cardigan, his fingertips rough against her skin. He kissed her, taking firm possession of her mouth as he deftly undid her bra. She felt his hands cupping her breasts and her whole body went tight. His fingers squeezed against her nipple, causing her to gasp.

She suddenly realized that he intended to take her right here in the garden. Where—in spite of the seven-foot-high stone walls—anyone could see them. Servants. Photographers with wide-angle lenses.

"No," she breathed, struggling to resist. "Not here."

"Here," he said, holding her wrists. "Now."

Tempted beyond belief, she watched the hard, handsome angles of his face in wonder. He was like a god of nature, she thought suddenly. A savage ruler of a wild, primeval kingdom. But there were traps beneath the lush beauty—poisonous flowers and animals with sharp claws. A civilized girl could wander into his kingdom and disappear. She'd be eaten, consumed, until only the flowers feasted upon her bones.

And yet still she hungered…

"We can't…" she gasped, trying to pull away. "We mustn't…"

His knee pressed between her legs. "You can't deny me."

"Let me go," she whispered.

His fingers cupped her breasts, rubbing her nipples gently against the cashmere. "In the night," he said darkly, "in my garden, you're no prim-and-proper princess. You're a woman. *My* woman."

Slowly he lowered his head, kissing her neck, sending spasms of pleasure up and down her body. Pulling away, he looked down at her. "Do you really want to go back to the villa? To close the windows and lock the door? To hide and stifle your cries of joy?"

She didn't even have to think about it. "Yes!"

"What a sad life you lead, Princess. A sad, lonely life."

"What do you want from me?" she cried, struggling to rip her wrist out of his iron grip. "To admit that I've missed you? To admit that I've spent ten years alone, night after night? To admit you're the only man I've ever been with?"

He grabbed her shoulders, his dark eyes searching hers. "Is it true? I'm the only man you've ever taken to your bed?"

"Go to hell!"

"Is it true?" he thundered.

"Yes!" she cried.

Anger gave her strength to pull away. Turning on her heel, she ran through the garden, away from the villa, tripping down the cliff steps to the shore. She was desperate to get away from the look in her eyes. He felt sorry for her. He *pitied* her. He'd spent a decade making love to countless women, while she'd just admitted she was a bitter, lonely spinster, pining for the one man she could never let herself have…

At the bottom of the steps was a secluded beach, an apron of white sand surrounded by rocky cliffs on three sides and the sea on the other. She turned her face toward the moonlight. The roar of the sea, the pounding surf of the rising tide, echoed the rapid beat of her heart.

"Isabelle!"

She pulled off her beige leather pumps, carrying them in her hands in the effort to run faster away from him across the sand.

He caught her.

"Don't be afraid of them, Isabelle," he said in a low

voice. "Never be afraid. I'll never let anyone hurt you. If any man tried, I would grab him by the throat and toss him into the sea."

But who would protect her from Paolo?

He pulled her into his arms. She wanted him with every drop of her blood, every beat of her heart, every longing of her soul. Even if it cost her marriage to Magnus. Even if she lost everything. She couldn't fight him anymore. She couldn't fight them both. She'd lost the will to resist…

But still, as he wrapped his hands around her naked waist, she trembled.

"I'm afraid," she whispered.

"You're with me," he said.

But that's what frightens me, she wanted to say. *I'm afraid I'll give you everything…*

"This is Anatole Beach." Paolo took her shoes from her hands and let them fall one by one. "Have you heard of it?"

"Yes." She could hear the cries of the gulls overhead, echoing strangely against the large boulders of the shore and the crevices of the cliffs, as if someone was weeping. "The Russian nobleman lost his wife…"

"She drowned on their honeymoon. The next day he threw himself off that cliff."

"He couldn't bear to live without her," she whispered.

Paolo unbuttoned her cardigan, dropping it onto the sand. "Love is destructive, Isabelle. You asked why I gave it up. That's why."

I won't love you, she vowed to herself desperately.
I won't.

He pulled off the cashmere shell over her head.
Kneeling at her feet, he gently pulled her skirt down past
her thighs, to her knees, finally dropping it to her feet.

Then he looked at her.

Wearing just her plain white silk bra and panties,
whipped by the wind on the moon-drenched beach, she
didn't feel cold. Not with Paolo here. Even surrounded
by long-ago ghosts, beneath the eerie cries of the gulls,
she felt warm and bright as a midsummer day as long
as he was with her…

He rose to his feet.

"I loved someone once," he said softly. "Just once."

Her heart vibrated as fast as a hummingbird's wing.

Slowly, he lowered his mouth to hers. His lips were
gentle. He kissed her languorously. Thoroughly. Until
her knees were so weak she couldn't have stopped
kissing him, even if every paparazzo on the Riviera
were madly snapping pictures.

He finally released her, and she opened her eyes,
exhaling. He pulled his white T-shirt off over his head,
revealing bare muscled shoulders and a taut chest laced
with dark hair. He pulled off his jeans, and his black
boxers, form-fitting against his hard thighs, revealed
how much he wanted her.

She looked into his face with stars in her eyes.

He suddenly smiled down at her. "I dare you to
follow me."

Turning without warning, he raced into the surf.

She obeyed without thought, following him across the sand, running barefoot into the sea. The cold water shocked her. Then it invigorated her. She laughed with the pure joy of freedom as she ran through the waves. Dipping her hands into the water, she splashed Paolo. Water dripped in rivulets down his hard-muscled body.

With a mock roar, he turned on her. He chased her, scooping her into his arms.

The laughter faded from their faces as they looked at each other, both breathing hard.

"Isabelle…" he said hoarsely.

Somehow, she was never sure how, they made it back to shore. He lowered her to the sand, all the while crushing her lips against his own.

He touched her everywhere, caressing her in the moonlight, making her body gasp and clench and cry. The roughness of the sand pressed beneath her, threatening to devour her beneath his weight. Her lips were bruised, her body aching. She moved beneath him, straining as she felt him between her legs.

With a curse, he rolled off her, yanking down his boxers. Ripping her white silk panties off with one pull of his powerful hand, he positioned himself between her legs. For a moment he hesitated. She arched her whole body against him. If he didn't take her now…

He shuddered as she moaned his name. Drawing back, he thrust into her.

She gasped. He filled her completely, stretching her to the limit and more; he was inside her so deeply. She bucked her hips, crying out in building pleasure as he rode her. Quickly. Urgently. The roar of the rising surf grew closer as he squeezed one taut breast in his hand, biting and suckling her nipple through the wet, clinging white silk.

Holding on to her shoulder and breast, he pushed into her harder. Faster. The tension coiled low in her belly, threatening to consume her. It was too much, too fast. She tried to pull back, to slow down.

He wouldn't let her. Grabbing her wrists, he forced them above her head, holding them into the sand as he thrust deeper still, taking his full pleasure and enticing her to do the same. He wouldn't let her escape everything he was giving her…

She started to writhe and shake, twisting her head as waves of joy lifted her in pleasure so intense it was almost pain. She felt water against her feet, rushed from the lifting tide of the sea. Her body detonated like an explosion, sending shockwaves that curled her toes into the sand.

She screamed, never once caring who might hear. With a simultaneous roar, he filled her with one deep final thrust, spilling his seed into her.

For several long moments afterward he held her close.

Dazed, she licked her swollen lips, tasting the salt of the sea. She could feel the beat of his heart against her skin, and smell the fragrant breeze, redolent of spices from distant lands. She felt the waves of the surf, cooling their wet, naked bodies with each rush of the rising tide. The sea lingered like a caress, lapping against their skin.

But each time the water fell away it stole more of the sand beneath her.

Paolo woke in his bed with a start.

Something wasn't right.

Sitting up, he shook his head, hazy and disoriented. A cool breeze was blowing through the open window, waving the long, translucent curtains. Birds were singing in nearby trees. Bright sunlight cast a golden patina through his enormous bedroom, from the gleaming hardwood floor to the Savonnerie rug.

"Paolo?" From the pillow next to his, Isabelle blinked up at him sleepily. "What's wrong?"

In a rush, everything came back. Making love to her in the pounding surf. Returning to the villa, sharing a shower and making love again. Falling into bed, still naked in each other's arms. But that had been hours and hours ago. That could only mean...

"I slept," he said in amazement.

She stretched her arms over her head, blinking with a pretty, kittenish yawn. "Do I need to explain the concept of nighttime?" she teased.

"I never sleep," he muttered, suddenly sweating in the cool morning air.

Looking as if she still weren't quite awake, she held

out her arms. "It's too early," she murmured. "Come back to sleep."

He turned his head to look at the gold clock over the marble fireplace mantel. "It's almost eight," he said in disbelief.

"Too early," she sighed, closing her eyes and turning against the soft pillow.

She didn't understand. How could she, without experiencing insomnia herself? She didn't know the helpless fury and rage he'd felt night after night. Paolo had always been able to fight anything and win—it was how he'd become rich, how he'd become powerful. But since the night he'd bought this villa he'd been powerless to do what all of his employees, from Valentina Novak to his fourth under-gardener, could do without effort.

Every night he'd stared at the shadowy ceiling, waiting to hear the birds cheerfully singing his doom, waiting to face the dim horizon of dawn more exhausted than the night before. Trapped.

But somehow Isabelle had changed everything.

He cursed under his breath. It was a coincidence. It had to be. All that vigorous lovemaking last night had worn him out. There could be no other explanation.

None of the other women you've bedded helped you sleep, a small voice pointed out.

He squashed down the voice, pummeled it into dust. He wouldn't—couldn't—accept that Isabelle de Luceran had that kind of power over him.

"Paolo," she called sleepily. "Come back to bed."

"*Sì*," he said automatically, rolling over to take her in his arms. She closed her eyes, sighing in satisfaction. He kissed her temple, then looked down at her.

Her skin glowed the color of cream, with warm roses in her cheeks; her long chestnut hair was wild, tumbling across his pillows in a riotous cascade of shiny waves. Contentment emanated from her like a house cat curled up in sunlight. She was naked. She had no makeup, no jewelry.

She was the most beautiful woman he'd ever seen. And all he knew was that he wanted more of it. More sleep. More lovemaking. More of her.

And he would have it. Not because he needed her, he told himself, but because he enjoyed her. Making love to her. Watching her laugh. Sleeping next to her. Possessing her in every way.

Even now she might be carrying his child.

He heard her suck in her breath. Her eyes, the color of rich caramel, flew open in horror. She clutched his shoulder. "Paolo!"

"Yes, *cara mia*?" he said, idly tracing her naked breast.

"We—we didn't…" She paused, swallowing, then blurted out, "We didn't use a condom!"

"Is that all?"

"Is that *all*?" she cried out. "Don't you realize what could happen?"

"Be calm," he said sharply, softening his tone with a smile. "You have nothing to worry about."

She blinked up at him, looking as if she wanted to

believe him so badly that she could barely breathe. "I don't?"

"No," he said firmly. "You will not end up pregnant and forced to raise a child alone. That is quite impossible."

"Oh," she said. Then, more quietly, "Oh." She turned to him, and her eyes were enormous. They were pools of light, teasing him with goodness and trust.

Yes, he thought, mesmerized by that light.

"Do you mean that you—?"

"Come here," he said, pulling her naked body to his.

He took her in his arms and made love to her again, this time more slowly. He caressed her satin skin, spread her wide, filling her. Slowly. Inch by inch. Until she begged for more. He held himself back, making her moan and writhe before bringing her to fulfillment—twice.

Only then did he let himself go, closing his eyes, pushing into her with a hard gasp. He didn't enjoy her for nearly as long as he'd planned, however. He'd intended to make her climax a third time, but she turned the tease back on him, grabbing his hips, stroking between his legs and up his body with feather-light touches. *Dio santo*, he was only a man.

Afterward, as he rose from the bed, he was glad he'd decided to make her his bride. A lifetime of such nights with her wouldn't be enough to satiate him.

Smiling to himself, he ordered breakfast on the intercom. As they waited for its arrival he dressed, pulling on a long-sleeved black shirt and fine-cut Italian pants. He could feel her watching him from the bed, where she was still tucked beneath his quilt, lazing with contentment like a Sunday morning.

Marrying her would be a honeymoon that never ended.

Oh, yes, he thought, congratulating himself on his choice. Mrs. Caretti. He liked the sound of it. His wife. In his bed. At his command.

His British butler brought in a tray of breakfast delicacies and placed it on the small round table near the fireplace. Smoothly he set plates and served the food before departing, never once showing any indication that he recognized Princess Isabelle de Luceran in his employer's bed.

But at the door the butler turned and said with a cough, "Sir?"

Frowning, Paolo went to him. "Riggins?"

"You asked for the newspapers, sir, as always. But… ah…I thought I might give them to you privately. For the sake of the lady."

As Riggins departed, closing the door behind him, Paolo looked down at the open papers in his hand.

And immediately closed them. He ground his teeth. Damn the paparazzi to hell. He cursed the photographers and their long-range lenses, and most of all he cursed his own arrogant certainty that they'd have privacy on his own damned beach…

"Don't look!" Isabelle cried.

"What?"

Without thinking, he looked. Isabelle had leapt naked

out of bed and run across the bedroom. She was standing on her tiptoes, stretching her lovely limbs to reach for his robe, hanging on the bathroom door. For a moment his eyes traced over her, helpless to do anything but savor the curving lines of her exquisite body. Only after she'd wrapped the tie twice around her waist, covering herself with white cotton terry from her neck to her ankle, did his brain start to work again.

She sat back down at the table, glancing at him with a flush of self-consciousness on her cheeks. "You didn't see anything, did you?"

He tucked the newspapers behind his back. "Nothing I didn't want to see."

Her blush deepened. "You're a beast, Paolo. A beast."

"*Sì*, I know." He gave her a wicked grin. "Although you didn't seem to mind that last night."

She smiled at him for a moment, glowing. "No, I didn't."

Her face grew serious.

"Our night is over," she said softly. "Our time is done."

No.

It was a visceral response from deep inside his soul, fierce and possessive. He put his hand over hers.

"I don't want our affair to end, Isabelle," he said in a low voice. "We are both free. Stay with me."

She looked down miserably at her plate, loaded with Spanish *jamón*, fried eggs, and two big, buttery slices of *tarte aux fraises*.

"You are free, Paolo," she said. "I am not."

His brows lowered like a stormcloud. "What do you mean?"

"I told you two days ago."

"You cannot still intend to marry him!"

"Magnus can give my country a future."

"Do you love him, then?" he demanded. "Are you really such a fool?"

"I'm Princess of San Piedro. My fate is to serve my people." She looked up at him, her light hazel eyes limpid and pure. "I have no choice but to accept it."

"You'd be sacrificing yourself for no good cause." Furious, Paolo tossed the newspapers across the table in all their lurid glory. "Perfect as he is, do you think he'll still want you when he sees this?"

She blanched as she read the headlines. Snatching up the first tabloid, she opened the pages to see pictures of them making love on the beach, fuzzy, but still distinct enough to reveal their faces. Gasping, she grabbed the next paper, which had a similar picture on the top right corner of the front page.

"You said we were safe!" she cried.

"I thought we were," he said grimly. "My mistake."

Her beautiful features crumpled. Tossing down the paper, she put her face in her hands, rubbing her forehead. "I've ruined everything. I never should have… Oh, my God. It looks like a deliberate insult!"

He clenched his jaw. "I'm sorry."

She bit her lip. "It's all right," she said in a small voice. "It wasn't your fault."

But it *was* his fault, and he felt it. He'd seduced her on the beach, promising her he would protect her. That he hadn't kept his promise felt like a knife-wound in his chest.

"I'll find that photographer and smash his camera," he added, barely joking.

She laughed, hiccoughing through her tears. "Yes, please. That would be lovely." Then she shook her head, furrowing her brow in anguish. "Magnus will have seen these pictures. My *mother* will have seen them!"

In a controlled motion, he poured himself a *tazza* of espresso. "I'll talk to them. Tell them it was my fault. Settle them down." *Tell them you're mine,* he added silently.

She stared at him. "Are you out of your mind? You can't do that!"

"Why not?"

"Well, you're not exactly my mother's favorite person, for a start. I doubt Magnus would even agree to meet you."

"He would," Paolo said tersely.

She shook her head in disbelief. "Because you always beat him in every motorcycle race? Just because you're rivals doesn't mean—"

"No. That's not why." He gulped down some espresso, barely feeling the burn against his tongue. "Magnus isn't just my rival, Isabelle. He's also my brother."

"Your *brother*?" she gasped.

But it suddenly all made sense. For the first time Isabelle saw the similarities between the two men. The same hard jaw, the same cleft in the chin. Magnus was more slender, more elegant. Paolo was darker, rougher, wider. But no wonder she'd once thought Magnus to be handsome—his coloring, the beauty of his dark eyes, had reminded her of Paolo.

"Brothers," she breathed. She shook her head. "How is that possible?"

"We had the same mother."

"Magnus's mother…the Princess von Trondhem? She was a society matron from an old New York family!"

"Yes, I know." He finished his espresso off in a gulp. "When she was sixteen she eloped with my father. By the time I was born she knew she'd made a huge mistake. My father was hard and dangerous, which she thought romantic. Until she lived with him." He gave her a thin smile. "She wanted to leave, but he wouldn't let her. So right after I was born they made a deal. He gave her a divorce. She gave him—me."

"Oh, Paolo," she whispered, her heart breaking for him.

He shrugged. "It apparently wasn't difficult for her to leave. Her family sent her to Europe to wait for the scandal to blow over, and she met a prince in Vienna. Within weeks she was married. A year later she had a new son." He stood up. "From the day my brother was born everything was given to him on a silver platter."

With a jaw like granite, he turned away.

"Paolo…" she whispered.

"I have some work to do," he said over his shoulder. "Finish your breakfast, and then we will talk." He stopped, looking back at her. "You're going to stay, Isabelle. We both know it. Don't waste your time fighting me."

He closed the door firmly behind him.

She stared after him, aghast. His mother had *left* him. As a baby. How did anyone ever get over that?

She suddenly had a horrible headache. Her own parents hadn't exactly created a warm home. Between her father's endless affairs and her mother's bitterness, their rare family dinners had been filled with many cold silences. But at least she'd had her brother, and later Karin. And at least Isabelle had always known that both her parents had wanted her.

She still remembered how horrible it had been to return to San Piedro ten years ago, pregnant, unwed, and apparently forgotten by her faithless lover. Her mother had spent the whole flight home alternating between sympathy and plotting to give away the baby. Isabelle had alternated between weeping and throwing up. Until Karin had come to her with a compromise.

"No one outside the family need ever know." Her sister-in-law's eyes had filled with tears. "Your brother needs an heir, and if I have another miscarriage I'll die of grief. Help us. Let us love your child as our own."

It had nearly killed her to give up Alexander, but she'd done it. For her family. For her country. And most of all—for Alexander.

But even though he'd never called her *Maman*, Isabelle had at least spent every day with the boy. She'd experienced his childhood, planned birthday parties, laughed at his knock-knock jokes and soothed his tears over skinned knees. She'd been the boy's confidante, his friend.

Paolo didn't even know he had a son.

She'd stolen his son away without even giving him the choice to be a father.

He obviously doesn't want children of his own, she argued fiercely. He'd told her yesterday that she would never end up pregnant and alone. It had taken her a few minutes to figure out what he meant, but of course a man like Paolo—working sixteen-hour days, spending his free time motorcycle-racing and romancing one glamorous mistress after another—wouldn't want to be slowed down by the responsibilities of a family.

He'd had a vasectomy.

But not wanting children and dealing with them if they came were two different things.

When he'd spoken about his mother she'd seen a vulnerability in his eyes that she'd never seen before. His jaw had been tense and angry, his shoulders tight, his body poised for a fight. But she'd still seen the truth: he'd never gotten over being abandoned as a newborn. It still angered him. Bewildered him.

It forced her to finally admit another truth to herself.

She was falling in love with Paolo all over again.

She was falling desperately, totally in love with a man she could never marry. Whom she'd hurt in the most cruel way possible.

"Oh, my God," she whispered from bloodless lips.

How would he feel if he found out that she'd forced him to unknowingly abandon a child—just as his mother had once abandoned him?

She couldn't love Paolo. She couldn't. The secret she carried would always be between them. What she'd done was unforgivable. If he ever found out he would hate her for all the days of his life.

And yet…he deserved to know. Even if it did make him hate her, he had to know he had a child.

If she told him, could she trust him to keep the secret? Could she trust him to protect Alexander above all else?

Suddenly she couldn't breathe. Then she rose to her feet. She squared her shoulders, tying Paolo's robe more firmly around her. Trying not to think about what she meant to do, she walked down the hallway and down the stairs.

She turned in the first door on the right and saw walls of books—the library. A man rose from the upholstered chair by the window.

"Oh!" she said surprised. "Excuse me, I—"

She started to turn away, then froze. As if in slow motion, she looked back at him.

Prince Magnus von Trondhem stood silhouetted in front of the wide, expansive windows in an elegant gray suit and purple silk tie.

"Hello, Isabelle," he said quietly.

His expression was calm, almost kind, but her cheeks went hot with shame. She was wearing Paolo's robe. Her hair was mussed with lovemaking. And since he was here he'd obviously already seen the pictures of her making love to his brother.

"Magnus," she whispered, barely able to speak over the lump in her throat. "I'm so sorry. I never meant to hurt you…"

"It's all right. He's the one to blame, not you." He held out his hand. "I came to tell you that you're making a mistake. And to offer a warning—get out before it's too late."

CHAPTER SEVEN

PAOLO stared blankly at his laptop screen.

With a sigh, he looked up at the wide window above his desk. It was a beautiful spring morning. Sunlight glittered against the sapphire water, and the fragrant breeze made the sailboats and yachts in the harbor dance and sway.

He'd just made love to the woman of his dreams three times. He had no doubt that his plans would be successful. Whether she realized it or not, she would soon be his bride.

So why wasn't he happy?

Closing his laptop in disgust, he rose from his desk and paced the length of his study. Going out onto the open balcony, Paolo stared at the blue water and the gently rocking boats. He raked a hand through his hair.

He never should have brought up his mother. Some secrets remained better buried. What difference did it make that she'd left? What difference did it make that she'd loved his perfect brother and not him? He didn't care. Being left alone had only made him stronger. He'd learned to fight. He'd learned to win.

"Sir?"

Turning around, he saw Riggins, red-faced behind him on the balcony. The usually dignified butler was breathing hard, as if he'd run across the length of the villa.

"*Sì?*"

"We've been looking for you," Riggins panted, then leaned forward, trying to catch his breath. "Prince Magnus von Trondhem—here. He's—waiting in—the library."

"Magnus is in my library?" Paolo demanded. "You just let him in?"

Riggins looked shocked. "Mr. Caretti, you said if the Prince ever should visit, you'd wish to see—"

"That was before." Paolo cut him off. Scowling, he strode back through his study without a backward glance.

Halfway down the hall, he heard a man's voice. He froze at the base of the wide, sweeping staircase. His hand clenched against the banister, every nerve taut as he listened to his half brother's muffled voice coming from the library.

"He'll never marry you, Isabelle. Never be faithful to you. He's dangerous—ruthless. He's not from our world. He doesn't have our code of honor. The way he wins on the Grand Prix circuit year after year—it's suspicious. And I wouldn't be surprised if the whole time he's been seducing you he's still been sleeping with that secretary of his…"

With a muttered growl, Paolo knocked the door aside

with a loud bang. He took in the scene at once: Magnus, suave and elegant, with his hand on her shoulder; Isabelle, still wrapped in his oversized robe, clutching the belt in her white-knuckled hands and looking stricken. Looking small. Fragile.

Paolo went straight for his brother.

"You had something to say to me?" he demanded.

"Just the truth," Magnus replied coldly. "If you really care about Isabelle you'll let her go, before you cause any more damage to her reputation."

Paolo's lip curled.

"I'm not giving her up. Not to you or anyone."

"That's for her to decide, isn't it?"

They both looked at her.

Isabelle's hazel eyes locked with Paolo's for a long minute before she finally turned to Magnus.

"It's all right," she said faintly. "Really. You can go, Magnus. I'll be fine."

He pressed his hand against hers. "When you change your mind, come to me," he said urgently. "I still want to marry you, Isabelle. Our union can be successful. When you finally realize what kind of man he really is, come to me—"

"Time to go," Paolo growled. Brother or no brother, he wasn't going to stand and watch the man try and convince her to leave him. He grabbed Magnus's shoulder and started walking, shoving him down the hall.

"But—"

"Thanks for the visit." Pushing him out the front

door none too gently, he closed the door behind him and turned to find Isabelle standing behind him.

"Is it true?" she whispered. "About the…the cheating?"

He clenched his fists. He should have punched his brother in the face for even daring to make that accusation. Damn his sense of family obligation anyway. He ground his jaw. "Since he can't beat me, he accuses me of cheating. He's a liar—and a loser. I work. I train. I never stop. So I win."

She took a long, deep breath. High above them in the foyer, the enormous crystal chandelier cast prisms of light and color across her lovely drawn face.

"That's not what I meant," she said. "What he said about your secretary. I met her in New York, remember? She's…beautiful."

"Yes, she is," he said tersely. "It doesn't mean I'm sleeping with her."

"I wouldn't blame you if you were. It's not like we're married." She swallowed, her troubled eyes translucent as amber. "It's not like you love me."

He met her gaze evenly. Honestly.

"No, I don't love you, Isabelle. And I never will."

His words should have given her a sense of relief. The last thing she wanted was for him to love her. Bad enough that she was already starting to fall for *him*.

If he loved her in return, she would never have the strength to pull away. Even knowing that staying with him would ultimately destroy her.

"Good," she said numbly. "I'm glad to hear that. Now, if you'll excuse me, I…I need some air…"

Turning on her bare heel, she all but ran out onto the balcony. Once she was alone, she turned her face toward the sea. She pulled the plush robe closer to her body, shivering in the fresh morning breeze. She could hear the cool wind through the palm trees, waving the green fronds above her in the bright blue sky.

She'd nearly made the biggest mistake of her life. If she'd told Paolo that he was Alexander's father their lives would have been tied together forever.

Would Paolo have demanded marriage? Would he have forced her to be his bride? Would he have used his charm and strength and body to make her love him forever, even against her will?

If he had, how long would it have been before he betrayed her? Immediately? By announcing to the world that he was Alexander's true father? Or ten years from now, by taking a young mistress when Isabelle started to lose the first blush of youth?

Magnus was right—there was no telling what Paolo might do. He wasn't of their world. He didn't have the same code of honor.

She'd be reckless to take the risk. Certifiably insane.

She had to marry Magnus as soon as possible. Because it terrified her that, in spite of everything, she was desperately trying to think of excuses to stay…

She heard Paolo come up behind her.

"I'm sorry if those weren't the words you wanted to hear," he said quietly. "I told you I'd never lie to you."

"You're wrong." She whirled to face him. "I'm glad you don't love me. It would only complicate things."

"Love is a waste of time," he agreed.

"Right," she managed over the lump in her throat. "And anyway, I'm leaving today."

"No, you're not." He came closer to her.

She lifted her chin. "You can't stop me, Paolo."

He stroked her cheek. Slowly he lowered his mouth to hers. His kiss was passionate. Tempting. His lips were hard, soft, sweet. His tongue stroked between her lips, teasing her, spreading her, and he drew a shuddering breath.

"You're mine, Isabelle," he whispered against her skin. "Magnus doesn't deserve you. You're a bright flame, a tropical bird of paradise. He isn't man enough to hold you."

"And you are?" she breathed.

"Yes," he said in a low voice. "I will hold you forever."

She wrenched her head away so he wouldn't see the confusion and desire and pain tumbling inside her. "I have to marry. I want a family, Paolo, someone of my own. Can't you understand that?"

He looked down at her. "That's why you're going to marry me."

"What?" she gasped.

His eyes were dark, mesmerizing. "I have factories

of my own. Influence of my own. Together we will be an unstoppable force. You will marry me."

She sucked in her breath. For a moment she was tempted. No man had ever affected her like Paolo. He could give her a life of excitement and joy, of racing motorcycles along the sea and making love all night long. Each morning would be better than the last. Every day would be bright and new with the man she loved beside her.

So he'd cheated on her, she thought suddenly. So what? He'd done it once, and he would likely do it again. Her mother had dealt with it. Couldn't she? Wasn't a lifetime of being Paolo's wife worth occasionally turning a blind eye to his infidelities? She could endure that private humiliation, couldn't she, if no one else ever knew?

She took a deep breath.

No.

She'd seen her mother's anguish too closely. Jealousy and bitterness poisoned a woman. Loving Paolo, and knowing he took pleasure in other women, would kill her.

If infidelity was inevitable, she wasn't going to make the mistake of marrying a man she loved. It was better to marry a man who left her cold. That was the safe choice. The only choice…

"Our marriage will be better without love," he said softly, stroking her cheek.

Better for you, she thought. Better so he could sleep with his gorgeous redheaded secretary and whomever else took his fancy with a clear conscience.

Heart in her throat, she turned her head away. "I can't."

"Can't?" he growled. "Or won't?"

"It's the same thing." She clenched her fists together, trying to stay strong. "When I marry, I must choose someone who can lead San Piedro."

"Someone royal," he said evenly. "Not someone like me."

Suddenly she felt like weeping. "Don't you realize what it would mean for you to marry me?"

"Sì," he said. "But I still want to."

"You'd make an awful prince!" she cried. "You'd never handle the public criticism. You'd go ballistic at the lack of privacy. And as for diplomacy—" She tried to smile. "You'd get mad and tell some head of state to go to hell."

"You still don't trust me," he said evenly. "You never have."

He'd told her the truth about not loving her. She had no choice but to return the favor.

"No, I don't," she said softly. "I can't. I'm sorry."

Muttering a curse under his breath, Paolo turned away. And watching him go, she felt a bolt of anguish crack her soul apart, like lightning scorching the dry earth.

Everything she'd said was true. It all made perfect sense.

But her instincts were screaming. Her whole body cried out for him. And her heart…

Paolo, I love you.

As if of its own accord, her hand flew out to grab his wrist. "Wait."

"For what?" he asked in a low voice, not looking at her. "You've made your opinion of me plain."

"Please." For a moment she couldn't breathe. "Just wait."

She felt herself standing on the edge of a precipice. She heard the voices of Magnus, of her mother and brother and Karin, and the ministers of San Piedro, all telling her to return to the palace at once. To be dignified. To be proper. To be good.

To follow the rules.

But it's the twenty-first century! she cried back to them. Dignity and sacrifice weren't what they used to be. A neighboring crown prince had lived openly with a commoner—a single unwed mother—before he'd made her his bride. Another crown prince had married a woman from a family so scandalous that her parents had been excluded from the wedding.

Why should Isabelle sacrifice every bit of personal happiness for old-fashioned standards that the rest of the world had long since left behind?

I can't give him up, she thought suddenly. *I won't. Not yet!*

She needed a taste of pleasure. A drink of joy. That was all she wanted. She was starving for it—gasping like a fish on sand. A few weeks of passion and excitement and laughter with the man she loved would fill her soul enough to sustain her for the lifetime of duty.

A vacation. That was what she needed. From being a princess. From being herself.

And then I'll go back, she promised herself desperately. *I'll marry Magnus. I'll be good and follow the rules the rest of my life.*

Perhaps it might even help. After a few weeks with Paolo she would surely see his faults and fall out of love. Or else he would grow tired of her and betray her. At any rate, she could then marry Magnus for the good of the country, knowing that she had left nothing behind—except, perhaps, her own heart.

And a heart, she thought, was something she was quite willing to live without…

Taking a deep breath, she came to her decision.

"I can't be your wife, but…"

"But?"

"I'll be your mistress," she whispered.

"My mistress?" Paolo's dark eyes were assessing her, luring her, scorching her whole body. "You would openly live with me? You would defy the whole world?"

"Yes." Looking up into his handsome hard-edged face, she said the words she'd longed to say her whole life. "Paolo, teach me how to live dangerously."

Isabelle wasn't the only one who soon found herself living dangerously.

Over the next few weeks, in spite of Paolo's warning instincts, he found himself starting to do something he'd sworn he would never let himself do again.

He found himself starting to like her.

Respect her.

And more…

He'd enjoyed teaching her to ride a motorcycle. She'd followed his instructions to the letter, screaming with joy as she took her first solo ride. With paparazzi following close behind, they'd had to drive fast.

He'd taken her to Paris for dinner—but with bodyguards and flashing photographers following them everywhere they went, they'd practically had to sit atop the *Tour Eiffel* to watch the sunset over the violet rooftops.

Finally, on her birthday, he'd been so fed up with the constant media assault that he'd kidnapped Isabelle on his yacht and taken her out onto the open sea. They'd had a candlelit dinner alone on deck, and he'd presented her with sapphires from Bulgari, emeralds from Van Cleef & Arpels. With fireworks exploding in the dark sky above his yacht, they'd made love until dawn. It had been perfect.

Until pictures taken from a long-range helicopter had appeared in a British tabloid the next day. So much for the open sea!

Damn it, how was a man supposed to seduce a woman into accepting his proposal if they could never be alone?

She would accept his proposal soon enough, he told himself. In his arms by day, in his bed by night, she would soon realize she could not challenge his will. She had no choice but to become his bride.

In the meantime, there was no reason to slow down on his plan to get her pregnant…

They spent a great deal of time in bed. A good thing,

because they couldn't leave the villa without an entourage. Paolo almost felt like a prisoner in his own house.

Still, she was worth it.

Isabelle, on the other hand, took the paparazzi in her stride. He admired her for that. She never complained. No matter the inconvenience or pain, she waved for the crowds, her smile always in place.

Paolo didn't take it nearly so well. She'd been right about one thing—the constant lack of privacy set his teeth on edge. But he'd wanted the most famous princess in the world, hadn't he? It was all part of the deal.

Still. He should have tossed that photographer into the sea when he had the chance, he thought with a growl. Then at least there would be one less of them.

He'd thought the frantic interest couldn't last. Their relationship was just scandalous and new. The hard-edged Italian-American tycoon stealing a virginal princess from another man on the eve of her reported engagement made great copy. Paolo told himself the interest would fade.

And yet the media furor only intensified. Two weeks ago a German tabloid had discovered that Prince Magnus von Trondhem was his secret half brother, and the news had landed like a bombshell all over the world. Since then reporters had camped along the road outside his villa, desperate for pictures, shouting questions at the closed windows of their limo when they left the gate:

"Princess Isabelle, why did you choose one brother over the other?"

"Yeah, was one better in bed?"

"Was it love at first sight?"

"Do you have any intention to marry?"

That last question was one that Paolo himself longed to answer—preferably while throttling the obnoxious reporter who'd asked it. *Yes,* he wanted to yell at them. *We're going to marry. Leave her the hell alone.*

But throughout it all Isabelle was calmness and grace personified. One hot day she even ordered lemonade and teacakes be taken to the reporters camped outside the villa's gate.

"Why?" Paolo had demanded incredulously. "Let them leave. Or die of thirst," he'd muttered, only half-joking.

She'd just given him a rather wistful smile. "Do you really want them to write stories about us in that mood? We can't control what they write about us. But we can try to influence their opinion."

Sure enough, the stories posted the next day were all about Isabelle the Kind, Isabelle the Bountiful, who still remembered poor reporters while living in sin with a rapacious Italian-American billionaire.

"See?" she'd said, flashing him a smile.

And he did see. Dealing with reporters and media was as much of a negotiation as sculpting a business deal. Only instead of trying to purchase a company, he was trying to gain percentage points in public approval.

Something he'd need to work on after they were married. But Isabelle had been doing it since birth. From now on, he decided, when it came to reporters he would follow her lead.

She managed reporters so well, he could hardly wait to see how well she'd raise their children…

Every day now he watched her. Wondering if she was pregnant. For weeks their lovemaking had been hot and furious. Each time he'd waited for her to ask for a condom, to ask why he wasn't worried about pregnancy. He'd already told her his intention. He would have gladly told her again.

But she didn't ask.

Which could mean only one thing. Part of her must want to marry him, in spite of all her stated objections.

Oh, yes. Their marriage would happen. Within weeks, if not sooner.

As he became wrapped up in their affair, playing hard and making love and sleeping in her arms each night, he respected her more and more. And he realized he didn't want Isabelle to just supervise his houses and rear his children.

He wanted her to be the heart of his home.

Home… He savored the thought. As a boy, he'd longed for a real home, the kind where people looked out for each other and celebrated holidays together. Family dinners. Teaching his son to play catch. Teaching his daughter to write her name. But to have a home he needed the right woman.

Now he had her.

Isabelle might not love him, but love came through in everything she did. She was all heart—and he realized that, foreign as it was to him, he needed that in his life.

Isabelle would be the heart of their family.

He would be the gate, keeping them safe, keeping them all from harm.

Isabelle was his now. No matter what she might believe, Paolo wouldn't let her marry any other man on earth. She belonged to him, and no other woman would do. No other woman had her grace, her fire. Her strength.

In Isabelle he'd finally found a worthy partner. A woman who challenged him both in and out of bed. A woman he could respect.

Finally he'd found a woman he could trust.

CHAPTER EIGHT

"WHERE have you been?"

Paolo's voice was teasing, almost tender, as he came up behind Isabelle in the foyer of the villa. He wrapped his arms around the waist of her demure white sundress of eyelet lace. "You've been gone for hours."

She whirled around in his arms, hiding the brown paper bag behind her back. "I was busy at the palace," she said, unable to look him in the eye. "I had breakfast with Alexander, then a meeting with the French ambassador."

Pulling back, he frowned at her. "I called the palace. They said you left an hour ago."

"Oh. Yes." She gave a feeble attempt at a laugh. "I forgot. After I finished speaking with Monsieur Fournier, I went out with Milly."

Alexander's nanny, only a few years older than Isabelle, was the one who'd gone to the drugstore to buy the test. She was the only one she could count on not to sell the story.

Isabelle's chic goddess sandals tapped nervously against the mosaic floor.

"Rough day at the palace?" His voice was sympathetic as he rubbed her shoulders with his strong hands. "Your mother keeps you busy."

"Avoiding her keeps me busy." She gave him a weak smile. "You've been busy too, training for the race and planning Caretti Motors' expansion."

"Valentina is bringing me construction bids right now," he said. "She should arrive in about an hour."

"Oh. Valentina. Good." Just what she needed—to be faced with Paolo's devastatingly gorgeous redheaded secretary at the very moment when she herself wanted to stick her head down the toilet. "Valentina is a charming person," she managed. "So stylish and…smart."

She despised the way her voice trembled. Would he notice? Would he dèmand to know what she was hiding behind her back? The telltale evidence was in her hand right now, barely covered by brown paper.

"So you don't mind if I work until the race starts?"

She gave him a faltering smile. "I have to spend the afternoon at the palace anyway. It's my mother's birthday. She'll disinherit me if I don't go for a visit."

"Ah. Guess it's time to bite the bullet." He gave her a cocky grin. "Think there's anything in particular she wants to discuss with you?"

With a gulp, she looked down at the floor. "Perhaps."

She was trying not to think about the conversation that awaited her—the lecture she'd managed to avoid for weeks. But at the moment even that seemed easy to endure compared to her newest fear…

"I'll miss you." His smile became sultry and predatory as he looked down at her. He looked handsome in a black T-shirt and dark jeans, tanned and fit from their hours spent sunbathing together on his yacht and driving along the coast. "It'll take at least an hour for me to properly bid you farewell."

She swallowed. Normally, spending an hour in bed with Paolo was the most exquisite enjoyment she could imagine, but she just couldn't do it. Not now. Not when her whole future was hanging by a thin line.

It's not possible, she told herself for the hundredth time. It can't be. Once I take the test I'll see I was ridiculous to even worry about it.

She couldn't be pregnant.

She was Princess of San Piedro, second in line to the throne. She couldn't have allowed herself to get pregnant again. By the same man.

Without love.

Without marriage.

She wasn't eighteen anymore. She was constantly followed by press. If she were pregnant, this time she wouldn't be able to hide it. She would be scorned and mocked around the world. Just taking Paolo as her lover had already created shock around the world, causing damage to her image. To her country. And, she feared, to Alexander.

Alexander—her cheeks flamed just picturing how

the scandal would affect him if she were pregnant by her Italian-American lover. How it would affect her innocent babe.

There's no baby! She shouted at herself. Paolo's had a vasectomy! But her hands shook, crumpling the top of the paper bag as she turned away from him.

"I'm…just not in the mood," she said, and it wasn't even a lie. "I'd better go. I'll see you at the Grand Prix."

She'd never turned Paolo down for sex before. Not once. She could feel his surprise as he watched her.

"As you wish," he said after a pause. His voice sounded awkward, stilted. "I need to test-drive the engine adjustments anyway. I'll give you a ride to the palace."

"That's not necessary," she said, still not meeting his gaze. "I'll see you at the race."

He grabbed her wrist as she turned to leave. "What's wrong, Isabelle?"

"Nothing." *Just that you have a secret child and might soon have another…*

"Really?" His tone was decidedly cooler in turn.

She had to get out of here. Once she took the test she would tell him her fears, and they'd both have a good laugh. Once she knew she wasn't pregnant everything would be all right again, and she could cheer him on to victory in the race.

She'd promised herself that she would end their romance after the Grand Prix, but now that it was here she couldn't do it. She wanted to put it off. Just a few more days. A few more weeks.

Nine more months?

Her breath caught in her throat.

If she were pregnant, it meant that Paolo had either casually risked pregnancy, not caring how it might affect her, or that he'd deliberately done it to cause her pain.

He wouldn't do that, she told herself angrily. He wouldn't ruin my life and an innocent child's life. I believed the worst about him once. I'm not going to do it again.

I love him…

"Bella?"

She ripped her arm from his grasp. She couldn't take the test here. She couldn't even look at Paolo's face until she knew for sure. "I have to go."

"Fine. I'll tell Yves and Serge that you want to leave."

She could feel hurt mixed with anger radiating in waves from him. But she didn't stop to wait for her bodyguards. She needed to be alone. Going to the garage, she climbed into her custom pink MINI COOPER convertible, put on her sunglasses and wrapped her hair in a scarf. As she drove past the paparazzi camped outside the villa, she was glad her face was hidden behind the big black lenses.

She didn't want anyone to see the fear in her eyes.

I'm not pregnant, she repeated to herself numbly. *I can't be.*

But she was late.

She drove faster along the coast road, evading a persistent photographer on a Vespa behind her. For a moment driving made her forget her fears as she focused on the skills Paolo had taught her.

Accelerate, brake, turn.

Accelerate, brake, turn.

But once she was behind the gate of the *palais*, safely past the cobblestoned courtyard with her car tucked into the royal stables, she picked up her carryall and stared at the crumpled brown paper inside with mounting fear. Then she slammed the car door behind her and started toward her private apartments in the palace.

She found her way blocked by Chancelier Florent, her mother's advisor.

"Thank you for coming, Your Serene Highness," he said sternly in French, in the tone that had used to terrify her in childhood. "The Queen Regent is anxious to discuss your marriage prospects."

She rubbed her forehead. "Yes, I know. I'll…be there in just a moment."

"It's Her Majesty's birthday. Perhaps you've forgotten?"

"No, I haven't forgotten. I just have something to do in my own apartments first…"

"I will follow you then, *mademoiselle*." His voice dripped disapproval. "And wait until I can escort you into the Queen Regent's presence."

Take the pregnancy test with dour-faced Florent waiting outside her bathroom door? She knew when she was beaten. "Very well." Tucking her handbag safely under her arm, she pulled the scarf off her head with a resigned sigh. "I will see her now."

Queen Clothilde's harsh lecture in the *salon de réception* soon made Isabelle long to return to Florent's friendly warmth.

"I cannot believe that any daughter of mine would be such a *fool*." The slender gray-haired woman paced back and forth across the dais. "He cheated on you once already. He nearly destroyed you. Was once not enough?"

"He's not going to hurt me, *Maman*." But even as she defended Paolo, Isabelle didn't know whether she could believe her own words. Was she pregnant? After all his talk about honesty, could he have lied about his vasectomy?

"That you would even *dream* of letting that man back into our lives…"

"He saved Alexander. Does that mean nothing to you?"

The Queen stopped. "Of course it means something," she snapped. "I am grateful beyond words that he saved my grandson from that kidnapper. But it would have been more appropriate to reward him with a note and a gift—not your virtue!"

Isabelle met her mother's steely gaze. "You know he took that long ago."

The Queen Regent clenched her jaw. "And while you flaunt your affair, our country is suffering. We need you to marry a man who can make difference."

"I love Paolo, *Maman*," she said quietly.

Her mother drew in a ragged breath, then sank wearily into the throne.

"He is a heartless playboy, *ma fille*. He will string you along and…"

"He's asked me to marry him," Isabelle said.

Clothilde looked at her in amazement. "And what was your answer?"

"It was no," she whispered.

"Thank the good stars for that." Her mother shook her head. "You cannot marry Paolo Caretti. You realized that long ago. It's why you gave away your child. Do you think to reverse your decision now, and make an alliance with his family? He has no manners. No morals. He's nothing. A *nouveau riche* motorcycle racer, barely fit to be a chauffeur. The son of a common thug—"

"But Paolo's not like his father!" she cried. "He's different. He can be trusted. I think. I hope…"

"Is that so?" The Queen Regent pressed her advantage. "Have you trusted him enough to tell him the truth about Alexander?"

Isabelle swallowed, fell silent.

Her mother waved a hand. "You've grown old before your time. I see now that you need time to enjoy yourself before settling down. So I forgive you. Your *paramour* is racing in the Motorcycle Grand Prix this afternoon, *oui*? His participation brings desirable attention to San Piedro. So wait until after the race. But tomorrow," she said sharply, "you will end it. You will go to Prince Magnus and beg him to take you back."

"But I don't love Magnus!"

"Consider that the best wedding gift you'll ever

receive," her mother said coldly. Florent came into the room, and she waved Isabelle's dismissal. "Go. I have no desire to watch you weep into my birthday cake all afternoon. Go and enjoy one last night with your mechanic. But tomorrow I expect you to do your duty."

Isabelle left the *salon de réception* feeling despondent and cold. It was exactly what she'd known her mother would say. And she couldn't even argue.

But Isabelle wanted to trust Paolo. She'd already given him her heart. After weeks of spending her days and nights with him she hadn't found a single flaw.

Except for the fact that he would never love her...

"Aunt Isabelle!"

She stopped when she heard the childish whisper. Turning, she saw Alexander peeking around a suit of armor down the hall. She held out her arms and the little boy threw himself into her embrace. She held him close for a moment, relishing the feel of his thin arms around her, the smell of his shampoo. After enduring her mother's tirade, Isabelle wanted to hold her son in her arms forever. But when he pulled back she reluctantly let him go.

Blinking back tears, she looked down at him in wonder. "How is it possible? I swear you've grown since breakfast!"

"I know," he said, straightening with dignity. "An inch in the last month. Milly has been letting me eat all the ice cream I want. Hard just keeping meat on my bones, she says."

"I'm glad," she replied with a smile. She couldn't stop looking at him. Her son. Her baby. At nine years old, he was still a child, but quickly growing into a man. And looking more like his father every day.

Alexander frowned. "Is *Grandmère* angry with you?"

"Yes."

"Why?"

She rubbed the boy's back with a sigh. "She wants me to marry someone. But now," she said wistfully, "I realize I want to marry someone else."

"You mean Paolo Caretti?"

She drew back in shock. "How do you know about him?"

"Of course I know him. I'm not a baby, Aunt Isabelle. He saved me in the farmhouse from that bad man. I like Signor Caretti. He's nice. And in the garden you seemed to like him too." He tilted his head. "Why doesn't *Grandmère* like him?"

She cleared her throat. "It's a long story."

Alexander squared his shoulders. "Well, if you want Signor Caretti, I will give you my permission. As your King," he said grandly. "Not just my permission—my *blessing*."

For a moment Isabelle just stared at him. Her son was giving her permission to marry.

Images of the last weeks of joy came rushing at her. She could marry Paolo? She could have that—for a lifetime?

Her whole idea of existence suddenly crashed down around her. Perhaps he didn't love her, but her love might be enough for both of them. He cared for her. Could that be enough? As long as she could trust him not to hurt her...as long as she could trust him to protect Alexander...

Mon dieu, she thought. The pregnancy test would prove he'd never lied to her. It would come back negative and prove she could trust him.

In a rush of emotion, she kissed the top of the boy's head.

"Thank you," she whispered.

But when she reached the elegant marble bathroom of her private apartments all thoughts of trusting Paolo flew from her mind. She took the test and realized her future didn't hang just on one thin line, but two.

She was pregnant.

Pregnant.

She whispered the word soundlessly, her hands trembling as she drove her MINI COOPER out of the palace gates. She'd wanted to trust Paolo. She'd almost convinced herself that she could.

And he'd lied to her.

Or had he? She searched her mind. He'd never *said* he'd had a vasectomy. He'd only said that she'd never find herself pregnant and alone.

That suddenly had a whole different meaning.

I'm planning to seduce you, get you pregnant with my child, and make you my bride.

He hadn't lied to her. He'd flat-out told her the truth from the beginning.

Her fingers clenched on the steering wheel as she drove down the steep cobblestoned street. Sunlight was everywhere, the warmth of the Riviera smiling on the southern Mediterranean port, but she felt ice-cold.

She saw a Vespa pull out from a corner to follow her. The paparazzi were relentless, as always.

She sucked in her breath.

What would the papers say when they found out she was pregnant?

What would her mother say?

And Alexander... Would he hear the whispered insults? Would he be forced to defend his aunt's apparently easy virtue?

She was suddenly desperate to feel Paolo's arms around her. She drove more quickly along the road, trying to outrun the Vespa behind her. Paolo would make this all better. He would solve everything. Somehow he would convince her to forgive him.

After all, he hadn't lied to her. He'd told her the truth. She just hadn't believed him.

Nothing had changed. She could still marry him. *Why shouldn't I?* She thought defiantly. She loved him. She was pregnant with his child.

She could perhaps endure a marriage with love only on her side—if only she could trust him not to betray her. As long as he was faithful, she thought she could love enough for both of them...

Paolo's not a liar, she whispered through chattering teeth as she arrived at San Cerini. *I can trust him.*

She parked near the stone fountain in the circular driveway. Her eyes fell upon the large statue of the phoenix rising from the waves, clutching a sea dragon in its sharp claws. The bird's beady stone eye seemed fixed on her as she walked toward the steps. As if it were trying to tell her something.

I can be that phoenix. I can rise above my fear, she told herself. *I can forget the past. I love Paolo. I can tell him everything. I can even tell him about Alexander. He will forgive me. I can trust him...*

Stepping from the sunlight into the shaded cool of the foyer, she felt a rush of strength and hope. She was pregnant, but it wasn't a disaster after all—it was her chance to do everything right. Just because every man she'd ever known had been faithless it was no reason to be afraid. Paolo was different. He was honorable and true and—

Where was he?

She stopped in the doorway of his empty study. He'd said he would be working with Valentina on the factory bids. He'd been so busy with Isabelle lately his work had started to suffer. He was probably trying to get through as much of it as possible so he could focus on the motorcycle race later. And then he'd be free for hours of laughter and making love...

"Paolo?" she called.

"I think he's upstairs, *signorina*," a passing maid told her shyly.

"Grazie." She ran up the stairs toward their bedroom.

Perhaps he was taking a nap; she'd certainly done her best to wear him out last night. If he was asleep, she would take off her clothes, climb in under the covers and thoroughly wake him. She grinned to herself happily. Then she would tell him her news, the way she'd dreamed of sharing similar news ten years ago...

"Don't worry," she heard him say. "She won't be back until tomorrow."

Isabelle stopped abruptly outside the bedroom door.

"Are you sure?" It was Valentina's voice, a sultry Czech purr.

"Of course I'm sure," he said impatiently. "Isabelle will never know. And even if she did, she likes to share. So come here. Yeah, there. This is what you want. I'm tired of hearing you beg. Do you want me to wait outside while you take off your clothes?"

"No," the woman sighed. "I trust you..."

Frost spread up and down Isabelle's body. She could barely feel her fingers or toes as she gently pushed the bedroom door aside.

The redheaded secretary was standing near the closet. Her blouse had been tossed carelessly to the floor. She was wearing only a skirt, high heels, and a sexy bra that pushed her enormous breasts halfway up to her neck.

Paolo was sitting by the window, his laptop on his knees. No doubt waiting for Valentina to come round and entertain him with a sexy striptease while she moaned out figures from the quarterly reports.

Isabelle's whole body felt like ice. Especially her heart.

Slowly, she turned to face Paolo.

"Isabelle." He rose to his feet. "You're home early." He cleared his throat with what he no doubt hoped was a charming grin. "I hope you don't mind, but I wanted Valentina—"

"Oh, but I do mind," she said hoarsely, swaying on her feet. Blood was rushing through her ears like a torrent of rain. She looked from the father of her children to his half-naked secretary. "How could you?" she whispered. "How could you do this to me?"

The expression on Paolo's face changed.

"No," he said sharply. "*No.* Wait."

But she couldn't wait. With a sob, she turned on her heel. She ran down the stairs and out the front door.

As she started the engine of her car, the large stone phoenix grinned down at her. Only now she realized her mistake.

She wasn't the phoenix.

She was the dragon in its claws.

"Isabelle!" she heard Paolo shout behind her. In her rearview mirror, she saw him running down the steps toward her. But she didn't wait. She gunned the motor and drove right out of the gate. She didn't slow down until she reached the von Trondhem villa half a mile away.

She would do her duty. She would marry Magnus.

She never, ever wanted to see Paolo again…

A whimper escaped her lips. She stopped her car, staring at the von Trondhem crest on the wrought-iron gate.

She couldn't do it.

No matter how Paolo had treated her. She loved him. She couldn't marry anyone else. She couldn't betray Paolo the way he'd betrayed her.

She pounded on her steering wheel in frustration, then with a sob she leaned her head against the dashboard and cried.

CHAPTER NINE

"WHERE's the Princess, *signore*?"

Paolo looked up from a motorcycle engine, a wrench still in his hand. His racing bike had already been taken to San Piedro by his team. For the last hour he'd been taking out his aggression on the 1962 Triumph Bonneville he'd been patiently restoring over the last year. Motor oil coated his fingers, slick like blood.

"I don't know where Isabelle is," he muttered, lowering himself back under the engine. "And I don't care."

He'd thought he'd been doing a kindness for Valentina by letting her try on Isabelle's dress. His secretary had gushed about it for an hour, and he'd been frankly sick of hearing her talk about the photos of Isabelle at Cannes. It was just a dress, for God's sake. Isabelle wouldn't care if she tried it on. She rarely wore the same thing twice anyway. Clothes were just a uniform for her—like his old mechanic's jumpsuit or his current Savile Row suits.

But of course Isabelle had taken one look at them in

their bedroom and believed the worst. Paolo had been facing the window, going through the numbers on his computer; he hadn't even *wanted* to turn around and look. Valentina Novak was a good secretary, but she wasn't his type—and even if she had been he never would have dishonored Isabelle that way. Not in a million years.

But when had Isabelle ever trusted him? Never. He'd never been anything but honest with her, but no matter what he did she refused to believe he was decent or true.

So fine. If she wanted to pout and run away, fine. He would be damned if he would explain a single thing to her.

Bertolli made a worried sound with his tongue. "I only ask about the *Principessa*'s whereabouts because I have just heard René Durand has escaped custody of the San Piedran police."

Paolo rolled out from under the engine. "What?"

"The police wanted to ask him about some recent art thefts, and he escaped during the transfer. It's probably nothing," Bertolli said hastily. "I'm sure he's halfway to Malta by now, on some fishing boat. Don't worry about it, *signore*. We should head for the race. It's almost time…"

Paolo's breathing suddenly came hard. "Does the palace know about Durand?"

Bertolli reluctantly nodded. "They're the ones who called me."

"Everyone is safe?"

"Yes." Bertolli paused. "But the *Principessa*'s convertible isn't here. Yves and Serge are trying to find her. You know that Durand had that grudge against her…"

"Maledizione," Paolo swore. Throwing down his wrench with a loud clatter, he leapt to his feet and headed for his fastest street-legal motorcycle. "Offer the police our assistance with Durand," he bit out. "If they don't want it, send some men out anyway. I want to know where he is. I want him found."

"Sì, signore."

As Paolo roared his motorcycle past his gate, he ground his teeth. *Damn her!* Why did she have to be so stubborn? Why couldn't she just trust him?

But beneath the anger his heart was pounding with a totally different question.

Why hadn't he gone after her?

Isabelle. Just thinking of her in Durand's clutches made him feel sick.

He loudly accelerated past the waiting paparazzi, who scattered like dead leaves in the wind. Once he hit the coastal road, he let out the throttle.

He passed her pink MINI convertible headed the other way. He had a brief vision of Isabelle: dark sunglasses, tight red lips, shiny chestnut hair blowing in the wind.

Then she was gone.

He turned his motorcycle so hard that he left a black scar against the pavement. Gravel scattered as he braced one leg against the ground in a tight hairpin turn. He caught up with her at San Cerini.

Not bothering to go past his driveway, Paolo brought

his motorcycle to a screeching halt. He knocked over the kickstand and stalked angrily through one of the open garage doors to where she was parking her car. Bertolli was gone and his mechanics had already left, so the garage was strangely empty.

Isabelle looked pale as she climbed out of her convertible. Her hand seemed to tremble against the gleaming pink paint. Looking at him, she slowly took off her sunglasses.

He wanted to yell at her. To demand that she never, ever go anywhere without him ever again. He wanted to knock sense into her.

Instead, he took one look at her miserable face and his whole body went rigid. Before she could say a word, he took her in his arms.

For a moment she tried to push him away. Then she sagged against him. He heard her choked sob, muffled against his chest.

"I didn't sleep with Valentina," he vowed, stroking her hair. "I've never touched her."

"I want to believe you," she whispered. "I want to."

"So believe me." He looked down at her. "You're the only woman for me, Isabelle."

Pulling away, she gave him a tremulous smile that didn't fool him for a second. She rubbed her nose, and her eyes were red. "I'm fine, really."

"Why are you crying?"

"It's hay fever."

"Like hell it is." He knew her now. Knew the way she

trembled, and the shape of her, and the way she cried out joyfully at night when he thrust into her. And he knew to his marrow that she was hiding something. "Tell me what's wrong."

She pushed back from him so violently that she stumbled and nearly dropped to the concrete floor.

He caught her. She weighed almost nothing at all. He had to convince her to eat more, he thought dimly. For the last few days she'd had no appetite, barely touching her food. He'd thought it wasn't his responsibility to make sure that she ate. Now he realized that it was. Everything concerning Isabelle's health and happiness was his responsibility.

"What is it?" he said quietly. "Tell me."

Covering her face with her hands, she fell against him with a sob. Shocked, he held her in his arms, rocking her gently against his chest like a child. Sunlight beamed through the garage's solitary window, shimmering on motes of dust floating softly through the air. At this moment even time seemed suspended.

And he realized how much he cared about her.

Enough to protect her from anyone—anything.

Even if she didn't trust him, he trusted her. She was the one person who would never lie to him.

The one woman he might even let himself…love?

"Did someone hurt you?" he asked in a low voice. "Was it Durand?"

If Durand had hurt her, Paolo would rip the man apart with his bare hands…

She drew back with a confused frown. "Durand? No. Why?"

"It's nothing," he said quickly. There would be plenty of time to share the news of the man's escape when her eyes weren't full of tears. As it was, seeing her cry was driving him so crazy he could barely think straight. He wanted to comfort her. He had to make her tears stop. "So where did you go?"

She licked her dry lips. "I went to see Magnus."

"Magnus?" His heart stopped in his chest. "Why?"

"To accept his proposal of marriage," she said quietly.

He stared at her for several seconds. His brain couldn't understand her words. It kept re-ordering them, but they didn't make sense.

He dimly looked at the tools spread across the garage, the wrenches and engines and pneumatic lifts. At the old Triumph Bonneville parked between his gleaming red Ferrari and brand-new white Lamborghini. They hadn't changed since the afternoon. They were still solidly the same.

So how was it possible that in that same space of time the rest of his world had been ripped apart without warning?

He wanted to hold Isabelle tight, to never let her go, to demand that she stay.

But he knew it was no use.

She'd made up her mind that he couldn't be trusted. And it was finally clear that nothing he did would ever change her opinion.

Abruptly, he let her go.

"Leave, then," he said. "I won't stop you."

Turning away, he started to walk out of the garage.

With a cry, she ran to him, blocking him from the door, throwing herself into his arms. "I couldn't do it! I couldn't even drive past his gate. I don't want Magnus. I never did. I want you, Paolo. *You!*"

His heart, which had been flash-frozen in his chest, abruptly started beating again. He could again feel his limbs, feel the blood rushing joyfully back through his body.

She didn't want to leave.

She trusted him enough to stay.

He sucked in his breath, looking down at her searchingly. "So you believe me, then? About Valentina?"

Biting her lip, she looked away. Her shoulders straightened as she seemed to come to a decision, and she looked him full in the face.

At last she was going to say she believed in him. That he was a man of his word. That he was nothing like his father.

That she trusted him the same way he trusted her.

The future was wide open before them. It wasn't too late. Perhaps they'd never be the same innocents they'd been during that long-ago summer in New York, but that was all right. Because now they both knew how rare it was, how precious a gift it truly was, to find someone who made you want to risk everything…

"You deserve to know." She closed her eyes and took

a deep breath. When she looked at him, her caramel-colored eyes swirled with emotion. "Whatever happens, you deserve to know," she repeated softly to herself. "You deserve to know."

"What is it?"

"I can't keep it secret anymore. I don't have the right. No matter what kind of husband you would be, you have the right to know about this."

"What?" he demanded, growing alarmed by her wide eyes, her pale expression. She looked as if she might faint. Instinctively, he braced her body with his own.

"Alexander isn't my nephew. He's my son." Taking his hands in hers, she clenched them to her chest and looked up at him fiercely. "Paolo—Alexander is your son."

"Son?"

She watched the blood drain from his face.

"Yes," she whispered. "It's true. Paolo, we have a child—"

His hands dropped hers. He staggered backward as if the concrete floor had just lurched beneath his feet.

She reached for him, trying to grab his hands, desperate to steady him. "I wanted to tell you. I tried to tell you!"

"No." His eyes were wild. He pulled away, not letting her touch him, leaving her hands grasping only air. "He can't be my son. He is nine years old. You wouldn't have…you couldn't have lied to me all this time."

"Please, Paolo. You have to listen!"

He turned to her, and his eyes burned like a raging

fire. "Your brother needed an heir to his throne, so you gave him our baby?"

"That's not how it happened!"

"You gave away my son!" he said, as if he didn't hear. "You took him from me. You tossed our baby away as if he meant nothing to you at all. What kind of heartless mother could do that?"

"Do you think I enjoyed it?" she cried. "Giving him away nearly killed me! Having him call me Aunt while he called someone else *Maman…*"

His eyes darkened, and she realized that she'd only reminded him that at least she'd seen their child grow up—he had not.

She took a deep breath, gathering her emotional strength. She had to stay rational and reasonable. It was the only way to make him understand. "I didn't know I was pregnant when I ended our affair. But we were young, and everything was against us. I was afraid to marry you. The differences in our social class. I knew you'd be mocked and scorned. You don't know what it is to be royal. You would have had to give up all your personal freedom…"

"And so instead you gave away our child?" he demanded.

"When I realized I was pregnant—" her voice quivered "—I tried to come back to you. I convinced my mother to give you a chance. I practically danced the whole way to your apartment…and then I saw…I saw you kissing that woman."

"That's your excuse for lying to me for ten years?" he said incredulously. "Because I sought comfort in a one-night stand?"

"I thought I couldn't trust you!" she cried.

"Right. Because I'm dangerous. The son of a criminal. You felt you had to protect our son...from *me*." He folded his arms, staring down at her with narrowed eyes. "And all this time you've been my lover, lying next to me in bed, you've never changed that opinion."

"I was afraid! Telling you meant risking Alexander's Kingship, his custody, his life! Did you expect me to ignore all that?"

"You stole my son!"

"I'm sorry!" she said, tears in her eyes. "I tried to tell you. But the more time I spent with you, the more I started to...care. I was afraid that if I told you the truth you would hate me!"

"You were right to be afraid." She could hear the hoarse rasp of his breath. "Because I will never forgive what you've done, Isabelle. *Never.* You abandoned our child. And by not telling me you forced me to abandon him too. You've lied to me for nearly ten years. Every day for the last month you've been in my arms. And still you kept your silence. Every night, sleeping next to me, you lied. Every smile, every kiss was a lie."

"I made a mistake," she whispered. When he still wouldn't look at her, she took her heart in her hands and slowly fell to one knee in front of him. The concrete floor felt cold against her skin. But not nearly so cold as the current of fear coursing through her body. Her teeth chattered and she barely contained a sob as she, Princess of San Piedro, did the unthinkable.

She knelt before him.

Clutching his hands in her own, she pressed them against a cheek wet with tears. "Please forgive me, Paolo. Please," she whispered. "You have to forgive me."

For a moment he was silent. She could feel him staring down at her. He pulled one hand down to touch her head, reaching to stroke her hair, as if to comfort her. Even now, after everything she'd done, his first instinct was to comfort her when she cried.

She held her breath, praying, aching to feel his touch…

But at the last second, a centimeter from touching her, his hand froze. "You still don't believe me about Valentina, do you? You still think I slept with her."

She looked up his body to meet his eyes pleadingly. "Just tell me the truth. I think I could forgive you if you would just respect me enough to tell me the truth."

"The truth?" He looked at her scornfully. "Why should I bother? You've already made up your mind."

"What else do you expect me to believe? I saw you in the bedroom—"

"I expected you to trust me," he said. "Believe in me. That's what I expected. But I see now that I was expecting the impossible." Grabbing her wrists, he yanked her to her feet. He quickly released her, as if touching her contaminated him.

"My God," he whispered, raking his hand through his dark hair. "I have a son. A son who thinks I abandoned him."

"Paolo—"

"Does the boy know?" he demanded.

"No. And I don't want him to. He adored his parents. He is still mourning them."

His dark eyes looked at her incredulously. "And you don't think he should know he has parents who are still alive? *Dio santo*, you want him to go through life believing he's an orphan?"

"The alternative would be to tell him that I gave him away before he was born, and that the parents he loved lied to him his whole life. Do you think that's better?"

Clenching his jaw, he looked away as if he couldn't even bear to look at her. "The truth is always better."

"You've never told me a lie?" she said quietly. "Not once?"

He ground his teeth. "No, Isabelle. Not once."

"You never had a vasectomy, did you?"

He stared at her. "What kind of question is that?"

"You didn't use a condom," she said bitterly. "And I never asked. I thought you were joking when you said you intended to get me pregnant."

"No," he lashed out. "I told you the truth from the beginning. I wanted you to be my wife. I wanted to get you pregnant." He gave a harsh laugh. "But it's a good thing I failed, isn't it? You'd likely have given our baby away to the first person you met."

It was like a slap in the face. "That's a horrible thing to say."

"You deserve it." His eyes were dark with hate as he looked at her. "Just the fact that I have one child with you is almost more than I can bear. Thank God we don't have more."

She could hardly breathe from the pain and hurt. How could she tell him that he had succeeded in getting her pregnant?

"You're so beautiful, Isabelle," he said. "But that's a lie, too. You're not beautiful. You're ugly through and through."

"Paolo, please—" Her voice choked on a sob. "I never meant—"

"Basta." He turned away. "I have to go. The motorcycle race is about to begin."

"No!" she said tearfully. "Forget the race, Paolo. Stay and talk with me."

He took his leather racing coat from the hook on the wall. "I'm not giving it up. Not for you or anyone." He gave her a hard, bright smile. "Racing is what I do. It's who I am. I don't have a wife to slow me down, so I'm the fastest in the world. I'm alone. So I win."

"Please." She clutched his sleeve, following him out of the garage. "You can't leave me like this."

"Oh, no? Why not?"

"Because I love you," she whispered.

For a split second his eyes widened. Then his expression grew hard, his eyes even darker and more full of angry shadows than before. "In that case there's one thing you can do for me."

"Anything," she said, her heart in her throat.

"You can pack all your belongings and get the hell out of my house." Climbing onto his motorcycle, he put the key in the ignition. "Expect a call from my lawyer about custody of Alexander."

And, gunning the motor, he left Isabelle choked by dust and tears in his driveway.

CHAPTER TEN

SHE'D gambled everything—and lost.

No. Isabelle put her hands over the flat belly of her white lace sundress. She hadn't gambled everything. She hadn't told him she was pregnant. He hadn't let her.

Just the fact that I have one child with you is more than I can bear. You're ugly through and through.

She covered her face with her hands as a sob rose to her lips. He didn't want another child with her. Fine. He would never know this child was his. She would run away, disappear, and he would never know…

But she couldn't do that. Alexander. Oh, my God. To hurt her, Paolo was going to try to get custody. He would destroy their son's life…

"Princess?"

A woman's voice, deep and breathless, spoke from behind her on the driveway. Not bothering to smooth the tangles of her hair or wipe away the tears streaming down her cheeks, Isabelle turned.

Valentina Novak stood in front of her, swaying nervously from one high-heeled foot to the other.

"What do you want?" Isabelle said hoarsely.

"I…I wanted to say I'm sorry. I just wanted to try on your dress. It was silly. I never should have…" She gave an embarrassed laugh as her cheeks turned bright red. "I never came close to fitting into it anyway. But you just have this perfect life. I thought if I tried on the dress I might feel…"

"Perfect life?" Isabelle gave a harsh laugh. "Which part of it do you envy? The paparazzi who stalk me to the bathroom? The counselors who arrange every aspect of my life? Or a palace that's cold even in summer, with threadbare antiques I'm not allowed to touch?"

"I meant Paolo," Valentina said quietly. "I would give anything to have a man love me the way he loves you."

Isabelle sucked in her breath. "Paolo doesn't love me."

"Anyone with eyes can see that he does."

"He doesn't, and he never will. He's said it to my face."

"Perhaps he's said that with words." Valentina tilted her head, blinking at her. "What has he said with his actions?"

A torrent of images went through Isabelle. Paolo's laughter, the way he held her at night. The way he insisted she follow her passions, whether it was making fettuccine or riding a motorcycle. The way he'd taught her to accept pleasure, to face her fears. The way he'd protected her. Believed in her. Respected her.

I will always protect you, Isabelle. I protect what's mine.

I'll always tell you the truth, even if it hurts.

Her knees suddenly felt weak. She nearly sank to the ground.

This whole time she'd been so afraid that he would betray her. But *he* wasn't the faithless one. *He* wasn't the criminal.

She was.

He'd loved her. And she'd betrayed him. Not just once, but many times.

Every time she'd kept silent about Alexander.

Every time she'd believed the worst of him.

Every time she'd run away from him rather than stay and fight for the truth....

He loved her.

She slowly lifted her chin. The warrior queens of her ancient line rose up in her blood. Power and strength flooded through her as she set her jaw.

She'd been a coward. But no more.

This time she would stay and fight. This time she would try to prove that she was worthy of him.

"Bless you, Valentina," she said, briefly grasping her hand. "Thank you."

She raced back to the garage. Climbing into her pink convertible, she dialed Magnus's number. When he didn't answer, she left him a message. "I'm sorry, Magnus, but I must decline your offer after all. I've realized I'm completely in love with your brother. I'll be there cheering for him today."

She dialed Paolo's number, but he didn't answer

either. Of course not—he was either lining up for the race or ignoring her. No matter. She put the key in the engine. She would go to the race. She would tell him the truth about her pregnancy at once. There would be no more secrets between them, ever.

She would make Paolo forgive her. If he scorned her apology today she would keep trying. Forever, if that was what it took.

She would prove that she was worthy of his trust.

And he would forgive her. He had to. He was her love. Her family. The father of her children.

He was her home.

She turned the key again, but the engine stubbornly refused to start. She tried again, then pounded the dashboard in frustration. She'd coasted back from Magnus's gate on gasoline fumes, but she'd been so upset at the time that she'd barely noticed. Now, with the race starting soon, the cliff roads would already be a tangle of snarled traffic and closed streets…

She looked past the Lamborghini and the Ferrari to Paolo's sleek chrome Caretti motorcycle by the garage door, the key still dangling from the ignition.

"Oh, no," Valentina said, following her gaze. "Surely you're not thinking…?"

"It's the only way I'll make it in time," Isabelle said, hoisting up the white skirt of her sundress and throwing one leg over the motorcycle. "He gave me lessons. I know what to do."

"Just a few lessons, and you're going to drive along

the edge of those cliffs?" The redhead shuddered. "Aren't you afraid?"

Isabelle blinked, then shook her head. "Only of losing Paolo," she realized aloud.

As she drove out of the gate she was surprised to see that the paparazzi were gone. No doubt they were camped by the finish line of the race, hoping to get a photo of the Princess and the motorcycle champion together. Blessing her unusual anonymity, she drove down the cliff road as quickly as she dared, weaving around the steadily increasing traffic.

She turned to take a short-cut on a gravel path that led beneath the cliffs—a secret way to the palace that only the royal family and their bodyguards knew about. She smiled to herself, knowing she'd arrive in plenty of time. Perhaps she could even kiss Paolo for good luck before the race…

But as she went past a thicket of trees, a scattering of long, sharp nails punctured her front tire. The tire blew out, causing the motorcycle to suddenly wobble and veer wildly to the left. She threw her hands up to protect her face as the cruiser careened straight into a thick pine tree. She had the experience of flying, falling. Pain searing her head and arms. When she woke a minute later she was lying in grass, and she blinked in confusion up at the sky.

A man's head suddenly looked down at her, blocking the sun. He was dark and dirty, as if he'd been hiding in the forest for days, and his face was half hidden in shadow. But she recognized him at once. He'd haunted her dreams ever since he'd kidnapped her son.

"Hello, Your Highness," René Durand said. He gave her a chilling smile. "I've been hoping to catch you."

"I hope you're happy."

Paolo was pacing inside his tent, strangely unsettled. He'd gone through the final checks on his engine. His bike was already at the line. But something didn't feel right. He was tapping his helmet against his leather-clad hip when he looked up and saw Magnus standing in the doorway.

"I'm ecstatic," Paolo growled back. "It's another chance to beat you."

His half brother folded his arms. "I meant about Isabelle."

Paolo was still reeling at the news that Alexander was his son. He had a child—a nine-year-old boy he'd *abandoned* thanks to her.

"I don't want to discuss her." Paolo could hardly believe she'd claimed to love him. *Love*, he thought bitterly. Grinding his jaw, he changed the subject. "Oh, and by the way, if you ever accuse me of cheating again, I'll smash your face."

Magnus looked at him in alarm, then sighed. "You can be ruthless, you know. In the business world. On the racing circuit. You're just so much more successful than everyone else. You can't blame me for wondering if—"

"I win honestly," Paolo bit out.

Magnus put his hand on his hip. His own racing suit was angelic white and blue—a stark contrast to Paolo's devilish black and red leather. "I'm starting to believe that."

"Terrific," Paolo said. "Now, do you mind getting the hell out so I can get ready for the race?"

"Where is she?" Magnus looked from side to side, as if he expected Paolo might have hidden Isabelle somewhere behind all the gear. "I just want to tell her there's no hard feelings."

"Packing to leave, I expect." Paolo's closet had become full of her clothes over the last month. Pretty dresses, matronly blouses, seductive lingerie. Tonight when he went home they would all be gone. He would return to an empty closet and an empty house.

Good, he told himself angrily. Love him? She didn't even respect him. She'd proved that more times than he could count.

But Magnus was shaking his head. "No, old chap. She's here. She left me a disgustingly cheerful message that she'd be cheering you on to victory." He sighed again. "Like you really need the help, *hein*?"

All Paolo's uneasiness came rushing back. "When did she leave that message?"

"An hour ago."

Even in traffic that should have been enough time. More than enough.

He stuck his head through the tent flap. "Bertolli?"

The man came to him at once. *"Sì, signore?"*

"Have you seen Princess Isabelle?"

Bertolli shook his head mournfully. "No, but Signor Caretti, the race is about to start. You need to go to the line."

"That's my cue," Magnus said. He gave Paolo an elegant salute. "Good luck to you. I'll see you at the finish."

"Wait," Paolo said sharply. He turned back to Bertolli. "Have the police found Durand?"

"They're trying, but he hasn't shown up on any plane, ship or train list. He's just disappeared. Shall I send more of our men to assist?"

A sick, hollow feeling filled Paolo's gut.

Durand.

And Isabelle.

Both missing…

"You need to go to the line, *signore*," Bertolli said. "You're going to be disqualified—"

"So I'll be disqualified!" Paolo shouted back. "It's just a race!"

Shaking his head, muttering under his breath in Italian, Bertolli disappeared.

But Magnus didn't move. He stood watching Paolo, his eyebrows raised.

"Just a race?" he asked quietly.

Clawing back his hair, Paolo took a deep breath. If anything had happened to Isabelle he'd never forgive himself. He'd promised to protect her. *Sworn* to protect her. And he'd failed. He hadn't protected her from the photographer on Anatole Beach. He hadn't made sure her bodyguards were with her when she left the villa. He hadn't warned her that Durand had escaped.

He'd just tried to get her pregnant without her consent.

Maybe she'd been right not to trust him. She'd betrayed him by not telling her about their child—yes. But he'd made a few mistakes of his own…

A sudden memory flickered through his mind. Her accusing eyes, her sad voice: *You never had a vasectomy, did you?*

He hadn't paid attention at the time, but now the obvious reason for such a question made him gasp. He hadn't failed. She *was* pregnant. Isabelle, their son, another child…all hanging in the balance because he'd been too stupidly proud to admit the truth.

"You *love* her," Magnus said. "I thought you were just playing, but you really do love her. Enough to lose what you value most."

"Yes," Paolo said wearily. And that was exactly why he hadn't wanted to love her. Love meant loss. He'd been determined to be alone forever. Hell, he'd become the fastest motorcycle racer in the world so no one would ever catch him. But he hadn't been fast enough. In spite of his best efforts he'd fallen in love with her. He knew that now.

Because he'd never felt loss like this.

Going back into the tent, he grabbed his cell phone off a table. "I think René Durand might have her."

"Durand? The art thief?"

"He's more than just an art thief—" But before Paolo could open his phone to call the police, it rang in his hand. He looked at down at the phone. An unidentified number.

"Hello?" he demanded.

"I have something you value."

Paolo recognized the sly voice. "If you hurt her, I'll kill you. Not even the vultures will find your bones."

"Write this number down. Are you ready?"

Holding the phone against his ear, he grabbed a pen from the table and looked for paper. He motioned sharply to Magnus, who ambled over with a bemused expression.

"*Sì,*" Paolo said tersely. "Go ahead."

Durand gave him a long number, which Paolo wrote on his brother's white leather sleeve.

"As soon as I get the money in my account," the ex-bodyguard said, "I will tell you where to find her." The line went dead.

"What's happened?" Magnus asked.

Paolo snapped the cell phone shut. "She's been kidnapped."

"Kidnapped?"

"Contact the police." He tossed him the phone. "See if they can trace the line."

"But…where are you going?"

Paolo thought of the seagulls he'd heard, the strange echo of Durand's voice. "I have an idea where they could be."

"I'll come with you."

"No. I could be wrong. Brother, I need you to help me. To take charge. Get the police, the palace bodyguards— everyone you can find." He went out of the tent. "Bertolli! Get our men. Follow Prince Magnus's orders until I return. But first—transfer this amount to this account."

Magnus was talking on the phone, so Paolo just pointed at the numbers on his sleeve. Bertolli's jaw dropped. *"Sì, signore,"* he said faintly.

Grabbing his motorcycle from the nearby start line, Paolo pushed it through the crowds.

"The police will be here in minutes," Magnus called. "You should just wait."

Paolo threw his leg over his sportbike. "I can't."

"They're already on their way."

Forget the race, Paolo, she'd begged. *Stay and talk with me.* And he'd turned his back on her. Threatened her. Abandoned her.

Would he be too late to save the woman he loved? Too late to save their unborn child?

Paolo started the engine. *I love you, Isabelle,* he told her silently. *Just hang on. I'm on my way.*

"What do you expect to accomplish alone?" Magnus demanded.

Paolo's fingers tightened around the throttle.

"I expect to get there faster," he said, and with a loud roar of his engine he accelerated his motorcycle past the crowds in the race he'd trained for all his life.

* * *

"Good news," Durand called to Isabelle from the lowest ledge of the cliff above her. "Your lover has decided to pay. He really must care for you. If someone demanded a hundred million euros for *my* mistress, I would tell him to take her and good riddance."

Isabelle tried to raise her chin and tell him to go to hell, but there wasn't enough fight left in her. After the accident, Durand had used a stolen car to take her to this beach. He'd tied her bruised, aching body to a rock overlooking the place where she and Paolo had famously made love. It amused his sense of irony, he'd said.

"So you'll let me go?" she said through cracked lips. He had to let her go. She had to survive for the sake of her child...

"Maybe. If the money arrives in my Swiss bank account before the tide." He shrugged. "But probably not. Easier just to let you stay where you are. No witnesses."

She wanted to plead for her unborn child, but she knew that telling him she was pregnant wouldn't make him merciful.

If she'd only been stronger, more able to fight him off. If only she'd heeded Paolo's repeated insistence that she always travel with bodyguards...

Blindly, she stared past Durand, past the rocky cliffs above. "Paolo will kill you for this. He will—"

But her last word ended on a gurgle as a wave crashed against the boulder where Durand had bound her against the rising tide of the sea.

"Don't worry, I wouldn't dream of separating you,"

he replied absently, plugging numbers into his cell phone. "As soon as I have my money I'll send him to join you."

At his words, Isabelle struggled against the cords that bound her wrists and ankles, but she'd spent the last hour being taunted by Durand and battered by the tide. The water was already up to her shoulders, and every wave splashed higher.

She had to stay calm and think. She had to save Paolo and the little life she was carrying inside her. She had to think of a way. Something. Anything.

Still staring down at his cell phone, Durand gave a sudden howl of triumph. "It's there. The money's there. He's paid it!" He snapped it shut with a laugh, then looked at her. "I'm afraid that means I have no more use for you, *ma chérie*. I'll bet you're wishing now you'd let me take that Monet, aren't you?"

Another powerful wave crashed into her, sending water into her mouth and nose and lungs. Salt water flooded her eyes, it drenched her ears, and she couldn't see or hear. She coughed and gagged, gasping for breath as the wave receded.

But then, as she opened her eyes, she saw a miracle in watery colors as blurred as an Impressionist painting.

Paolo came out behind Durand from the dark shade of the trees. With a roar of fury he knocked the ex-bodyguard into the dirt. His cell phone skittered off the cliff, slipping noiselessly into the sea.

With a curse, the ex-bodyguard fumbled in his pocket,

drawing a pistol that gleamed black in the sun. "You're too late, you tricky Italian bastard. The money is mine—"

Paolo knocked the pistol aside. The two men fought, rolling back and forth on the edge of the cliffs above her. René Durand, with his broad shoulders and hard muscle, was a tough fighter, and wasn't afraid to fight dirty. But Paolo didn't seem to feel the man's punches or kicks. He was grim. Relentless.

"You should have just come after me." Paolo pushed him against the ground, bashing his head against the hard-packed earth. He punched Durand so hard that Isabelle could hear the impact against the bone. "You bastard—why couldn't you just come after me?"

"Paolo!" Isabelle screamed, and another wave crashed against her, longer this time. She couldn't see. Couldn't breathe. She couldn't escape her ropes. "I'm down here! Hurry!" The wave slowly receded, but only to her chin. "Save our baby," she said softly.

She took two long, deep breaths as another wave slowly built...

"Isabelle!" Paolo shouted. Tossing Durand aside like a ragdoll, he sprinted down the cliff path toward her, nearly skidding off the edge in his desperation to reach her.

Their eyes met, and she knew he wouldn't make it in time.

She was going to die. She and her unborn babe with her.

"I love you," she whispered, knowing he wouldn't be able to hear her over the waves and the pounding of his running feet.

The wave hit her, water caressing her face all the way up to her forehead. She held her breath as long as she could, but to no avail. She felt Paolo splashing around her, beneath the sea, desperately trying to free her from the cords that bound her to the boulder. She felt his frustration, his terror. She wanted to tell him that she loved him. That she was sorry she'd ever chosen duty over love. Sorry she'd ever doubted his courage and honor. She wanted to tell him that she was sorry she'd never given them the chance to raise their children...

But it was too late. Too late for anything. Her body took over. She opened her mouth and took a deep breath of the water.

It seized her lungs, drowning her.

Her body collapsed in a seizure and the world went black.

Paolo felt her die in his arms as he wrenched her free.

Carrying her through the water, he used every bit of his strength to reach the shore. But as he put her down on the slim margin of white sandy beach beyond the tide he knew it was too late. He'd lost her.

No.

He dropped to his knees. Turning her on her side, he pounded on her back. He rolled her faceup against the sand. He gave her two quick breaths, then started chest compressions, counting aloud. More breaths. More compressions.

She didn't respond.

She was gone.

"No!" he screamed.

He pounded her back, cursing at her, shouting at her. Finally he just crushed her against his chest as a sob rose in his throat he couldn't control.

"Don't," he whispered. "Don't leave me…"

He looked down at her pale, beautiful, lifeless face.

Suddenly she drew in a shuddering breath. She coughed, then fell back onto the sand, retching seawater.

She looked up at him wanly, pale as a ghost. "Paolo…"

Tears streamed unchecked down his face as he stared at a living, breathing miracle. "Isabelle. You came back."

"I'm pregnant," she choked out. "You deserve to know. And no matter how long it takes for you to forgive me—"

"I forgive you." He silenced her with a gentle kiss. "I love you, Isabelle. I was a fool. All I can hope now is that you'll forgive me for failing to protect you…"

"You didn't fail!" she said indignantly. "I'm alive!" Weak as a kitten, she coughed more saltwater onto the sand, then shook her head, sagging against his soaking wet chest. "At least I *think* I'm alive. I must be. Everything hurts."

He looked into her beautiful face, so bright with life, and at that instant it was like a lifetime of missed Christmas mornings distilled into one perfect moment of joy. "I'll call the doctor to make sure."

She snorted out a weak laugh, then clutched his shirt.

"I'm sorry, Paolo. Sorry I ever doubted you. I will never doubt you again. I love you…"

"How touching."

Durand's sneer caused them both to look up. He stood high above them, pointing his pistol at them from the edge of the cliff. "Since you love her so much, Caretti, I'll let you decide. Which one of you should I shoot first? You, or the Princess?"

Cold fury ripped through Paolo.

"Let her go, Durand." He rose slowly to his feet, stepping in front of Isabelle, who was still too weak to rise. "You have your money," he said fiercely. "Let her go."

"So all the *carabiniers* can hunt me down like a criminal for the rest of my life? I don't think so." He raised the pistol. "Which one first? You have thirty seconds to decide."

Paolo took a deep breath, clenching his fists. He knew he could rush the cliffs and take his chance with Durand at close range, but that would leave Isabelle and his unborn child vulnerable and unprotected on the sand.

That left only one choice…

He spoke in a low voice, for Isabelle's ears alone. "When he shoots me, try and make it to the water. Swim out to where he can't reach you."

"No," she gasped. "No…"

"Save our child." He looked down at her and smiled. "Tell him about me."

"No!" she whimpered.

"Time's up," Durand said.

"Shoot me," Paolo said.

"No!" Isabelle screamed.

But as Durand aimed his pistol Paolo saw a sudden flash of movement and color behind him. Two hulking shadows rushed him, and Durand was suddenly the one screaming.

"Over the side," a woman's cold voice commanded.

The rocks slid beneath Durand's feet. He tripped on the gorse, stumbling as the ground fell away beneath him. For a moment his hands lashed out, desperately trying to grab something other than air. The pistol fired into the sky, echoing against his long, loud scream as he fell.

The faithless bodyguard bounced against the rocks once, twice. His screaming stopped long before he was finally swallowed by the unforgiving sea.

Paolo recognized Isabelle's two bodyguards. An elegant gray-haired woman stood behind them, glaring at the sea with narrowed eyes, dignified and fierce with a mother's vengeful fury.

"No one hurts my daughter," the woman said. She looked at Paolo, then slowly smiled. "No one."

Two months later, Isabelle was pacing Alexander's private room inside the palace.

"Stop that, will you?" her husband said, glancing at her above his copy of the *Wall Street Journal*. "You're wearing tracks into the marble."

"I can't help it." Flopping into a chair—she'd grown

happily accustomed to stretchy, comfortable clothes, and the large velvet maternity dress she'd worn to Alexander's coronation was no exception—she glared at him. "We're newlyweds. I'm pregnant. I'd think you'd be more sympathetic."

"We all deal with stress in different ways," he said mildly, flipping the page. "Right now I'm coping by reading the business page."

She nearly believed him—until she saw the way his sleek leather shoes were tapping the floor. He was as nervous as she.

When Alexander finally entered the room, they both leapt to their feet like recalcitrant schoolchildren facing the headmaster. Their son was no longer wearing the ancient jeweled crown that had so recently been placed on his head by the archbishop—that had already been reverently taken to the vault that held all the de Luceran crown jewels. But after seeing his solemn dignity that morning, when he'd been crowned in the cathedral in a coronation ceremony attended by royalty and heads of state from all over the world, Isabelle thought that even without the crown Alexander looked taller. Older. Somehow he'd gained the stature of inches and years within space of a single hour.

"I'm sorry I had to keep you both waiting," he said with a formal nod. "Please sit down."

"That's quite all right," Isabelle said, feeling awkward.

"We know you're busy," Paolo said, tapping his heel.

Once they were seated, Alexander sat back against

his chair and folded his legs against the cushion. "I'm exhausted. I believe I'll send for some ice cream, if you don't mind."

"Of course," Paolo said.

Suddenly, Isabelle couldn't take it anymore. "Alexander, we have something we want to tell you." Licking her lips, she glanced over at Paolo.

He cleared his throat. "Yes. We do."

He looked back at her.

A lot of help he was, she thought in affectionate exasperation.

"What is it?" Alexander said. "Some problem with the factory?"

"No, the factory is fine," Paolo hastened to assure him. "We've hired half of San Piedro to get it done, and there's more new business every day."

"Then let me guess." The boy turned to her. "*Grandmère* has convinced you to have another wedding so she can turn it into a state occasion? I'll admit, Aunt Isabelle, that I was surprised you insisted on such a small ceremony. I was sure you'd be clamoring for the hugest wedding cake ever seen on earth."

Paolo snickered under his breath, no doubt remembering the four slices of chocolate cake she'd eaten last night in her first real pregnancy craving. But it was *his* fault she'd eaten so much, she thought indignantly. Paolo and her mother were in cahoots, always bringing her tempting treats to get her to eat a little more for the sake of the baby. It was a wonder that Isabelle still fit into anything at *all*.

Shaking her head with a sigh, she said, "Alexander, we've agonized about whether to tell you this, but—" she glanced at her husband "—we've decided the truth is always best. And so we have to tell you… That is, you should know…"

She looked helplessly at Paolo.

He reached over to take her hand. Immediately she relaxed. Ever since that day on the beach when he'd saved her life there had been no secrets between them. He was her protector, her lover, her husband. The father of her children. He comforted her in every way.

Except, of course, when he thrilled her. As he'd done in bed last night. Three times. She didn't know if it was pregnancy hormones, or the fact that he knew just how to touch her, but she couldn't get enough.

And, luckily for her, Paolo loved nothing more than bringing her to indecent shuddering satisfaction again and again…

She felt her cheeks go hot. He gave her a wicked answering grin that told her she'd have more to enjoy tonight than just dessert.

Then Paolo's face sobered. For a long moment they looked at each other, gathering strength.

He turned to face Alexander.

"The truth is, Alexander, you're our son," he said gently.

The boy stared at them, wide-eyed.

"I know this might be a bit of a shock," Paolo said, then rubbed the back of his head. "I only found out about this a few months ago myself…"

Isabelle knelt before their child, touching his arm. "I know there's so much to explain, but please, you have to know that Maxim and Karin loved you. Just as we do."

"I know." He looked at them, blinking in surprise. "I just thought we weren't supposed to talk about it."

Isabelle fell back against her haunches. "You *know*? What do you mean, you know?"

"Mama and Papa told me the truth a few months before they died. They said I was old enough to know that you gave birth to me. But they said never to speak of it, that even though they loved me with all their hearts it had broken yours to give me up." He glanced at Paolo. "From the moment you saved me in that Provençal farmhouse I wondered if you might be my father. We look so much alike. I wanted to ask, but I'd given my parents my word. But now—" he gave a sudden, impish grin "—you're the ones who brought it up, so I'm free to discuss it as much as I like. But first—ice cream. All this business of ruling a nation is exhausting."

Isabelle watched her son as he rang the bell. When a servant came, he requested, "Ice cream for three. No." He glanced at Isabelle's curving belly. "Four."

Isabelle sat against her husband, watching their son in wonder. Alexander already knew. He'd known all along.

And she realized then that everything was going to be all right. Better than all right.

Paolo's arms wrapped around her, and she felt him

kiss her cheek. "We're a family," he whispered. "That means forever."

"Forever," she agreed with a sigh.

And, leaning back against the man she adored, she could hardly imagine anything better than living in a palace with the sexiest man on earth, the son they loved, and a baby on the way—all that, with cake and ice cream too.

Her Royal Bed

LAURA WRIGHT

Laura Wright is passionate about romantic fiction. Though she has spent most of her life immersed in acting, singing and competitive ballroom dancing, when she found the world of writing and books and endless cups of coffee she knew she was home. Laura lives in Los Angeles with her husband, two young children and three loveable dogs.

One

Jane Hefner affixed an easy smile to her face as she walked into the entryway of Rolley Estate, her heels clicking against the white marble. One month ago, the Turnbolts' grand Texas compound would have made her normally confident manner wilt slightly. But that was one month ago, when she'd been a regular girl, living in a modest duplex on a quiet street of an even quieter beach town in California, working as a chef in a quaint little restaurant for a meager salary—a salary she'd hoped would someday earn her enough to open her own sand-side eatery.

One month ago, when she'd been just Jane Hefner—not Jane Hefner Al-Nayhal, the long-lost princess of a small but wealthy country named Emand.

With only four weeks worth of instructed grace and

poise to her credit, Jane shouldered her way through the thick crowd now milling about the Turnbolts' mahogany-paneled living room snatching up a variety of hors d'oeuvres and what her mother always referred to as "stiff drinks."

Rolley Estate was a magnificent place, a massive hunting-lodge-style home that sat atop a twelve-hundred-foot tall mesa overlooking four thousand acres of prime wildlife habitat. Just thirty minutes outside of Paradise, Texas, Rolley felt a world away from the big city with its quiet serenity, native game and rugged beauty. Jane had learned from her brother that the owners, Mary Beth and Hal Turnbolt, had purchased the property five years previously and had quickly transformed the once-unhurried surroundings into a modern showplace complete with three guesthouses, a lake and gazebo, a show barn, an indoor arena and a helipad.

Finding a relatively quiet spot near the brick fireplace, Jane sat, the gentle blaze behind her warming the skin of her back, which was laid bare due to the low sweep of her emerald-green silk dress. Lord, it felt wonderful to be alone. Even for just a few hours. She adored her new brothers and her sister-in-law, Rita, but in four weeks the only time she hadn't been engaged in conversation or some type of royal duty was in bed—and even then her dreams seemed to be just as active as her daily life.

"Shrimp?"

Jane glanced up and smiled at the friendly-looking waiter, remembering why she was attending the Turnbolts' party—to check out the high-society Tex-Mex

party food, wait staff and chefs in Dallas. She had a staff
to hire and a menu of her own to create. Baby Daya Al-
Nayhal's Welcome to the World party was just three
weeks away, and Jane was determined to make Sakir's
and Rita's jaws drop when they saw the spread.

Reaching for a large grilled shrimp, Jane eyed a small
bowl of untouched sauce beside the fan of prawns.
"What's this?"

"Oh." The young man bit his lip, his gaze flickering
from Jane to the sauce, then back again. "That's cilan-
tro. A cream sauce, I think."

He thinks?

Jane grimaced. If this guy worked in her kitchen
she'd be reading him the riot act right now. But she
didn't have a kitchen of her own anymore.

"Would you like to try it?" The question held a touch
of worry, as if the man hadn't tried the sauce himself
and wasn't altogether sure about the freshness of the
main ingredients.

"Thank you," Jane said, sliding a half dozen shrimp
onto her plate.

The sauce was divine, spicy and creamy and a definite asset to the shrimp. As she watched her uninformed
waiter walk away, then sidle up to an older couple with
his silver tray, Jane shook her head. She felt for the chef
whose delicious concoction was going unnoticed as the
waiter not only forgot to offer it, but also looked uneasy
about ingredients he couldn't even name.

Finishing off one large prawn, Jane wondered if her
search for catering staff might prove more difficult than
she had once thought. If the past week was any indica-

tion, then she ought to start worrying. Three parties in seven days and she'd found only one server who had made an impression on her. There was no doubt about it. She had to focus every ounce of her time and energy on the search, with no other interests to distract her. The problem was, she was finding herself distracted a lot lately. Granted, she was happy to offer herself as caterer to her new family for this one event, but that fulfilling surge of pride and purpose wasn't there, as it had been when she was a chef.

Jane's thoughts faltered as around her the noise in the room dropped to a dull roar. She glanced up and saw a woman in her late sixties with dark eyes and a very long, beakish nose standing at a makeshift podium, two priceless abstract oil paintings hanging impertinently on either side of her. It was their hostess, Mary Beth Turnbolt. She stared at the crowd as though she would dearly love to press some invisible mute button and get everyone to quit talking. But she did just as well by lifting her hands in the air and pursing her thin lips.

"Ladies and gentlemen," she began to say in a husky, though surprisingly friendly voice. "I would like to thank you for coming tonight. It's wonderful to see so many friends who support this cause. As most of you know, our housekeeper Beatrice's son, Jesse, is afflicted with Down's Syndrome, and Hal and I are just as passionate as his parents about funding research and treatments."

Jane saw Mary Beth turn and smile at a round, apple-cheeked blond woman sitting on the couch. A man Jane could only assume was Beatrice's husband sat beside her, his hand clamped tightly over hers.

Jane felt a pull of emotion as she fully realized the weight of the evening's benefit.

"We have a special guest tonight," Mary Beth continued, drawing Jane's gaze back to the podium. "He rarely comes to these events, though we all try to persuade him."

A trickle of soft feminine laughter followed this comment, and Jane's brows drew together in confusion.

Mary Beth beamed, her smile large and toothy. "Please help me welcome one of my dear friends, and the man who trained all nine of our horses, Bobby Callahan."

Jane followed the gazes of the party guests as all eyes flew to the doorway. It didn't take long to see what all the tittering and whispering was about. Promptly forgetting about the three remaining shrimp drowning in delectable sauce on her plate, Jane stared at the man walking through the crowd and up to the podium. He was in his early thirties, at least six-foot-three, brawny and barrel-chested, and wearing a black tuxedo that could barely contain him.

Jane's heart began to thump, and the easy blaze behind her suddenly felt like an all-consuming forest fire.

Unlike most of the dressed-up testosterone in the room, this was no society gentleman who stood before her. His cowboy swagger and rugged, untamed features under a short crop of dark-brown hair, clearly stated that this man worked outside, pushed his body to the limit and didn't give a damn about designer labels or fancy shrimp.

Jane remembered to swallow as Bobby Callahan faced the crowd with a self-assured, denim-blue stare.

He was far from classically handsome, but the air he gave off—that gust of leather and sunshine and pure-blooded male—easily made him the sexiest man in the room.

Jane watched as he adjusted the microphone to accommodate his height, then placed his large hands on either side of the podium. "First off, I want to thank Mary Beth and Hal for giving this party to help Down's Syndrome and KC Ranch. And I want to thank them for inviting me here tonight and allowing me to speak to y'all. Especially knowing how long-winded I can get." He paused, gave a decidedly roguish smile.

Jane stood and on bizarrely unsteady legs, moved into the crowd, closer to the podium.

"My daddy used to say," Bobby began to say, his sexy Texan drawl as big as the rest of him. "'If it don't seem like it's worth the effort, it probably ain't.' Those words have stuck with me, made me look real close, find out what's important in this life." He inhaled deeply, then continued talking in a powerful voice, "Most of you know that my sister, Kimmy, died one month ago today. She was the inspiration for KC ranch, and the most important thing in my life, and I miss her every damn minute. But her memory gives me a reason, a kick in the backside actually, to get up in the morning. Sure, she had Down's, but she never let that stop her. She was a tough one, bossed me around somethin' awful. But she was my best friend, and my inspiration." His voice fell from booming to restrained, and his grin vanished. He looked around, nodded at a few people before resuming. "Some of you know about KC Ranch—the morning grooming programs we offer for the little kids, the after-school assisted-riding programs and overnight summer camps for developmentally challenged, hearing-impaired, learning-disabled, physically challenged and visually impaired kids. Some of you have been real generous over the years, and some of you may decide to get real generous tonight."

There was a collective chuckle sprinkled throughout the room, though the sound was respectfully muffled. Bobby Callahan was absolutely riveting, grabbing the men's attention with his humor and easy speech, and the women's with his honorable words, and the loyalty and love he had for his sister.

"I believe, and I know my dad would've felt the same, that KC Ranch is worth every effort." His jaw tightened as he nodded. "Hope y'all do, too. Have a good night now."

The room erupted into applause, and Jane noticed that some of the women were dabbing at their eyes, trying to stop their fifty-dollar mascara from running. But she didn't keep her gaze on the crowd for long. Standing on her tiptoes, she strained to find Bobby Callahan, to see where he was, and if he was with anyone.

She couldn't get over his speech, those words, they'd torn into the open wound of her soul, the one that had never healed since her mother had told her so many years ago that she was going blind. It was odd. Many people had tried to talk with Jane about her mother, about her feelings and fears over the years. But Jane always had stuffed her emotions. She'd never had the time or the fortitude to go there in her mind and heart. But tonight, for some strange reason, Bobby Callahan had dug up all of those long-buried feelings.

Her pulse jumping in her blood, Jane spotted him shaking hands with a few people at the bar before grabbing two beers and heading out of the room.

Jane waited to see if anyone would follow him, and when no one did, she made her move.

"Spare rib in a port-wine glaze?" A girl in her early twenties with a killer tan and wide green eyes, a shade lighter than Jane's, held out a silver tray. "Goes wonderfully with the dry merlot we're serving tonight."

Jane shook her head, distracted. "No, thank-you." The server was perfect—in appearance, attitude and professionalism—and if Jane was on top of things, she would have found out the girl's name and phone number for the Welcome to the World party. But the focus she'd sworn to uphold just moments ago had evaporated when Bobby Callahan had taken the stage.

Normally she wasn't this interested. Normally she looked at men as a consideration for the future, possible husband material, a father to the three children she wanted to have someday. Normally she didn't leave a party to hunt down a tall, tanned and highly altruistic cowboy. But tonight she was pulled from the room by some unknown force she was too mortified, and frankly too scared, to name.

Ten minutes of searching and careful inquiries later, she found him. One floor up, and down a long hallway, a large flagstone terrace jutted out over the preserve. A soft, though oddly cool breeze for early fall, rustled in the trees beyond, and made Jane hug her arms.

The man whose words had been so heartfelt and animated downstairs was now standing against the railing, reveling in the silence of the landscape, drinking a beer, his back to her. Like some kind of deranged spy, Jane crept onto the deck and ducked behind a large potted plant. With no clue as to what her next move should be, she just watched him for a good five minutes as he downed both of his beers and stared into the black night.

Her right foot went tingly and her knees ached with the strain of her weight as she crouched there. She wondered what the hell she was thinking. Where had her good, practical and highly steady sense escaped to?

She glanced behind her. If someone saw her out here like this, she'd be the laughing stock of Paradise, Texas, and the surrounding counties, while embarrassing her brother and sister-in-law to no end.

What she needed to do was stand up, silently edge her way out of the plant and return to the party. Hey, if she really was desperate to meet Bobby Callahan there were about five more sensible ways of going about it.

"My daddy used to say," came a deep, masculine drawl, "'Never approach a bull from the front, a horse from the rear'." He turned around and eyed the potted plant as if he could see straight through it. "'Or a fool from any direction.' Which one you reckon I am?"

Jane went cold and her breath caught in her throat as a leaf pitilessly tickled her back.

"If you've got something to say, darlin', I suggest you come out from behind those weeds and say it."

Sweat broke out at the base of her skull where her dark brown hair was pinned neatly in a knot. It trickled down her neck into the bodice of her gown. What should she do now? Run for her life? Pretend she wasn't there? What if he stalked over to the plant, wrenched the leaves apart and caught her sitting there like an enormous ladybug?

Closing her eyes, taking a deep breath, she attempted to slow her thudding heart. But the yoga technique did nothing, and she forced herself to stand. Embarrassed to her very core, she parted the green foliage and stepped out of the massive plant. Shaking her head, she managed to say a lame, "I'm sorry."

Jane quickly saw that Bobby Callahan had a way of assessing a person with one easy sweep from toe to top. "Who are you?" he asked.

"Jane," she answered him, brushing a small clot of dirt from her dress.

He lifted one dark brow. "Just Jane?"

"Wouldn't that be easier?" she said dryly. "For us both?"

"Maybe, but I don't like being at a disadvantage when I'm talking to someone." Seeing her confused expression, he grinned. "You know my name? Front and back?"

"Yes."

"All right then." He crossed his powerful arms over his chest. "Out with it."

"Jane. Hefner."

A surly grunt came from Bobby's throat. "Hefner?"

She shook her head. "Don't look so hopeful. There's no relationship to the man who runs the naked bunny magazine."

He chuckled, the smooth, low sound reverberating off her skin. "You get that a lot, huh?"

"You have no idea." A thought of changing her name to Al-Nayhal had crossed Jane's mind a time or two in the past month, but Hefner had been who she was for too long now. It was her mother's name, after all.

"So, Jane Hefner, you spy on people a lot?"

"No," she stated, quite serious in both tone and expression. And yet, he looked doubtful.

"I don't think I believe that," he said.

"It's true. In fact, you're my first." The words were out of her mouth in a blink, but she still hoped she could somehow retrieve them because Bobby's brows drifted upward suggestively.

His grin widened. "Your first, huh? How was I?"

She let out a groan. "This situation is becoming more and more humiliating every second I stand here."

"Does that mean you won't be doing this kind of thing again?"

"Not a chance."

"An end to the spying?"

She nodded. "I think that would be best. Obviously I can't handle the outcome."

"And which outcome is that? The verbal sparring or the mild inquisition?"

"Mild?" she asked with a touch of humor in her tone.

"Oh, c'mon," said Bobby, his eyes glinting with a dangerous blue fire. "A man has the right—no, the obligation, to find why he's being tailed. Even when it's a beautiful woman who's doing the tailing."

He was unbearably attractive, rough and used and slightly broken in spirit. Jane stood there, brazenly staring at him, wondering what it would be like to touch him, to run her fingers over his face, that stubborn jaw, that slash of a scar on his upper lip. She wondered if he would be rough with a woman in bed or achingly slow and deliberate. She wondered if he allowed anyone to comfort him when he grieved for his sister.

Such strange, diverse thoughts worried her, made her heart thud in her chest, made her belly feel warm and liquid, as though she'd swallowed a cup of sweet honey.

"So, was there something you wanted?" he asked, cutting into her private reverie, a faint smile playing on his lips.

"No," she said quickly, then retreated, shook her head. "Well, that's not true." How did she put it? "I was…interested in you."

"Was?"

"Am," she said without thinking.

"Is that so?" Smiling lazily, he leaned back against the railing.

"What you said tonight," she began, walking gingerly toward him. "What you said…about your sister, and how you feel about her…it really moved me."

His expression changed in an instant. Where there had been an easy, roguish grin, a dark, thin line now etched his mouth. "So you're not really interested in me. You came to find me out of pity."

"No," she said at once, wondering how he could have

misunderstood her so, wondering what was pushing her even to continue with this conversation.

He took a swallow of his beer, then muttered tersely, "The sad dog with no tail, right?"

"That's not it at all."

"Darlin', I've seen it before, and I'm not looking for anyone's pity."

Above them, the wind played with the clouds, blowing the pale-gray poufs over the stars and moon, while casting Bobby Callahan's face in an eerily sensual shadow. But Jane could see his eyes clearly enough. Dark, and hot with emotion. A quick shiver traveled her spine. She'd seen that look before, seen eyes that masked great pain and regret. She'd seen that look in herself and in her mother, right before Tara Hefner had lost her sight.

She took another step toward him. "You have it all wrong, Mr. Callahan—"

"I doubt it," he interrupted.

"I wasn't offering you pity."

"What are you offering then, Jane Hefner?"

The question startled her. So did his expression. Unmasked passion—though from anger or sexual curiosity, she wasn't sure.

She stood on legs filled with water and listened to her heart pound in her chest. What *did* she want from this man? To talk? To exchange painful histories and hopes for the future? That was an incredibly brazen thing to expect from a stranger, now wasn't it?

A pang of need snaked through her, through her belly, up to her breasts. It was a completely insane moment for her as she realized she wanted him to touch her, hold her against him.

She looked him straight in the eye and said in apologetic tones, "I feel like an idiot here. This kind of thing is all new to me. Like I said, I don't usually follow men out of parties, spy on them and offer to—"

"Again the offer," he broke in, his gaze riveted on her, his eyes an almost stormy shade of blue. "What is it you're offering, darlin'?"

A picture of his body against hers flashed into her brain, but she rejected it. For the moment. "I just thought you might want to talk."

He stared at her blankly. The deep-cut shadows beneath his eyes hinted at nights not spent in sleep. Was it grief that kept him awake or the soft body of a woman?

"I know what it feels like to lose someone," she said, in a quiet voice. She hadn't lost her mother physically, but in her own way she had. They hadn't been able to do the same things, share the same things. "I know the pressures of a family member who has a disability."

He said nothing at first, just looked at her…or straight through her, she couldn't tell which. Then he shook his head and muttered a terse, "Not into talking, Miss Hefner. Thanks, but no thanks."

"Mr. Callahan—"

"I'm not looking for a soulmate, and I sure as hell ain't looking for pity."

"You keep misunderstanding—"

He pushed away from the wall and covered the few feet between them. "Have a beer on you?"

"No."

"How 'bout a whiskey?"

She shook her head, tried mentally to slow her pulse as his closeness, his scent, had her heart in her throat. "No."

He shrugged, then suddenly reached out, took hold of her arm and hauled her against him. "Well, this'll do, I suppose."

Jane never had a chance to think, much less react as Bobby Callahan dipped his head and covered her mouth with his. As his lips crushed against hers, she felt her belly tighten, felt her knees cease to hold her weight. There was no slow sweetness about his kiss. He was all passion and fireworks, hungry as a wolf and frighteningly demanding.

For the first time in a month, Jane felt her mind go. His passion, anger, fear, whatever it was that had called her to him tonight, fused into her skin, branding her.

He moved impossibly closer. He was incredibly tall, and although Jane stood five-foot-eight, she still had to roll up to her toes to gain full contact. When she did, Bobby growled, deepened his kiss, clearly spurred on by her interest. Gripping her waist and back, he tilted his head and eased his tongue into her mouth.

When he pulled back, left her mouth, his gaze was fierce, but vulnerable. "Unless you can give me more of that, darlin', we're done here."

Breathless, her body shocked with electricity and heat, Jane tried to find her sense of reason, but it was lost. Completely evaporated into a sky of need. She had been kissed with such desperation, passion and ferocity, it was as though Bobby Callahan wanted to consume her. It was as though she'd been offered a chance to morph into a hawk for one night and fly without any fear or reason. Her thighs trembled, for God's sake.

She'd never offered herself to a man. Not like this. Brazen and uncomplicated.

Swallowing every last bit of unease, Jane curled a hand around his neck and tugged his head lower. But before Bobby reached her mouth, he uttered, "You sure?"

"Yes," she said in breathless tones.

"Because this'll go way past a kiss."

"I'm counting on it."

His dark gaze flickered to the doorway behind her. "We can't do this here."

Truth be told, she didn't care where they ended up. On the deck, in a bathroom, against the tiles of a shower. She wanted this man, this stranger. A raw desperation filled her, rationalized her actions. It was complete and utter madness, but she wanted to fuse herself with the one person who had unknowingly touched her soul, the place she hadn't allowed anyone to touch in years.

"Come with me."

He practically carried her away from the deck and down the hall, his mouth ravaging hers, nipping at her lips, tasting her. Several times, he pushed her back against the wall and kissed her, his thigh pressing between hers, nudging at the pulsing center of her body. Time seemed to slow as they rolled and jostled their way to wherever Bobby was leading. Then Jane heard a muffled click as a door opened. The room was dim, just a faint cast of moonlight through an open window. She had no idea if they were in a bedroom or an office, and she didn't care. Bobby's mouth was on hers again.

She heard him kick the door closed with his foot. "It's not locked," she uttered, her skin itching to be touched by large, rough hands.

"I know." He eased her onto the bed, then shouldered out of his tuxedo jacket and white shirt. Jane stared, her lips parted. Bobby's face remained in shadow, but his chest, that tanned, thickly muscled chest, lay bare, greedy fingers of moonlight washing over him.

When he lowered his head and Jane found his gaze, she smiled. "This will be far better than a beer, I can promise you that."

"Better be," Bobby said with a lazy grin, though the muscles in his arms were as taut as pulled rope.

"You'll let me know…"

"I'll guide you every step of the way, darlin'." Bobby was over her in seconds, his mouth on hers. But he only allotted her a few deep kisses before his head dipped, finding her pulse at the base of her neck. He nibbled at the spot, drew his tongue up the band of muscle. Jane sucked air between her teeth and plunged her fingers into his hair. Down he moved to her collarbone, his teeth grazing over the sensitive skin.

A hungry growl escaped his throat as he tugged the top of her dress down. She wore no bra, and he quickly bent his head, took one stiff nipple into his mouth and suckled deeply. Jane gasped in pleasure and dug her nails into his skull.

Bobby tugged and suckled her steadily, making her toes point and her thighs tremble. Jane squirmed and pressed her hips up, against the mound of his erection.

Bobby eased down her dress and discarded it somewhere on the floor, then returned to her breast, laving slow circles around her aching nipple. His hand slipped down, over her ribs where her heart thudded violently, over her flat belly and under the slip of underwear at her hips. Pure instinct took her, and Jane opened her thighs in response. It had been so long—two and half years to be exact—since a man had touched her. She'd almost forgotten what it felt like.

Though she wasn't sure she'd really been touched before now. Bobby Callahan was an expert. He had skill and an erotic passion she'd never experienced. His emotions were raw and exposed as he ravished her body, acting as though he wanted to consume her.

His mouth was on her jaw, her neck, as his hand moved over the curls between her legs, his middle finger dipping into the wet seam beneath. Jane's skin prickled, and her womb pulsed in anticipation. She pumped her hips, urging him to use his hands, his mouth, anything. She wanted him on top of her, splaying her thighs as wide as they would go. She wanted him inside her.

But he had other plans.

Chuckling softly, he found the swollen peak hidden inside her slick folds, and flicked the pink cleft lightly between his thumb and middle finger.

"Oh…please…" Jane uttered, her hips and legs jerking wildly as she felt herself on the brink of orgasm.

"That's right," he whispered in her ear, quickly slipping off her underwear. "Let it come, darlin'. Let yourself come."

Her hips thrust up, over and over as he nipped her

earlobe and skillfully circled the pulsing, ultra-sensitive nub. Jane's breathing went ragged, and sensing her urgency, Bobby thrust two fingers inside her.

Jane's breath hitched, and she closed around him, her buttocks squeezing as electric currents ran through her, faster and stronger until she cried out, her hands digging into the flesh of his chest.

Her climax softened only a touch while Bobby ripped off his pants and sheathed himself. Without missing a beat, his mouth found hers as one powerful hand caught her wrists and lifted her arms over her head. She felt him hard and thick against her, pressing solidly against the opening to her body. With one long driving stroke, he was inside her. He was large, but her muscles clamped around him, took him fully.

No slow thrusts followed. No soft kisses or whisperings of what was coming next. Bobby was really worked up, ready to take his own release and Jane wanted to hear how he sounded when he came.

She wrapped her legs around his waist and thrust upward, meeting every stroke he gave her. He felt like heaven, so powerful, hitting a spot inside her womb so foreign she bit her lip. She tasted blood, but didn't care. Bobby was riding her hard and she was close to climaxing again. She lowered her legs, then slapped her thighs together under his body so she was holding him inside her as tightly as possible, while he bucked against the ridge of her sex.

It was too much for them both. Jane went first, her climax harder and richer the second time, and Bobby followed, pumping furiously into the tight glove of her body until he thrust hard upward and held, releasing a dark groan along with the wet heat of his orgasm.

Sweat dampened the sheets, held their bodies together as outside the moon once again escaped the cover of a cloud and brilliant yellow light beamed into the room, as if to remind them that their encounter was coming to a close.

But Bobby didn't seem to have the same interpretation of the moon's movement. He gathered Jane against him, held her tightly and brushed a kiss over her forehead.

Jane rested her cheek on his chest, listening to the beat of his heart. "We should probably get up, get dressed and go back down to the party," she whispered, the hair on his chest tickling her cheek.

"Probably," he uttered.

But that was all he would say as the minutes ticked by and his breathing slowed. He'd given in to sleep, and for a moment, she wholeheartedly wished she could do the same. To wake up with Bobby, maybe make love a second time before this whole mad fantasy of an evening came to a close. But then reality started to pinch at her. She'd wanted to be close to this man, feel his energy, his pain, his mouth, and she had. What she needed to do now was rise, brush off the tiny flecks of shame she felt for allowing such a tryst to happen and leave.

Her breathing shallow, she disentangled herself from Bobby's warm and heavenly grasp and sat up. It took her only moments to slip back into her panties and her dress, which had been in a rumpled pile on the floor. Then she looked back at Bobby Callahan. He looked so appealing in the washed light of the moon, his dark, powerful body wrapped in the sheets.

A flash of memory assaulted her, brought shivers to her skin—hands, strong and large, exploring, tantalizing.

She almost cast aside all her good sense and crawled back into bed with him. But instead she covered him gently with a blanket, grabbed her heels and slipped from the room.

Two

She was an untamed beast with a spirited attitude, but it was her elegance and beauty that had his muscles flexing and his pulse pounding in his blood.

The burnt-orange sun dipped into the horizon as Bobby came to a quick stop in the dirt. The charcoal-gray mare trotting beside him followed suit, snorting and smacking the ground with her hoof. Breaking two-year-olds could be a boring process; weeks of training on the ground before you even thought about riding. And even after you did get to ride, there was still not all that much excitement in store. Very little bucking, and a rare thing to take a tumble.

But this lady, Bobby mused, giving the mare at his right an appreciative look—she was spectacular. Her eyes darted with excitement, as if she wanted him to challenge her nature and instincts.

Bobby reached around, pushed his finger into the horse's shoulder, then ribs and hip, grinning when she quickly understood to calmly step away from the pressure. Not a day went by when he wasn't breaking or training a horse for someone. It was how he made his living, how he kept the ranch going and the kids coming. Sure, the private donations were large, but they were also few and far between.

Bobby pulled on each side of the mare's mouth, softening her jaw. This mare was for Charlie Docks, a sweet old man who had a place just north of Paradise, and to whom Bobby had turned for help and humbling support when his father had died all those years ago. He wouldn't be seeing a bundle of cash for breaking Charlie's mare, though. The man didn't have much, but he had offered Bobby a nice, reliable old nag for the kids in exchange.

"That Charlie's gal?"

Bobby glanced up, pushed his Stetson back. "Yep."

Standing at the corral gate, his foot propped up on a steel rung, was Abel Garret. KC Ranch's foreman was almost as big as Bobby, but a sight older with short, graying blond hair, pale-green eyes and a time-worn face. Abel had never told Bobby his exact age, but Bobby had guessed he was somewhere in his fifties. Thing was, he could stick on a grizzly attitude if he had a mind to, and sometimes it made him seem older. Folks thought he was a curmudgeon, but losing a wife to another man could do that to a person.

"Pretty thing," Abel remarked.

Saddle pad in hand, Bobby gently and rhythmically slapped the dusty pad against the horse's side. "Sure is. Smart as a whip, too."

Abel lifted a brow. "You're getting paid for this, right?"

"So to speak."

Abel chuckled, took off his Stetson and plowed a hand through his hair. "Couple chickens and a quilt?"

"C'mon, now. The man's got nothing but a good wife and ten head of Angus. He needs a respectable horse."

"Sure he does. But we don't got all that much more."

Bobby scrubbed a hand over his face, barbed with a day's growth of beard. He wasn't a rich man, but he was comfortable, had food on his table and a good business that did good work. "We've got thirty-two head," Bobby said to Abel, an easy grin playing about his mouth. "And you've been more than a good wife to me."

Abel frowned. "Shut yer face, will ya?"

Chuckling, Bobby said, "You know that you're talking to your boss?"

"Yeah, I know it."

Bobby moved down the mare's body, gently slapping the pad against her muscular legs. "Janice Young is coming by today."

"Who?"

"Woman I met at the Turnbolts' charity event last week." A shot of heat went through Bobby at the memory. But it had nothing to do with Janice Young. As far as Bobby was concerned, he'd noticed only one woman that night. A woman with smoky-green eyes, hair down her back and legs so long he'd have sworn she could've wrapped them around him twice—a woman who had taken over his mind and his body for the past seven nights. Hell, he'd barely dropped on his bed at night before the visions of her slammed into his brain, before sweat broke out on his forehead and the lower half of him went hard as steel.

"Right," Abel said, the late-afternoon sun still pounding him full force. "Forgot to ask you about that shindig. How'd it go?"

"Pretty dull." Bobby was closemouthed about women, even with Abel.

"So why's this gal coming by?"

"Her husband's law firm is donating ten grand to KC Ranch."

"Well, we can sure use it," Abel uttered, then paused, eyed Bobby with an amused expression. "She want anything in return?"

Bobby swatted away a nagging fly. "She's pushing seventy, Abel."

"Don't matter. Every time you come back from one of them things the phone is ringing off the hook. And I always end up talking to 'em, trying to make them lovesick fillies understand you ain't at home." He shook his head, rolled his lips under his teeth. "Won't be your damn secretary, Callahan. Didn't sign on for that."

"No one asked you to talk to them, Abel. Just tell them to call back."

Abel muttered something unintelligible that involved him ripping off his Stetson and swatting it against his worn jeans.

Bobby stared pointedly at the older man. "We're

lucky people are calling, and we're damn lucky to get the funds. It's for the kids, and don't you forget it."

Abel looked as if Bobby had sucker-punched him. "I'd never forget that and you know it!"

Bobby tossed the pad on the ground. "Yeah, I know."

Neither one of them said anything, just stood there, uncomfortable. It was strange. When Kimmy was alive, they'd been a family—the three of them together for dinner and holidays, working the ranch. She'd always made them laugh, made sure they didn't take themselves so seriously. Bobby and Abel had struggled somewhat since her death, trying to find their footing, trying not to be so serious.

The memory of Kimmy, of her beautiful wide face and huge grin, those sky-blue eyes and her bossy ways, slammed into Bobby, made him feel breathless with pain for the recent loss.

Clearing his throat, Abel, pushed away from the steel gate. "I could use a beer. How 'bout you?"

Bobby gave a clipped nod and muttered, "Sounds good."

Beside Bobby, the mare snorted, her eyes flashing with a readiness for freedom Bobby understood all too clearly. She'd done well today. He gave her thigh a light smack and hollered. She took off toward Abel, who quickly opened the gate and allowed her to run past him, out into the pasture.

The men walked side by side toward the main house, their strides equally long and purposeful.

"Got another one 'round the corner, don't you?" Abel asked.

"What's that?" Bobby said.

"Another one of them charity things."

"Friday night." Bobby was dirty and dusty as hell. Not fit to look at, kind of like most days, but he wanted to see that woman again, right here, right now. He wondered if she'd be at that charity event. He wanted to see if she was real, if those emerald-green eyes of hers would once again streak with gray when he kissed her. He wanted to taste her again, do things he'd fantasized about doing ever since he'd woken up in an empty bed.

He sniffed and rolled his eyes as they went into the house and headed for the kitchen. He was acting like a real jackass with all this frilly thinking. He liked women, liked taking them to bed, and that night at the Turnbolts' shouldn't have been any different.

Except that it was.

He grabbed two cold beers from the fridge. On most occasions, one night of good, mutually pleasurable sex was enough for him. But Jane Hefner had wreaked havoc inside Bobby, and he wanted to see her again. Not only because he wanted to touch her, but because he wanted to know why the hell she'd left him. The question consumed him.

"Is it a tea party or fancy-dress ball?" Abel said, taking a chug of his beer.

Bobby's mouth tugged with humor as he leaned back against the counter. "Barbecue, actually."

Abel snorted. "Pulled pork and Oscar de la Whatshisname."

"I'm going to plug KC Ranch. That's all."

"'Course."

Bobby tipped his beer in Abel's direction and grinned. "You want to go?"

"I'll work for you, Bobby," Abel said, real slow and deliberate, "I'll even answer the phone for you on occasion—but I sure as hell won't date you."

"I have never seen you so nervous. What is wrong, my sister?"

The man before Jane was tall, dark, wealthy, charming and decadently handsome—he also had her eyes.

Sakir Al-Nayhal offered Jane his hand as she stepped out of the limousine. "I'm fine, Sakir, just keyed up."

"Keyed up?" Under his brand-new brown Stetson, his thick black brows drew together. "What is this, *keyed up?*"

Sakir's wife, Rita, laughed and slipped her arm through his. "She's excited, sweetheart."

"Why are you excited?" Sakir asked as they walked the short pathway to the Gregers' massive ranch house.

Jane mentally rolled her eyes. If her brother only knew what was making her pulse pound furiously and her breath hitch. But of course he didn't. With all of his focus going to his new daughter, his wife and his work, he'd barely acknowledged that his sister had gone to a charity function last week.

Jane, on the other hand, hadn't been able to stop thinking about the affair at the Turnbolts', and about Bobby Callahan. Those raw blue eyes haunted her dreams, as did that scar on his lip that she'd traced with her tongue, and the hot-blooded, hungry way he'd made love to her. If that was not enough, her thoughts would stray from his physical attributes to the more emotional queries, such as, had she done the right thing leaving without a word? And was that why he hadn't tried to find her, to ask her out again? Maybe he wasn't all that thrilled with her or the time they'd shared.

Her heart dropped into the brown distressed-leather boots she'd bought just that morning, along with a pair of jeans and a faded denim jacket. She wasn't all that experienced in the ways of lovemaking, but she knew this much—she'd been dangerously passionate with him that night.

It was a risky thing to let your imagination run wild, she decided as they stepped inside the Gregers' home and settled into the jovial crowd of exceedingly wealthy cowboys and cowgirls.

The interior of the ranch house looked like something out of *Home and Garden,* the Texas edition. This was no easy homestead as she'd imagined Bobby Callahan's KC Ranch to be, but an elegantly rustic home with beamed ceilings, gleaming hardwood floors covered in colorful rugs, a massive brick fireplace and a wall of glass that was now retracted to allow partygoers to use the sprawling backyard.

As Sakir led them outside where the real party seemed to be taking place, Jane's gaze darted here and there, looking for the tallest, largest and sexiest *real* cowboy in the crowd. He'd be here, wouldn't he? Texas society went to everything, didn't they? And he was a pretty sought-after member of the Dallas crowd, though selective about which parties he attended. She only knew this because of what Mary Beth Turnbolt had said in her speech that night, and the few articles she'd read about Bobby Callahan and his ranch on the Internet.

Excitement and nerves were forming mini tornados in her stomach as a concerned female voice uttered, "Jane?"

Jane forced her gaze back to her family. Rita was watching her, curiosity lighting her eyes. And Sakir seemed to be assessing her. Jane gave them both a bright smile. "You two enjoy yourselves. I'm going to work now, see if I can scrounge up some barbecue to taste, and a staff to interrogate."

"We don't want you working the whole party, Jane," Rita said, smoothing the skirt of her denim dress. "Do we, Sakir?"

"Jane must do as she thinks best, but it is fact that Al-Nayhals are most content when they are working."

Rita lifted an amused eyebrow. "Most content working, huh?"

A slow grin worked its way to Sakir's full mouth. "Work is contentment," he acknowledged, nodding, "while pleasure, amusement and overwhelming happiness are what I get from you, dearest."

On a laugh, Rita said, "That's better."

For a moment, Jane watched the pair. Just as it was with her eldest brother Zayad and Jane's best friend, Mariah, Sakir and Rita made love look so wonderful, so safe. She envied them all, wondered if such a blissful state would ever befall her.

"I'll see you both later, okay?"

Sakir nodded, and Rita smiled, said, "We'll meet you by the dance floor for dinner in, say, an hour?"

Jane nodded. "Sounds good."

As they walked away, Jane grinned at her brother in his jeans and boots, so completely bizarre-looking on a man who wore suits, expensive sportswear or a formal kaftan 24/7.

But they were both a long way from Emand and its edicts, weren't they? she thought, walking around the backyard, through the gardens and over to a circle of barbecues, where a crowd had gathered, inhaling the mouthwatering scents of hickory, beef and pork. Yes, she was away from her father's homeland and her mother's place in California. She was here in Texas, trying to decide where her life was going, where she belonged and if she was ever going to realize her dream of opening her own restaurant.

She looked around. She didn't see any sign of Bobby Callahan, and with a flood of disappointment, she wondered if he might not be coming. She'd dressed with such care, too, wearing a pretty green silk blouse, and she'd even spent a good twenty minutes on her hair and makeup.

Forcing back the melancholy snaking through her, she decided to concentrate on the real reason she was at the Gregers' party—to taste and talk, and potentially to employ.

By eight o'clock, she'd hired two waiters and an assistant chef for Sakir and Rita's party. She'd also tasted some of the best barbecue in her life. She was very pleased with herself, and quite preoccupied as she made her way to the dance floor to meet her brother and sister-in-law—so preoccupied in fact that she hardly noticed when someone put a hand on her shoulder.

But the voice, that deep, sensual timbre, sent her reeling back to a night of careless, heedless passion—one of the best nights of her life.

"You look beautiful tonight, darlin'."

Jane turned around, her breath hitching. He stood before her, the man she'd given up hope she'd see tonight, an easy smile on his face. She looked him over greedily. He wore a pair of worn dress boots with faded jeans that hugged his powerful thighs and, under a caramel suede jacket, a blue shirt made his chest look a mile wide, while the color made his eyes pop.

He pinched the tip of his stone-colored Stetson and gave her a nod.

She felt like a teenager, all nervousness and thrill. "Hello."

"Hello?" he repeated, his grin, sexy. "That's all I get?"

Playing along, she cocked her head to the side. "What more do you want?"

He shrugged. "How about a few answers to a few questions?"

"I'll do my best."

"Want to tell me why you up and left me in the middle of the night?"

The question took the breath from her, and she forced a smile. "Jumping right into it, are we?"

"Why not?"

"All right." She shook her head. "I thought it might be best if I wasn't caught in nothing more than a sheet in the house of—"

"You were in more than a sheet, darlin'," he interrupted with a grin. "Had my arms around you, didn't I?"

She laughed. "Is my face red? Because it sure feels like it is."

"Your face is fine. Beautiful actually."

Warmth curled in her belly, and around them the room spun slowly, the noise of the crowd dulled. "As I was saying, I thought it might be best if I wasn't caught in nothing more than a sheet…et cetera." She grinned as he laughed again. "We were in a stranger's bedroom, after all."

"Hardly a stranger," Bobby corrected. "Hal and Mary Beth have been friends of mine for a long time."

"*Your* friends, not mine," she pointed out.

"They're very nice people. They'd have embraced you."

"Something that would've been good to know nine days ago."

"Ten," he corrected.

Jane stared at him, into those soulful blue eyes of his, and felt her breasts tighten, felt the muscles between her thighs tingle. So, he had thought about her, had counted the days, had wanted to see her again.

She cleared her throat. "So the Turnbolts didn't ask why you'd fallen asleep in one of their guest rooms? Naked?"

"They thought I'd just tied one on."

"Ah."

"They were real hospitable. Eggs, bacon and fresh-squeezed orange juice in the morning."

"Sounds good," said Jane, as behind her, the band leader announced a two-step.

"Not as good as a different morning activity might've been." He laughed at her stunned expression. "Before I scare you away with all my innuendo and good-old-boy frankness, have a dance with me."

"I don't know this kind of dancing."

He took her hand in his and led her out on the floor. "Trust me, Jane Hefner."

She smiled at him and slipped her hand in his. "But I hardly know you, Bobby Callahan."

He grinned. "Boy, we're gonna have to remedy that, don't you think?"

"Yes, I think so." She'd never flirted so outrageously in her life—but of course, as far as Bobby Callahan went, she seemed to be racking up a laundry list of firsts.

He moved with masculine grace, slow, sexy, making sure she was taken care of as they circled the floor. At one point the music came to a twangy crescendo and he led her into a slow turn, then pulled her back into his arms. "So you know why I come to these things—to help out my ranch—but why are you here? You're not a society lady, are you?"

"No," she said, slightly breathless as she felt his chest brush against the tips of her breasts. "I'm a chef."

"Oh, a woman who can cook," he said with a slight growl. "Be still my heart."

She grimaced and said with mock severity, "That sounds a little nineteen-fifties, Bobby."

"It's Mr. Callahan." He grinned. "Maybe it does sound a bit old-fashioned, but it's a lost art."

"What exactly? Cooking? Or cooking for your man?"

He released her hand, and touched the brim of his hat. "Don't get me wrong. This goes both ways. Women don't have the time to take care of their men anymore, and the men won't take the time to please and care for their women."

Jane opened her mouth to reproach this statement, but she promptly shut it. He was right, she'd just never heard anyone say something quite like that. In fact, she'd never heard anyone speak the way he did—honest, forthright and just plain sexy.

"So you're a chef," he said, giving her another twirl. "Where do you work?"

"So, you didn't try and find out about me, huh?" she chided. But deep-down, she held her breath for his answer.

"As a matter of fact I did. But the Turnbolts didn't know a Jane Hefner." His eyes narrowed. "Did you crash that party or something?"

She laughed. No, the Turnbolts wouldn't have recognized her name. They'd only known her as an Al-Nayhal, and if Bobby had tried to describe her that might not have worked, either, as they'd only seen and spoken to her briefly. "The truth is, I'd heard who the guest speaker was going to be, and I just had to get in to see him, no matter what the danger."

He grinned. "Well, I'm flattered, darlin'."

If he wanted to, he could say *darlin'* at the end of every sentence.

"So you didn't tell me," he said, catching her attention, once again. "Where do you work, so I can come in and—"

"Heckle me?" she joked.

"Have a bite," he said slowly, his eyes hooded and

slightly dangerous as they swayed slow and easy into the strains of the music.

Ripples of excitement ran through her, and she knew she was powerless to resist this man. They had serious chemistry, the kind the women's magazines were always having you take a poll to help you find. "Unfortunately, I don't work at a restaurant here. I was working in California for a long time, but I've recently acquired some new family members here, and a quasi-catering gig." She shook her head. "It's a strange situation, and probably dull for you—"

"Stop right there." He laced his fingers with hers, stepped closer, even as the music ended and couples left the dance floor. "Dull is the very last thing you are."

"Jane?"

Jane heard her name being called, recognized the man who spoke it, but had a hell of a time turning away from Bobby to face him.

"I think we've interrupted something," Jane heard Rita say softly, but with a ring of a smile, behind her.

"And I am glad of that," Sakir said coldly. "Jane?"

This time Jane turned, saw her brother and sister-in-law standing there and smiled apologetically. Rita looked bright-eyed and interested. Sakir, on the other hand, appeared intense and irritated.

Unsure of what was bothering her brother, Jane made quick introductions. "Sakir, Rita, I'd like you to meet—"

Sakir cut her off. "We know each other."

"Oh," Rita said, confused.

"Unfortunately," Bobby muttered, from beside her.

Jane turned to look at Bobby Callahan. Gone was the

charming, funny and highly sensual man she'd just danced with, and in his place stood a man of stone, a thick vein pounding in his temple.

"What's wrong?" she whispered to him.

Bobby acted as though he hadn't heard her. He stared at Sakir, his gaze hooded like a predatory hawk.

"Is it possible for us to behave like civilized gentlemen tonight, Callahan?" Sakir said, ice threading his tone as he stuck out a hand in Bobby's direction.

Eyes narrowed, Bobby stared at Sakir. "It'll be a cold day in hell before I shake the hand of the man who stole my father's land and helped put him in the ground."

Three

It had been close to eight years since his father's death, yet the anger that now burned in Bobby's blood was stronger and more dangerous than ever.

His fierce gaze never left Sakir Al-Nayhal as they seemed to circle each other, challenging each other, without moving a muscle. The party went on around them. Guests ate and drank, women flirted with men and the host and hostess gave their tenth tour of the night.

Beside Bobby, Jane tugged at his hand and asked, her voice threaded with concern, "What in the world is going on?"

Gesturing to Sakir, Bobby muttered a terse, "This man, this friend of yours, is a thief and a liar."

"What?" said Jane in shocked tones. "What are you talking about?"

"A rich and powerful thief, but a thief nonetheless."

"Careful, Callahan," Sakir warned, his mouth grim with dislike.

"Sakir?" Al-Nayhal's wife spoke, her tone even, but concerned. "Maybe we should discuss this at another time? This doesn't seem like the place to—"

"Discuss what?" Jane demanded, this time looking at Sakir.

"He is angry because his father lost his family's land," Sakir explained to Jane.

"He didn't lose anything," Bobby growled with deep menace, not caring who overheard him. "You set out to destroy him, and you did."

"Destroy him?" Sakir repeated, sniffing as if that were the silliest idea in the world.

"How many times did you approach my father about buying his property, Al-Nayhal?"

"I will not go over this again—"

"What was it? Five, six times?"

"Sakir, what is he saying?" Jane demanded, alarm threading her tone now.

Sakir sighed with annoyance. "When I came to Texas I wanted to acquire several acres of land. The oil industry here was on the decline. Callahan's land was on the auction block, and in dire need of environmental changes I might add, so I acquired it."

Bobby snorted bitterly. "You're getting so good at spouting off that story, somebody'll think you actually believe it." His voice dropped, and through gritted teeth he uttered, "Bottom line is, my father wouldn't sell you his land, so you went about getting it any way you could."

"Rita's right," Jane said as people began to stare. "Maybe we should take this conversation inside."

"Or better yet, let us postpone the discussion altogether," Sakir suggested tightly. "It grows tiresome."

Bobby finally turned to look at Jane, who appeared pinched and uneasy. "How do you know this guy?" he asked her, not caring that she'd stepped back a few inches.

She didn't answer him at first, looked from him to Sakir, then back again.

"She is my sister," Sakir supplied for her.

"What?" A slow, sinking feeling pushed into Bobby's gut.

Sakir raised his already tipped chin. "She is Al-Nayhal."

"I told you that I had family here," Jane said slowly, her green gaze—so like her *brother's*—filled with worry.

But Bobby was in no mood to offer her any comfort. "You also said that your name was Hefner."

"It is. Sakir's my half-brother. I didn't know he existed until just a few months ago."

Bobby sniffed derisively. "I'm sorry for you."

Sakir spoke in a quiet, though ultra-threatening, tone. "Again, I caution you to be careful, Mr. Callahan."

"Or what?" Bobby spat. "You'll try and take the measly twenty-five acres of my father's land you left behind? Not going to happen. I've paid you every last cent for the place, including interest."

Sakir acknowledged this with a nod. "So you have." He placed a hand protectively around his wife's shoulders. "Understand, Mr. Callahan, that, like you, I feel impassioned over the well-being of my family."

Dark, blood-red heat tumbled through Bobby's chest and gut. He looked at Jane, at the beautiful, seductive woman who had captured his mind and body, had made him feel alive for the first time in a month, with new eyes. Was it possible that this whole thing had been nothing more than a game to her? Did she know about his history with the Al-Nayhals?

Bitterness flooded him. He had to remember that this woman belonged to a family who apparently thought it was nothing to use and hurt others—all in the name of acquisition.

"Jane is part of my family," Sakir continued ominously, in the same tone he'd used eight years previous to tell Bobby he'd never sell the Callahan's land back to a Callahan. "And I ask you not to forget that."

"Believe me, I won't," Bobby said without emotion before he turned and walked away.

When Jane sat down next to Rita at a nearby table a moment later, she felt as though she'd just been tossed into an emotional whirlpool. Bobby had stalked off in one direction and, when she'd tried to speak to Sakir to ask him a few questions, he'd taken off in the other direction, leaving Jane with bits and pieces of a cruel, wicked, time-worn story. The man she was desperately interested in getting to know on one side and her newly found brother on the other.

The dry heat from the barbecues moved over and through her, making her feel breathless and very weary. What in the world did she do now? Try to find out both sides of this tale? Or give up on a potential relationship, give up on something that seemed real—give up on a chance for something of her own? Because this thing between her and Bobby was tainted with her new life, a life she hadn't even come to grips with, much less embraced.

A deep longing for the familiar moved over her in smooth, uncomplicated waves. She knew it was a childish thought, but she missed her mother, missed how the woman had held her and kissed her hair when she felt unsure of the world.

"I'm so sorry about all of this, Jane." Beside her, Rita inched closer, her forced smile uneasy.

"What just happened?" Jane asked.

"That was pretty much business as usual for Sakir." Rita grimaced. "I only know Bobby by reputation, but that was a very different view of the charming cowboy I've heard the women around town go on about."

Very different from the man Jane had made love to ten days ago and flirted with tonight. "Do you know what really happened to his father's land?"

"Sakir's only talked about it once. Supposedly, Bobby's father made some foolish deal with a shady oil-drilling company. They never paid, and much of the land was ruined because of their bad drilling practices. Soon after, the property was seized by the bank and put on the auction block. Sakir was just getting started here. He wanted to buy some property for grazing land for cattle. There was nothing spiteful in the purchase, I don't think."

Mixed emotions flooded Jane as she listened to her sister-in-law. Bobby's loss and Sakir's gain. Nothing seemed right, but she wasn't certain of what was wrong or who was in the wrong. "Bobby accused Sakir of putting his father in the ground. What did that mean?"

Rita looked pained. "Bobby's father passed away just a few months after the land was sold."

"Oh, God." Jane could hardly make sense of all of this. Losing your land, then your father. Caring for your sister alone. Wasn't he entitled to some anger and hostility?

But was that anger misplaced?

She didn't know.

"Bobby also spoke about twenty-five acres?" Jane prompted.

Rita nodded. "Sakir did let Bobby buy back a few acres, along with the old house he'd grown up in."

"Why?"

"I don't know."

"And why not let him buy back the whole thing if he could?" Jane asked, as much to herself as to Rita.

Rita shook her head, played with a silver fork. "I honestly don't know. Sakir won't go into that, and I didn't want to push him. It's a sore subject."

"For them both." The heat from the barbecues was almost irritatingly suffocating now. "Why won't Sakir talk about this with me?"

"Sakir doesn't like his honor questioned."

Jane released a breath. Sakir was just like his eldest brother, Zayad, the Sultan of Emand. Business was done in a strict fashion, no games. But they were both very honorable, very good, kind men. She couldn't imagine Sakir doing something underhanded.

"By the way," Rita said with quiet familiarity. "How

do you know Bobby Callahan? You didn't just meet to-night, did you? You seemed…close."

Her sister-in-law's words ripped at her heart. They had been, in a crazy, short time, oddly connected. By a mutual desire, a steady interest and a similar pain. "We met at the Turnbolts' charity function."

"And?"

"And what?"

A soft, knowing smile touched Rita's lips.

Jane laughed half heartedly, shook her head. "You're very good at this."

Leaning in, Rita whispered, "I have a sister. Ava can never keep a secret from me, either."

Jane looked out over the crowd, tried to spot Bobby Callahan, but he was nowhere to be found. Odds were good that he'd already taken off. When Jane found Rita's gaze once again, she studied the woman. "How good is our friendship?"

A warm smile touched Rita's mouth. "Well, I'd say we're sisters now."

Jane nodded, then lowered her voice and said, "Bobby and I were together at the Turnbolts' charity do."

"Together?" Rita repeated.

Jane raised her brows suggestively.

"Oh," Rita said, surprised.

"It was one night, amazing, wonderful…" She put her head in her hands and groaned.

"I understand," Rita said comfortingly.

"Sakir can't know this," Jane said gravely.

"Sakir doesn't need to know this," Rita assured her. "It's your business, your relationship."

Jane looked up and heaved a sigh, tracing the edges of the white china plate before her. "Well, I think any chance of a relationship was just—"

"Tossed out the window?" Rita supplied.

Feeling overwhelmingly grievous, Jane shook her head. "Try catapulted."

He could go to hell for thoughts like this.

But as Bobby Callahan rode like the devil over his land, he felt defiantly resolute.

Finally, he would have his revenge on Sakir Al-Nayhal. Finally, he would honor the memory of his father.

On Josiah Callahan's deathbed, he'd asked just two things of his son, to take care of his sister, Kimmy, and to pay back the man who had stolen so much from them. There was nothing Bobby wouldn't do for his father, for the man who had felt honored to be the parent of a handicapped daughter, the man who had considered his life to be the easiest and most rewarding a man could have.

The part of Bobby that felt angry at his dad for giving up and leaving him and Kimmy alone, would forever be buried in his heart.

He hauled back the reins in his fist, brought his horse to a stop just inches from the property line he'd spent years memorizing. The line that separated his land from the land Sakir Al-Nayhal had stolen. For the first three years after his father's death, Bobby had sat on this imaginary line, his butt in the dirt, his heart and soul wrecked. He'd imagined all sorts of ways to get his revenge. He'd fantasized about getting even with Sakir Al-Nayhal. Making him pay, making him realize what pain really was.

The woman who'd called herself Jane Hefner entered his mind with a quick shot of desire. Bobby wasn't altogether sure if she'd lied to him or not, if she'd known who he was all along and had been playing him—after all, he wouldn't put anything past that family.

But he almost didn't care.

Jane Hefner Al-Nayhal was going to be the answer to his eight-year quest. She liked him, he knew it, and he was going to make her fall in love with him, desperately in love with him, then toss her back into the arms of her brother, rejected and shattered. Then her brother would see what it was like to watch someone he loved fall apart.

Sakir Al-Nayhal had destroyed Bobby's family.

Now Bobby was going to destroy Al-Nayhal's.

Four

Jane hadn't touched a drop of alcohol the night before. She hadn't danced into the wee hours with her heels in one hand and the palm of a gorgeous man in the other. And yet, she felt as though she was suffering the worst hangover of her life.

Was it possible to get drunk on confusion and disappointment?

Jane rolled to her back and faced the morning sun that slammed into her bedroom with ferocious intensity. Much like a spotlight, she mused glumly. She had come to Texas in hopes of redefining her future, but eleven days ago a major roadblock had been thrust out in front of her in the glorious shape of a six-foot-three cowboy. The truth of it was, she was still intrigued by him, attracted to him. She still liked him—a lot—despite the feud between him and her brother. But if she pursued her desires, regardless of what she'd heard and seen last night, would both Bobby and her brother reject her?

She closed her eyes and sighed. At this point, she realized dolefully, she couldn't decide whose rejection would pain her the most.

A soft knock at the door interrupted her thoughts, and she unfolded the covers and pushed her tired self out of bed as she called, "Come in."

Sakir and Rita's housekeeper, a very serious-looking woman in her mid-fifties entered the room, too perfectly starched and coifed for 8:00 a.m. She inclined her head. "Good morning, Miss Al-Nayhal."

Jane smiled at the older woman as she reached for her robe. "Good morning, Marian. Would you please call me Jane?"

"His Highness wouldn't like that."

Jane pulled the belt of her white robe with a little too much force. "We don't have to tell him."

The woman frowned deeply, and ignored Jane's comment. "You have a phone call, Miss."

Jane glanced over her shoulder, her gaze settling on the nightstand where she expected to see a telephone. But oddly, there wasn't one. She hadn't noticed this before, and thought it strange in an enormous house like this that guest rooms weren't equipped with phones.

Seeming to read her thoughts, Marian simply said, "Mrs. Al-Nayhal hasn't had time to install telephones in every room."

"Of course not," said Jane, feeling sheepish, her toes

sinking into the thick cream carpeting. "With the new baby and all."

Marian neither agreed nor disagreed with this. Instead she thrust the cordless phone at Jane, who took it from her with another quick, "Thank you."

After a pert nod, the older woman turned on her perfectly polished black shoes and left the room.

Wondering if whoever was calling her still remained on the line after all of that nonsense, Jane cradled the phone to her ear and said hopefully, "Hello?"

"Well, that was one helluva party last night, wasn't it?"

Her heart dropped into her stomach, and she actually felt herself beam with pleasure and relief. The rough timbre of his voice, edged with that slow charm made her smile, made her recall their first night together. She was surprised by the intense reaction, albeit a little worried about this undeniable need she had to hear his voice again.

"One helluva party?" she repeated with a trace of sarcasm. "I suppose. If you like a little conflict with your barbecue."

His chuckle lacked real mirth. "Yeah, well, we took things too far."

"You and Sakir, you mean?"

He paused, then sighed. "It's all water under the bridge now."

"Is it?" she asked in a small voice. The way Bobby had glared at Sakir last night suggested the opposite.

"It has to be. We both have to get over all this past BS." She could practically hear him shrug. "Well, I do anyway."

Not that she didn't want him to feel this magnanimous spirit, but she couldn't help wondering how, after such a display of hatred last night, he could make such a turnaround. "Why the sudden change of heart?"

"This feud is getting in the way of something real important."

"What's that?"

"Me asking you out."

Jane grinned gleefully, and snuggled her ear closer into the phone. This was an answer she liked. "Would it appear too desperate to say that I'm really glad you called?"

He laughed, and the sound was genuine this time, not forced. "No, darlin'. Sounds honest."

"Honest is good." The simple phrase was a mantra for Jane, had been ever since she could remember. Even as a child, her mother had always led her to believe that honesty was the only way to live her life. Painful or painfree. Ironic as her mother was holding onto a very deep secret regarding Jane's father during that time.

"Pick you up in an hour?"

Bobby's query shot her back into reality, and she muttered swiftly, "I'm sorry, what?"

"I said I'll come by, pick you up in an hour," he repeated.

She glanced at the clock, then down at her robe. "It's only eight o'clock."

"All right," he acquiesced with a trace of mock annoyance. "Two hours."

"So bossy," she chided playfully. "And would you like to tell me what to wear, as well, Mr. Callahan?"

His voice dropped to a husky whisper. "Damn right I would, but with the suggestion I'd make you might just get arrested the minute you step out your front door."

She laughed. "Casual elegant, it is then."

"Fine," he muttered dolefully.

"Are we really going to do this, Bobby? Are we really going to *date* after…well, after last week?"

"You bet. And we're going to do it the right way."

"The right way?"

"Hand-holding, then maybe a kiss or two…we're going slowly this time."

Little shots of thrill twirled in her belly, and she leaned closer to the phone, her lips brushing over the receiver, her mind conjuring images of that sweet, soft kiss. "Like courting?"

"Sure, but I won't be asking your brother for permission."

"No." His shot of cold humor put a slight damper on her romantic feeling, but she brushed it away.

"See you in an hour?"

"I thought you said two."

"I don't want to wait that long. Do you?"

"No." The excitement that ran a marathon through her blood mingled irritatingly with caution, brought on by last night, and her judgment and blind hope that he was trustworthy.

"Bye, darlin'"

"Bye." As Jane hung up the phone, slipped out of her robe and headed for the bathroom, she wondered what she was in for downstairs. She wondered if her brother would raise holy hell when he found out what she was doing.

But as soon as she stepped under the hot spray of the shower, she let her mind fall to more appealing queries, such as what delights awaited her on her first real date with Bobby Callahan.

Forty minutes later, down in Sakir's very masculine, very brown leather- and mahogany-paneled library, Jane got the answer to her first question.

Not *holy hell,* but definite displeasure.

"He is using you, Jane."

Dressed in a white kaftan, her brother looked impenetrable and uncompromising sitting behind his desk.

Jane stood before him wearing a pale-green sweater, white jeans and a determined set to her chin. "I don't think so, Sakir, but even if that were true, it's my choice to make."

"Rita has told me that she spoke to you regarding the history of Bobby Callahan and myself."

"Yes."

"The man will do anything to get back at me, including hurting the members of my family, I am certain of it." He leaned forward, lifted his brows. "He despises me that much."

"Does he have a right to?" The question fell from her mouth without thought, and she quickly added, "In the short time I've gotten to know you, I see a great man, an honorable, caring man. But we all do things that live in the gray. Was this deal with Callahan one of those moments?"

His mouth set in a thin line, Sakir uttered, "You ask your brother such a question?"

"I ask my brother for the truth, that's all." She sighed,

sat in the chair opposite him and laid a hand over his. "I'm a big girl, Sakir. I can handle the truth. Whatever it is."

The ire in his eyes and the tight expression of a businessman he wore, softened. "You will always receive the truth from me. Be assured of that."

She offered him a gentle smile. "Thank you."

He nodded, then exhaled heavily. "There was no maliciousness in the procurement of Bobby Callahan's land. After the drilling company left, the land was in a bad state. They had dug and torn the soil and spilled oil everywhere. It was an environmental nightmare. The elder Callahan could not care for, or repair, the property, and the bank was foreclosing. If it had not been I who made the purchase, it would have been someone else. And I have no doubt that buyer would not have been as generous in the end."

"You're talking about how you allowed Bobby to buy back a few acres of the land?"

"Correct. I am sorry about his father's death, but the anger he has for me is misplaced. And his unreasonable manner and quick anger make him dangerous."

"That's ridiculous," Jane tossed out, but in the back of her mind she couldn't help but wonder. Her stomach tightened with worry, and the reaction irritated her no end.

"You saw him last night," Sakir continued. "He was acting like a madman."

"He was angry, and he clearly holds a grudge the size of Texas against you. But a madman? No way."

"I will not allow you to walk into that fire, Jane."

She slipped her hand from his and laughed. "Allow me?"

It had been close to ten years since she'd heard words like that, and even then she'd rejected them. Most of the time. Coming from a man, a command such as this one really made her blood simmer. After all, she'd had no father, no male figure of authority in her life, and she wasn't looking for one now.

Leaning back in his chair, Sakir stared at her, his eyebrows set. "You must understand. You are Al-Nayhal. You are my sister, and I—" He broke off, looking rather embarrassed, but continued at any rate. "I have come to care for you a great deal."

An understanding smile nudged at the corner of her mouth. Clearly, it was far easier for her to show emotion than Sakir. "I love you, too, big brother."

"I do not want to see you hurt. Can you not understand this?"

"Of course."

"Then you will abide by my decision."

"No." She wasn't about to roll over and play the "little sister," no matter what judgments Sakir had made about Bobby's motives in asking her out.

"You are as stubborn as my wife," Sakir grumbled.

She laughed and stood. "Thank you. I take that as a compliment. Rita's wonderful."

"Yes."

"Listen, I've been making my own choices for ten years now, and I've done a pretty good job of it." She walked around his desk, leaned over and kissed his cheek. "Trust me, okay?"

His gaze found hers, and there was unabashed worry there. "It is Bobby Callahan I do not trust."

The doorbell rang just then, and Jane offered Sakir one last, faith-inducing smile before she turned her back on him and left the room.

If it were possible, Jane looked even more beautiful in a pair of form-fitting white jeans than she had in all that finery she'd worn the first night they'd met. Course, that could be just his taste, Bobby thought, shoving his truck into third as he shot up Hollyhock Drive. Sure, he liked dresses on a woman, but nothing could beat denim on curves.

Forcing his gaze onto the road and away from her slim thighs, he asked, "Have you had breakfast?"

"You hardly gave me time," she replied, a smile in her voice.

"Sorry about that."

"No, you're not."

He turned to her, grinned sinfully. "No, I'm not. I wanted to see you."

A slight pink blush crept up her neck, matching the haze around the morning sun before them. Bobby thought it was just about the sexiest sight he'd ever seen, and he wondered if he'd be able to pull this off— stay unaffected with this woman.

"So," she said, tugging him from his thoughts. "Where are we going?"

"A great place with real Texas ambiance and one helluva chef."

"Sounds good."

But when they turned into a driveway marked Private Property and drove through a set of weathered iron gates emblazoned with the letters *KC* Jane turned to him, her dark eyebrows raised. "What are the specials today, chef?"

He chuckled. "Bacon, eggs, maybe a slice or two of toast if I manage not to burn it."

Her gaze shifted to the landscape around his home. The pasture land, grazing horses, miles of sky above. No matter what the size of his property now, Bobby thought with a deep sense of melancholy, it was still home and it always felt right to be there.

She turned back to him. "Breakfast at your house. That's pretty intimate." Her full lips curved up at the corners. "And I thought we were taking things slow."

Bobby just grinned as he brought the truck to a dusty halt in front of his ranch house. The last thing he wanted with this woman was slow. Ever since they'd made love, he'd ached to touch her again, have her beneath him, on top of him, in front of him. But for his plan to come off, he needed to take his time, give her a little romance. Hell, he might even enjoy it.

He was quick to step out the driver's side and walk around the truck. He helped Jane out, then took her hand. "Well, I suppose I'd better admit it. I didn't bring you here *just* for breakfast."

Mock shock settled over her features. "No kidding."

"You implying I'm some kind of rogue cowboy?" Bobby asked lightly as they walked around the side of the house and down the stone pathway.

"I wouldn't dare."

Shifting the Stetson on his head, he laughed. "Well, it'd be the truth, on most days."

"But not today?"

"Today, I brought you here so you could see who I was. After last night, I don't think you got a pretty clear picture."

The air around them cooled, and Jane's voice dropped. "Maybe not."

She had reservations about him, he knew. And rightly so. It was also clear as river water that she was confused, not sure what he was about and what he was after.

Dammit.

Every time he looked into those dark-jade eyes of hers, Bobby had the same problem. He needed to keep his cool, stay in control of the situation and himself if he was going to finish this mess with the Al-Nayhals and get his father's ghost off his back once and for all.

"This." They reached the corral then, and Bobby released her hand and pointed into the ring. "This is who I am. This is why I cling tight to this land, and its past. Here's my passion, Jane."

With curious eyes, Bobby watched her take in the sight before her, then turned to see what she was seeing. While three children waited atop their horses, Abel helped sixteen-year-old Eli Harrison up the ramp and out of his wheelchair, then onto the back of Sweet Grace, a gray mare. Eli laughed and patted his horse, and while the other kids whooped and clapped excitedly around him, one of the ranch assistants belted Eli securely into place.

With a deep inhale, Jane turned her gaze from the corral and gave him a brilliant smile. "I'd like to meet them."

A shot of surprise registered in Bobby's gut, and he returned her smile. He hadn't expected her to say that.

Maybe how wonderful the place was or what great work he was doing—the usual thing women said when they stopped by the ranch. But as he'd suspected from the first night they'd met, Jane Hefner Al-Nayhal was far from the usual.

"How about after breakfast?" he asked, taking her hand again. "And after they finish their lesson?"

She squeezed his hand. "Okay."

With a wave to Abel, Bobby led Jane away from the corral, back down the path and through the yard. When they entered the house, Deacon, Abel's ancient dog, was asleep on the rug in the large kitchen. The spotted brown mutt barely raised his lids when they walked in.

Bobby motioned for her to have a seat at the nicked wood table over by the bay window. "Make yourself comfortable and I'll get to work in here."

"Weren't you the one who wanted the woman doing all the cooking in the kitchen?" Jane teased, sitting down at the table and smiling.

"That's not what I said and you know it."

Elbows on the table, chin resting on the back of her hand, she looked too comfortable in his house, at his kitchen table. "Okay, you said something like you appreciate it when a woman can cook."

"Damn right." He turned back to the counter and cracked a few eggs into a bowl, then grabbed a fork. "Just as you get to appreciate a man who can cook."

"Only if he doesn't burn the toast."

He tossed her a wicked glare, and she laughed.

"You sure you don't need any help?"

"I can make bacon and eggs with my eyes closed, darlin'."

She gave a soft whistle. "Now, that's something I'd like to see," she said, easing herself out of her chair and onto the floor, where she hunkered down next to the dog.

With a grand yawn, Deacon opened his eyes and rolled to his back, ready for a few scratches from the pretty lady who was visiting his bit of rug. The scene was a nice one—easy conversation as Bobby stirred eggs, Jane kissing Deacon's dusty face as she rubbed his pink belly. For just a moment, Bobby almost forgot the reason she was here.

Almost.

Ten minutes later, they were sitting across from each other at the table, eggs and bacon before them. Though she ate heartily, Jane kept glancing out the window at the yard and corral beyond. "Must be comforting to know your future."

The statement had Bobby pausing, a slice of toast poised at his lips. "What do you mean?"

She gestured around the kitchen. "You have this place, and a clear purpose. You know who you are and what you want and where you're going to be in ten years."

Bobby bit into the charred toast. He'd never thought of himself as set in his life, sure of his future. Maybe because he was so damn obsessed with the past. He caught her eye and raised an eyebrow. "You don't know what you want, Jane?"

"I thought I did."

"You're a member of a royal family now, you can probably do whatever you want."

"If we're talking about money, sure, but that's never where true happiness and fulfillment lie, is it?"

True happiness? Christ, he didn't know. He hadn't known true happiness since he was a kid, hanging out with his family, back when they were whole and happy. Bobby probably wouldn't know true happiness now if it rose up and bit him on the chin. And if it did, he'd push it away. He didn't deserve to feel good—not yet.

Jane continued, "The thing is, money and situation can't bring about purpose. That has to come from inside your gut." She placed her fork on her plate and sighed. "I thought opening my own restaurant was the be-all and end-all for me, but now I'm not so sure. What gets to me is that I was so sure of it before, back in California. The restaurant of my own, a family of my own some-day. That was my passion, what drove me. Then this man comes along and tells me he's my brother—that back when my mother worked in politics, she met a man and had a short-term affair with him, and that this man was my father. Oh, and right, he also happened to be the Sultan of Emand—"

"What?" Bobby prompted, watching her mouth drop into a apprehensive frown before his eyes. The sight bothered him far more than it should.

"Well," she said, shrugging. "I was sort of tossed into someone else's life—a life that would probably thrill most people. I mean, Emand is beautiful and the people are great and I want to *want* to be a part of them. But I found myself only feeling discontented there, and then guilty because of all the wonderful things my brothers have given me, offered to me. But, honestly, that life—their life—makes me uncomfortable. I've never been out in front, you know? Celebrity holds no appeal for me. I like simple. I like being behind the scenes."

"In the kitchen," he said, following her thought, though the mutual joke made her smile.

"Don't get me wrong, I'm glad I know the truth about where I come from, and having brothers is a gift, but my life doesn't seem to be my own anymore."

"Are your brothers making the decisions for you?" he said, his smile wavering as a thread of contempt lined his query.

Her large, almond-shaped eyes held understanding. "No, Bobby. There's no forcing me to do what I don't want to do. But I do feel obligated to try to be an Al-Nayhal. That's why I went to Emand, to experience the life and the culture, to learn as much as I could about my father and his family. And it was wonderful. But I felt like a tourist. I felt like I wanted to go home."

Bobby stared at her. Not since his parents were alive had there been such a conversation at his kitchen table. Most meals, he and Abel just talked about familiar things—the ranch, the food, the past, what had to be done the following day. On occasion a local politician's name would be tossed around, dragged through the mud, but that was about it. Never were there feelings and hopes and flowery stuff like that mentioned.

"Maybe you just want what every woman wants," Bobby pointed out, leaning back in his chair.

Her gaze moved over him in a slow, covetous way that made his chest and groin tighten simultaneously.

"What's that?" she asked.

"Security."

"In love or money?"

"In life."

She smiled then, a deep, warm smile that cut into his gut like a hot knife. "How did you get so insightful?" she asked.

"My sister probably," he said without giving it much thought. "Despite her disability, that girl had wisdom beyond her years. She always knew what was really important."

Kimmy had tried to make Bobby see what was important in life, too. But trying to teach a dead heart to beat again was an impossible task and he'd failed her time and time again in everything but the ranch.

Bobby stared into the green eyes of the woman who made his pulse shift erratically. In this, he wouldn't fail his sister or his father. Jane Hefner Al-Nayhal had complimented him on the direction he'd taken with his choices and his future. Little did she know that Bobby was attempting to navigate her future as well, but in a direction not nearly as successful.

Five

Sara, Eli, Daniel and May.

They were four of the most wonderful children Jane had ever met. Talking with them and hearing how much they enjoyed coming to KC Ranch made her heart twist with admiration for the man who had made it all possible.

Bobby Callahan was a few feet away, saying good-bye to May and her parents. The bright and beautiful teenage girl, who had lost her sight just ten months ago, was a new student at the ranch. Bobby's ranch foreman, Abel, had told Jane that the family traveled three hours each way to come to KC Ranch because of its reputation. He'd also told her that the girl had been completely closed down when she'd first arrived at the ranch. But the horses and the care of the staff had helped her crawl out of the dark place she was living in.

"Ready to go?" Bobby asked her.

Jane let her gaze travel over the sea of green and gravel, the trees and horses, and the sweet little ranch house that had felt warm and comfortable to a girl who regularly got lost in both the palace in Emand and Sakir's home outside of Paradise. "Not really, but I do have plans this afternoon."

"Another date?" Bobby asked casually, though the harsh grooves around his mouth hinted at his irritation at the thought.

A bolt of satisfaction knocked around in Jane's belly, and she wondered if he was going to make good on his promise and give her a kiss. He'd already held her hand, a kiss was the natural progression—even for a man bent on *slow moving*.

"Yes," she said seriously. "I do have a date. With my sister-in-law and a shopping mall."

His expression changed like quicksilver. Rigidity morphed into that lazy, roguish grin that made her knees buckle. He took her hand. "Let's go."

Jane waved goodbye to Abel and the kids and headed toward the truck with Bobby. On the way back to Sakir and Rita's house, Jane reflected on her time at KC Ranch and how she'd felt so alive there surrounded by the kids, air and life that was being nurtured every day. And once again, she thought how lucky Bobby was to have made such a valuable choice.

"The kids liked you."

Bobby's husky voice stole her from her thoughts, and she looked at him and smiled. "And I liked them. Maybe next time I can volunteer…maybe help out in the corral or make lunches or something."

"We welcome any and all help," he intoned seriously.

"You might regret saying that," she said sardonically rolling down her window for a shot of the sweet, early-fall wind. "You just might be seeing me every day."

"No regrets here," he said, his voice oddly gentle.

The hungry expression in his blue eyes made Jane's throat tighten, made her feel as though she couldn't swallow properly. She cleared her throat. "I had a great time today."

"Not disappointed in the humble surroundings?"

"Don't be silly," she admonished halfheartedly. "I'm a simple girl. I don't need fancy, never have—just clean and comfortable and homey."

His dark head tilted, his voice dropped. "Is that so?"

"That's so," she insisted. "Except…"

He frowned. "Except what?"

"The next time," she began as they turned into Sakir and Rita's long driveway, "why don't I make the toast?"

Bobby grinned suddenly. "I did warn you, darlin'."

The mall was fifteen minutes outside of Paradise. The massive lump of concrete consisted of two department stores, ten specialty shops and a small food court. Not exactly the ideal place to shop for elegant linens, china and flatware. Jane had suggested they travel to Dallas or rent what they needed, but Rita had assured her that she wanted the party to be as warm and rustic as it was stylish, and rented settings might feel too impersonal.

Jane had been more than happy to hear that Rita didn't want a stuffy affair, but as she combed through burgundy placemats that were made from a material she'd never heard of, she wondered if a happy medium were even possible here.

She tossed the items back onto the shelf and walked toward Rita, who was sitting on a bench holding Daya. Their faces were very close together and Rita was whispering something to her two-month old daughter. A combination of emotions swelled inside Jane—jealousy, affection, happiness, hope.

"How do you not eat her right up?" Jane said, coming to stand before them.

Rita kissed Daya. "I eat a large meal right before I pick her up to snuggle."

Jane laughed. "Is having a baby the best thing in the world?"

"Definitely. Of course, it helps having a husband."

"Yeah, and I bet Sakir changes her diapers," Jane said sardonically.

"Actually he does. And in the middle of the night, too."

"No way," Jane said, aghast. She couldn't imagine her stoic brother changing poopy diapers at one in the morning.

"Men are funny, aren't they?" Rita stood up, cuddled the baby against her chest. "They only let you see one side of them until they trust you."

As Jane helped her sister-in-law reorganize her stroller, shopping bags, diaper bag and blankets, she wondered if Bobby was only allowing her to see one side of him. She guessed he was. After all, they hadn't known each other very long. But that only led Jane to wonder what the other side of him looked like. Was it the angry, bitter man she'd seen the other night or someone else?

"Let's walk, shall we?" Rita suggested.

"Sure. We could head over to Young's. I hear they have a wider selection and a china department. And on the way we can talk more about the menu."

As the baby cooed and shoppers around them grabbed for the deals of the day, Rita explained, "I want something fun and interesting. Same as the food. Can that be any broader?" She laughed at herself. "My sister, Ava, has made me promise to have ribs, so we have to have those."

Jane nodded. "I've never met your sister."

"Nope, not yet. Ava and her husband, Jared and their little girl, Lily, have been away, in Florida. Disneyworld, actually." Ava rolled her eyes. "I can't even imagine Jared there, riding in teacups, standing next to Mickey for a photo op. Jared's great, but he's a pretty uptight guy."

Jane laughed. "Can't wait to meet them."

"You will. The whole gang will be at the party. Jared's grandmother, Muna, too. She's a trip."

They were just crossing the threshold into Young's department store when Rita spotted something in the distance and gave a little gasp. She turned to Jane and grinned widely. "We're being followed."

"What?"

"Well, actually, you're being followed." Rita poked her finger in the direction of women's nightgowns and lingerie. "Over there."

Jane looked in the direction that Rita indicated and

felt her heart drop into her shoes. That strange breathlessness she'd felt when she'd first seen him at the Turnbolts' party hit her again—and oddly just a few hours after she'd left him standing on her doorstep. Walking toward them, far too tall, dark and masculine to be shouldering through racks of white lace and silk, was Bobby Callahan. He was dressed in the same faded jeans, T-shirt, Stetson and boots, and he looked good enough to eat.

Bobby grinned at the two of them as he approached. "Afternoon, ladies."

Jane smiled brilliantly at him. "Afternoon, Mr. Callahan."

"How are you, Bobby?" Rita asked, a slight wariness threading her tone.

Bobby nodded. "Real good, thanks."

"Shopping for undergarments?" Jane asked, eyeing the row of silk and cotton he'd just emerged from.

"Don't wear undergarments." He winked at her, and when she blushed he laughed. He turned to Rita, saw her balancing the baby in one arm and a large shopping bag that hadn't been able to fit under the stroller in the other, and said immediately, "Let me help you with those, Mrs. Al-Nayhal."

"Thanks," Rita said, still sounding slightly uneasy, though she smiled pleasantly as he took the bag, then pushed the stroller through the store as they all walked along.

"So what are you shopping for?" Jane asked him, clearly wondering why he had come to search her out just hours after they'd seen each other.

"A new toaster."

At his grin, Jane laughed.

Bobby felt like the back end of an ass right now. He hated lying, especially as he stared straight into those bright-green eyes of Jane's, but his vow demanded that he use whatever means necessary to accomplish his goal. He knew that Sakir hated him, which probably meant that his wife felt less than fine with Bobby dating Jane. And Bobby needed to see Jane without any chance of interference. If Rita approved of him, helped Jane to cast aside any doubts about his sincerity, then they would have the time it took for a woman to fall in love. Just the thought of having Rita Al-Nayhal on his side, thinking him a good man—even telling her husband so—made a warlike smile break on his face.

"You missed me, didn't you?"

Jane's query ripped him away from his thoughts. When he raised his eyebrows to her teasing smile, she added, "It's okay to admit. It won't crush your masculinity."

Bobby chuckled. "I'm in a ladies' department store. I think my masculinity's already been compromised."

Beside them, Rita cuddled Daya and sang softly to her as Bobby continued, though he felt the woman's gaze on him from time to time. "Truth is, darlin', after I dropped you off, I realized that we hadn't decided what we're doing tonight."

"Doing tonight?" Jane repeated, rubbing her chin in mock thoughtfulness. "I don't recall—"

"Oh, c'mon, Jane," Bobby interrupted with an arrogant smile. "You know as well as I do that we're spending the night together." He turned to Rita then, gave her a wicked grin. "Pardon me, ma'am."

For a moment Bobby wondered if his take-what-you-want attitude offended Rita, but it didn't seem to. And after all, she *was* married to Sakir Al-Nayhal.

"No pardons necessary," Rita said at last, a cautious, though far more friendly smile tugging at her mouth. "This old married woman with a baby is gonna take off for a little bit. Be over here if you need me." She turned away from them and pushed the stroller over to the linens section.

A wave of triumph moved through Bobby. He'd made some headway here, made a few new and improved impressions that Rita would no doubt share with her husband. He turned back to Jane. She was smiling at him, familiar and open, with that touch of humor that made him want to kiss her and talk to her at the same time. Damn, why did he have to want her this way? Why couldn't she have been anybody but who she was?

"Something you wanna ask me, cowboy?" she teased.

"How about dinner tonight, maybe a moonlit ride?"

"I'm not the greatest horsewoman."

"You'll be fine," he insisted.

"How can you be so sure?"

"Because," he said, moving closer to her, his voice dropping to a husky whisper. "I'm going to teach you how to ride."

Jane felt her skin turn hot with his blatant innuendo. Here they were, standing in the middle of a crowded store with sales people pushing half-price sweaters, laughter and cries emerging from the many baby strollers around them, and all Jane could think about was lying horizontal on something moderately soft, with Bobby's mouth on hers.

"Come with me now," he murmured, his eyes liquid and hot.

The push to say yes was almost torturous, but Jane forced herself to decline. "I can't," she explained with a soft smile. "We're not finished here. I've got to work on this party. We have china and linens to buy today. This gathering is really important for my family, but most of all, it's important to my niece. It's her special day."

He looked thoughtful for a moment, then nodded. "I can wait."

Those words curled inside her, and the wicked smile he shot her only added fuel to an already blazing fire. It was a good thing Rita walked over then, because Jane was tempted to forgo the soft place to fall and kiss him rather obscenely against a rack of maroon table runners.

Little Daya was fussing, scrunching her face up and squirming in Rita's arms. Rita shrugged. "She's a little cranky. I'm thinking maybe we should go."

Jane glanced at Bobby. It would have been the perfect opportunity for him to get his wish. Baby crying, baby and mommy go home, Jane and Bobby start date right now.

But instead of waiting for the inevitable wail from Daya, Bobby said, "Let me try, Rita."

Jane gaped at him, so did Rita. It was a pretty well-known fact that men normally ran from a fussing baby unless they were biologically linked to the child.

"Are you sure, Bobby?" Rita asked, looking totally convinced that he was wasting his time.

He nodded and reached for Daya. "Trust me," he said confidently, wrapping the fussy little girl in his arms and tucking her against his massive chest. "I'll have her cooing in no time. Babies love me."

For a moment, Jane actually thought Daya was going to smile, but the flicker she saw on either side of the baby's mouth was step one of a full-on freak-out. As Bobby rocked her gently, Daya began to cry. When he tried making "shushing" sounds, Daya's cries turned to wails. And when he stopped moving altogether, a sound so painful and pitiful exploded from the little girl that both Jane and Rita reached for her.

Bobby looked dumbstruck as he handed the baby back to Rita. He kept on repeating the words, "I don't get it," over and over.

"It's all right, Bobby," Rita said over Daya's slowly deflating din, her gaze as concerned for him as for her daughter. "She's a little skittish with new people." Rita turned to Jane and rolled her eyes. "Just like Sakir."

Jane shifted her gaze to Bobby, who appeared a little detached, though he still had that crestfallen expression in his eyes. "Hey," she began, tucking her arm through his. "We need a big strong man to help us to the car. You up for it?"

"And you're bigger than most, Bobby," Rita said encouragingly, Daya now sans tears in her arms.

"No, you're the biggest," Jane amended, and the two women smiled at him affectionately.

Releasing a breath, Bobby shrugged. "All the compliments in the world can't make up for being rejected by a two-month-old, but I suppose I'll just have to take what I can get."

Jane smiled at him as he gathered the packages. Poor guy, she mused as she followed him and Rita out of the department store and into the parking lot. She knew it was a ridiculous notion, but she couldn't help wondering if the animosity Sakir had for Bobby might have somehow infected his daughter.

"Do you wish to torment me, my love?"

"Always," Rita said lovingly, sitting in her husband's lap, her arms around his neck.

Sakir pushed the leather captain's chair away from his desk and around to face the office's floor-to-ceiling windows. Holding his wife tightly, he looked out at the unending land of his backyard. "So, Callahan shows up at the shops, and you allow him to hold our child?"

"Yes."

"Why?" He eased her away a few inches so that he could look into her eyes. "You know how I feel about the man."

"And I know how Jane feels about the man," Rita said, strength in her tone. "And how he feels about her."

Sakir shook his head. "He is toying with her."

"I don't think so."

"What makes you so certain?"

Her hands cupped his face. The sun, hanging low in the horizon, bathed his handsome face in a reddish glow. "I know what need and longing look like in a man's eyes."

A slow grin worked its way to Sakir's face. "Yes, it would seem you do, dearest."

She leaned in and kissed him, warm and slow. "We had our struggles, too, Sakir," she said against his mouth. "But we overcame them and look at us now. Happy, in love, our beautiful child sleeping upstairs."

"Yes. I am a most fortunate man. I am proud of what we are and what we have. But Jane is my family now, too. She is Al-Nayhal."

"Jane is a strong woman with a great head on her shoulders."

"She will always be my little sister, dearest, and I would die before I let anyone hurt her."

"I know." Rita wrapped her arms around him, kissed him deeply, passionately. "That's why I love you so much."

"And I love you." His mouth covered hers hard then, his hands fisted her sweater.

"What can I do to take your mind off this?" she asked against his mouth.

"Off what?" he muttered, lifting her up and placing her on his desk. A sinful smile tugged at his mouth as he eased her back and lifted her skirt.

Six

"What's the big idea?"

The playfully gruff tone of voice made Jane grin. Poised at the stove, towel over her shoulder, she glanced over at Bobby, who was wearing a sexy pair of black jeans, a white shirt and a bewitching scowl on his handsome face. "Is there some problem, Mr. Callahan?"

"Yes." He crossed his arms over his chest and nodded at the steaming pan of chicken marsala she was working on. "Here I thought my eggs and bacon—"

"And toast," she teased. "Don't forget about the toast."

He rolled his eyes. "And my slightly charred toast…"

She laughed.

"Well," he muttered darkly, "I thought my meal was pretty damn impressive."

"It was," she assured him, turning back to the stove.

"But look at this." He gestured to the steaming pan of chicken and mushrooms in a wine and butter sauce. "It looks...professional."

"I did happen to mention that I am a chef, right?"

"Well, sure, but you didn't say what a big show-off you are."

She turned to glare at him, even tried to look shocked, but the sexy twinkle in his eyes had her busting out laughing again. "You won't care when you taste this, along with the penne and pine nuts."

"What, no dessert?" he said sullenly.

"I saw that ice cream in your freezer, Callahan. Ice cream trumps all other desserts, even the fancy ones."

He tossed a stray mushroom into his mouth. "I didn't know that."

"It's a chef thing." The late-afternoon sun settled over the house, bathing the spacious kitchen in a friendly, yellow light. "You know, some of my fellow chefs back in California actually prefer a hot dog with the works to sea bass and pesto butter."

"Yeah, well, who wouldn't?" Fork in hand, he stabbed a tender piece of chicken and popped it into his mouth. He groaned, and tossed her a hungry look. "I don't want this to sound sexist, but damn, lady, your place *is* in the kitchen."

Feeling incredibly close to him in that moment, she smiled a little shyly. "Thank you. I think."

Upon Bobby's insistence, and the fact that they were both starved and didn't want to wait until the food was plated, they stood side by side at the stove, eating chicken marsala and penne with pine nuts right out of their respective pans. As a chef, it was a fairly normal thing to do—skip the table and just go for the good stuff. But she'd certainly never tried it with a man before.

And such a man.

Bobby made no secret about his feelings—well, for her food anyway. He ate with gusto, showering her with praise after every bite. Pleasure coursed through her at his words and his passionate expression. This was why she'd gotten into culinary arts in the first place. Good food for people who really enjoyed it.

When Bobby'd had enough, he leaned against the counter and raised a brow at her. "You're amazing."

She flushed happily. "I'm glad you enjoyed it."

"I'm enjoying a few things lately." He gave her a wink. "You ready for a ride?"

Her breath caught in her throat as a mental image popped into her head that had nothing whatsoever to do with horses.

"Only take a minute to saddle up a couple of ponies." He pushed away from the counter.

And just as quickly, the sensual image faded. She had to bite her lip to stop herself from laughing. She really was growing desperate. Sad but true. She wanted to know when that kiss was coming—wanted to know why they had to take things slow when they'd started out so gloriously fast. She hoped he wasn't playing with her….

Sakir's warning was always there, under the surface of her skin, making her second-guess herself and Bobby.

"C'mon," he said, taking her hand and leading her

away from the kitchen and toward the front door. "The sunset can be real shocking it's so pretty."

"But we just ate," she warned, humor lacing her tone.

He chuckled. "It's not like swimming, Jane."

Any thread of worry she'd had disappeared and she laughed with him. "All right, lead on, cowboy. Into the barn and onto the back of the oldest and slowest horse you got."

A man and his horse were a sacred thing.

Bobby Callahan had always ridden solo. It was sort of a rule he had. No females behind him or in front of him. But tonight he had a woman sitting behind him, her arms wrapped around his waist, tight and warm, her thighs pressed against his, and she felt damn good. Lucky for him, Jane hadn't felt all that comfortable on Frankie, the horse he'd originally picked out for her, and Bobby wasn't about to walk the whole property alongside Ol' Dolly Parton, an aging blond mare who walked as though she were stepping in and out of a bucket of molasses, so he'd suggested riding double.

Beneath him, his gray stallion, Rip, tore up the ground while his gait remained as smooth as an ocean wave. The Texas landscape whizzed past, the air growing cooler with every dip of the sun into the horizon.

When Bobby had reached his destination, he slowed and let the stallion walk. "The sun's falling fast."

From behind him came a sigh, then the words, "It's beautiful."

"The land or the sunset?"

"Yes," she replied, a smile in her tone.

He chuckled. "Careful. Or you'll get bit."

"Bit by what?"

"The Texas bug."

"Oh, that."

"Think you could live here?"

The question was a basic one, simple actually when they were discussing sunsets and pretty scenery, their mood light and humorous. But the question also held a dot of intimacy that made Bobby real uncomfortable. Things were hopping around in his mind as of late, poking at his heart and gut over this woman. He liked her, liked her mind, her up-front way of talking. He was over the moon for her cooking, and those full lips and long legs….

Sweat broke out on his neck.

He had to keep reminding himself why he was pursuing her or there would be some real trouble ahead.

"Texas is already growing on me, Bobby. For many reasons." Jane shifted against him, her arms loosening slightly. "But in the end, I believe the place picks the person."

He snorted. "That's a bunch of bull, you know."

She laughed, let her head drop against his back. "Yeah, I know, but with a philosophy like that I don't have to make any decisions for myself."

"Looking for someone to make decisions for you, are you?" He hated the race of thrill and tension that snaked through him. And before she could answer him, Bobby twisted to the right, scooped her up and planted her in front of him on the horse.

Another rule broken, he mused. But hell, it was all

in the name of revenge, wasn't it? The darkly sarcastic thought made his gut twist, as did the hot look she sent him.

Her eyebrow arched over her left eye. "Is this standard horse protocol, Mr. Callahan?"

"No, but I wanted you in front of me, and instead of asking, I thought I'd make the decision for you." He kicked the horse forward into an easy walk.

With a grin, she wrapped one leg over his and inched herself closer. "So we're just going to keep riding this way?"

"Nope, we'll stop at that tree and turn around."

"Why?" She glanced over her shoulder, saw the massive tree, then turned back and curled into his chest. "Amazingly, I'm really enjoying this. I'd like to go farther."

"We can't."

Emotions were shooting off inside him like out-of-control firecrackers. With the center of her snuggled into him, fitting him perfectly, he wanted her, any way he could get her. Desire warred with an irritating wash of chivalry. He could feel her heart pounding against his chest. Was she excited, was she nervous? He wanted to protect her. But how did he protect her from himself?

She looked up. "Why can't we go farther?"

"Beyond that tree…" The words weren't as easy to speak as they were to think.

"What?" she asked, concern etching her features.

"That's your brother's land, darlin'."

For a moment, she just stared at him, then she nodded. "But I'm sure he wouldn't mind us—"

"I mind," Bobby said firmly, his gut tight now. "I've

never passed this boundary since the day the land was sold, and I don't intend to trespass now."

He brought the horse to a stop beneath the tree. They sat there, Rip shifting his weight beneath them. Bobby stared up at the massive trunk and pale-yellow leaves as though it was something to revile, wondering, as he always did, just how long it would take him to chop it down.

Jane's soft voice cut through his black thoughts. "Bobby, I've heard one side of this story. I'm smart enough to know that there's a lot more to it than just one side."

"'Course there is."

"You want to tell me?"

Bobby stilled. Sure, he wanted to tell her, every last bit. From his father's phone call telling Bobby in a miserable voice that Callahan land no longer belonged to the Callahans, to Bobby's nightly agony over a promise he wished he'd never made. But he couldn't say anything about that last bit, could he? Just like he couldn't change what was promised. He'd made the vow, and what he said here would need to work in his favor with regards to wooing Jane Hefner Al-Nayhal.

"You had to come home, right?" she prompted, "Leave your work when your father…"

"Had his land ripped from him?" Bobby finished for her. "That's right. Working the rodeo circuit was the best life a young man could know, but Dad needed the help. He was starting to really lose it. And with Kimmy… well, they both needed me."

"So you put your own life aside for your family."

He sniffed. "It's not as benevolent as it sounds, I promise you."

"Sounds like a sacrifice to me."

Admiration lit her eyes, and the sweet, honest smile she gave him nearly undid him. Why couldn't she have been a cold, unfeeling liar like her brother?

He looked away, looked deep into the land that would never again be his and begged to feel the comforting wave of anger. "Family takes care of family, simple as that."

"This whole thing sounds anything but simple." The wind blew over them, and Bobby tightened his hold on her. She released a weighty breath. "Have you ever thought about going back to the rodeo circuit?"

"My life is here now," he answered, his voice ripe with an acceptance he'd come to terms with long ago.

"And you never regret the sacrifice you made?"

"Hell, no." He didn't altogether believe the bold statement himself. Sure, he missed the circuit, the traveling. "How did we get on this subject? I thought you wanted to hear how your brother swooped in like a ravenous hawk and snatched up my father's land. You know, this property had been in the family for over fifty years."

"Did your father have to sell the land?"

"Yes," he said through gritted teeth.

"Why?"

"Made some deal with a seedy oil company." One that Bobby had always thought might have connections with Sakir Al-Nayhal, though he could never prove it.

"So Sakir didn't actually steal the land, he—"

Bobby interrupted caustically, "He tried to buy this land several times and my father told him to get lost. Your brother was proud and pissed off when he was rejected, and first chance he got, he took what he wanted."

She pushed away from his rigid body. "Why do you think he wanted this land so badly?"

Bobby shrugged, gave a derisive snort. "He said the land had major environmental issues that needed to be addressed."

"And that wasn't true?"

What was the point of this? Bobby thought angrily. With all the questions? It was like a damn inquisition. She was following a path that made Al-Nayhal look innocent, and Bobby wasn't going there with her. "It's getting dark, and so's my mood."

Her face was filled with contrition. "I'm sorry, Bobby. I just want to get to the truth."

"Why? Why do you care?" And didn't she know that the truth had many sides to it? Hell, if he really looked at the truth, turned away from supposition and what he believed in his heart, he might not be so quick to keep his word to his father.

"I care because I like you." She bit her lip, but didn't look nervous, just desperate to understand. "And you hate my brother. That's a problem for me."

"Yeah, I get that."

"I'm trying to build a bridge here."

As Rip shifted beneath them, his muscular body ready to fly again after the short rest, Bobby snaked his hand behind her neck and pulled her to him. His kiss was hard and unyielding. When he eased back, he found her gaze and said in a hushed, though ultra-serious whisper, "Sakir Al-Nayhal and I will never be friends. No matter how close you and I get, that fact will never change. Understand?"

Tipping up her chin, she nodded. "Yes."

"Can you handle that?"

"I don't know."

His hand tightened possessively around her neck. He wanted to kiss her again, nip her lower lip with his teeth—brand her somehow before he was forced to give her back to her brother. But the rabid hunger he felt worried him, and he released her, lifted her up and placed her behind him once again.

"Put your arm around me, Jane," he commanded.

Seconds after she wrapped her arms about his waist, he led Rip into a half turn, then kicked the gray stallion into a heart-jolting gallop toward the ranch house.

The sky had turned an eggplant color as the sun disappeared completely, giving in to the black night.

Jane sat beside Bobby on a white porch swing, a heavy quilt over their legs as they dipped spoons into a bowl of ice cream that Bobby held in his fist. Jane ate the sweet chocolate slowly, thinking about the passion that ran between her and Bobby. Not a romantic passion, but heat and walled-up anger and a need for redemption.

This relationship, if she could even call it that, was growing dangerous with every moment they spent together. Bobby clearly was swimming in a sea of bitterness. He turned away from the realities of his past, clung to his own beliefs. For what reason, she wasn't sure. But she feared she had a weakness for men with injured souls, men who loved her cooking and made her laugh. She suspected that in some way her brother had it right. Bobby Callahan could very well break her heart. And what a fool she was for taking that chance.

Her gaze flew to his face. So rough, so sexy, with eyes that held a thousand emotions, five hundred of which were happiness and hopefulness and caring for others and a deep sense of compassion. She wondered if the truth would ever set his soul free.

She took another bite of ice cream and said thoughtfully, "Romeo and Juliet."

Bobby turned to stare at her, eyebrows raised. "Pardon?"

"That's what's happening here. With us. Did you read that play in high school?"

"Sure. Boy and girl fall in love, then off themselves."

She grinned, pointed her cleaned spoon at his chest. "They *off* themselves, as you so delicately put it, because their families are bitter enemies and they'll never allow Romeo and Juliet to be together."

"I don't have any family, darlin'."

"It's the principle of the thing," she explained.

"So, what's your point? That we're going to end up dead if we continue to see each other?"

She laughed. "No, of course not." The laughter melted into a reluctant smile. "But we might end up hurt."

His expression changed from playful to cryptic in a nanosecond. "Anything's possible, I suppose. Found that out a long time ago." He dug his spoon into the frozen treat. "But…"

"But what?"

His gaze found hers. "Is the possibility of pain later on worth the pleasure now?"

"Wow, that's a question."

"All I'm saying is that we've got something here, happening between us. Why worry about the future?"

With her spoon mining into the ice cream, Jane replied, "Well, I guess because I'm a woman and that's what we do. Worry. About the future and a hundred other things."

Bobby set the bowl on the table beside the swing and pulled Jane onto his lap. "I think about you too damn much, you know?"

"I don't know if I'd put it that way, but I think about you, too."

"Yeah?"

"Yeah," she replied, grinning, allowing the heaviness of their ride and all conversation about family to fall away.

Bobby repositioned the blanket over her shoulders and let it cover him. "What do you think about?"

She smiled. "That night."

"Ah, yes. That night."

"Your eyes," she whispered.

He found her neck, grazed his lips over her pulse point, and uttered, "Your skin…"

She smiled, closed her eyes. "Your mouth…"

He pulled her face down to his and covered her mouth. This time, there was no anger in his kiss, only desire. He tasted like chocolate and cold, and the sound of his breathing, heavy and hungry, made every nerve in her body jump with excitement. When his tongue darted out, lapped at her upper lip, she opened for him, her breasts tightening in response. Such a heady reaction to just a kiss was new for her.

With a hungry whimper, she curled her arms around his neck and pulled his head closer so their kiss could go deeper. Running on pure instinct, Jane closed her lips around his tongue and sucked.

Bobby went stiff, then shuddered. He pulled away from her, and she saw that his eyes were near-black with need, his breathing labored.

"Did I hurt you?" she asked, concerned.

"Not yet, Juliet."

A strange blow of emotion sank into her chest. Why would he be the one to say that? To pull away and say something like that? He wasn't the one taking the chance here…was he? He was the one who didn't want to worry about the future. She closed her eyes for a moment, deeply confused, desire and frustration running a race in her blood.

He gently lifted her off him. "I'll take you home now."

"I didn't ask you to."

"I know." He took her hand and led her off the porch.

Seven

When Jane walked through her brother's front door that night, she felt weary, aroused and more confused than ever. What had started out as a light affair had shifted into something far more than casual fun. Bobby seemed to be agonizing over moments of intimacy, limited though they were, and Jane couldn't figure out why. Was it that he really didn't want her? Had that one amazing night they'd shared taken all the mystery out of their relationship?

Melancholy twisted around her heart. She felt the exact opposite. That one night had been an awakening for her, a moment where she'd come to realize that there might be a man out there for her—and the thought of exploring more nights in his arms made her breathless with anticipation.

As she walked into the living room, she felt a heavy gloom cover her, then noticed that it was the house that had brought on the feeling. Sakir and Rita's home was unusually quiet and dark for nine o'clock. No Marian, no Rasan, Sakir's assistant. Had everyone gone to bed? she wondered, following a dimly-lit hallway toward the kitchen. A nice cup of hot chocolate sounded like just the thing to take up to her room to aid her as she tried to get Bobby Callahan's blue eyes and hard mouth out of her head.

But before she reached the kitchen, a chunk of yellow light purged into the hallway ahead. Soft laughter followed. Both light and sound were coming from Sakir's library. There was something in the sound that drew Jane toward it like a tired body to a soft bed. She paused in the doorway, found Sakir and Rita sitting hand in hand on a brown leather couch. They were chatting with someone Jane couldn't see due to a white-leather high-back chair.

Sakir looked up when Jane entered the room and seemed to fight between a welcoming smile and a worried gaze. Jane wanted to tell him irritably that he didn't need to worry—that Bobby Callahan had barely touched her tonight, but she didn't get the chance when he quickly said, "You have a visitor. And a very charming one."

Rita nodded to the person before her, and Jane, eyebrows furrowed, stepped farther into the room. Rounding the chair, she nearly fainted with pleasure when she saw the beautiful, long-legged blonde.

"Mom!" she exclaimed, running straight for her like a lost toddler.

Crushed in her daughter's zealous embrace, Tara Hefner laughed. "How are you, sweetie?"

"I'm fine. But why didn't you call to tell me you were coming early? You weren't supposed to be here for another week."

"I wanted to surprise you."

Sakir nodded deferentially. "And a very welcome surprise it is."

Rita smiled in agreement.

Jane appreciated her brother and sister-in-law's kind welcome. She'd expected Sakir to be aloof, like their brother Zayad, maybe even a little cynical upon meeting the woman who'd long ago had an affair with his father. But if he felt anything at all on that front, he masked it very well.

"I've missed you so much," Jane said with undisguised passion.

"And I've missed you," Tara said, easing her daughter onto her lap. The blind woman let her fingers loose on Jane's face. "You feel tense. What's going on? Are you all right?"

The fact that her mother could feel her mood always unnerved Jane. Even after her mother had lost her sight, Jane had never been able to get away with anything.

Tara took Jane's hand and squeezed it. "Mr. Al-Nayhal was just telling me that you were out with a man who might not be the best company."

Jane tossed Sakir a semi-irritated glare. "Don't listen to my big brother, Mom. He's just being over-protective."

Rita laughed. "I'm afraid you're going to have to get used to that, Jane."

An eyebrow lifted in Jane's direction, Sakir shrugged lightly. "I merely was telling your mother the truth. And please, Tara, I wish for you to call me Sakir. We are family now."

Tara looked toward him, her unseeing eyes bright. "Thank you. It's good to have family."

"Sometimes," Jane said with a dry smile.

Everyone laughed, except Sakir, who managed a tight grin. For the next forty-five minutes, they sipped wine and talked about Jane's time in Emand, little Daya's entrance into the world and her upcoming party. When the clock in Sakir's library struck ten, Jane noticed her mother's well-disguised yawn.

"Are you tired?" Jane asked. "You had a long trip."

Tara nodded. "I am tired."

"I'll take you up," Rita offered kindly.

But Jane was already helping her mother to her feet. "No, thanks, Rita. I'll go with her."

"Your bags have been taken to your room," Sakir said, then turned to Jane. "Tara is in the blue room, just down the hall from you, yes?"

Jane nodded.

"Goodnight, Tara," Rita said warmly.

Her arm through her mother's, Jane guided the older woman upstairs. They walked several hallways chatting softly about the size of Rita and Sakir's home, and how they could have fitted their entire house inside the main hall.

The blue room was large and comfortable and, true

to its name, had bed linens, pillows and walls done in different shades of blue. The first thing that Tara wanted to do was unpack, but, as Jane had expected, her clothes and personal effects had already been put away.

With an easy sigh, Tara sat on the bed, her back resting against the headboard, and gestured for her daughter. "Come here, sweetie."

Feeling six years old, Jane crawled onto the bed and curled up beside her mother. She smelled like lavender and vanilla, and Jane let her head fall into the woman's lap.

"Now, tell me what's going on," Tara pressed gently.

Jane told her mom about her dates with Bobby Callahan, naturally omitting the night they'd shared at the Turnbolts' charity event. Then she went on to explain the situation between Sakir and Bobby.

Tara took a moment before answering, but when she did her voice was soft and wise. "It seems that neither Sakir nor Bobby is in the wrong here."

"I know."

"Bobby's story is a hard one. That's a lot for one soul to bear in a lifetime."

"And he hides the pain well."

"Through bitterness and a good defense?"

Jane looked up, surprised. "Yes."

"Well, that's a natural response to happiness or pleasure or anything good that happens."

"Why?" Jane asked.

Tara shook her head and said almost wistfully, "You feel guilty enjoying life when your other family members can't." Lovingly, she kissed Jane's forehead. "Don't you remember when we went to the beach for the first time after I'd lost my sight? Don't you remember how you felt?"

Undeserving, guilty. Yes, Tara was right. "Well, I don't know if it's anger or guilt that he feels, but whatever it is, it drives him." Jane sat up, took her mother's hands. "I really like him, Mom, but I can't help wondering if Sakir's right. Is Bobby Callahan out for more than just a few dates?" With her thoughts running over the night's events, Jane shrugged. "Maybe it's better if I just stay away from him."

Tara smiled. "Only you can make that choice."

"What would you do?"

"Oh, sweetie," Tara said on a laugh. "I couldn't make that call. I'm in the same boat as Bobby Callahan, still steeped in bitterness."

"What?" Jane stared at her mother. "That's not true."

"Like your friend, I hide it well. Perhaps better than most." Tara eased Jane's head back down to her lap. "But unlike your friend, I think I'm too old to change that part of myself."

Her mother's words settled over Jane, making her feel more confused and on edge than she had when she'd entered the house earlier that night. The admission from her mother was bizarre. Jane had never imagined Tara pining and wallowing over her affliction. Jane had only seen her strong, and spouting off wise words about survival and acceptance.

Good Lord, if her mother could fool her so, what should she think about Bobby Callahan? Would he ever change? Could he let go of his bitterness and embrace life? Did he even want to?

Jane couldn't help but wonder if she was seeing things, people clearly anymore—or through some rosy filter of her own making.

"Well," Jane began to say tightly, "it seems that I'm falling hard for a man who I'm fairly convinced can never offer me a future."

"It's strange," said Tara in an emotional voice. "Strange that our lives should follow such a similar path."

"What do you mean?"

"I, too, fell in love with a man who couldn't give me a future.

Sakir and Zayad's father. Yes, he'd been married, the leader of a country. Totally unavailable.

"But I have no regrets," Tara said, leaning down and giving her daughter another kiss on the forehead. "After all, he did give me you."

"You call that girl of yours. Tell her to get herself out here."

Bobby ignored Abel's ridiculous demand as he helped Laura Parker with her riding helmet. It was close to eight o'clock in the morning, the sun was shining brightly, and Bobby had an excited group of riders ready and waiting. For the first time since he'd taken Jane home last night, his mind wasn't on her.

But thanks to Abel, she was back to the forefront.

"Said she wanted to help, didn't she?" Abel persisted.

"She did," Bobby muttered.

"Well, we're going to need it later on today. Twice as many students as usual."

"We can handle things just fine."

"Don't be stupid."

Bobby threw the older man a dangerous glare. "She wouldn't come anyway. Something tells me she doesn't want to see me today."

"Why's that? What did you do?"

"What I always do." He'd found a reason to distance himself from any feeling that wasn't productive. He could handle anger or irritation or despair—even plain and simple sexual pleasure—but forging a connection between his black heart and another's strong, healthy one had him backing off to get his bearings, and once again reaffirm what he was doing with her. Damn, why couldn't he and Jane have stopped this the night he'd found out who she was? Bobby cussed under his breath as the reason stabbed at him. He hadn't stopped this tryst with Jane because he had payback on his mind.

Thing was, he hadn't bargained on liking the woman—wanting her, yes, but liking her, no.

The mare beside Abel shifted and stepped on the edge of the old man's foot. Abel swore darkly, then looked sheepish as the teenager he was helping brush down the horse lifted his eyebrows. He lowered his voice and leaned into Bobby. "You're going to end up a lonely old goat."

"Look who's talking," Bobby shot back.

The teenage boy chuckled, then stopped when Abel sent him a testy glare. Again, he leaned into Bobby and whispered, "That wasn't my choice and you damn well know it."

Bobby swatted at a fly. "Fine."

"But you do have a choice, boy."

Bobby looked Abel straight in the eye, prepared to utter some stay-out-of-my-business comment. The older man had been with Bobby for too long. He knew too much, spoke whatever was on his mind with little thought of the impact. But Abel also had been a good friend, so Bobby curbed the need to argue and muttered a quick, "I don't have time for this. As you said, we have a big group today," then walked away.

"Are you sure it's all right if I tag along?"

"Of course," Jane assured her mother as she pulled one of Sakir's cars into the driveway of KC Ranch. "Bobby's foreman said he'd love another set of hands helping the kids with their gear and lining them up and things like that."

"Because I don't want to be a burden."

The warm morning sun filtered through the passenger-side window, setting her mother's pretty face in a flattering pale-yellow glow. "Mom, why are you talking like this? It's not like you to be so—"

"Self-pitying? I know." Tara laughed weakly. "I'm feeling a little lonely lately."

"Even with all of your friends?" Jane asked as she parked the car in one of the vacant spots in front of Bobby's house.

Tara shrugged. "I suppose they're not the kind of friends I want."

Realization dawned. "Oh." In twenty-some years, Jane had never known Tara to be lonely, to want the comfort of a male "friend" in her life. She had always been so caught up in life, in her art and in Jane. But of course she'd want companionship, love.

Really, who didn't?

Jane walked around the car and opened the door for her mother. Tara took her daughter's hand and they walked up the path toward the house. "It's been a long time since I put my oar in, so to speak."

"I don't think much has changed. There still are sharks out there." Jane grinned. "But every once in a while you snag a great catch."

Tara laughed. "I like this metaphor. Goes well with my Piscean nature." She squeezed Jane's hand, then said softly, "So you don't mind? I have your blessing to date?"

"Not that you need it, but of course you do. Go fishing, Mom."

"Fishing!" came a weathered, though highly masculine voice from the porch.

Jane looked up and saw Abel Garret leaning against the railing. He smiled at them both. "You two have plans with a few horses today. No skipping out for trout, understand?"

If he only knew to what they referred, Jane mused with a laugh. She turned to Tara, who looked a little flushed all of a sudden. "Mom, this is Abel Garret. Abel's the foreman here at KC Ranch."

"Among other things." Abel, aware that Tara was blind, shot down the stairs like a man half his age and took Tara's hand in his own. "Pleasure, ma'am."

Tara groaned, then laughed.

"What'd I say?" Abel asked Jane, perplexed.

Jane grimaced. "Ma'am."

"Makes me feel very old, Mr. Garret," Tara said, her face shining with humor and good health.

"Ah, I see." Abel's gaze remained on Tara, smiling at her as if she could see him. "Don't look a day over twenty-nine, but how bout this? How about I call you Tara and you can call me Abel?"

Tara grinned. "Deal…Abel."

All of a sudden, Jane felt like a third wheel. She'd heard of such a feeling, but had never experienced it. Abel and Tara were standing close, seemingly unaware of her presence, talking quietly about the ranch and Abel's job. They seemed not to even know that Jane was still there.

Jane didn't want to interrupt them, but she wanted to find Bobby. She was glad he'd had Abel call and invite her to the ranch today, glad that he'd let his wall and his pride crumble a little and admit that he wanted to see her again. Granted, she still wasn't exactly sure what was going to happen with them, but just the fact that he'd made this step gave her some hope.

Turning to Abel she asked, "Is Bobby around?"

Abel came out of his dream-like state long enough to nod, though his gaze remained on Tara. "At the paddock. Why don't you head down there?"

"Mom?" Jane said, touching her mother's arm. "Ready?"

"I got some lemonade up here on the porch," Abel put in quickly. "Tara, if you're interested…"

"Fresh-squeezed?" Tara asked.

Abel tried to look aghast. "This is the country, little lady. Is there anything else?"

Tara shook her head, then said, "And by the way, I like 'little lady.' Much better than ma'am."

They both laughed, and it was Jane's turn to shake her head. Her mother was actually flirting, full-on. Jane wasn't sure if Abel was a shark or a good catch, but she'd definitely find out the answer from his boss.

"All right," she said finally. "I'll go and find Bobby."

They both waved at her as she walked away, then Abel took Tara's hand and led her up the porch steps. Jane went around the side of the house and down the path.

The ranch was quiet, and she wondered where all the children were. Abel had told her they were understaffed today with an extra-large group of kids. Come to think of it, she mused, there weren't many cars parked in front of the house.

As she headed down the path and toward the paddock, she ran smack into Bobby. Surprise registered on his face. So did discomfiture and, if she wasn't mistaken, a desperate hunger.

"Jane."

"Hi."

He stared at her, then said a little too caustically, "What are you doing here?"

Eight

Jane was like a breath of cool air on his hot and sweaty skin. She made the sun shine frustratingly brighter and made his gut tighten with a need he knew would only keep intensifying in her company.

"Abel said you could use another pair of hands." She studied his face, a slow disappointment settling deeper and deeper into her wide green eyes. "You didn't do the inviting, did you?"

His jaw worked. "No."

She said nothing, just nodded slowly, then turned around and walked away from him.

Bobby followed her. "Jane, wait a minute."

Stumbling over a large rock, she righted herself and muttered a terse, "No."

"Where are you going?"

"To the car," she said, her chin lifted as she stalked down the path.

"Why? You're here now. Stay." He cursed under his breath. "I want you to stay."

She whirled around and eyed him critically. "Look, I don't play games. Never have. I think they're a total waste of time. You either want to see me or you don't. And after last night, I think I deserve an answer."

Frustration seeped into Bobby's pores. He spotted the barn to his right and grabbed her hand. "Come with me."

"I don't think so."

But he wasn't listening. She struggled to free her hand as he tugged her toward the barn, as he kicked open the door and as he pulled her inside. Once there, he eased her back against an empty stall door, his hands falling to either side of her shoulders as he gave her no way out and only one thing to look at.

His eyes blazed into hers. "Just because I didn't do the inviting, doesn't mean I don't want you here."

"Doesn't it?" she tossed back at him.

"Hell, Jane, I wanted you all night long. I just…"

"You just what?" she prompted brusquely, her eyes narrowed. "Because I'd really like to know why you took me home after what I thought was a really great night."

What did he say? That he was freaked out? That their conversation had traveled a road that made him wince, that he liked her, craved her, wanted nothing more than to kick his plans to the curb and jump on this idea of him and her, together…?

Jane crossed her arms over her chest. "Either answer me or let me go."

Her green eyes sparked with anger, her tall, toned body was rigid, and her mouth—that sexy, full mouth— quirked. Bobby struggled with the tension that was building inside him, and lost. He didn't think, just reacted. His mouth closed on hers, hard and demanding, as his hands left the stall door and curled around her waist and back.

At first, Jane remained still under him, her lips tight and closed, then she seemed to crumple, her lips parting, her breath quickening as she gave in to the pressure of his mouth.

Lightning fire shot up between his thighs at her response, and he tightened his hold on her. This was why he hadn't asked her to come to KC Ranch today. This was why he'd taken her home far earlier than he'd wanted to last night. She did something to him, made him forget who he was and what he had to do.

The ire inside him only fueled his desire further, and he opened his mouth, let his tongue explore the seam between her lips, so soft, so smooth, so tantalizing. She groaned with satisfaction and plunged her fingers into his hair, gripping his scalp.

Just when he thought she was going to press his face closer, she did the opposite. She pulled his head away, and raised an eyebrow at him.

"Was that an apology?" she asked, her breathing labored, her eyes liquid with the same desire that was running through his blood.

"Could be."

"Better be."

The exchange amused him, and he grinned. "Did it work? Am I forgiven?"

"I don't know," she said slowly, the pads of her thumbs caressing the tops of his cheekbones. "The punishment for being a closed-off jackass last night should be more than a little kiss."

"Little kiss?" he repeated arrogantly, his fingers gripping her back.

"You heard me." She stared at him. "No more mixed signals, Callahan."

"No." That promise was going to be the death of him. He slid his thigh between her legs and nudged at the soft V. "You want to go riding?"

A smile touched her lips. "Are we talking horses or something else?"

He gave her a wicked smile, his thigh shifting back and forth over the core of her. "First one, then the other."

"What about the work I was called here to do?" she whispered, her cheeks flushed.

"Next group is in two hours."

"Two hours?" Jane repeated, smiling. "Abel failed to mention that."

Bobby leaned in, nuzzled her neck, and reveled in the quick smack of her pulse against his mouth. "He's got a notion he needs to matchmake."

On a soft sigh, Jane managed to say, "We're way past that."

"Yes" he muttered, nipping, suckling his way back to her mouth. "We're into soul mate territory now."

Jane's breath hitched.

Bobby held her steady gaze for a moment.

What the hell had made him say something like that?

After all, he didn't believe in all that romantic, greeting-card baloney.

Teeth gritted, he meditated on an alarming query. Was it possible that his two worlds were suddenly colliding—the fact and the fantasy?

He never got the time to seek an answer. Jane had snaked her arms around his neck and was pulling his mouth down, down, down atop hers once again.

The sun beat down on Jane's back, hot and inescapable.

Today, she had her own horse. Though she'd loved sitting behind Bobby yesterday, her arms wrapped around his waist, her cheek to his back, she'd wanted to experience something new, to learn and to impress the man beside her with her fabulous equestrian skills.

And she'd only fallen off once.

Oddly, her horse had stopped short in front of a particularly large cactus. Thank goodness they'd only been walking, or no doubt she'd have ended up with more than a scratch on the hand.

"Let's give the horses a rest," Bobby said after they'd ridden for a while. "There's a lake just over that rise. We could have a swim."

She grinned. "No showers out here, I suppose?"

"City gal," Bobby needled playfully, looking entirely too sexy in his worn jeans and white T-shirt, every inch of him bronzed skin and hard muscle as he rode his gray stallion as though he'd been born atop him. "You know, if you want to be a real cowgirl, you can't expect any fancy showers on the trail."

"Who says I want to be a cowgirl?" She tossed the

words out as they rode over the rise and down to a kidney-bean-shaped lake, its water very clear and calm.

"That's right," he said, finding her gaze. "You're not sure you're going to end up in Texas, are you?"

She shook her head, sighed. "Not sure where I'm going to end up, period."

Bobby turned his gaze from her, and pointed to the lake. "You know, you can't go in there with your clothes on."

"No, I suppose not."

"Water looks great, though," he remarked, swinging his leg over the saddle and jumping down.

"I have no aversion to skinny-dipping, Mr. Callahan," Jane said as Bobby helped her down from the beautiful chestnut mare. He tethered the horses then returned to stand close in front of her.

"And I have no aversion to watching you," said Bobby in delighted, wicked tones. "Although, joining you sounds damn good, too."

"Hmm. I don't know about skinny-dipping with company," she teased. "That's a whole different matter."

His mouth curved into a sexy smile as he found the edge of her pale-blue tank top and slowly inched it upward. "There's mean fish in that lake."

"Is that so?"

He nodded, mock concern threading his tone. "Who'll protect you?"

"Good point." She raised her arms above her head and, with her heart smacking excitedly against her ribs, she allowed him to remove her tank top.

Bobby tossed the fabric onto a rock, then shifted his gaze to the top button of her jeans. "Shall I continue?"

"I think I can handle it from here," she said, unzipping her jeans, wondering when Bobby would follow suit, wondering how he would look naked under all this sunshine. "So, what's the probability of anyone seeing us?"

"Zero," Bobby told her. "No one comes out this far but me and Abel and, as you said, he's pretty occupied with your mother."

Jane forgot about her bra and panties. In fact, she forgot to breathe as she watched Bobby remove his shirt. Ridiculously, time seemed to slow, and the faint strains of an Al Green love song played in her head. Cut and bronzed, Bobby Callahan was a sight to behold. The only time she'd seen him without his clothes had been their evening in bed at the Turnbolts' where it had been dark, and she'd had to feel her way. With greedy eyes, she surveyed him—barrel-chested, with just a sprinkling of dark hair around his nipples and down to his navel. She swallowed thickly, her breasts tingling as she imagined brushing the hard tips back and forth against his chest.

Her fingers ached to grab at his stomach, so rockhard, it looked as though he'd been slashed with a woman's fingernails. She watched his hands move lower, to his belt buckle. Off went the strip of worn leather, down went the zipper. Her throat was strained, her chest, too, as she watched him remove his jeans and the tight cotton shorts beneath. She sucked in a breath as her gaze moved up. Solid calves, powerful thighs and the thick, demanding muscle in between.

"Hey there."

She looked up, dazed, her cheeks as hot as the rest of her.

He was grinning at her. "This ain't no peep show."

"Right," was all she could manage.

"Get those skivvies off and let's go swimming."

He was at the water's edge in seconds, then dove beneath the clear blue before Jane could even register what he'd said.

Waiting until he dove under once again, Jane quickly removed her bra and panties and hurried down to the water. But she was only up to her ankles in the cool lake, when Bobby surfaced. When he saw her, her breasts moving as she walked, the dark curls between her legs, sexual awareness darkened his face.

He dove under the water again and resurfaced before her. Without a word, he eased her into his arms and held her to him, though his eyes remained fixed on hers. "I don't think I've seen you until today."

She laughed, wrapped her legs lightly around his waist. "I was thinking the same thing."

"Disappointed?" he asked with a devilish grin, as if he knew the answer.

"Get serious," she said, every inch of her electrified with the sensation of his wet skin against hers, and the center of him now hard as steel at her belly.

He pushed a strand of hair out of her eye. "You know, Kimmy and I used to swim here when we were kids. Dad taught her, was real careful with her, but she didn't want any of it."

"She sounds like she was an amazing girl."

"Yeah. Tough girl. Real loving, too."

"I wish I could've met her."

His eyes went soft, and he caressed her cheek with the pad of his thumb. "She would've liked you."

"Why do you say that?"

"Kimmy had a soft spot for funny, kind…good people, I guess."

A bashful smile tugged at Jane's mouth. The way he talked to her, about her, made her feel so cared for, and the way he touched her, gently yet possessively, made her want only to kiss him. Her arms went around his neck and she pressed herself closer to the blunt, plum-shaped tip of him. "Do you have a soft spot, Bobby?" she whispered close to his mouth, near that slash of a scar that so intrigued her.

"I'm looking at her."

His hand moved down her back, rolled over her buttocks and underneath where fine hair gave way to the slick entrance to her body. Jane arched her back, closed her eyes as she felt his fingers get closer.

"This is another one of my soft spots," Bobby whispered in her ear as he slipped one thick finger inside her.

A moan escaped Jane's throat and she pumped her hips, back and forth, taking him in and out of her body. Bobby's tongue lapped lightly at her ear, a sensation that was entirely new to Jane—a sensation that had her on the verge of orgasm in seconds.

"And this," he breathed into her ear. "This is very, very soft."

He continued to lick and nibble at her ear as he

pushed a second and third finger inside her. He was so deep, the tips of his fingers flicking back and forth against a spot so highly sensitive, Jane thought she might pass out.

She gripped his shoulder, needed the support, then felt a desperate urge to touch him as he was touching her. Down her hand raked, over his chest and belly until she found him, his erection, thick and pulsing. She wrapped her hand around him, stroked from the base to the top, circling her thumb over the smooth hood until she felt something hot and sticky-wet, so different from the lake water, drip from the tip.

"So soft, so hard," she uttered, feeling weak and ready to give in.

Her sex pulsed as he thrust his fingers inside her, smacked and teased and tormented at the spot that ached and felt electric. Despite the cool water, she was sweltering. She pumped him as he pumped her, and listened to his breath run ragged. She arched, hovered on the brink....

"Come with me," Bobby whispered against her throat as he placed the pad of his thumb on the plump ridge of nerves beneath her dark hair.

Yes. Yes.

She couldn't speak. Climax was upon her. Her muscles stiffened, inside and out, and she released an unabashed cry into the sunshine and blue sky. Bobby followed, his body convulsing in ocean-like waves, his shaft throbbing in her hand.

Passion spread like wildfire over his face, made his eyes burn blue flames as he gave in, his mouth capturing hers in such an all-consuming way, Jane would have sworn she was having her soul ripped from her body.

They lay together in a patch of sunlight, feeling lazy and comfortable and not at all ready to leave, but…

"The horses are restless," Jane said, drowsily.

Bobby rose up on an elbow and looked down at her, so bone-weakeningly sexy in nothing more than a few specks of grass. "I hate to say it—God knows I do—but it is getting late. We should head back."

"We could always come again," Jane said, then realized the double meaning in her words and laughed.

"And again and again and again." Bobby followed, chuckling.

Her gaze moved over him in a way that had his laughter turning to awareness. "All right, now," he began warily. "You better put some clothes on or I'll forget I have a bunch of kids waiting for me."

She looked horrified. "You can't do that."

"I know." He pitched her tank top at her, along with her jeans. "Hurry it up now."

They both dressed quickly and were back atop their horses riding for home when Bobby turned to her and asked, "Do you still want to help out with the kids? You don't have to. After all, Abel really tricked—"

"I want to stay, Bobby," she told him in all sincerity.

He nodded, feeling as if he'd won the lottery today. The lake had never felt so cool, the sun had never been so pleasingly warm and he'd never felt so wanted by anyone in his life. Jane was a woman without inhibitions. She didn't need rose petals or Frank Sinatra. She gave of herself, totally and freely. She took what she needed, but made certain her partner felt every ounce of her pleasure in his own.

She was rare.

And he didn't deserve to touch her.

They arrived back at the ranch in just under twenty minutes. The first thing Bobby saw was a tall blond woman in her fifties standing outside the corral fence with Abel. She was brushing down Missy, a sweet black Morgan. She looked unsure of herself with the horse, but she was laughing with Abel—as though they'd known each other for much longer than an hour or two.

Bobby hadn't met her, but he was pretty sure the woman was Jane's mother, Tara Hefner. And upon closer inspection, he saw that she had Jane's mouth and her long, lean body.

Jane was off her horse as soon as they reached the pair. "Mom, what are you doing?"

"What does it look like I'm doing?" Tara said with a laugh, looking in Jane's direction.

"But you're afraid of horses. I thought you were just going to get the kids ready with helmets and stuff."

Abel smiled at Tara and patted Missy. "Is that so, Tar? 'Fraid of horses? Well, you sure fooled me. I thought you'd been around these lugs your whole life."

Tara blushed and shook her head. "Oh, Abel."

Clearly shocked, and maybe even a little bothered by the expeditious intimacy of the pair, Jane took her mother's hand and led her over to Bobby. "Mom, I'd like you to meet someone. This is Bobby Callahan."

Like her daughter, Tara Hefner was a very beautiful,

fine-figured woman. She stuck her hand out, and said in a warm voice, "Hi, Bobby."

Bobby softened in Tara's presence, couldn't help it. She had a Southern femaleness about her, and he understood right away why Abel was acting crazy. Heck, her daughter had that sweet openness, too.

He shook her hand. "It's good to know you, Mrs. Hefner."

"I hope you don't mind another assistant?"

"Not at all. In fact, my daddy used to say, 'It don't take a genius to spot a ready angel in a flock of weary sheep.'"

That made her smile, and she leaned close to him, whispering, "Your father sounds like a good man."

"I like to think so," Bobby said tightly, not missing the quizzical look Jane gave him.

Little more was said as the children arrived. Bobby put Jane to work immediately, assisting with the preparations and mounting. From time to time, he'd glance her way, his gut tightening with pride as he watched her, so gentle as she encouraged a young girl from her wheelchair and onto the back of Dandy, an old white mare. She was comfortable here already, comfortable with him, his life and his body. Heat surged into his blood as a flash of memory from this afternoon entered his mind.

He forced his gaze away, onto Abel and Tara, who were working as a team. While Abel led two horses around the paddock, Tara held onto the top of the stirrup, talking to the young boy in the saddle.

It was a sight for sad eyes.

This place hadn't seen the likes of Tara and Jane for a long time and everything here, kids, horses and staff alike seemed to blossom under their care.

Bobby lifted Kitty Johnson onto the back of an old quarter horse, his gut twisting painfully as he realized that the promise he'd made to his father would soon rip this wonderful, short-lived reality from his sights for good.

Nine

It was close to sundown when a weary Tara and a beaming Jane returned to the house of Al-Nayhal. The lush and highly polished surroundings felt just a little chilly after the warm modesty of KC Ranch. Especially when Sakir Al-Nayhal, dressed in a flowing white kaftan, met them at the front door, his face set with grim determination.

"Good evening, sister, Tara." He nodded at each of them, his gaze so stern it caused Jane's cheerful mood to fade slightly.

It was no mystery what was about to happen. Under the priceless chandelier, another confrontation between her and her brother over Jane's choice of man was about to take place. But after the wonderful time she'd had today, she was more than armed to fight him.

"Good evening, Sakir," Tara said quickly, obviously sensing the tension in the air. "Is Rita with us?"

"No, she is with the baby. Daya is having trouble sleeping."

"Ah," Tara said sagely, turning toward Jane. "I remember many a night walking the hallway with you in my arms."

"Just didn't want to sleep," Jane explained to Sakir. "I was always a problem child."

"That's not true," Tara defended passionately.

Jane laughed. "But I grew out of it."

"I am not so sure," Sakir said softly, then when he had captured Jane's attention, continued, "You worked at KC Ranch this afternoon, did you not?"

"Yes."

A heavy sigh was followed by a glance in Tara's direction. "Please talk some sense into your daughter, Tara."

Tara smiled patiently. "It's not that simple, Sakir."

"It must be."

"Just wait until your Daya grows up. You'll see that once they are adults, you have little influence over their decisions."

Sakir lifted his chin and stated proudly, "It will not be so with my daughter."

Tara's smile widened. "Well, I think I'm going to head upstairs. It's been a long day."

"Wait," Jane said, reaching for her mother's hand. "I'll take you up."

"That is not necessary." Sakir clapped his hands three times and Marian appeared in the doorway. "Please take Ms. Hefner to her room."

Marian inclined her head, then went to Tara's side, rested her hand on the older woman's arm. "Ms. Hefner?"

"Goodnight," Tara said to the both of them with a touch of hesitancy in her voice. "Be kind to each other."

Knowing it was important to reassure her mother that everything was going to be all right, Jane used a phrase from her childhood. "Sleep tight, Mom."

Tara granted her a nod and a loving smile before following the housekeeper up the stairs.

When she was gone, Sakir motioned for Jane to follow him into the living room, where a healthy blaze crackled and snapped in the fireplace. Jane sat beside him on a long, gray chenille sofa and waited for him to say whatever it was that he needed to say.

It didn't take long.

"You are falling for him, yes?"

Eyebrows knit together, Jane laughed. "Where did you hear that expression?"

"My wife has said this. About you and…Callahan."

"Has she?"

"She thinks you are in love." He leaned back, crossed his arms over his chest. "I cannot allow this, Jane. I only accepted your dates with Bobby Callahan because I thought that would be all of it. Just a few casual outings. After all, the man has never taken any woman seriously since I have known him."

Alert now, Jane straightened in her seat. "How would you know that?"

With a dismissive flip of the hand, Sakir uttered, "I have ways of finding out information."

The heat from the fire seemed to intensify as Jane absorbed this news. If all Bobby Callahan had been able to manage until now was a date or two, then she was in luck. Aside from the dates they'd shared, Bobby had actually sought her out—at the mall with Rita—and had shared his personal history with her. Those were not the acts of a casual affair.

"Jane?"

She looked into her brother's dark eyes with their wary expression, and grinned like a teenager. "So, he had no serious girlfriends in the past, huh?"

Realizing that the information he'd given her as a warning had only managed to spur her on, Sakir shot her a penetrating stare. "You do not take this matter seriously."

"Oh, believe me, Sakir, I take this very seriously."

Clearly he didn't believe her, because a moment later he was shaking his head and muttering foolish threats. "I am afraid I will have to forbid you from seeing him again."

Unable to stop herself, Jane burst out laughing. "Oh, c'mon, Sakir."

"I am in earnest."

"You're talking like it's the nineteenth century and you're my guardian."

"As your brother I have the right to make decisions, even demands."

Suddenly Jane's laughter died, and so did her smile. She looked at him. Really looked. He wasn't kidding. And this wasn't a quirky brother-sister squabble over what was best for Jane. This was Sheikh Al-Nayhal making an edict.

Her gaze fixed to his, Jane spoke gravely to her brother. "Understand something, please. You have no rights over me. I love you, Sakir, but I'm an adult."

As if he hadn't heard her, Sakir continued, "While you are under my roof—"

"Please don't go there."

"Jane."

"I'm serious, Sakir. That's a dangerous road to take."

"So is the one you are traveling on," he snapped. "Our father would not allow this—"

"I have no father," she interrupted, her tone dotted with a sourness she never knew she possessed. But the truth of the matter was she would never consider the wishes of a parent who had not been in her life—or a brother who hardly knew her, yet believed he knew what was best for her.

"You may not have known the great sultan," Sakir said tightly. "But he would not have allowed such a thing to continue, and I'm afraid I cannot allow it, either."

They stared at each other, stubborn green eyes to dictatorial ones. Finally, Jane stood and nodded. "I'll leave first thing in the morning."

A dark-red stain moved over Sakir's face. "I will not allow that, either."

She said nothing, couldn't say anything with the lump of misery in her throat. Her new family was causing her tremendous pain, forcing her to look at difficult choices.

But the choice to walk away from Sakir, in that moment, was the easiest one she knew she'd ever make.

"We're a couple of sorry saps."

"How do you figure that?" Bobby asked. He and Abel sat on the porch steps, stars flickering in the sky above, beers in hand, just as they'd done almost every night since the older man had come to work at KC Ranch.

Gloom curled through Abel's voice. "Another night with no women."

"Speak for yourself. I was out last night," Bobby reminded him.

"And where's that pretty little filly tonight?"

"Back at Al-Nayhal's."

Hearing the irritation in Bobby's voice, Abel rolled his lips under his teeth. "You know, that Tara's a nice-looking woman."

"You think so, do you?"

"I do. Nicest-looking woman I've seen since..." Abel's voice drifted off and he looked slightly pained at the near mention of his ex-wife, and understandably so. He'd loved her something awful.

"Maybe you should do something about it," Bobby suggested, thinking that the man deserved some home and hearth after what he'd been through.

"Maybe."

"What's the problem?" Bobby asked, his tone threaded with a challenge. "You scared to go under the knife again?"

Abel tipped his beer bottle back and took a swig. "Too old to get my guts ripped out."

"Yeah, I can see that."

Catching the grin on Bobby's face, Abel chuckled. "But then again, I don't want to end up like you, either."

Shifting on the creaky wooden step, Bobby shot Abel a glare of reproach. "What the hell does that mean?"

"One woman to the next. You hardly get to know 'em before you say adios."

Bobby gave a defensive shrug. "Haven't found the right girl, that's all. Not that it's any of your business."

As usual, Abel ignored the last comment. "Jane looks pretty right to me."

To Bobby, too.

Damn her.

Visions of tangled legs, wet fingers and a strange familiarity that went far past the physical, shot into his brain.

Damn her.

There was nothing wrong with good old-fashioned sex. Nothing wrong with a day of fun out on the lake. Nothing, except the ties that bind you, force you closer, worm their way inside your brain and stop you from thinking about anything else.

That's what was happening with Jane. He couldn't think about anything or anyone else. He wanted more— more of her hands on him, more of the laughter in her eyes, more of that heart that practically sang with compassion and truth.

On a trashy curse, he shoved his empty beer can into Abel's hand and mumbled, "I'll see you later."

As he stalked down the path to the driveway, Abel called after him, "Where you going?"

"Need to clear my head," Bobby shot back over his shoulder.

"If it were only that easy," Bobby heard the man say with a dry chuckle as he headed for his truck.

The weight of him pressing down on her body nearly had her breathless.

Wet, wonderful kisses blanketed Jane's mouth as she

wrapped her legs around his waist and thrust her hips up. Bobby entered her slowly, inch by glorious inch, and she reveled in the sweet invasion.

Then, in a red flash, they were fully clothed and Bobby was ripped from her by Sakir. In one disjointed movement, Sakir plowed his fist into Bobby's gut. A low groan erupted from Bobby's throat, and he went at Sakir like a defensive lineman. Jane watched helplessly as the two men fought without fear and without tiring for what seemed like an eternity.

Suddenly she was Bobby, and she was the one fighting her brother with all the strength of a man. She felt his bone-crushing blows to her jaw and ribs. She felt the sadness, horror and adrenaline that kept her from running, kept her fighting even when her body cried in pain, even as tears washed her cheeks....

"Hey, hey there, darlin'."

Jane's eyes flew open; she was instantly relieved of her nightmare. She was in her room, the scents of fresh bed linen and night air curling through her senses.

But there was something else.

Someone else.

Her heart smacked against her ribs and she sat up, stared into the blue gaze of the very man she had been dreaming about. "Ohmigod, Bobby."

"Shhh…" he said, placing a finger to her lips, looking around at the door and the window.

Jane glanced at the clock. Eleven forty-five. Then back at him. "How did you get into my room?"

"Through the window."

Not sure she'd heard him correctly, she tilted her

head to see past him to the open window. "I'm on the second floor, and there's a guard and dogs."

"That's right." His gaze, so dark and intense, slipped to her mouth. He reached out, traced the edge of her jaw with his fingertip. "That's how badly I needed to see you?"

Reality dawned. He was really here, in her room, on her bed. "Is something wrong or—"

His finger moved up, flicked gently over her lower lip. "Nothing's wrong, darlin'. I just needed to give you something."

"What is it?"

"This." With gentle hands, he eased her back to the mattress once again. His eyes filled with wicked intent, he hovered above her, his thigh nestled between her legs.

"And this," he uttered, his mouth greedily descending on hers.

Ten

All that Jane wanted was to have him inside her.

Ever since that night—that party at the Turnbolts'—she'd wondered if those delicious quakes and shivers she'd experienced lying beneath Bobby, the way her blood had roared in her brain like a starved animal, had been real, or just a product of her overly romantic thought processes.

Jane gazed down and sucked air between her teeth, her skin hot and electric at the sight before her. Bobby lay cradled between her legs, blazing a trail of kisses from her knee to her trembling inner thigh.

Her womb ached at the sight—there was no other way to describe the feeling, but it was one she'd never experienced before. Strong and pulsing, running straight from brain to blood.

She realized that the Turnbolts' party had been just a prequel to this night. A fusion of not just two bodies, but two souls, two minds and, if she got her way, two hearts.

"You're so sweet, Jane," whispered Bobby against the hot skin of her thigh as he nuzzled his way, nipping and suckling, to the center of her.

Perhaps it was a purely sexual urge, perhaps she was desperate to connect with him, but Jane rose up on her elbows to watch him. With gentle hands he splayed her thighs and dipped his head.

Electric heat shot through her as tongue met the hard band of her sex. The groans and breathy sounds didn't feel as though they were coming from her, but the strain of her throat proved otherwise. Her gaze moved over Bobby. His hands on her hips, the pads of his fingers digging deliciously into the flesh of her buttocks, his dark head buried between her thighs.

His tongue was creating a trail of fire as he raked up and down the hooded tangle of nerves. His movements were ruthless and hungry, and Jane felt her hips lift, felt them pump against his mouth, move and jerk out of instinct alone.

She let her head fall back, her hand fisting his hair, slamming him harder against her.

Bobby had never had a woman take what she wanted in such a bold, open way. As Jane pumped and writhed against his mouth, she left no doubt of her need for him, and he adored her for it.

"Please," she breathed.

"How do you want this, darlin'?" said Bobby, his

groin tight, his cock straining against the zipper of his jeans as the salty tang of her invaded his nostrils. "My mouth or my—"

"I want *you*. Inside me."

That's what Bobby wanted, too. Maybe he was a fool for caring so much, for needing this woman the way he did. But he couldn't help himself. As he slipped on a condom, he realized how much he wanted to remember tonight, the way he'd loved her, the way he'd given himself to her as he knew he could never do out of bed.

But all his thoughts and sorry hopes vanished as Jane wriggled beneath him, her hips arching with a need that hadn't yet been fulfilled. Bobby's gaze slipped to the entrance to her body, glistening wet and pink. Fear mingled with the rock-hard need possessing every muscle in his body. Joining with her, pushing into the tight, scalding glove of her body, meant more to him than he'd ever thought possible.

For one brief moment, he thought about burying his head once again between her beautiful thighs, sending her to the heavens with his tongue and fingers. But her eyes were on him, burning with a raging fire that ran through his blood, as well.

She spread her legs wide and reached for him. "Please, Bobby."

"Yes. Yes, sweetheart." With one sure thrust, he pushed through the tight passageway and found heaven.

"Bobby," she uttered, her muscles closing around him in a gentle fist.

Bobby's mind went numb, blood pounded in his ears. All thoughts of revenge and guilt and lust and hope seeped out of his mind and left him with nothing but a soothing euphoria.

His mouth tucked into her neck, his erection poised deep inside her body, he whispered, "Tell me you're not going to leave this time."

"No. I'm not going anywhere," she said, clinging to him, pumping her hips slowly, urging him to move.

And he could deny himself no longer. He rose up and slammed back down. Over and over, he thrust inside her. Damp flesh slapping against damp flesh. The sound, mingled with Jane's cries, drove him mad.

Bobby knew they could be heard, and muffled the sounds of her pleasure with his mouth. A red haze blanketed the room, coated his mind. And he shook, hard and long. Felt Jane shudder, the muscles around him quaked as she climaxed. Then he was coming, intense and hot, his own shout of pleasure softened by her deep kiss.

Minutes rolled by, maybe longer, Bobby wasn't certain. He felt drained, and as though he never wanted to move again. He couldn't recall ever feeling so satisfied, so alive. And the feeling scared the hell out of him.

"Bobby?"

His gaze found hers, sleepy and lush. "Yes, darlin'?"

She cupped his cheek in her palm. "There's something I've got to ask you."

"All right."

Her smile was slow and not a little bit sensual. "Were you infiltrating the enemy's fortress tonight?"

He matched her smile, though his gut twisted with a twinge of guilt. "It's no secret that I'm not welcome here. And yes, I feel some satisfaction that I got up here, to you, without being detected. But believe me when I say that my reason for climbing that tree was all about seeing you, darlin'."

"You missed me?"

"Damn right."

"Good." She kissed him, slow and sexy, then whispered, "But maybe you should go now."

Rolling to his back on the bed, Bobby chuckled. "Not the thing a man wants to hear right after making love."

The playfulness in her eyes vanished, and her shoulders fell. "I know, but I can't handle another confrontation tonight."

"What do you mean, another?"

She sighed. "Sakir and I got into a fight earlier."

"About me?"

She gave him a grim smile. "No, about me. He wants to impose his brotherly wisdom on me."

Irritation slammed into him as her discord became his. "He wants you to stay away from the cowboy on his land."

"*Wants* is the relaxed version," said Jane. "He actually demanded that I never see you again, as if I was twelve."

"Maybe to him you are," said Bobby, suddenly feeling as though he'd made a mistake in coming here tonight. He hated that he'd caused her pain, caused a rift between her and her brother. He was actually beginning to despise himself more than he did Sakir.

"So, what did you tell him?" said Bobby, self-recrimination making his tone sharper than he wanted. "Because this won't be our last meeting."

Her eyebrows rose at the obvious possessiveness in his tone, but she didn't refute it. "I told him I was an adult, and that I'll make my own decisions, choices and mistakes."

Mistakes. The word cut through Bobby like a chainsaw.

With a shrug, Jane said, "I just need some space from him, that's all."

Bobby glanced around. "Well, this house is big enough for it."

"I don't think so. I told him I was leaving."

Bobby was so shocked he actually sat up. "What?" he said angrily. "Where are you going?"

"Probably to a hotel for a few days."

Relief that she wasn't leaving town altogether spread through him like warm honey, and he relaxed momentarily. But only momentarily because a realization assaulted him. He wasn't angry over the thought that her absence meant his plan failing. No, he was angry at the thought of days and nights without her.

He was in the deep end, swimming with sharks.

Big trouble.

"I have the baby's party on Saturday to plan," Jane was saying. "So, I have to stay close."

"You're still going to do that party?"

"Of course I am," she said strongly. "Daya is my niece. Granted, this whole thing with Sakir puts a damper on matters, but I've never been one to walk away from a commitment."

No, he'd just bet she hadn't.

"You're not going to any hotel, Jane." The words and

their meaning were out of his mouth before he could take them back.

She sighed and moved away from him to the edge of the bed. "Don't you start, too."

"I'm not bossing, Jane, I'm asking you to stay with me."

The smile she granted him could have lit a dark, Texas sky. "Bobby, that's sweet of you, but—"

"The hell with sweet," he barked good-naturedly, shoving off the bed and coming to his feet. "It's purely selfish. I may've made it sound like it was easy before, but if I have to climb up that trellis one more time I might just end up losing my best bits."

As she watched him yank on his jeans, she laughed. "And we can't have that."

"No, indeed."

She inhaled deeply, shrugged. "I don't know. My mom's got to be with—"

"You and Tara can stay in Abel's house," Bobby told her quickly. "It's private, but close enough to the main house for whatever you might need."

"Bobby, I don't know…"

"Yes, you do." He grinned, tucking in his flannel shirt. "It's a damn good plan and you know it."

Bobby watched as ten different emotions crossed her face while she weighed the pros and cons of such an offer. Then finally, she smiled. "Okay."

"Good. I'll be by for you around seven."

"No. We'll come to you."

Understanding her need for independence right now, Bobby nodded, then leaned over and gave her a kiss before heading out the window and down the trellis. A grin tugged at his mouth. He couldn't have asked for anything more. Jane close by, at his home and on his land, and the sweet knowledge that they were both making Sakir Al-Nayhal pay for his commands and arrogance.

For Jane, leaving her brother's house had been an incredibly difficult move. Rita had been angry with her husband for his foolishness and had on several occasions that morning tried to make him see reason and retract his demands on Jane. But he was resolute. He believed Bobby was out to hurt Jane, and Sakir had made it clear that he wouldn't stand by and watch it happen.

For just a brief moment, Sakir's resolve had caused Jane to wonder about the man she was falling in love with, had caused her heart to flip-flop with fear. But she'd forced herself to look at the reality of the past few weeks, and had come to the conclusion that her fear was just her insecurity talking.

As she'd walked Jane to the rental car, Rita had made her promise that this move would be temporary. While Jane made her sister-in-law see that it was Sakir's decision and fence to mend, Jane assured Rita that she would continue to plan little Daya's party from Bobby's place.

Tara stayed relatively silent on the drive, though she kept her hand over Jane's for most of the way in reassurance and support. After all, when it came down to it, they had been family forever, and nothing would divide them.

Pulling into KC Ranch felt good, felt right. Jane had thought she might feel beholden to Bobby, but she didn't. She was excited to see him and to be on the ranch where so much good was happening—where she felt of use to the world.

Bobby and Abel met them when they came to a dusty halt in front of the house, and helped them both out of the car.

"Welcome," Bobby said, taking Jane's hand and giving her a kiss on the cheek. "Had breakfast yet?"

"No," said Jane, her heart warming at the endearing greeting. "I'm not all that hungry, though."

Abel took Tara's hand as well and gave her a grin. "How 'bout I take you up to the house for some coffee and eggs?"

Tara glanced in Jane's direction, a wistful expression on her face. Jane recognized it at once. Whenever Tara had been away from her beloved pottery for too long, she wore that expression. "I should help Jane get unpacked."

"No, Mom," Jane assured her. "You go."

"Don't you worry, Tara," said Bobby magnanimously, heading for the trunk of the car. "I'll give her a hand."

"All right." Tara walked up the front steps with Abel, looking very pleased.

"Looks like my mother's got one heck of a crush," said Jane as she followed Bobby around the side of the house.

Carrying all three suitcases as though they were nothing more than three matchboxes, Bobby chuckled. "She's not the only one."

"Abel's got it bad?"

"Like a slap in the neck, darlin'."

They were still laughing when Bobby stopped in front of a sweet little cottage. Painted white with dark-green trim, the place was lovely. Big enough for two with lots of flowers and plants and trees, even a small vegetable garden along the side that was boasting two rows of ruby-red tomatoes.

They walked up the porch steps and Jane eyed a white porch swing. "Abel lives here?" she asked, surprise evident in her voice.

"I know. Ruddy old bachelor lives like a peacock."

"It's so neat and clean."

"His former wife's influence. Never been able to shed that thick skin." Bobby set the bags down on stripped hardwood floor. "We gave it a good cleaning, put fresh linens and towels out."

"Thank you." Feeling suddenly weary, Jane sat on the couch and rubbed her eyes.

Bobby sat beside her. "Everything'll be okay, Jane."

"You think so?"

He didn't answer her.

"A few months ago, my life ran a perfectly straight track, and now it's a damn mess. Found out about my real father, about this whole royalty thing…Emand… my brothers." Through an open window, the faint scent of hay and earth wafted in on a breeze. Jane looked up at Bobby, her head heavy, her heart, too. "I feel lost. I thought if I came to Texas—if I left Emand and that life for a while—I'd gain some perspective, be able to see that clear path again. Maybe settle into a life."

"You will," Bobby assured her, though his eyes were slow to echo that statement. "It'll come. You have to give it time. You can't expect things to jump into place minutes after they're tossed around."

A grin tugged at her mouth. "Another one of your dad's sayings?"

"Nope. That one's all me."

Her gaze ran over him, from knocked-around boots to weathered jeans and white T-shirt. He looked like the best thing she'd ever seen, and she hoped to God her brother was wrong. "Thanks, Bobby."

"For what?" he asked.

"Being a friend."

Something dark and undefined moved over his eyes and he looked away. The look unnerved her to her very bones. "Well, maybe I should unpack."

"Right." He stood quickly. "I have a few chores to finish. You'll be all right here?"

"Sure."

After he left, Jane unpacked, refusing to think about what could be. Before she went to work on her own future, she had one important task to complete.

With a steaming cup of tea in her hand, she sat at a little desk beside the open bay window and jumped into the party plans for the daughter of the man she wasn't speaking to—but the man she had come to love as a brother.

Eleven

Bobby had never had a girl in his bed before.

Sounded crazy for a man his age, but he'd always made it a practice to keep women away from his home. It had started out as a protection for his sister, but had continued as a protection for himself. And until Jane Hefner had come into his life, he'd succeeded with that practice. Hell, until Jane, he'd climbed in and out of women's beds, between their starched sheets and beside their fancy pillows.

Didn't want that anymore. Didn't want other women, and didn't want to keep his bed cold.

"So what do you think?"

Lying on the mattress, head on a pillow, Bobby gazed at the woman who had stolen his heart. She sat, legs crossed, sheet tangled, on his bed, holding a pen and a pad of paper. Bobby hated the paper. It was one of those big, yellow legal pads that blocked his view of her pale breasts and pink nipples.

He sighed, the heaviness of a day spent in lovemaking still clinging to his body. As Abel had taken Tara back to the cottage to get her settled and pack a picnic lunch, Jane had come to the main house to work on her menu for the party. But she'd only got as far as the wine and beer list before Bobby had asked her to his bed.

"Read it over again," he said, craning his neck to see over the yellow legal pad.

Jane's pen moved down the paper as she spoke. "Tender smoked brisket, cheese enchiladas, mesquite-grilled chicken, beef flautas with a red-pepper cream sauce. Beans and rice, of course, and Tara's cloverleaf rolls."

"Don't forget about the salads. Got to have a fancy coleslaw and potato salad. Those uppity types love potato salad, but they won't admit it." He took one of her soft feet in his hand and rubbed the instep. "They're so tight in the hind-parts they won't put it on their plate unless it's gourmet—like with red or purple potatoes or some such nonsense."

"Got it. Nonsense potatoes." She laughed as she wrote.

"What about desserts?"

"We're having hot peach cobbler, vanilla buttermilk pie and chocolate fudge pecan pie."

"Oh, darlin', my mouth's watering." Abandoning her foot, he reached for the yellow legal pad and pulled it down an inch or two so he could see her face, and the supple rise of her breasts. "Or maybe that's just because I'm looking at you."

She grinned. "You know your flattery will get you everywhere?"

"I'm counting on it."

Hard as stone, Bobby flipped back the sheet and grinned. Jane laughed and held her notebook up as a shield. "I still have three staff members to hire." She pointed at the ancient clock on the bedside table. "And I have to meet them in one hour."

Bobby seized her ankles and pulled her to him. "Plenty of time."

The notebook slipped from Jane's hand and landed with a dull thud on the rug as Bobby splayed her thighs, and with a wicked grin, lowered his head.

Luck was with her.

Out of the five people Jane had interviewed, she'd found three new fabulous staff members to hire. One young man who worked for his mother's restaurant, but wanted some experience elsewhere was not only going to cook, but also was actually going to act as Jane's buyer since he knew the best butchers, farmers and wholesale suppliers in town.

Things were falling into place, and Daya was going to have a wonderful party, despite all the family craziness surrounding the festivities.

"Jane?"

With a start, Jane turned. Walking up Delano Street, baby Daya in tow, was Rita. Dressed in a pale-pink track suit, the woman smiled warmly and gave Jane a big hug when they met.

Her lips tucked under her teeth contemplatively, Rita asked, "Everything okay?"

"Fine. Great, in fact." For the next several minutes, Jane filled Rita in on the new staff and the menu she'd concocted that morning in Bobby's bed. "We'll be ready to go on Saturday. I'll probably need to come over on Friday to set up."

Rita cocked her head to the side. "You're welcome anytime, you know that."

As people milled up and down the street, gazing in shop windows, laughing or scolding their children, Jane looked directly at her sister-in-law with a sad smile. "How's my brother?"

"Doesn't show his feelings much, but I can tell that he's very upset."

"I'm sure."

"He won't budge."

"He's stubborn."

Rita gave a melancholy laugh and nodded. "Yes. Please don't hate him, Jane."

"Oh, God." Shaking her head, Jane tried to explain what was so heavy on her heart. "I don't hate him. I'm not even mad at him. I just won't be dictated to. Even if this relationship with Bobby turns out exactly the way Sakir believes it will, it'll be my doing, my choice."

A proud gleam twinkled in Rita's blue eyes. "He had to get used to one strong woman in his life, and he'll do it again." She smiled at her baby. "And again, no doubt."

Jane laughed. "No doubt."

"So, how are things with Bobby?" asked Rita gingerly, her eyes twinkling once again.

Jane knew she was beaming, but she didn't care. "Wonderful."

Rita smiled. "I'm happy for you."

"Thanks." Little Daya started to fuss and the three of them walked down the street toward Market Place. The question that weighed heavily on Jane's heart finally inched its way to her lips. "Do you think it's possible to heal this rift between Sakir and Bobby?"

With a shrug, Rita said, "I don't know. Over time, maybe."

"I hope so."

A full minute passed as they crossed the street. Once at the other side, Rita paused and gave Jane a knowing smile. "So, when did you realize you were in love with him?"

Jane actually pretended to look confused for a moment, which made Rita break out into a fit of laughter. "Oh, c'mon, sis."

Tucking her arm through Rita's, Jane sighed as they walked up Grand Avenue. "Well, I guess it was the night he sneaked into your house and into my bed."

When Abel Garret had something serious on his mind, he stood stock-still, his legs splayed, his arms crossed over his chest and his eyes fixed into two narrow slits. It was a look Bobby normally paid attention to, maybe even questioned if he had the time. But today, he had a feeling Abel's mood wasn't related to troubles with KC Ranch.

"Something to say?" asked Bobby in a dry voice.

A sound close to a grunt echoed from Abel's throat. "What's going on between you two?

With a glare, Bobby pointed to himself, then the animal beside him. "Trainer, horse."

Abel scowled. "I'm talking about you and Jane."

"Right. That makes more sense."

"Callahan, you answer me."

Bobby gave the mare beside him a pat and faced his foreman. The man wore his troubled fatherly expression—the one that made Bobby experience equal parts of frustration and fondness. "I like the girl, okay?"

"I think it's far more than that, and so does her mama."

Bobby pulled off his Stetson. He felt damn hot for a relatively cool fall day. "Hasn't Jane made it clear? She doesn't want anyone interfering in this…this…whatever we got going here—and neither do I."

"Tough," said Abel brusquely.

Bobby cursed and walked away from him, toward the corral gate.

Abel followed him. "Family's always involved. May not like it, but there it is."

Swatting at an irritating pair of flies, Bobby whirled on Abel. "I don't have any family."

Abel looked as if he'd been punched, and the sight made Bobby's insides kick. He had this angry streak in him, born out of a promise he'd made to a man whose vow for vengeance wasn't altogether sure he believed in anymore, and fed by a vile bag of revenge he was about to dump on the woman who had made his life livable again.

"Listen, Abel—" he began, but the older man was having none of it.

Through gritted teeth, Abel said, "Say whatever you

want to me, but I'm serious about this girl. She's in love with you, Bobby. Sure as a shot."

Bobby's jaw tightened. He didn't want to hear it, yet he already knew that what Abel said was true.

"Just take care," Abel added with a shrug, opening the gate.

Noncommittally, Bobby nodded. "Yeah."

"I think you'd be feeling something strong for her, too, but you'll stamp that out, won't you?"

"None of your business." Abel didn't know about the vow Bobby had made to his father, but he was sure acting like he knew something.

"Fine. Fine." The older man waved him off and went down the path toward the house.

"Hey." Bobby called after him. "Where you going?"

Abel stopped, glanced over his shoulder. "Tara and I are camping out by the lake tonight. She wants to lie on her back and see the stars."

"See the stars…"

Abel smiled a little sadly. "Through me. You know, that woman may be blind, but she sees a helluva lot more than the rest of us."

Tipping his Stetson, Abel turned and headed toward the house. Leaning against the fence, Bobby reached into his pocket, took out the watch his father had given him, the one with the old man's picture inside. Bobby stared into the rugged face and felt as though the weight of his stallion leaned heavily on his back. Felt a powerful struggle deep within his heart.

What was he doing? His life, once simple and uncomplicated, had turned into a web of lies and lust and, more than possibly, love. He didn't want to look at that last part, didn't want to admit that he was going to bring down the woman he needed above all others for a man who no longer walked the earth.

But the promise—that goddamn vow—couldn't be laid to rest without acting on it.

The sound of tires on gravel had him looking up. Someone was coming up the drive. He headed in that direction, arriving just in time to see a long, black car come to an easy, money-soft stop in front of the ranch house.

At first, Bobby thought it was Sakir, and he was glad. He was ready for a war of words, maybe a few punches. He felt wired as hell.

But the man who stepped out of the Mercedes wasn't Sakir, though he sure had the look of him.

"Bobby Callahan?"

Bobby nodded. "That's right."

"I am Zayad Al-Nayhal. I wish to see my sister."

Twelve

The first thing Jane saw when she got back to KC Ranch that afternoon was Bobby, sweaty and serious out in the ring, training a particularly lovely jet-black stallion.

The second was Zayad Al-Nayhal.

Her eldest brother, the reigning Sultan of Emand, stood regally beside the steel fence in a stark-white kaftan, his chin hard, and his dark gaze intent on the animal and rider before him.

Jane's heart gave a nervous lurch, which irritated the heck out of her. She hated feeling anxious. But even though her best friend, Mariah, had softened Zayad a little, he was still an intimidating presence. Jane knew that if Zayad had come to Bobby's ranch to try to force the royal Al-Nayhal will on her, she was going to need every ounce of strength she possessed to stand up to him.

She watched him watch Bobby, an air of superiority affixed to his handsome countenance—or was it interest? She couldn't tell. But the former would no doubt be the surest guess. Zayad could not help his attitude. After all, he'd grown up in a palace with an armload of servants to do his every bidding.

What was he doing here? Jane wondered, biting her lip thoughtfully. He wasn't supposed to have arrived in Texas until Friday. Sakir must have called him, told him what had happened and asked him to come and take control of their little sister.

With a forced smile that slowly morphed into a real one, she walked up to her brother and laid a hand on his shoulder. "Well, what do we have here?"

Rarely startled, Zayad turned easily. "Hello, Jane," he said, his dark eyes intent, his tone warm. "Mr. Callahan was kind enough to allow me to watch his training session, and show me a few of his stallions. This one is a particularly beautiful beast."

He wrapped her in his arms and gave her a kiss on the cheek. "My brother has told me what transpired between you."

So, Sakir *had* called him. Not much of a shock there. "I'm sorry I wasn't at the house to greet you, but my mother and I—"

"Yes, I know," interrupted Zayad before releasing a weighty breath. "Sakir is acting the fool."

Just as Jane was about to agree, Bobby took that particular moment to ride up. He slipped from the stallion's back and joined them. "Who's a fool?"

"I was saying this about our brother," Zayad told

Bobby, his chin lifted as though he was the only human being alive who was allowed to say so.

Leaning against the fence, Jane looked at the ground. "He's no fool. He's just being protective—in his own irritating way, of course."

"Does he have reason to be protective?"

Jane's head came up. Zayad was staring at her, then he turned to look at Bobby, one dark eyebrow raised.

Bobby's mouth thinned with anger. "Your sister is more than capable of handling whatever's thrown her way."

Zayad nodded slowly. "Yes, I believe she is. She is Al-Nayhal, after all."

"Yes, she is," Bobby agreed.

A heavy weight sat on Jane's shoulders, on her heart and soul, as well. Bobby had offered neither a yes nor a no to Zayad's question about her needing to be protected. It was possible that Bobby thought the query insulting or maybe he was just too angry at the Al-Nayhals to give any of them a sign of his sincere feelings regarding their sister—Jane didn't know. But that quick, jabbing fear she seemed to experience every time she thought about Sakir's warning and Bobby's feelings reared its unwelcome head once again.

"Mariah is downtown at a restaurant called the Willow Tree." Zayad's words broke through Jane's uneasy fog. "Will you join us for a late lunch? Tara as well, if she is free."

"My mother's with a friend right now," Jane explained, thinking of Tara around the small kitchen table smiling as Abel read her another chapter of *Don Quixote*. "And there isn't much that'll tear her away from him."

Zayad gave a nod of understanding, then turned to look at Bobby. "Mr. Callahan, would you care to join us?"

"I don't think so," Bobby said, his face stoic.

"Yes, that would be wonderful," Jane said, true excitement in her tone. She turned to Bobby. "C'mon, Bobby. Mariah's my very best friend in the world. She's beautiful and pregnant and funny and a great lawyer." A wide grin split her features. "And if you're real lucky, maybe she'll tell you how she and Zayad met. He moved in next door to us in California and pretended to be just an average Joe. It's a very funny story."

With a quick roll of the eyes, Zayad explained, "Not one of my finer moments. But I received a most precious gift. My wife and a mother for my son, Redet, and our baby to come."

"So deception brought you good fortune," Bobby said, his voice threaded with a lighthearted antagonism that made Jane's stomach churn.

Zayad's face turned to stone. "Pardon me?"

Around them a breeze blew. It was neither cool nor hot, and was scented with aging hay. "Just remarking that deceit for profit seems to run in your family, that's all."

"Bobby!" Jane said sharply, shocked at his rudeness. But she was allowed nothing else as Zayad turned on the cowboy.

"You do not insult the family of Al-Nayhal," Zayad warned.

With a cold frown, Bobby nodded. "Whenever I can."

As Jane tried to think of what to say next, her belly as tight as a trap, the two men stared at each other. Both exceptionally tall, one all lean muscle, the other brawny and steeped in a bitterness he refused to climb out of.

"Bobby," Jane began hesitantly, not exactly sure what to say or do to diffuse the situation. She hardly thought a good punch in the stomach would be appropriate, but she was so frustrated at his attitude, she wished she could.

But Bobby didn't stay long enough for a word or a jab. "I have work to do," he uttered, then turned away, led the stallion toward the other end of the ring, tossing a tart, "Enjoy your lunch," over his shoulder.

Jane didn't want to look at her brother. She knew what was coming, what he was about to say, and she didn't blame him. When Zayad touched her shoulder, she found his gaze. "Jane, I do not wish to say this, but I think Sakir may be right."

She shook her head. "No. You don't understand. Bobby's had a hard time of it, Zayad. He's lost his land, his father, his sister. He's lashing out at the family he thinks is responsible for his destruction."

"Yes, I agree. And you, my girl, will no doubt get caught in the crossfire."

"I don't believe that," said Jane, not thoroughly convinced. "But even if I do, it's my choice to make."

Zayad nodded at long last. "On this point, we agree."

"I want to help him."

"You love him that much?"

She nodded. "Will you wait for me in the car?" With a quick, grim smile Jane excused herself from Zayad and went after Bobby. She found him at the other end of the corral, lightly slapping a dusty pad against the horse's side. She wasted no time, her anger now free to show itself.

"What was that?"

He didn't look at her. "That was pissed off."

"At what? Zayad's done nothing to you."

"It's the attitude, Jane," he said, glancing up, his blue eyes filled with the same ire she always saw when they spoke about the past. "It's the belief that good things come to those who lie and cheat. If someone's going to deceive someone else…" he paused, shook his head.

"What?" asked Jane uneasily. She felt desperate to understand him, help him, heal him. If only he'd let her. If only she could grasp the real Bobby, the one who cared for her, and stamp out the one who hated her family, maybe they'd have a chance.

"Well, they should only expect to get their ears boxed," said Bobby, his fist tight around the pad. "Get what they deserve for hurting someone else."

"When Zayad came to California to see me, he was only trying to find out who I was. He knew that deceiving us about his identity was wrong and immoral, and he asked Mariah and me to forgive him. He's more than paid his debt to Mariah."

Grabbing the rope that had been tossed over the fence, Bobby said sullenly, "The particulars are none of my business."

"Maybe not, but when you make judgments—"

"They're fair judgments, Jane," said Bobby, turning on her, his gaze fierce. "A lie is a lie."

"The world's not that black and white," said Jane in apple-crisp tones.

"It is to me."

She stared at him, her heart pounding furiously in her chest. His conviction for the truth impressed her, but the solid sourness that resided in his eyes made her wince in frustration. "We're obviously at an impasse," she said finally, feeling a wave a gloom move through her gut. Did they even stand a chance of making it? "I'm going to go now."

When she turned on her heel and started away from him, he reached out, grabbed her hand and pulled her back to him. For several moments, he held her close, his breathing slow and steady. Jane closed her eyes and allowed herself to melt into him.

"Darlin'?"

The husky endearment caused the cold navy blue of Jane's heart to warm into a soft pink. "Yes?"

"I'm sorry."

"I know."

"Come back. After you see your friend." He eased back, bent his head and nuzzled her mouth. "I'm an angry bastard, but I need you, Jane. I need you so damn much."

The torture in his voice, the desperation in his tone, and the love she had for him in her heart made her weak. She let him hold her, let his mouth cover hers, let her weariness of spirit turn into a tumbling sense of desire. "I'll be back."

Twisted and confused, Jane pushed away from him. The walk from the corral to the driveway to the man waiting for her in his shiny, black Mercedes was one of the longest and, strangely, the loneliest, of her life.

* * *

"May I say it again?"

Jane laughed at her glowing best friend as they walked down Grand Avenue after their late lunch. The day was slowly turning into evening, but the warm sun filtered through the trees lining the sidewalk with fierce determination. "Okay. Say it again if you feel you must."

With a dramatic sigh, Mariah put a hand to her growing belly and said wistfully, "I miss your tapioca pudding something awful."

Again, Jane laughed, and the sound moved through her like music. Ever since she'd found out that the man living next door to her and Mariah was not only the sultan of a foreign land, but her brother, ever since she'd left her home in California, Jane had been walking on a tenuous cloud. She'd missed the girlfriend banter with her childhood friend. It felt comfortable and familiar and it made her feel as though she could open up in ways she never could in Emand—or at Sakir's home.

"So, no pudding in Emand?" Jane asked.

"Of course," Mariah said as she proceeded to count off on her fingers. "Mango pudding, coconut pudding, the chef even managed a pretty fabulous chocolate pudding. But when he attempted tapioca…" She said no more, only rolled her lips under her teeth and shook her head.

"Well, we'll have to remedy that right now," Jane told her, giving her a wry wink. "But first, butter pecan."

"Oh, I thank you and my baby thanks you," Mariah said with a greedy little giggle as she tucked her arm in Jane's. There was a moment of silence as they headed toward the ice cream shop, then Mariah inhaled and said slowly, "Just so I know, when I do get my pudding, where do I need to pick it up?"

Shaking her head, Jane chuckled. "That was a smooth segue."

"Thank you," said Mariah proudly, flipping her blond hair. "I'm learning quite a bit from Redet, and from that old windbag of a P.R. man at the palace."

"Not to mention the kids you represent in court, right?"

"Kids are the very best at changing the subject—but I have to say that you come in a close second."

Jane gave her friend a wide grin. "All right. I'm staying with Bobby Callahan."

"Yes, I've heard the reports. You sure you know what you're doing?"

"Nope." The unease that had been running through Jane's blood on a daily basis didn't feel nearly as frightening to admit when she was with Mariah. "But I'm in love."

"Yeah, that'll pretty much wipe out all good sense." Mariah wiggled her eyebrows. "And I only know this from personal experience."

"The thing is, he's a good man, Mariah. Loving and kind and sexy and, well…he makes me feel needed and desired. I've never felt like this about anyone in my life. I want to be his other half, share his life here…if he wants me."

"Really? You think you might want to stay in Texas? No Emand with your best friend?"

"Tara is really starting to love it here, and…well," A

warm flush surged into Jane's cheeks and belly. "Emand makes a great honeymoon destination."

Mariah came to an abrupt halt in front of the ice-cream store. Totally unaware of the throngs of people herding in and out of the glass doors with their double scoops and banana splits, she asked, in all seriousness this time, "Do you think he's going to ask you to marry him?"

Jane shook her head. "I honestly don't know. It's what I fantasize about, if that means anything. Bobby cares about me, I know that much. But he has a lot to work through, people to forgive—his father's choices to come to terms with. But the way Sakir and Zayad talk, it'll be a miracle if Bobby and I end up together."

In all good friendships, there comes a point in time when one party needs to hear a word or two of encouragement, whether the other person believes what she's saying or not. This was one of those times, and as always, Mariah curled around her friend in an emotionally indulgent way.

"I don't care what anyone says, Jane—or what they believe to be true. I want you to be happy. If you love this man, then you have to fight for that love, right?"

Hope swelled within Jane and she nodded. "Right."

"Now," Mariah began with a tough smile. "With that said, if Bobby Callahan ever hurts you, Sakir and Zayad will have to climb over me to get to him."

Jane couldn't help herself. She burst out laughing.

"Let's get that ice cream," said Mariah, making for the doors. "If this child doesn't get a nutritious meal soon, he or she is going to kick me into oblivion."

Thirteen

The days leading up to little Daya's Welcome to the World party rolled over on each other like a carpet. By Friday, Jane thought her head might explode with all the information, recipes, times and worries she had crammed into her brain. Her body felt slightly drained from so much prepping, cooking and discussions/arguments with the decorator. But it looked as though the party would go off without a hitch and, though tired, Jane felt very pleased with herself.

Her relationship with Sakir, however, was not doing nearly as well. Jane had wondered if she and her brother would have some time to talk, maybe settle a few matters, since she worked under his roof nearly every day. But Sakir stayed in his office most of the time, and when he did emerge, all he offered her was a quick hello as they passed each other in the house. Even as she was immersed in party planning, she missed their talks, his funny, starchy ways and his brotherly presence.

As she drove away from his home the night before the party, she wondered if they'd ever be friends again, if he'd ever welcome her into his home as his family.

The weathered KC Ranch sign gave her a dusty, encouraging smile as she passed through the gates. If she were to be honest with herself, she'd admit that Sakir's house would only be a place to visit now anyway. How she viewed "home" had changed the moment she'd moved into Bobby's house. Against her better judgment, she'd been referring to the ranch as her home for some time now, and actually felt a thrill when she pulled up and saw the lights flicker in the open windows.

She didn't even bother heading over to the cabin. Three days ago, when Tara and Abel had returned from their night under the stars with looks of total adoration on their happy faces, they'd all made a silent agreement. Tara and Abel would have the cabin and Jane and Bobby would have the house. Sometimes they took meals together, sometimes not. It was smooth and easy and Jane had never seen her mother so happy.

Jane pulled back the screen door and sighed as she entered the house. "Do I smell pizza?"

"You do."

The sight before her was like something out of a dream. Looking thoroughly pleased with himself, Bobby stood beside the couch, big and sexy and rough in his faded jeans and pale-green T-shirt, a delicious smile on his lips. And in front of him, on the coffee table, was a hot mushroom and pepperoni pizza, a bottle of wine and a few videos stacked up on top of each other.

"Oh, I love you!" she said in a rush, then glanced up sheepishly.

Bobby raised an eyebrow and grinned.

"You know what I mean," Jane said, forcing a casual tone to her voice.

"No. What do you mean?"

Acting coy, she strolled over the kitchen table and dropped her things on the rough wood surface. "A starving woman will say anything. She's got a mental block that only nourishment will banish."

"Only nourishment?"

She grinned as she watched him move toward her, take her hand in his. "I didn't say what I was hungry for."

"Yes, you did, darlin'. It's in your eyes." He guided her over to the couch and motioned for her to have a seat. "Haven't eaten a thing all day, have you?"

"I think I had some peanuts around ten," said Jane, dropping onto the soft cushion.

"Pathetic."

"They were organic."

He chuckled, opened the pizza box, took out a slice and slipped it onto a plate. "Here." He handed her the plate, then filled a glass with wine.

As she ate her slice with gusto, she said, "You better be careful, Callahan."

"Why's that?"

"I could get used to this."

With an easy grin, he handed her the glass of wine. "Drink up."

The slow, delicate currant flavor of the merlot went to work in a hurry. Feeling relaxed and happy, Jane fell back against the couch cushions and eyed her hunky cowboy. "I want to ask you something, and I want you to promise to think about it before you fly off the handle."

He snorted. "I don't fly off the handle."

"On this subject you do."

"You want me to teach one of your brothers to ride?" he asked, his eyes filled with grim amusement.

"Something easier than that." She grinned, her eyebrows rising hopefully. "Come to the party tomorrow night."

"No," said Bobby succinctly. He smiled brightly. "See, no flying off the handle."

"There was also none of the suggested thinking, either."

"C'mon, Jane," said Bobby, tossing a second slice of pizza onto his plate. "Why would you want another batch of stress added to your night?"

"I don't. I want you." The limb she was going out on felt shaky, but she pressed on. "I want you there, supporting me."

He sighed.

"All-you-can-eat desserts," she tempted, grinning.

"Even if I did agree, I wouldn't be welcome there."

"You're my guest," said Jane, sliding her plate back on the coffee table and inching closer to him. "All that needs to be said, okay?"

His gaze bored into her, a struggle going on behind his eyes. One she couldn't name. But when she smiled at him, he returned it and shook his head. "All right. One condition."

She gave him a quick kiss, then eased back. "Anything."

He took the glass of wine from her and placed it on the table, then took her in his arms. "The dessert sampling starts tonight."

He had her shirt unbuttoned, bra around her waist and his tongue circling her nipple before she could say another word.

The pearly-gray light outside his bedroom window signaled the dawn of a day he'd both anticipated and dreaded for some time. Until now, Bobby hadn't decided when the day of reckoning—the day he destroyed the woman beside him—would come, but Jane's invitation, her plea for his support last night, had offered him the opportunity on a cold, calculating platter.

Bobby shifted under the sheets, Jane following his movement without waking, her arms tightening around him, making him feel claustrophobic and beloved all at the same time.

He was a monster.

A cold-blooded, unfeeling asshole, and yet he knew he would close all passageways to his heart and follow through with his plan.

He owed it to his father. The final payback. Then maybe he'd be free, be able to breathe again—let go of all the anger that fisted around him.

"It's barely morning," said Jane in a husky whisper against his chest.

"I know." He cuddled her deep into his chest and kissed the top of her dark head. It would be the last time

he would feel her beside him. Her warmth, her scent.
"Go back to sleep, darlin'."

She was quiet for a moment and he thought she'd
fallen asleep, but once again she stirred. "Bobby?"

"Yes?"

"I really do love you, you know."

Bobby died inside.

His gut twisted in pain, a sick, shallow feeling moved
through every vein, every bone, every muscle. He
wanted to pull away from her, or push her off him before she branded him with her words of love.

But he lay there, listening to her breathing turn slow
and shallow as she crept back into sleep.

The mattress felt soft, too soft, ready to swallow him
whole, and all he could think about was taking her with
him, escaping his burden together.

He stared at the ceiling, at the morning light as it
turned from gray to the color of sun-bleached hay. Not
only was this the last time he would hold Jane, but also
it was the last time she'd ever speak to him with love in
her voice. The thought cut him deep.

He never would have believed it.

From one wild night at the Turnbolts' to this,
this…something real. He'd just never counted on how
much it would hurt to lose her.

Fourteen

"**B**eautiful." "Elegant". "Delicious." "Outstanding."

These were the comments that Jane heard as she walked the ancient Armenian carpets scattered over the hardwood floors of the Al-Nayhals' massive living room. Three crystal chandeliers blazed a lovely light throughout the room, making the bronze statues, Italian and Spanish artwork and the beautiful photograph of Daya and Rita catch the eye.

A young man held out a glass of Cristal to her and smiled. She took it and thanked him. Her staff was exceeding her expectations. With wall-to-wall guests, the servers seemed to be moving at the speed of sound to take care of everyone's drink requests. They were even caring for the children, though the little ones had their own party going on in the corner of the room. Anticipating the needs of the guests' children, Jane had set up a kiddie table, with every yummy treat imaginable, all surrounded by toys, puzzles, crayons and miniature sofas.

Jane glanced over at the extra-long table overflowing with flowers, food and candles set up in the adjoining room and smiled. The room was still packed with people who were going for seconds. The party was a success.

She was a success.

She knew now that her dream of opening a restaurant had been with her all along, had been a part of her, but alas, it had just taken her a while to rediscover that passion. It was hard to see clearly through a fog of sudden insecurity, which was what she had suffered from the moment Zayad had revealed who she was. But now her confidence had returned in a marvelous rush. Now she recognized her future once again. Only one question remained—where would she unlock that dream? Where would she open her restaurant?

With a quick glance in the direction of the entryway, Jane bit her lip. Bobby was supposed to have been here over an hour ago. She'd called the ranch, but there had been no answer. He was not the kind of guy to go back on his word, and she didn't believe he'd come to any harm on his way over here.

Looking gorgeous in a pale-blue silk dress, Rita strolled over to her, baby in her arms and someone Jane could only assume was Rita's sister by her side. "Jane, I'd like you to meet my sister, Ava."

"It's nice to meet you," said Jane, shaking the striking blond woman's hand.

"You, too," Ava said warmly. "I've heard so much about you."

Giving her sister an affectionate smile, Rita told Jane, "Ava brought her husband, Jared, his mother, Muna, and my niece, Lily, but they're out in the gardens right now. You'll meet them later. For now," she said dramatically, "I want Daya to give her auntie a kiss. She's a genius chef."

Daya was fast asleep, and Jane leaned down and brushed a thumb over her soft cheek. "How about I give you one, precious?"

"Seriously, Jane," said Rita warmly, her blue eyes flashing with pleasure. "This is fantastic." And Ava nodded in agreement.

Flushing proudly, Jane said, "I'm glad."

"Sakir thinks so, too." She gave Jane a sheepish smile. "I have a feeling he's making his way over here to tell you so himself."

And when Jane looked past Rita she saw just that. Sakir, shouldered by Zayad, was talking with an older couple a few feet away, though Sakir's gaze kept flickering toward Jane.

"So," Rita said, lowering her voice. "Are you enjoying yourself?"

"Sure." That was almost the same thing as being proud of herself, wasn't it?

Rita glanced at Ava, then back again to Jane. "Well, that's not very convincing."

Jane chuckled. "No, I guess not."

It was true that with every wonderful thing that happened tonight, she missed having Bobby to share it with. Jane tried to think back to this morning and Bobby's mood. She'd been distracted with plans, and had left for Sakir's around nine. But before then, at the breakfast table, Bobby hadn't said much to her. In fact, he'd had a tense expression on his face when she'd kissed him goodbye.

A cold shiver moved up her spine, and she reached in her purse for her cell phone. But Rita's words and the smile that accompanied it stopped her.

"Someone is here to see you, Jane."

Jane glanced toward the doorway. Relief spread over her, along with a wave of possessiveness. He'd come. For her, he'd braved the censure of her brother and come.

Dressed simply for a semi-formal affair in black jeans and a white shirt, he still looked overbearing and sexy, though more than a little tense. But that was to be expected as a guest of Sakir Al-Nayhal.

She quickly smoothed down the skirt of her pale-gold silk dress and gave him her most charming smile. She could feel Sakir's and Zayad's eyes on her, but she didn't care. All she could think about was telling Bobby of her success here tonight, of how rooted and self-confident she felt again—how she finally understood where her career was going.

His mouth set in a tense line, Bobby strode right up to her, didn't acknowledge Rita, Ava or Mariah, who had just joined them.

"You look handsome tonight, Mr. Callahan," she said, reaching for his hand. "Thank you for coming."

But he didn't give her his hand, and there was something strange in his gaze, something blank—almost dead. "I have something to say to you."

His cold tone hit her hard, made her shiver. "Okay."

Around her, the small gang of women seemed to stop breathing, and Jane's heart began to thump loudly in her chest as the taste of fear blocked out her earlier taste of success.

"These past few weeks have been a mistake," said Bobby roughly. "I wanted you and I took you, but that's all there was."

Someone put a supportive arm around her waist, but in her shock, Jane couldn't tell who it was.

"I've come here to tell you that I don't want you anymore, Jane."

Their gazes clashed and held, and the shock evaporated from Jane's mind. Through gritted teeth, she uttered, "Is that so?"

He nodded. "I could never love you."

"You're probably right," Jane countered, realizing with a flash just what was happening here, what Bobby Callahan was doing.

"I think you should leave, Mr. Callahan," said Rita in a disgusted voice.

He nodded, but not at Rita, at Jane. And for one brief second she swore she detected a flash of misery in his lifeless gaze, but it was gone in an instant.

And so was Bobby Callahan.

Anger unlike anything she had ever known flooded Jane's senses as she watched him walk away. Around her, Rita, Ava and Mariah were trying to comfort her, offering answers and angry excuses for Bobby's insanity and flagrant disregard for her feelings. But Jane wasn't listening. She shoved her gaze to where Sakir and Zayad stood just feet away. They weren't talking to the older couple anymore. Zayad looked murderous and ready to spring. Sakir was staring at Jane, a brother's grief in his eyes.

She pushed away from her family and headed after Bobby. If he really didn't want her, fine. But that's not what was going on here, and she was going to make him face that truth before he walked away from what they had so easily.

"Jane," she heard Sakir call after her as she rushed to the front door and yanked it open.

"I don't have time right now, Sakir."

"I am sorry."

She whirled around, her anger at Bobby—at this whole stupid, wasteful situation—coming to a head. "For what exactly? Not being able to rub Bobby's rejection in my face, or for pushing me out of your life when I was just getting used to having a brother?"

She watched the effect of her words as they burned into his face, made his lips thin and his jaw tighten. "I could not see you get hurt."

"Well, you see it now, don't you?" she countered, feeling the cool night air wash over her heated skin and temper. "What's the difference?"

When he didn't answer, she turned around and fled down the front steps toward her rental car.

"Jane. Wait."

With a sigh, she managed one last glance over her shoulder. "What?"

His green eyes heavy with concern, Sakir asked, "Where are you going?"

"To help one stupid man get over the past once and for all. Maybe while I'm gone the other man will have the balls to get over it, too."

She left Sakir with his mouth hanging open.

A first.

There wasn't enough alcohol in the whole state of Texas to block out the words he'd just uttered to Jane. Or the look on her face when he'd said them. So Bobby remained sober, his gut, soul and what remained of his heart aching.

In the shelter of the barn, he sat on a pile of fragrant hay, in the back of an empty stall and wondered when the relief of a vow completed would overtake him.

Would it be tomorrow? Next week? Next year?

Ever?

Or would this new pain, this loss of a woman who had come to mean everything to him take the place of his grief over losing his father and sister?

"So, did it work?"

Only mildly startled, he glanced up, saw an angel dressed in pale gold, her dark hair swirling around her shoulders, her eyes filled with a passion he understood only too well. "Did what work?"

"Your plan."

"I don't know what you're talking about."

"Get off it, Bobby. The plan to win back your self-respect and gain a little revenge in the process?"

"Why are you here?"

She ignored his question, moved farther into the stall. "Please tell me that you're happy now."

He cursed, forgot his stoic, unaffected mood and just let loose. "The plan was never to be happy, darlin'. I'll never be happy. But yes, I've finally avenged my family's honor by destroying your brother's family."

Jane cocked her head to the side. "My family's not destroyed." She shook her head. "Yes, you hurt me. Deeply and intolerably. But my family's fine."

"Even you and Sakir?" he asked darkly.

She flinched, but steadied herself and lifted her chin. "Maybe not today or tomorrow, but we'll get over it, and I'll forgive him for being a jerk."

She'd forgive him, but no doubt she'd never forgive Bobby. So, Al-Nayhal would win once again. Land, livelihood and the girl of Bobby's dreams. "So, through all the lies comes a happy ending for the Al-Nayhals," he spat out, wishing now he had gotten disgustingly drunk. "Figures."

"Don't speak to me about lies, Callahan," she countered angrily. "What did you say the other day? 'If someone's going to deceive someone else they should expect to get their ears boxed? Get what they deserve for hurting someone else?'"

"Damn right." He scrambled to his feet and stalked over to her, his heart slamming against his ribs. "Hit me."

"Don't tempt me."

He stood close to her, the heat of their bodies intense. He wanted to pull her into his arms, make love to her mouth, make them both forget what had happened tonight, but he knew that was impossible.

She stared at him with those large green eyes. "I want you to face the truth, your past and all those demons that drive you, and move on."

"I did that tonight."

"No, you acted like a child tonight. It takes a man to stand up for what he really wants and to say to hell with anyone who asks you to deny it."

Bobby froze where he stood. No one had ever said anything like that to him—called him a child. The words made his blood boil, made his mind go numb. He was no child. He was a man who had to make good on a promise, and that was that.

"Is there anything more you want to say, Jane?" he asked, icicles clinging to his tone.

He saw her chin tremble, her eyes fill with tears, but she shook her head, looked up until the tears were gone. When she found his gaze again, she said softly, simply, "I love you, Bobby. I may be a fool for saying it, for coming here, trying again…"

The words, and the tender, devoted tone in her voice, pierced his hard, cold shell—but what followed had every muscle in his body stiff with ire.

"I want you as my family."

As memories of his father, his sister and the battles he'd had with Sakir Al-Nayhal over the years slammed into his mind, Bobby felt his face contort into a mask of rage.

A member of the Al-Nayhal family!

Teeth gritted, he practically hissed, "I'd rather die first."

He watched as the blood drained from Jane's face,

the breath squeezed from her body. Hands shaking, eyes filling with tears once again, she said clearly, "If I leave here, I'm not coming back."

The full impact of her words was lost on Bobby. All he felt was hatred for her brother in that moment, not the love that surely dwelled in his heart. "Goodbye, Jane."

Tears slipping down her face, Jane nodded. "I'll get my things and be out of here in no time."

She turned around and walked away.

And he was alone.

Again.

The airplane engines rumbled, readying themselves for takeoff. With a book lying open and unread on her lap, Jane stared out the window, and wished she were already in Emand. The long flight would be difficult with nothing to do but think about what had happened last night, what had been said at the party and in Bobby's barn. There was also no one to talk to on the flight, to keep her mind occupied with trivial matters. Due to a few business engagements, Mariah and Zayad hadn't been ready to leave, but had offered Jane the private plane, understanding her haste to get away. Jane's mother had suggested that she go with her, but Jane could plainly see that Tara was in love with Abel, and wanted to remain with him. Jane had told her mother that she would call her when she got to Emand, and they could decide what to do from there. Sakir, on the other hand, had tried to reason with Jane, urging her to stay at his home until she figured out what she wanted.

But Jane was determined.

Right now, she needed as much distance as possible between herself and Bobby Callahan. Odds were she wouldn't get over him in a lifetime, but the thousands of miles, oceans and deserts might help a little.

She closed her eyes, knowing that the events of last night would play in her mind and ears. Sinking into the grief, Jane let the shots and jabs he'd uttered, his eyes dark with a lifetime of indignation, poke at her. He'd rather die than be her family. He wanted nothing to do with her.

She believed it all.

Except for one thing.

She knew he loved her, and that truth hurt worst of all. Bobby Callahan could love her and yet dump her because of her family.

She supposed she hadn't really known him at all.

Around her, the airplane's engines whirled, the tires rotated and they were off down the runway and away from Paradise, Texas.

Fifteen

"You got a death wish, Al-Nayhal?"

It had been one week since Jane had left, since Bobby had exacted his revenge, and had put an end to his duty to his father. He'd expected to feel a helluva lot lighter, at peace, maybe. But he only felt angrier, raw, as though he'd like very much to slam his fist through a wall—or through the man standing before him wearing a white kaftan and an arrogant expression.

Looking perfectly out of place in KC Ranch's dusty barn, Sakir lifted his chin. "Do not toss about threats you cannot possibly follow through on."

Bobby stabbed his pitchfork into a mound of hay. "Oh, I can follow through."

Sakir glanced at the makeshift weapon as though it were a thin twig. "As much as I would love to demonstrate all my years of training with both sword and staff, I have more important matters to discuss."

The sight of the man made Bobby's blood boil, made him think about Jane. "Make it quick. You're trespassing, and I have work to do."

"I have brought you this."

Bobby eyed the sheets of white paper Al-Nayhal thrust toward him. "What is it? Something to force me off this land now?"

It appeared as though Sakir were trying to hold on to his patience. "Something that will help you to understand why this land was lost in the first place."

A heaviness settled in Bobby's gut. "What the hell are you talking about? I know why we lost this land."

"You know only part of the reason." When Bobby said nothing, Sakir's eyebrow lifted. "Are you going to take this or not?"

With an indignant growl, Bobby fairly ripped the papers from Sakir's hand. His eyes scanned the documents. The first was a statement from the drilling company who had botched the job on his land, claiming they had no affiliation whatsoever with Al-Nayhal Corporation, squashing Bobby's almost decade-long conspiracy theory. The other papers consisted of five notices from environmental agencies warning Bobby's father about the instability of the land, warning him that if actions weren't taken to bring the land up to code, he would never be allowed to run cattle or horses, or to drill on his land.

A slow sick feeling came over Bobby as he stared at the date of the first and second notice. Six years before his father had lost the property. And he'd still allowed drilling, knowing what could happen, knowing that the drilling could ruin not only the land, but also his family. And afterward, the man had forced Bobby to come home from the road—a life he'd loved with all his heart—to fix a problem that could have been fixed long before.

And through it all, his father had made him believe that Sakir Al-Nayhal was to blame. Worse still, his father had made Bobby promise to carry a burden of revenge for years—while life went on around him, while a woman had found him and helped him to breathe, love life and care about someone again.

Bobby's hand fisted around the papers. If this was true, Bobby's father could have saved the property. If this was true, Kimmy and Bobby would have had their home without having to beg for a tiny portion of it back.

"Mr. Callahan, I—" Sakir began, but was cut off.

"This is a fake," said Bobby, unwilling to believe that his father would have done something like this. The man had been a great father, a good rancher, a respected member of the community. "You have the money to do it, and you'll stop at nothing to defame my father—"

Sakir actually appeared empathetic. "You can check for yourself. Local county offices and state offices have all these records on file."

Bobby started to shake, with fury for his father, for Sakir, for himself and for Jane. But the anger in his heart came out as anguish in his tone. "If this is really true, why would you keep this a secret? Why wouldn't you tell me? I spent years blaming you...."

With a heavy sigh, Sakir said, "I loved my father. I did not want to know of his mistakes or misdeeds. You and your sister thought much of your father." He shrugged, though his chin never dropped. "I thought it best you both hate me and not him."

Bobby couldn't believe what he was hearing. There was no way that Sakir Al-Nayhal was a good guy. No way! Bobby had spent too many years despising him. "And why are you telling me this now? After all these years?"

"I never thought you would try and avenge your father with something I could not handle." Sakir's eyes darkened. "My sister's heart is something I cannot control."

Jane. His beloved Jane. Caught up in a scheme based on lies told by an old man because he didn't want to deal with his mistakes. Bobby fell against the stall door and stared at the rafters.

"I love my sister, Mr. Callahan. And she loves you. I will not attempt to make choices for her again."

Shaking his head, Bobby uttered, "She said she'll never step foot on my land again."

"No, but perhaps if you went to her first."

Bobby came awake in an instant. "Emand?"

Sakir nodded. "It is her land now. Perhaps you will both find peace there."

The palace gardens were scented with citrus and roses, a heavenly combination that sought to soothe Jane's restless mind. But neither the roses nor the spectacular pink sunset before her could manage to curb her sadness. It had been this way for almost two weeks, she mused dejectedly as she sat on an iron bench and sipped her tea. She hated herself for feeling so downcast, missing Bobby the way she did, as though he were an appendage that still felt very much attached.

If she were wise, she'd force him to the back of her mind and concentrate on her future. Over the past week, she'd managed to make a list of restaurants, all bearing her name, some menu ideas, even thoughts on decor. But what she couldn't get down on paper was where this restaurant might be.

"Hi, sweetie."

Jane glanced up and saw her mother on the arm of Abel Garret walking toward her. Tara and Abel had arrived two days ago. Jane hadn't been surprised to see Abel with her mother when Jane had met them at the airplane. The two were most definitely inseparable, and their obvious devotion to one another made Jane's heart seize up every time she saw them.

"We have a surprise for you, Janie," said Abel, tossing her a crooked grin.

Jane returned the smile, half-hearted though it was. "Thank you, guys, but I'm not really up for surprises today." Or any day, for that matter.

"You'll love this one," Tara said with deep conviction, then glanced over her shoulder.

The low, masculine voice echoed throughout the garden, causing all the night insects to still. "You said you wouldn't come to me, so I came to you."

Jane's heart dropped into her shoes, and she whirled around. The man coming toward her was dressed in jeans and a pale-blue shirt, his chest as wide as the pathway on which he walked. His eyes glowed with regret and happiness and love, and his look nearly caused Jane to break down into tears.

Without a word, Abel and Tara slipped away, and Bobby Callahan stood before her. He took a deep breath, his gaze moving possessively over every inch of her until at last, he stared into her eyes. "You look beautiful."

"Bobby…"

"God, I've missed you. I've never ached like this before, in my body and my soul."

She knew exactly what he meant. Nights of loneliness and endless days with nothing to look forward to, a deep ache that nothing would ease. But Bobby had hurt her beyond measure, and no matter how much she still loved him, he wouldn't gain her forgiveness easily.

As if he saw the reticent glow in her eyes, he nodded. "I don't deserve this, just standing before you."

Jane's gaze flickered, her legs felt suddenly water-filled.

"I don't deserve it, but I'm taking it because I love you, Jane. I love you with every part of me, and I had to tell you so. I had to come here and apologize for what I did to you and your family." He reached out, tentatively brushed her hand. His eyes were a deep shade of blue. "Oh, Jane, darlin'. You belong back in Paradise. We belong together. You belong with me."

"I don't know if I do," she uttered, pain slashing her heart, tears pricking her eyes. "I'm scared, Bobby. I gave you everything, my love and trust…my heart and soul, and you tore them up and threw them back in my face. How am I supposed to believe in you again?"

Pain flickered in his eyes. "I'm not asking you to believe in me, Jane. But maybe you could believe in us."

Tears fell down her cheeks.

"Hear me out, darlin', please," he beseeched her, taking her hands in his, his eyes imploring to listen—really hear him. "Guilt and shame are funny things. They make you desperate. They make you do things that you know are wrong. They make you hurt people you love. In my case, they made me turn a blind eye to the weakness of a father I loved dearly, a man I wanted to believe was beyond reproach. A man I was sure had put the needs of his family ahead of his own."

The undisguised misery in his eyes made her heart ache, her throat tighten.

"I made a vow to my father on his deathbed," Bobby continued to say, "to avenge his honor, to hurt the Al-Nayhals as we'd been hurt." He shook his head. "I didn't know the truth of it. I didn't know that it was really my father, through all his mistakes, his blind eye, who had lost our land. I didn't want to believe that. Neither did he, obviously. He was a good man, Jane. He was Kimmy's savior, her touchstone. It broke her heart when he died. Mine, too. So, I blamed Sakir for every one of my losses." With a curse, Bobby pulled her into his arms. "I'm so sorry. I was such a fool. I hurt you, pushed you away after the love and the life you gave me, gave back to me, really. God, you'll never know how sorry I am."

"Yes, I do." Jane couldn't stop the tears, the sobs. She cried against his chest.

He held her for a moment, rocked her, crushed her in his embrace. "Will you forgive me, Jane? Can you forgive me? All I ask for is another chance." He placed a finger under her chin and lifted her bleary-eyed gaze to his. "I want to be your family. I want the babies we're going to have. I want you." With the pad of his thumb, he wiped a fat tear from her cheek. "I love you."

Even through tears, through the pain of what had been said in the past, Jane felt alive and tall and purposeful for the first time in almost two weeks. She understood his past, and now, so did he. When she spoke, her voice rang true and joyful. "I love you. More than ever, and I know what's in your heart. I see it."

A smile broke out on his face, so bright with relief and adoration it squeezed at Jane's heart. "Marry me, darlin'," said Bobby, lowering his head, giving her a tender kiss. "Marry me and teach me everyday how to be a better man."

His words gripped her tightly, curled around her, made her feel safe and filled with love. Finding his way through a wounded past, Bobby's heart had finally opened. He was ready to embrace a future, and Jane knew where she belonged—in his arms, her mouth to his, their breath as one.

"Yes," she whispered between kisses as the pink sun slowly set before them. "We will teach each other, my love."

Epilogue

Six months later

"Do you take this man to be your husband?"

Jane held her breath, her heart seizing with emotion. She'd always wanted this day to come, always hoped that there was a future to look forward to.

Standing proudly at the makeshift altar, Tara smiled at Abel and said, "I do."

"Then I pronounce you husband and wife," the preacher said with a wide smile. "You may kiss your bride, Abel."

In the field beside the lake where Bobby and Jane had swum, and where Abel and Tara had looked at the stars in their own beautiful way, two people committed their lives to one another.

Bobby took Jane's hand in his and squeezed it, his own wedding band rubbing softly against her fingers. "Want to do that all over again?"

Remembering their emotional wedding ceremony in Emand a month earlier, Jane grinned at her husband as he lifted her onto his gray stallion. "In a heartbeat. But maybe we should wait until our anniversary."

Climbing up behind her, Bobby kissed her ear and whispered, "It is our anniversary. One month today."

She snuggled against him as they rode back to the ranch house, back home, all of their family and friends behind them. "Who'd have believed that a six-foot-three, barrel-chested cowboy would be such a romantic?" she called over her shoulder.

"Anyone who looks at the woman he's married to," Bobby shouted over the thunder of horse's hooves.

"I love you, Bobby Callahan."

"I love you, and tonight we're going to say those vows all over again." As Rip galloped beneath them, Bobby held her tightly to his chest, brushed a kiss over her ear and uttered, "When I'm inside you."

She laughed, true happiness enveloping her as the fresh Texas air pelted her face. "I'm not sure I can wait until tonight for that."

"'Fraid you'll have to, darlin'," Bobby said as they pulled up to the ranch house, and the brand-new structure beside it. "Got a wedding feast to go to. And it's at my favorite restaurant in town."

Her heart full, Jane stared up at the sign above the

restaurant, her restaurant. "It's not set to open for three weeks. How is it your favorite already?"

He winked at her. "I've sampled the goods."

Around them, the whole gang, her whole new family rode up to The Darlin', ready and hungry for a full Texas feast. It was beyond her wildest imaginings, but Jane had everything she'd ever wanted—Bobby, a restaurant of her own and a true purpose, as KC Ranch was expanding, taking on more students, staff and wonderful programs. And Jane would nourish them all not only with her food, but her heart.

"Do I smell cornbread?" Ava's husband Jared asked as he jumped down from his horse.

"I love cornbread," said their daughter Lily, still sitting in front of her grandmother Muna, who cooed at the girl and said, "You just love food, Little Star."

"Like the rest of her family," Rita commented, stepping out of her car and handing Daya to Sakir, who promptly kissed the little girl's forehead.

"You did make coleslaw, my sister?" Zayad asked, helping Mariah from the same car as she was too pregnant to ride a horse now. "I do so enjoy that salad."

"Hope you made that brisket of yours," called Abel as he walked up the restaurant steps hand in hand with his new bride.

After assuring them all that their Texas favorites had indeed been prepared, Jane escaped into The Darlin' and into her beloved kitchen. And as she removed macaroni and cheese, beef brisket, potatoes and a chocolate sheet cake from their respective ovens, she smiled. Crowding noisily into her restaurant was her family. Happy, healthy and so much wiser.

Her heart swelled. She did indeed have it all.

*****